P9-DWT-807

CONTENTS

Year after year Donald A. Wollheim's Annual World's Best SF receives praise like this from reviewers. And it is praise well deserved by a series that has brought you each year's most memorable stories, many of them award winners, all of them by either top established authors or the most exciting newcomers in the field.

So welcome to this year's star-spanning tour of the many realms of science fiction, and now join your tour guide—publisher, editor, writer—Donald A. Wollheim as he introduces you to the World's Best SF.

Look for these other exciting
anthologies from DAW Books:

ASIMOV PRESENTS THE GREAT STORIES
The best stories from the
  golden age of science fiction.
Edited by Isaac Asimov and Martin H. Greenberg

THE ANNUAL WORLD'S BEST SF
The finest stories of the current year.
Edited by Donald A. Wollheim with Arthur W. Saha

THE YEAR'S BEST HORROR STORIES
Guaranteed to keep you awake at night!
Edited by Karl Edward Wagner

THE YEAR'S BEST FANTASY STORIES
The finest magical tales of the year.
Edited by Arthur W. Saha

SWORD AND SORCERESS
Stories of magic and derring-do
  from a woman's point of view.
Edited by Marion Zimmer Bradley

THE 1986 ANNUAL WORLD'S BEST SF

**Edited by
DONALD A. WOLLHEIM
with Arthur W. Saha**

DAW BOOKS, INC.
DONALD A. WOLLHEIM, PUBLISHER

1633 Broadway, New York, NY 10019

DAW Collectors Book No. 675.

First Printing, June 1986

1 2 3 4 5 6 7 8 9

PRINTED IN THE U.S.A.

INTRODUCTION

The world is in transition. The process has been going on for some years but it seems now to be entering what may become a qualitative change. The barrier to reasonable discussions of the problems of war and peace, apparent during the past years, seems slowly to be giving way to a time for talking. It is obvious that the accumulation of nuclear weapons has reached a saturation point beyond which anything more becomes lunacy. Actually it has been at that stage for twenty years, but political leaders—and economic interests—are reluctant to admit this. Nevertheless it is happening.

The so-called "Star Wars" project is the scheme by which the military industry hopes to alleviate the nuclear evil and still retain its own super-inflated prosperity. Some hold that money spent on space research and construction, whatever the ostensible military purpose, will open further outer space to mankind. Possibly so. In fact, almost inevitably so.

Others feel that this still keeps the war industry in power—and that all that money could be better spent on improving the planet on which we all must live. There are innumerable things that need to be done in agriculture, housing, health, education, research. Practically, however, it seems unlikely that anything is going to get priority for benevolent works. The armies of the world still stand, in the eyes of the common man, as protection against the unknown and alien outside their national borders. So humanity may continue on its doom course. But there is indeed some transitional hope and evidence for it. Even the mere mention of reducing atomic stocks is a big step.

In the world of fantastic literature, transition is also evi-

dent. The trend away from science fiction to fantasy continues, and on best-selling lists from the specialist book shops,
fantasy appears to outnumber the science fiction titles almost
two to one. We have mentioned in previous introduction to
earlier volumes in this series that there has been a steady
feminization of readership. What was once a predominantly
male readership has almost evened out. Many of the best new
writers coming into print turn out to be females. And what
most of them write is fantasy, not science fiction.

In these days of acute consciousness of so-called gender
roles, I hesitate to ascribe this to any essential difference
between the sexes. But the fact is that the old social roles and
social upbringing of the two sexes still persist in the great
majority and there are two differing outlooks on the individual and social futures displayed.

Fantasy, it always seems to me, is not forward looking. It
all too often takes the form of adult fairy tales, and such tales
take place either in a never-never land of the present or of a
mythical past. Feudalism is a prime background for much of
this—princesses and kings, dragons and witches, the legend
and lore of a thousand years ago. All too often we read
adventures on Earth-twin worlds that come to exist from out
of nowhere—no effort being made to claim star colonies or
such. This is simple escapism. It is also very prone to roman-
ticism, to romance, or to Amazonian feats of courage displayed by heroines who otherwise do not resemble the real
types of today's women who join police and military forces.

Science fiction, on the other hand, does not rejoice in the
present and past. It has always been forward looking, discuss-
ing the future, attempting to outguess the advance of science
and human progress, fascinated with the exploration of the
endless frontier of space.

What we have, then, is that fantasy and science fiction are
back to back—one looking one way, one the other. But there
are other reasons for the rise of fantasy and its escapism. The
real crisis of the twentieth and twenty-first centuries still
remains, "To be or not to be." Much science fiction is laid
in the far future where somehow, usually unstated, this crisis
has been resolved without the destruction of civilization.
Many years ago, writers attempted to wrestle directly with
the immediate future—but most have given that up. Of the

stories included in this new selection of the year past, there are two such stories. The rest are far future visions.

Read, enjoy, and think.

—DONALD A. WOLLHEIM

EARTHGATE

by J. Brian Clarke

Gates between worlds is hardly a new idea—it has become a favorite by-pass in many adventure novels, saving time from the years that star flight may require. From Andre Norton to C. J. Cherryh's Morgaine *novels, the gate has been with us. However, here is still a new approach to this intriguing subject. For if gates can exist at all, why isn't there one somewhere on Earth?*

"We have a problem." Peter Digonness said.

"Don't we all." Gia Mayland was in no mood to be sympathetic. She was still smarting because of the abrupt recall that had brought her from a beach in the Bahamas.

"It's about our search for the Earthgate," the Deputy Director of Expediters went on. "It seems someone does not want us to find it."

Gia raised a delicate eyebrow. "Now isn't that interesting."

He frowned. "More than you think, Jules Evien was murdered yesterday."

"Oh my God." Her face white, she sat down. "How?"

"Very neatly. At long range with a laser rifle. Strictly a professional job."

There was silence. Stricken, Gia was remembering an old lover and a good friend. Then, "Could it have been for another reason? Other than Earthgate? "

"I doubt it. Jules is the third member of the Earthgate team

10

to expire within the last two years. Heidi Jonson fell off a mountain in the Canadian Selkirks. Lynn Quoa died of apparently natural causes in a Denver hospital. Three out of the original seven who drew the assignment.'' Digonness shook his head. "Pretty long odds, Gia.''

"But that makes Jules's murder a pretty stupid blunder, doesn't it? Now you are suspicious enough to wonder about what happened to those other two.''

"The murderer was pressed for time. Three days from now, Jules is scheduled for deep sleep aboard the *Farway*. I told him I thought we had been concentrating too much on the Earth end, and he agreed. He was going to set up an investigation on the Shouter.''

Brown eyes blank with thought, Gia slumped back in her chair. The Shouter, the instantaneous gateway to nearly twenty thousand destinations throughout the galaxy, was six hundred light years and twenty-six months travel time from Earth. For Earth's sorely crowded billions, the Shouter was the access to unrealized dreams; a way to empty lands under clean skies and by unpolluted seas. But the waiting time was long; currently nearly twelve years to gain passage on one of the few dozen phase ships capable of making the trip. Millions more would undoubtedly apply if they did not have to wait a large portion of a lifetime just to get on a ship. So as long as that transportation bottleneck existed, the dream of Earth's being able to reduce its population to something less than bearable limits would remain a fantasy.

Her eyes strayed to the famous "Earthgate Summary,'' framed and hung on the wall above the D.D.'s desk. Ornately lettered and presented to Digonness before he was transferred back to Earth from the Shouter, the Summary was a constant reminder that:

Item: Someone, somewhen, somehow, established the terminal for an instantaneous galactic transport system almost exactly between the home worlds of the only two known star-faring races.

Item: It takes more than two years for even the fastest ships to reach the Shouter from either of the two worlds.

*   *   *

Item: Of the nearly twenty thousand gates on the Shouter, there are two which do not lead anywhere.

Conclusion: That AAs 6093 and 11852 are the gates to Phuili and Earth.

Questions: Which of the two is Earth's? On Earth, where is the corresponding "Shoutergate"? And how is the system activated?

Neat, concise and definitely logical. But like most of her colleagues in Expediters, Gia accepted the Summary as much on faith as on reason—because if there was any justice in the universe, it simply had to be true. If it were otherwise, populating the thousands of available worlds would be comparable to transferring Earth's deserts a few hundred grains of sand at a time.

Out of nowhere and completely irrelevent to her train of thought, a name popped into Gia's mind. "Transtar," she said.

"I beg your pardon?"

Her eyes widened. "That's it. The motive! Except for a few ships servicing the old worlds, Transtar has committed just about all of its resources to the Shouter run. So if Earthgate is opened up, it'll ruin them. The giant of the business will become a corporate has-been overnight. Can you imagine a better reason to stop our finding Earthgate? Even if it involves murder?"

"Frankly, no," Digonness admitted smoothly. "But with a motive that obvious, Transtar—*if* they are guilty—will have concealed their involvement behind false leads and middlemen enough to drown an entire army of investigators for years. So forget it, Gia. I did not bring you here to play gumshoe."

"Neither did you bring me here just to tell me bad news!" she shot back. "Or did you?"

He looked at her. After a few moments, Gia's eyes dropped from his steady gaze. "Sorry, I should not have said that."

"No," He said briefly. "You shouldn't." He did something behind his desk and the room darkened. A circle of light appeared and expanded. In the center of the field, set in a red-hued desert under an infinite sky, a huge saucer was balanced horizontally atop an incredibly slender pylon. Above the saucer, a pale sphere of flickering light. "You know what that is, of course," Digonness said.

Gia smiled into the darkness. "You'd fire me if I didn't.
Even kinder-schoolers can recognize a stargate."

"Officially still an AA, alien artifact," he reminded her.
"That happens to be AA One, my own favorite."

Gia nodded as she remembered the story. Peter Digonness
had been one of the early recruits to Expediters; the organization set up to "expedite" scientific cooperation. In the same
way a translator facilitates verbal communication, a trained
expediter can join a cacophony of scientific specialists into an
efficient unity; often in the face of mutual suspicions and
misunderstandings. Assigned to the Permanent Earth Research
Unit on the Shouter, the young expediter triggered events
involving PERU and the nearby Phuili base which were still
reverberating across three worlds and into the galaxy. Within
days of his arrival, Digonness not only proved to the condescending Phuili that humans are much more than primitives
with a lopsided aptitude for technology, but in Partnership
with one of the Phuili he also convincingly demonstrated the
true purpose of the gigantic AAs—by flying into the light
above AA One and instantly arriving at a lovely world now
appropriately know as Serendipity.

It made him famous of course. Which was not to the liking
of this mild mannered man, who elected to remain on the
Shouter while manned and unmanned vehicles began probing
the thousands of worlds beyond the AAs. But talent often
pushes an individual further than he wants to go, and after
unrelenting pressure from Expediters Central on Earth.
Digonness finally—though reluctantly—returned home to take
charge of the Earthgate search.

He pointed at the holographic image of the AA. "That is
the main reason I am convinced we are wasting our time,
Earthside. Three kilometers high and two wide—if such a
thing exists on this planet, then every human being has been
blind for—how many thousand years? OK, so perhaps it's
disguised as something else, though God knows what. A
thing that big would have to be concealed inside a mountain.
The point is, if we don't know what we are looking for, then
what are we looking for? If there is an answer at all, it can
only be on the Shouter. Which, young lady, is where you
come in. I want you to go in Jules's place."

Gia was not surprised. She and Jules were the only two
who had been recruited into Expediters from the World Union

Council's Security Service, so it was natural that the Deputy Director would seek her investigative talents. Nevertheless she decided to play cautious.

"To do what?"

"I would think that is pretty obvious. I want you to find out how to open the Earthgate."

She frowned. "Not what I would call a modest assignment."

Digonness folded his hands together and leaned forward on his desk. His gray eyes were intent, probing. "Believe me, if I could assign this mission to myself, I wouldn't hesitate. I have friends on the Shouter, of both races. But in their wisdom, the powers that be have decided the answer is on this planet, and that I must continue to direct the search. But at least I was able to persuade them to assign one of *Farway*'s sleep tanks to Expediters, so you won't have to put up with two years of boredom aboard an interstellar people-freighter. And because you have no close relatives—"

"—or emotional entanglements," Gia interrupted with a smile. "But you know that, don't you?"

Digonness looked slightly embarrassed. "I could not be sure of course. But I'm glad that you confirmed it."

"That's nice of me," the girl said sadly.

"Dammit Gia, I'm offering the opportunity of a lifetime! Whoever or whatever put the AAs on the Shouter obviously intended them to be used. Which means that in some logical way there must exist a switch to turn on one of the two blank AAs to Earth. I'm even willing to lay down hard money that that switch is there for the eye to see, in full view. So please girl, use your special talents to find it, huh? Turn on the Earthgate!"

Sleep tanks were such hugely expensive and complex pieces of equipment, most emigrants to the new worlds still had to suffer through more than two years of confined existence aboard one of the fleet of ships built specifically for the Shouter run. So when Gia Mayland was revived a week before the *Farway* arrived off the Shouter, she was not surprised at the hostility of her fellow passengers. The fact that she was an expediter made little difference. That once glamorous profession was now merely respectable, another way to make a good living. But the hostility was not really a hardship. The crew were cooperative, and in any case Communications had a backlog of tachyon-wave messages for her. Most were routine, though the most recent one from the Deputy Director was ominous.

UP TILL RECENTLY WE HAVE REMAINED COMPLETELY BAFFLED IN THE MATTER OF EVIEN'S DEATH. BUT LAST MONTH'S ARREST OF A KNOWN ASSASSIN ON AN UNRELATED CHARGE HAS VERY DEFINITELY RE-OPENED THE CASE. NOT ONLY HAS THE MAN CONFESSED TO JULES'S KILLING, BUT HE REVEALED ENOUGH ABOUT THE MANNER HE RECEIVED PAYMENT TO LEAD US TO A PERSON NAMED JOPHREM GENESE, WHO IS EMPLOYED BY A SALES ORGANIZATION WHICH HAPPENS TO BE A SUBSIDIARY OF—YOU GUESSED IT—TRANSTAR INTERSTELLAR. BEYOND THAT, THE ONLY INFORMATION I HAVE IS THAT GENESE HAS NOT BEEN SEEN OR HEARD FROM SINCE EVEN BEFORE THE ASSASSIN COLLECTED HIS FEE. SO HE COULD BE ANYWHERE ON EARTH, OR PERHAPS OFF IT.

GIA, AS I REMINDED YOU BEFORE YOU SHUTTLED OUT, YOUR PRIMARY MISSION CONCERNS THE EARTHGATE. BUT PERHAPS IT WOULD BE WISE TO LOOK OVER YOUR SHOULDER ONCE IN A WHILE. EVEN TO EXAMINE THE LISTS OF YOUR FELLOW PASSENGERS. I HESITATE TO ADVISE MORE, BECAUSE IN THAT GAME YOU ARE MORE QUALIFIED THAN I.

P.D.

It was a complication the young expediter would rather have done without. But she appreciated Digonness's warning to "look over her shoulder" occasionally, especially during the weeks until *Farway*'s complement of settlers were shipped out to their various destinations across the galaxy. If nothing untoward happened while the hundreds of families were being processed and prepared for their great adventure, then it was probable nothing would. Unless there is a crowd to merge into after he has earned his pay, a careful assassin would probably prefer to wait for a safer assignment.

The day before disembarkation, Gia determinedly deposited her worries in temporary storage and settled into one of the observation blisters on the side of the orbiting ship. A few hundred kilometers away, the Shouter's Mars-like landscapes rolled grandly by, the sparks of the stargates resembling randomly scattered tinsel. Even as she watched, she knew aircraft were plunging into those sparks of light and emerging hundreds, thousands, perhaps even a hundred thousand light

years away on the far rim of the galaxy. Or perhaps returning, bearing crews who only minutes before had said fare-
wells to those who even now were turning to a new life under
an alien sun.

Sunk in revery she did not notice the man who quietly
entered the blister and joined her contemplation of this strang-
est of worlds. "Fascinating," he said. "Quite fascinating."

Startled, she turned. It was not, as she expected, a crew-
man. He was a drably dressed civilian; plump, totally bald,
and with a wide, pink-cheeked smile. Incredibly the smile
broadened. "They don't like me either. I'm the other tanknaut."

Gia blinked. Tanknaut? Suddenly his meaning caught on,
and she laughed delightedly. "So you are the one? I wondered who I have been sleeping with."

He blushed, like a small boy accused of liking girls. "Sorry
we were not introduced. Endart Grimes of P.L.S.—Penders
Life Support Systems." He added, as if apologetically, "Once
in a while we do use our own products."

She accepted his hand. His grip was firm. "Gia Mayland.
I'm with Expediters."

"Ah." He looked at her with interest. "Expediters. Wasn't
Peter Digonness one when he—?" He gestured at the planet.

"He was. Now he's my boss." Curiously, Gia asked.
"Are you heading for one of the new worlds?"

He shook his head. "Unfortunately no. I am merely an
unattached person who can afford a few years away from
Earth while I check out a few refinements in our . . . ah . . .
process." He frowned. "Too bad it remains so damned
complicated and cumbersome as well as expensive."

"Can't that be changed?"

The fat man shrugged. "Naturally we are trying. Trouble
is, the system is not only innately unreliable, it is field
unserviceable. So we have split it into eight replaceable
modules. With a life expectancy per module of only a few
months, that of course means a lot of spares. On this trip for
instance, there are thirty such replacement units in the system. *Farway*'s two sleep tanks are, in fact, wired and piped to
about one hundred and eighty thousand kilos of equipment.
Did you know that?"

"My God," Gia was shocked. "No wonder the colonists
are unfriendly!"

Grimes regarded her thoughtfully. "A few days of social ostracism is a small price, I think."

He was right of course. Twenty-six months of communal living in a crowded steel shell was tough for even the most ardent gregarian. So Gia dismissed guilt in favor of gratitude for her good fortune, and settled down again to watch the unfolding scene.

Grimes said, "I understand it is called the Shouter because the emissions of the stargates make it one of the most detectable objects in the galaxy. True?"

"True," Gia agreed.

"Then why isn't the Shouter detectable from Earth?"

Gia sighed. *The ignorance of some people*. She pointed at a nebula-hazed cluster of stars rising beyond the planet's rim. "The Pleiades. Draw a straight line from here to Sol, and it passes exactly through the middle of those stars. For some peculiar reason, their nebulosity is opaque to the frequencies emitted by the stargates. So the Shouter was not detected until *Far Seeker* cruised out from beyond the Pleiades' shadow back in twenty-four-oh-six, thirty years ago."

Grimes gazed at the legendary star cluster, so familiar despite its reversed configuration of suns. Then, quietly: "So perhaps the Pleiades is the reason there cannot be an instantaneous transport link to Earth. An Earthgate. What do you think, Ms. Mayland?"

It took eight shuttle trips to ferry *Farway*'s hundreds of passengers down to the surface, which again did not endear Gia to those who knew she had ridden one of the P.L.S. tanks and now saw her assigned to the first flight. But she had become used to their resentment, though she wished she were free to disclose her mission so she could turn some of that hostility into friendship. Even Endart Grimes, despite his affability, had seemed oddly distant—a bland exterior that did not match what she sensed was behind the man's pale blue eyes. In any case he was not on the shuttle, so she supposed he had surrendered his priority so he could tinker within the maze of plumbing and electronics that served the two life suspension chambers.

A few minutes after the shuttle rode its jets down to a gentle touchdown, two pressurized buses coupled to the exit locks and everyone cautiously filed into the transparent-topped vehicles. As her bus began to bump along the graveled road toward the semi-underground complex of the Colonization Authority's Reception Center, Gia gazed across a rocky plain at the domes and pyramids of the Phuili base. Some of those graceful structures were centuries old, yet they all gleamed a crisp white under the light of the Shouter's distant sun. About halfway between the base and the Center, incongruous in its straightlaced economy of construction, the four-story home of PERU rose slab-sided against the sky.

Somewhere there was a throaty roar, and suddenly a broad-winged shape rose into sight from behind the Center. It accelerated swiftly, climbing higher and then banking toward the sun. Shading her eyes, Gia saw the incredible structure toward which the aircraft was heading: the vast saucer, the almost line-thin pylon that supported it. The sun was too bright for her to see the sphere of light that was the actual stargate, and for the same reason she did not see the aircraft enter. But the rumble of jets ceased as if cut by a switch, and Gia knew yet another load of passengers had arrived at a distant world.

"Where did it go?" shrilled a child's voice. "Mamma, where did it go?"

"To a place called Serendipity, dear."

"Is that where we're going?"

"No, dear. We are going to New Kent."

"Why aren't we going to Serendiddy?"

"Because it's not New Kent," the mother replied testily, and left it at that. But in her mind, Gia continued the explanation.

Because Serendipity was the first world to be reached through a stargate, humans and Phuili jointly decided that it would remain as they found it, unsettled and unspoiled. Scientists were on that aircraft, perhaps a few media people and even some tourists. But they will not be allowed to stay. In weeks, or at the most, months, they must reemerge out of AA One just as Petter Digonness and his Phuili companion did eighteen years ago. It's not such a bad trade, really. One world for thousands. . . .

Genevieve Hagan, the Assistant Research Administrator of PERU, was a small woman with intense green eyes. Rumor was that she and Peter Digonness had had something going during his years on the Shouter, and somehow Gia thought that quite fitting. Aside from her undoubted charm and keen intelligence, the A.R.A. also had an outgoing femininity that would have been the perfect complement to Digonness' reputed reserve.

After instructing the new arrival always to address her as "Jenny," the A.R.A. returned behind her desk, shuffled a few papers and shyly asked, "How is Peter? Is he holding up behind that Earth-bound desk of his?"

"He's trying to. But he did tell me he would prefer to be on the Shouter."

Jenny nodded. "We wish he could be." Gia noticed the unconscious emphasis of "We." *I think she still misses the man. Even after more than three years!* Abruptly the softness firmed and the green-eyed woman became the cool professional. "Now then. You received Peter's message about Jophrem Genese?"

"It was given to me after I was revived."

"Then you understand why I ask this question. Did anyone aboard *Farway* seem particularly interested in you?"

Gia smiled. "The other tanknaut."

"Tanknaut?"

"The man in the other tank. Endart Grimes of P.L.S."

"Oh, I see. Yes, I know about Grimes. But I was thinking more along the lines of someone connected with Transtar."

Gia frowned. "That's a bit unlikely, isn't it? If Transtar wants to stop us finding the Earthgate, their agent is hardly likely to advertise his connection by being listed as one of their own."

"He'd have no choice. Other than Grimes and yourself, the only people from the *Farway* who don't work for Transtar are the colonists. And they will be confined to the Center until they are shipped out."

"So if Genese—or whoever—was aboard, he has to be a member of the crew. Is that it?"

The older woman pushed a file across the desk. "Here are the idents of all fifty-two crew members. Also a likeness of Jophrem Genese, facsimiled from Central a few months ago."

Gia flipped open the file. On the top, a head and shoulders picture of a thin faced man with dark skin and slightly protruding eyes. She leafed through the rest of the sheets, each a single page summary with a small picture of the person described. The only one who even slightly resembled the thin faced man was a female crew member.

"Not much help, is it?" Jenny said.

Gia closed the file and handed it back to the A.R.A. "I am here to find the Earthgate," she said firmly. "I don't intend to be diverted by some hypothetical mystery man."

Thoughtfully, the A.R.A. studied the young expediter. "I'd take Peter's warning quite seriously. Whatever else he is, he is definitely not the paranoid type."

"I know. And believe me, I intend to take all the basic precautions. But beyond that, I will be working full time on my primary assignment."

"Well, it's your decision of course." Jenny balanced the file in one hand for a moment, then dropped it into a drawer and closed the drawer with a slam of finality. "Now that's done with—I hope—let's you and I get down to specifics. How can PERU help Gia Mayland find the Earthgate?"

"For a start, Gia Mayland needs updating," Gia replied promptly. "I have been somewhat out of touch during the last couple of years."

Jenny chuckled. "So you have. OK, two words. Nothing new."

Gia was astonished. "Nothing? Nothing at all?"

"What did you expect? Digger continues to spend government money looking for what he knows cannot be found, while on the Shouter we don't have the resources even to start looking. But I am glad you are here, because I also happen to agree with Digger that the answer—if there is one—is on the Shouter. Which is, I am afraid, my devious way of telling you not to expect too much from us. With all the teams going out from here, PERU is already spread far too thin."

Gia shrugged. "Which means we'll do what we can with what we've got, I suppose. Which is—?"

"Use of our T-Com facilities, of course. I have already arranged fifteen minutes of open channel for you once every day at sixteen hours. It's expensive, but at least you will be able to keep in touch with Peter and the rest of the high-priced talent at E Central. Further to that, I have assigned someone to be your guide and helper. Meet Galvic Hagan."

He must have been waiting outside, because he walked in almost before the A.R.A. had released the key on the intercom. He was young, sturdy, and red haired. And his grin was infectious. "Is this the lady, Ma?"

The A.R.A. sighed. "Don't you think that joke's getting a little thin?" She looked apologetically at Gia. "He is not even related. But somehow he has got half the people here thinking I am his mother." She shuddered. "God forbid."

"Poor lady doesn't know what she's been missing," the young man said, shaking Gia's hand. He stepped back and eyed her critically. "Have you eaten lately?"

Gia knew what he meant. "The sleep tanks are not one hundred percent efficient," she explained. "I guess I lost a little weight."

He nodded. "Then I suggest we go down to the commissary and put some substance back on that nice bod of yours. Between mouthfuls you can ask any question you like, and if we're both lucky I may come up with some right answers."

"Good idea," Jenny agreed. "Gia, take it easy for the rest of the day. Have Vic show you around the facility and introduce you to people. And then get a good night's sleep. Tomorrow, you will meet David."

"David?"

"Oh, didn't I mention him? He is your Phuili opposite number here. His job is to find the Phuiligate."

"David" was short and humanoid, with a pink-fleshed canine head. Gia's first reaction to the little alien was to be nervous and at the same time curious, though negative feelings soon evaporated under the scrutiny of the large eyes, which were violet in color with a hint of humor in their depths. Also, the clasp of the rough-skinned hand with its two fingers and two opposed thumbs, was friendly. "I am Davakinapwottapellazanzis," he announced in a rapid flow of syllables. "But to human fwiends, I am David."

Gia licked her lips. *How does one make conversation with a being who looks like an upright bull terrier?* "Er, have you been on this assignment very long?"

"Since five of your monz. I come to Shouter after not finding gate on Phuili."

"Do you think there is a gate on Phuili?"

"If zere is gate on Shouter, zere is gate on Phuili. But not get much help on Phuili."

For a moment Gia did not understand. Vic looked just as

uncomprehending, while Jenny merely shrugged and allowed herself a slight smile. They were in the A.R.A.'s office, the alien perched awkwardly on a low stool brought in to accommodate his diminutive short-legged frame. Trying to ignore the two interested spectators, the expediter looked directly into the violet eyes. They stared back unwinking. "Do you mean that other Phuili are not interested enough to help? Or that there was direct opposition?"

David looked puzzled. At least, it was the impression given by a slackening of his flexible muzzle. "Not understand. What mean opposition?"

Gia carefully explained. "If the Phuiligate is found, there will be no further need for the ships and crews that journey between your world and the Shouter. Wouldn't those who run the ships want to stop you?"

The "puzzlement"—if that was what it was—deepened. "If gate found, ships go ozer places. Cwews go where ships go."

Is greed peculiarly human? Gia wondered, ashamed of her race's larcenous instincts and envious of Phuili innocence. But romantics do not make good expediters, and she quickly realized that simplistic judgments are self defeating as well as downright silly. Because the Phuili were subject to the same natural laws as humanity, then somewhere down the line they had undoubtedly learned the same lesson: that angels are for the next universe, not the harsh realities of this one.

It was as if David were reading her thoughts. "Phuili develop over long time. Phuili young few, so planet still have much woom. Old ways not need to change. Yet gate will change old ways because much will come fwom outside. Humans cwowded, zey need new worlds. Not Phuili. We go only to look. Not to stay."

Even Genevieve Hagan was surprised. In her years of dealing with the Phuili, never could she remember such a confession of unease; like a hermit fearing his castle of solitude is about to be invaded by hordes of tourists. Undoubtedly David's "much will come in fwom outside" was a reference to humans, those—by Phuili standards—unpredictable beings with their unholy devotion to change. At the same time, however, the little alien's disjointed statement was also a contradiction.

The A.R.A. was not the only one who recognized the contradiction. "If the Phuili did not want the gate," Gia said puzzledly, "then why, David, do you seek to open it?" Even as she asked the question she sensed distress where earlier there had been humor. It was a strange feeling. Even with people, she had never been able to sense mood like she seemed to be doing with this little alien.

David's reply echoed the mood. "Humans use gate even if Phuili not," he said sadly. "Soon zis zen become human galaxy. Maybe Phuili ways saved, but Phuili people lost."

Phuili people lost. Perhaps it was his awkward use of the human language, but nevertheless it conjured a poignant image of an ancient race relegated to a galactic backwater. Gia was beginning to appreciate the dilemma faced by the Phuili, the "go" or "no go" situation which was almost Aristotelean in its terrible simplicity. Either to accept the challenge offered by the gates and as a consequence endure the shattering effects of change on the fragile underbody of their monolithic society, or to turn inward and eventually be humbled into obscurity by a species that was still living in caves when the Phuili culture had already matured into something resembling its present form.

The expediter moved closer to the Phuili and the mood of distress intensified. It surrounded him like an invisible aura, a form of communication as alien as he was. Telepathy, she wondered? *David, do you understand me? Can you read what I am thinking?*

There was no answer. Only the sorrow.

Despite Vic Hagan's protests, Gia borrowed a runabout and went out on her own the next day. After bordering the shuttle landing complex, the graveled road terminated a few kilometers farther on below the huge bowl of AA One. The bowl was supported by a three-kilometer pylon that was so slender it seemed barely capable of supporting itself, let alone the mass that loomed incredibly overhead. For a while Gia sat in the artifact's shadow, not thinking of anything in particular but letting impressions soak gradually into her brain. At this stage she did not expect to learn anything scientists on at least three worlds did not already know, but she knew this small pilgrimage marked the true beginning of her mission. Finally she clambered out of the runabout and wandered around for a while, uncomfortable in her pressure suit but happily enjoying the same feelings of awe Peter Digonness had undoubtedly experienced when he first came.

It was difficult to think of appropriate superlatives. The sheer scale of the enormous artifact was such that, though the pylon seemed incredibly frail from a distance, the close-up sixty-eight meters across its base suggested the comfortable solidity of a concrete monument. It had already been explained to Gia that the faint marks impressed on the smooth gray surface up to about the three-meter level, were in fact as much as Phuili science could do in an attempt to remove a material sample for analysis. It was while she was marveling at this unbelievable resistance to even the sun-heat of a laser torch, that Gia became aware of a second vehicle parked near her own, and a stolid human figure trudging toward her. She waited, irritated at this intrusion yet curious as to the stranger's identity.

"How do you do," a familiar voice puffed in her helmet phones. "Guess we're both doing what all the new people do when they first come to the Shouter. Right, Ms. Mayland?"

She smiled. "Right, Mr. Grimes. When did you come down?"

"On the early morning shuttle. And please call me Endart. Or even En if you like to be so informal. I don't mind."

Is he kidding? "And I'm Gia," she said politely. She waited as Grimes stared at the AA, then agreed as he voiced an appropriate expression of awe. Suddenly something reminded her of a remark he had made yesterday, in the *Farway* observation blister. Strange it had not registered before, but how in blazes had he known about the Earthgate? She asked him.

The question puzzled him. "Why is Heaven called Heaven? You may not believe in it, but it has to have a name just so you can identify what you don't believe. Right? Anyway, I know I saw "Earthgate" mentioned somewhere. Or heard it, I'm a bit of a sucker for that kind of thing, you know. Ghosts, Atlantis, UFO's, even the Bermuda Triangle. Nonsense of course, but fun. Guess I'm a bit of a romantic at heart."

It was a very human explanation. Not too glib and therefore having a ring of truth. So Gia decided not to pursue the matter. In any case Expediters did not own title to the somewhat unimaginative term "Earthgate," which to the uninformed could mean a lot of things, real or otherwise. It seemed Digonness's warning about the mysterious Jophrem Genese had affected her more than she realized, and she wondered if she were becoming paranoid.

Not if I can help it, she told herself grimly.

However, the subject was not so easily dropped. Grimes's curiosity had been piqued. "Why did you ask that? Is it possible there is such a thing as an Earthgate? Are you somehow involved?"

Gia tried not to overreact. "Of course not. As you said, it's nonsense. My job is to expedite, not to spend public money chasing fantasies."

He seemed relieved. "How glad I am to hear that. So what are you currently . . . ah . . . expediting?"

The man was becoming a nuisance. "Not very much at the moment. We're waiting for one of the teams to come in, from Gaylord. It's apparently one of the better worlds, though no decision to colonize will be made until we have evaluated the team's report. Believe me, Endart, being a sort of scientific mediator is only part of my work. The rest is mostly dull routine, as in any profession." Gia began to walk back to her runabout, and after a moment's hesitation, Grimes hurried after her.

At the vehicles, he turned again to the towering AA. "Such a shame really," he murmured. "All those thousands of worlds, as accessible from the Shouter as stepping through a doorway. While on our poor, overcrowded Earth . . ." Shaking his head, he clambered into his runabout, waved and drove off. Like a careless tourist he had forgotten to turn off his transmitter, and his muttering remained even after he was no more than a cloud of dust.

" . . . such a shame. Such a terrible, *terrible* shame . . ."

Gia asked for photographs. Of AA One, and of 6093 and 11852. Galvic Hagan delivered them to her and watched curiously as she spread the prints in three groups on the library table. "Comparing?" he asked.

"No, I just like looking at pretty pictures," she said irritably after she had arranged the collection to her satisfaction.

"It's already been done, you know."

Gia picked up one of the prints and held it closer to the light. "So?"

He spread his hands. "So nothing was found. Every AA on this planet is exactly the same as every other AA. Same dimensions, same markings, even the same spectral signatures."

"Hmm." Though she was not about to admit it, Gia knew the young man was right. She had slept badly the previous night and was feeling physically and mentally sluggish. At that moment fresh ideas seemed as rare as a Sahara iceberg. Again she looked at the print in her hand. It was of 6093, one of the two non-functioning AAs. "Vic."

"Yes, ma'am."

She pointed at the light above 6093. "Have you flown through that? Or through the one above eleven-eight-five-two?"

He nodded. "Several times. Through both."

"What does it feel like?"

He shrugged. "Same as any other AA. We just didn't get anywhere, that's all."

"Vic, I have only heard Digger's description of the sensation. I want to know if it is the same for everyone. So let me repeat the question. As you are transported through a stargate, what does it *feel* like?"

"OK, now I get you." Vic considered a moment. "It's being torn apart and then squeezed together again, that's what it feels like. But like everything else you get used to it."

"Are you a pilot? I mean, of an aircraft?"

He blinked at the abrupt change of subject. "Sure. Where do you want to go?"

She glanced at the wall map. "To six-oh-nine-three, I think. It's the closest, isn't it?"

"A tad under six hundred klicks. About seventy minutes flight time."

"Arrange it as soon as possible. For tomorrow, if you can. I would also like to take David along."

Vic shook his head. "Sorry. Both ships are already booked for tomorrow." He glanced at his watch. "But what's wrong with now? There is still time to give you two or three hours of daylight at the site." As he spoke he turned to the com unit and punched a three-digit number.

"*Phuili*," said an alien voice.

"Is that David?"

"*Not David.*"

"This is Hagan. I am about to fly Gia Mayland to six-oh-nine-three. She wants David to come."

"*David, come.*" There was a click as the Phuili broke contact.

"Just like that?" Gia asked, surprised. "Don't they even think to ask him if he's free?"

Hagan chuckled as he held the door open. "That is something else you'll have to get used to. Though to us the Phuili may act like individuals, sometimes they seem parts of one organism."

She stopped close to him. Though he knew she was at least ten years older, he felt a sudden protectiveness. He swallowed. "They're aliens," he said.

She nodded, thoughtfully. "As we are to them."

David met them as they pushed the aircraft out of the hangar. Clad in a silvery pressure suit with an elongated helmet, he looked more like a cuddly space toy than a member of a species older than man. But his assistance as he and the young human male unfolded and locked the wings was that of an experienced professional. Which was not surprising considering the machine was a human adaptation of an original Phuili design. Finally the ill-assorted threesome strapped themselves into the narrow cockpit, and with a surge from its jets the *Eloise Three* floated smoothly into the thin air.

Though seemingly a frail assembly of tubing and stretched plastfilm, this was actually a rugged and durable craft that had already proved its worth on hundreds of flights. Nevertheless Gia found herself breathing a little easier as they approached the slender column below AA 6093. "Can we spiral downward from the bowl?" she asked the pilot as she readied her camera.

"No problem," Vic replied, resetting the controls. As they entered into the enormous bowl's shadow, he tilted the machine into a slow descending circuit. Gia started taking her pictures, carefully spacing the shots to encompass all four sides of the pylon from bowl to base.

"You zink you find what ozers not find after doing same?" David asked interestedly from the rear seat.

"The pictures I have seen were all taken from the ground,"

Gia said, clicking away. "Nothing from this close, or from this angle."

"Still same," the Phuili commented.

He was probably right. Though the camera was the state of the art in electronic imaging, Gia suspected the ground based holograms contained as much information in four shots as she could obtain with dozens. But such was the strangeness of this world, she had decided that yesterday's truth is not necessarily today's. Digonness's own early experiences on the Shouter had demonstrated the fragility of several rigidly-held absolutes, and Gia was immodest enough to allow the possibility that she could also fracture a few. Especially if she found the Earthgate.

As they finally sped away from the pylon a few meters above the barren ground, Vic guided *Eloise Three* into a wide climbing turn. "Do you want to go through the light?"

"Of course. It's one of the reasons we're here, isn't it?"

"OK. But be warned. For first timers, it ain't pleasant."

"I'm aware of that." Gia remembered how Digonness had described it. *It's being exploded apart, spread all over the universe and then being imploded together again.* She turned to the other passenger. "Have you done this before?"

"Not wiz zis one. AA One only. Because zis AA not work, I wonder if hurt same. I come to compare."

Still same, Gia was tempted to say facetiously, having already been told by just about everyone in PERU that the "hurt" was equally unpleasant whichever AA one went through. But that was only the human experience. Perhaps to Phuili senses there would be a difference, though how that knowledge could help the search was problematical. In any case, how does one describe a subjective impression to an alien? She doubted David could do that any more than she could.

Again she remembered Digonness. *I'm willing to bet hard cash the switch is there to see,* he had told her. Well, maybe. But if he was right, then something had recently changed. Otherwise, she did not doubt the magic toggle would have been found long ago. She patted the camera. So perhaps her picture-taking made some sense after all.

They were above the bowl now, about a kilometer away and turning toward the pale radiance that shimmered above it like concentrated electricity. The bowl's inner surface was the most intense black she had ever seen, an effect infinitely more than a mere absence of light. Despite her heated suit, Gia shivered. Nevertheless, even before Galvic Hagan's exuberant "Tally Ho!" as he dove *Eloise Three* into the light, she was already taking more shots, hoping the camera could cope with the incredible contrasts of the unreal scene. Her concentration was so intense, it was almost unexpected when everything vanished in a sudden blaze of radiance.

" . . . ohhhh—!"

Seconds, minutes, or perhaps years later—her confused senses seemed momentarily flung aside from time—AA6093 was behind them as the aircraft hummed smoothly through the thin air. Digonness, and more recently Vic, had tried to describe how it felt, but Gia now knew that words would always be totally inadequate to describe what she had just experienced. In real space and time she supposed they were a few kilometers and two or three minutes beyond the gate, in the same sky and above the same desert where they had entered. But deep inside herself Gia knew without doubt that they had been *elsewhere*, that within the span of a moment they had journeyed beyond the universe and returned.

"Shall we do it again?" Vic asked cheerfully.

"Yes," Gia replied, surprising herself. "Yes!"

He swung around in his seat, and even behind the helmet visors he saw his astonished face. "You're kidding!" Then, plaintively, "Aren't you?"

"I too want do again," David said. "But also I zink we stop inside light for while. You have auto?"

Even Gia was shocked by the request. To extend that ultra-schizoid splitting to a virtual infinity of moments would be worse than the most malevolent concept of hell. That the Phuili could be such a masochist . . .

"When we in six-o-nine-zwee, we go ozer place and come out again. No time between, so in and out one moment. But if auto stay us, zen in and out separwated by short time. Hurt not differwent, just two smallers. We twy?"

. . . *or on the other hand, a useful friend to have around. We need a few of his kind in Expediters.* Her thoughts whirling at David's penetrating logic, Gia asked, "Can it be done?" *My God, perhaps the other place is Earth. Deputy Director Digonness, are you in for a surprise!*

The pilot began setting switches. "In, stop, hover for

about fifteen seconds, and then out again. If I could set it for as low as five seconds, I would. At least she'll stay on an even keel for a while, long enough for me—hopefully—to regain my senses. Dammit David, are you expecting this to be the quick way back to Phuili?''

"Iss not logical? But if human world, not matter. Ozer AA zen lead to Phuili.''

Fifteen minutes later *Eloise Three* was parked on the desert a few kilometers from AA 6093. Aboard the aircraft, its pilot and two passengers sat quietly. But their thoughts crackled like lightning.

. . . *telepathy for God's sake!*

. . . *it is what happened to my next level ancestor after he and the human named Digonness first went through AA One.*

. . . *David! It was your father who was Digger's companion?*

. . . *it is true. It is also true the thoughtspeak faded rapidly after they returned to the Shouter. So I suggest most strongly we exchange our impressions before we are also returned to the inadequacies of speech.*

. . . *I agree. Question. Where were we?*

. . . *God knows,* the pilot thought. *But it certainly was not any place I know. Or am likely to.*

. . . *Galvic dear, it was just too easy to persuade you. Which makes me suspect we were being influenced even before we re-entered the gates.*

. . . *damn right! By every standard I can think of, what we did was insane. But we survived, and now we're yakking like three animated radios.*

. . . *did you see anything? Feel anything?*

. . . *see anything, no. Feel anything! Well it's hard to say. I do know I received a pretty lucid message from . . . whoever. For some reason, I am to examine* Eloise's *tail section.*

. . . *interesting. Do you know why?*

. . . *I only know I am supposed to do it before we take off again. Would you believe it, they even knew I'd ground her after re-entry.*

. . . *it seems they know a lot of things.* David pondered a moment. Gia, do you agree there were other entities?

. . . *absolutely. I even tried to . . . er . . . converse with them.*

. . . yes?

. . . I asked about Earthgate.

. . . how strange. I asked about the gate to Phuili.

. . . ahha! Did they answer you?

. . . with an image. Very strong, very clear. It was of a pair of human hands framing a circle. They were smaller hands, smooth. A female's, I think.

. . . mine?

. . . it would seem logical.

. . . all I got was an impression of a white dot.

. . . nothing else?

. . . I did not understand it either. It seems we—

It was not as if a switch had been opened. At least, not exactly. But with breathtaking suddenness the three found themselves returned to their separate shells, their few minutes of warm sharing a fading memory. Galvic Hagan descended from the aircraft and began to inspect the wires and struts of its spidery rear section.

"Am glad it not last more." David said at last.

Gia turned in her seat. "Why?"

"At moment zis one not happy at loss of zought-speak. But zis one also know time make normal. If zought-speak last longer than did, zen I zink time not make normal. Me and you and Hagan stay always in loss."

"I see," Indeed, Gia did see. Like sex, their intimate sharing had been a sweet agony. Literally, a "high." Much longer, and it would have become an addiction for the rest of their lives, like a potent drug with no antidote except the drug itself. And that, she knew, was gone forever.

Her wistful reminiscence was interrupted by an exploded epithet. "Well I'll be . . . !" Muttering angrily, Vic came forward to the cockpit and handed up to her a putty-like blob about as big as a thumb nail. "Bloody murderer!" he snarled.

Gia rolled the substance between gloved finger tips. Her throat was tight. "Explosive?"

"And how! See those little gold flecks? That means it's denzonite, a plastique normally as inert as a stone until it's zapped with a precisely tuned radio signal. It doesn't need a receiver, or a detonator. It's its own trigger."

"Take it please," Gia said, feeling slightly sick. She flinched as she watched him grind the ugly substance into the ground with his boot heel. "We're OK, I hope?"

"We'd better be," Vic said as he returned behind the controls and turned on the power.

"Wait a minute."

He turned. "What now?"

"We took this flight at a moment's notice. Right? So how could—whoever it was—have known? Even which of the aircraft we would use?"

The jets whined and *Eloise Three* surged upward. "He didn't have to know," the pilot replied as he banked the machine in a wide circle about AA 6093 and then set the course toward home. "Presuming you are the target—which seems entirely likely—it required no great feat of the imagination to figure out you would sooner or later need one of the aircraft. So our nasty friend simply took advantage of an early opportunity and attached a package on both Eloises. By now he certainly knows you are on a flight somewhere, so I presume he and his button are just waiting for us to sail gracefully over the horizon." Vic chuckled. "You know, I feel real bad about how we're going to disappoint him."

"Maybe assassin Phuili," came a quiet comment from the rear seat.

The two humans were astonished. The aircraft wobbled as in his surprise Vic twitched the controls. "Phuili don't do things like that," he said. And then his doubts surfaced. "Do they?"

"Not before," David replied. Sadly, he added, "But zis time Phuili life can change much. I zink some might twy kill to stop change."

It was an astonishing admission. But at that moment Gia was thinking of beings who were neither human nor Phuili. Perhaps it would be easier to think of them as gods: all-seeing and all-powerful, as much cognizant of the rules which guide the universe as they were of a sabotage device aboard *Eloise Three*.

The mysterious entities beyond the AA were apparently benign beings. But if human and Phuili were being manipulated—even for their own good—where did that leave free will? The joy of achievement and discovery?

Behind them the sun sank below the horizon as the aircraft raced over a shadowy landscape rapidly deepening to blackness. Stars were appearing in numbers and brilliance far beyond that which could be seen from under Earth's dusty skies, but the mind of the human female was being turned inward, away from the external world.

Whatever their powers, they are nevertheless mortal.

Coming from within herself though not originating with herself, the statement was a true one. Gia did not know why she knew that, but she had no difficulty accepting it as incontrovertible fact. It had a corollary: that because the entities were physical beings, then like most life forms they had originated in the organic soup of some primeval ocean. They had traveled the same road man and Phuili were now traveling, so knew the value of the painful learning experience which is true progress.

Then why their intercession?

Because for us, there were no others.

The rise to intelligence of the entities had been a freakish circumstance during the dawning eons of the galaxy. Life should not have happened but did, on a world on which evolution somehow avoided the side-tracks, dead ends, and natural catastrophes that make normal evolution a spasmodic sequence of fits and starts. So when they looked for their peers among the stars, they found they had arrived too soon; that only a mere handful of primitive life-bearing worlds existed among literally thousands that were still condensing from the accretion discs of countless young solar systems.

With "others" there could have been a new view point, an exciting consensus of opposites. It was a special mathematics in which *two* is infinitely greater than *one*—an equation which for the entities was tragically incomplete. So a decision was made. If they could not be part of that equation . . .

. . . they would become the mathematician.

The equation was now—finally—almost complete.
Man plus Phuili.
The new duality.

"Interesting," the A.R.A. said after Gia had finished.

Gia nervously bit her underlip. "Don't you think it's a bit more than that?"

"Perhaps." Green eyes thoughtful, the older woman leaned back in her chair. "Well, Galvic? What do you have to say about all of this?"

The young man shrugged. "I'm not so sure about the last

part. But the rest I can vouch for. Especially the telepathy. That's how they told me about the denzonite.''

"As I said. Interesting." Jenny held up a speckled blob. "This was found in the tail section of *Eloise One*." She grinned. "Don't worry. It's been neutralized."

"It had better be!" He took the blob and looked at it sourly. "I don't know how much you know about this stuff, but even a few molecules are pretty potent."

"Oh yes." Wickedly. "The scorch marks on your aircraft prove that."

Vic stared. "Then he . . . it . . ." Abruptly he subsided. "Oh what the hell."

Gia shared the sense of narrowly avoided disaster. "They saved our lives, you know." She shivered. "Wish I knew who. Or what. And who did—?" She gestured at the substance in Vic's hand. As if it had suddenly acquired legs and a sting, he threw it down on the corner of the A.R.A.'s desk. It adhered obscenely.

"Second question first," Jenny said. She produced a photograph. "Gia, do you remember this person?"

The girl studied the picture. "You showed this to me before. Isn't she one of *Farway*'s crew?"

"That's right. Carmen Klaus is the one with a family resemblance to Digger's mysterious Mr. Genese."

"Now I remember," Gia looked up. "So?"

"A few hours ago, Klaus booked out a runabout and was last seen heading toward Pock Hill."

"Yes?"

"Pock Hill is an excellent vantage point in the direction of six-oh-nine-three."

Gia's stomach did a flip. "Interesting," she said, in unconscious parody of the A.R.A.'s recent reaction. Not so restrained, Galvic let out a long whistle. "A woman, by God!" He spread his hands wide. "And why not?"

A good question. Gia felt she could kick herself for overlooking the possibility. History after all was full of accounts of women impersonating men and getting away with it, sometimes for years. So it seemed one riddle (and presumably its accompanying threat) was finally about to be exorcised.

The A.R.A. could be excused for her air of satisfaction. "I have already dispatched a security patrol," she said, anticipating the obvious question. "I think that is one lady who is about to be withdrawn from circulation for a while."

"Provided she is the assassin of course," Gia said, still faintly tasting sour grapes. She rose to her feet.

"Going somewhere?"

The expediter nodded. "I need to think for a while."

"About how to tell illusion from reality?"

Gia hesitated. "Something like that."

"Your description of the beings' history, their promotion of a "duality" between us and the Phuili. Why didn't Vic pick that up?"

"For the same reason I did not get the message about the denzonite, I suppose," Gia said. "It depended on who was being talked to."

Galvic blinked with surprised realization. "Say, that's right! Whatever was said to us, it was never via an open three way—"

Gia laid a restraining hand on his arm. "Vic, it's not what happened on the other side of the gate that bothers me. It's what happened on *this* side, during the return flight. If I was not hallucinating, then we and the Phuili are on the verge of something pretty incredible, right? But if I was merely the victim of an over-stimulated imagination, then how do we avoid proving to the Phuili hardliners what they have always preferred to believe—that we humans are not only inferior, but unstable?"

"Did you discuss this with David?" Jenny asked.

"Would you?" Gia retorted.

The A.R.A. regarded the younger woman thoughtfully. "Put yourself in David's shoes. If he picked up the same message, and had the same doubts, do you think he would have discussed it with any human before he talked to his own kind?"

Gia's jaw dropped. "You think . . . ?"

"*You* think about it," Jenny said.

She was studying the pictures she had taken of 6093, when the little alien entered the lab and watched her for a moment. Then, "I speak Jenny."

Gia turned and looked at him. "About what, David?"

"About ozers ozer side of AA. About humans and Phuili togezer being more zan humans and Phuili not togezer."

Gia had a sinking feeling. "She told you."

"Not twue. I told her." The jaws flexed in the Phuili equivalent of a smile. "Zen she told me."

In her excitement the expediter knocked some of the prints off the table.

"Glory," she whispered. "What a day this has turned out to be."

"I wish not tell you until I say to ozer Phuili. After I say, I am told human female perhaps hear same. But not tell me for same weason I not tell her." The large eyes twinkled humorously. "Perhaps humans and Phuili should more twust ozers of each."

"Yes," Gia said fervently. "Oh yes."

With the rolling gait characteristic of his short legs and splayed feet, David walked across the room and picked the prints off the floor. As he handed them to her, he pointed to the top one. "I see zat before."

Putting the others aside, she looked at the print. Showing the bowl as seen from above, it was the one she had been studying when he came in.

"Put the picture on table," the Phuili instructed. "Hold wiz hands as you just doing."

Puzzled, Gia did as he asked. "I don't understand—" Wide-eyed, she stopped. The thumb and index finger of each hand had automatically spread apart, holding the print down by the corners and framing the image of the bowl between. *A pair of human hands framing a circle.* Smaller hands, smooth . . . It was part of what she would never forget, part of the warmly silent communicating they had shared and then lost. And there was something else.

"A white dot," Gia whispered. "They showed me a white dot."

David nodded. "Me ask about Phuili gate, zey show me circle. You ask gate your world, zey show little dot. What means?"

Gia was staring at an enlarged photograph on the wall of the lab. Apparently put there either as a measure of frustration or because someone had a peculiar sense of humor, it was a rectangle of unrelieved black. She pointed. "I suppose you know what that is."

The alien nodded. "We have same, zough we not waste spaces on walls wiz pictures we know show nozing. Many pictures taken fwom above bowl AA One to twy find twansmitter fwom where energy come. Zat picture and many more taken by wobot flyers vewy close to middle of bowl. Much time waste.''

"Perhaps because they were examining the wrong AA," the expediter said, pulling the sensing head of the projection magnifier toward her and carefully inserting the print of AA 6093. She turned on the magnifier, and as the room lights dimmed she began to rotate the zoom control. The round black image swelled beyond the edges of the lab's two-meter screen, causing the room to become stygian as the Shouter's brighter landscape was swallowed beyond the frame. Suddenly, at the center of the screen, a point of light appeared and then diffused as the magnification limit was exceeded. Gia reversed the zoom until the light contracted to a sharp, bright point. "There!" she said triumphantly.

It was more than an hour since Galvic Hagan had dropped out of *Eloise One*, the jets of his harness brilliant until he vanished beyond the rim of the bowl. Commentary from the pilot of the circling aircraft remained spasmodic, as he flew in as close as he dared to watch Vic's progress, then retreated to a distance where his signal was not completely blanked by 6093's radio interference.

". . . *crawled almost up to the edge of the bowl, slow as hell but sure. Seems those adhesion pads really work, huh? Whatever gizmo he found must be pretty small; his abandoned lift harness looking a lot more conscpicuous there in the center. Going back in now . . .*"

Undoubtedly he saw Vic step off the edge, but by the time he was able to transmit the news, everyone on the ground was already watching the tiny figure drift downward under its huge canopy. It took time to descend three kilometers of vertical distance, and when Vic landed it was amid a crowd. But by pre-arrangement everyone held back to allow one human and one Phuili to approach the parachutist.

"Please don't expect me to do that again!" Vic said breathlessly as he returned Gia's hug and clasped David's extended paw. "The harness worked fine, the chute worked even better, but getting up the slope of the bowl—" He shuddered. "Now I know what frictionless means." After discarding the suction discs attached to his knees and elbows, he reached

into the voluminous pouch on the front of his suit and withdrew a glittering object about thirty centimeters long. "Here,
lady. It's your bauble."

Gia gasped in wonder as she held it. A flat ended cylinder
of material which refracted light in brilliant colors, its translucent heart contained a tiny three-dimensional image of an
AA. "It's beautiful. But what does it do?"

"S'for you and David to figure that one out," Vic replied
with ill-concealed smugness as he watched her pass the object
to her Phuili colleague. "But I lay you a hundred to one
another of those is in the bowl of eleven-eight-five-two."

"Zat is logical," David agreed as he examined the crystal-
enclosed miniature.

By this time the mixed group of humans and Phuili had
crowded around, and exclamations of human astonishment
were interspersed with Phuili gutturals. David returned the
object to Gia and fired a burst of syllables to an attentive
member of his own team. Immediately the other Phuili turned
about and trotted toward a tiny single-seat aircraft parked
apart from the other machines. "He weturn base and awange
Phuili mission to ozer AA," David explained to the humans.
"Soon we know if same in zat bowl."

"If it is, which I do not doubt," Genevieve Hagan said as
she took the object from Gia and held it up to the light, "then
our mysterious benefactors will have put two rabbits into the
hat." She looked at Gia. "You know, of course, this pretty
paper weight was not there a month ago?"

The expediter nodded. "I've looked at the last series of
photographs. Clean as a whistle." Gia turned to David. "Do
you mind if we take this back to PERU?"

"You take," the Phuili agreed. "I come talk later."

By this time *Eloise One* had spiraled down to a dusty
landing, and Vic immediately persuaded the pilot to return as
passenger on another machine so he himself could fly the two
women and the "gizmo" back to PERU. Not unexpectedly
nothing was solved during the seventy minute flight, though
Gia and Jenny exchanged the trophy at least a dozen times as
they attempted to fathom its purpose.

"We'll just have to see what the lab can do with it," Jenny
said finally as the cluster of buildings rose over the horizon.
She sighed. "Gia, presuming this is Peter's 'key'—in full
view, as he said—now what? I have an uneasy feeling that

instead of an answer we have uncovered an even larger question. And right now, my dear, more questions are what I don't need.''

The A.R.A.'s foreboding was not misplaced. Two hours later they met in her office and heard a harrassed-looking technician describe a scientific impossibility.

''What ever it is, it certainly isn't matter as we know it,'' he reported, staring at the object with distaste. ''It doesn't chip, it doesn't scratch, and it reacted in absolutely neutral fashion to every frequency I could throw at or through it.''

''Solidified energy,'' Gia murmured, intending to be facetious. Galvic started to chuckle, but subsided as the technician said angrily, ''Why not? Tell me Earth's moon really is made of green cheese, or that the universe is smaller than the head of a pin, and right now I won't argue. Because that . . . that . . . *thing* has screwed up scientific logic in a way nothing short of shameful!'' Still red faced, the man stamped out of the room and slammed the door behind him.

''Well,'' Jenny said after a moment.

''The poor chap was almost violent,'' Vic picked up the object and hefted it. ''Energy? Green cheese?'' He put it back on the desk. ''Shameful!''

The A.R.A. smiled, but faintly. ''Gia, have you contacted Earth yet?''

''Haven't had a chance.'' Gia hesitated. ''Aside from the fact there has not been enough reason.''

''Well there is now, isn't there? And there is the matter of the late Carmen Klaus.''

Vic started. ''Our denzonite suspect?''

''More than a suspect, I think. She apparently blew herself to bits as you flew over Pock Hill. One of the bits—her hand—was still holding a button transmitter.''

''I don't understand—'' Gia began.

''I think I do,'' Vic said. ''The stupid broad must still have had some denzonite with her when she tried to blow us out of the sky.'' He shook his head in disbelief. ''Even the best of us make mistakes. But . . . *that*?''

It had been an awful death, even for one whose trade was bringing death to others, but Gia experienced a lifting of spirits as she realized she was finally free of a disturbing threat. Later, as she sat before a T-Com console, fingers aching from ten minutes of unaccustomed typing, she wondered if she had been out of the security game too long. Expediters were not, after all, supposed to be risk takers, yet for days that ancient bony finger had not been far from her shoulder.

Suddenly a new pattern of lights swept the console and Digonness's reply began tracking across the display:

JOPHREM GENESE'S BEING A WOMAN CERTAINLY EXPLAINS THE EASE WITH WHICH SHE ELUDED ARREST. AT LEAST WE ARE WELL RID OF HER, THOOUGH IT IS TOO BAD HER DEMISE HAS EFFECTIVELY SEVERED POSSIBLE LEADS TO HER EMPLOYER. I KNOW WE HAVE OUR SUSPICIONS IN THAT REGARD, BUT SUSPICIONS ARE NOT EVIDENCE, SO PLEASE KEEP THAT PART OF IT TO YOURSELVES FOR NOW.

"Agreed," the A.R.A. murmured. Squeezing into the seat alongside Gia, she typed, THIS IS JENNY. ANY IDEAS OF WHAT TO DO WITH THE GIZMO? SO FAR, IT SEEMS ABOUT AS USEFUL AS A BOOKEND.

WHAT ABOUT THE PHUILI? HAVE THEY RETRIEVED A SECOND UNIT?
NOT YET, BUT I AM CERTAIN IT IS THERE.

IN THAT CASE, SUGGEST TO THEM THEY KEEP THEIR UNIT ON THE SHOUTER, THEIR LAB IS LARGER AND BETTER EQUIPPED THAN PERU'S, SO IT IS LOGICAL THEY TACKLE THE PROBLEM USING THEIR SHOUTER-BASED FACILITIES. MEANWHILE SHIP YOUR UNIT OUT ON THE FARWAY. IF THAT THING REALLY IS A KEY, IT IS STILL POSSIBLE THE LOCK IS HERE ON EARTH.

Galvic whistled. "But we'll lose two years! The Phuili could be off and running while the *Farway* is still this side of the Pleiades!"

MAKE THAT FOUR YEARS, Digonness came back, BECAUSE IF THE ANSWER IS AT YOUR END, THE UNIT WILL HAVE TO MAKE THE ROUND TRIP. NEVERTHELESS I AM CONVINCED WHAT I SUGGEST WILL SERVE THE GREATER GOOD. THINK OF THE PHUILI AS MEMBERS OF A PARALLEL SCIENTIFIC TEAM, NOT AS COMPETITORS.

"What a nice idea," Jenny said. She chuckled. "Now if we could just persuade the Phuili to think the same way."

Later they met with David. The two units, one labeled *6093* and the other marked with a Phuili hieroglyphic, stood side by side on the table. They were identical; the same shimmering yet nonreactive substance of the cylinder, the same tiny AA replica embedded within. Jenny had passed on Digonness's proposal and the response was an extended exchange of gutturals between David and his two Phuili colleagues. Finally, "If we find before ship weturn your world, Phuili gate open much sooner."

"We accept that possibility," the A.R.A. said.

David nodded. There was approval and a hint of respect in his large eyes. "In short time zis way perhaps better for Phuili. But in long time I zink it better for humans and Phuili togezer. Zerefore we agwee."

Just like that. Gia thought her mixed-up feelings were hidden, but she had forgotten the legendary emphathetic sense of the Phuili. For the sake of inter-species harmony, Peter Digonness and his Phuili opposite number had long ago concluded an agreement in which the Phuili would respect the human need for emotional privacy, in exchange for human acceptance that "haste" is not in the Phuili lexicon. By definition the human side of the agreement was the more difficult, especially considering the dragging pace of most joint projects. So to say that Gia was surprised at David's alacrity in accepting the proposal, was an understatement. Equally unsettling was the inescapable fact that once the unit from 11852 disappeared into the Phuili research lab, her own role on the Shouter would become redundant. David, recognizing the human female's aura of confusion, and apparently deciding this was a moment to bend the rules, was sympathetic.

"Gia, you not like zis. You not zink we do wight?"

Gia blinked at the little alien. Perhaps it was innate or perhaps it was a residue of what they had shared beyond the AA, but she had no doubt he knew her feelings. And the fact that she knew he knew, hinted at a still open two-way. But she did not mind.

"You are doing what must be done," Gia told David sincerely. She turned to the A.R.A. "It's just that as things start becoming interesting, I find myself sort of—"

". . . out of it?" Jenny queried, her eyes twinkling.

The expediter shrugged. "As far as Earthgate is concerned, anyway."

"Well, you are wrong," Jenny said.

Gia was revived as the *Farway* reentered normal space three days' travel time from Earth. After thirty minutes of painful exercise, followed by an even more painful experience of being required to swallow an evil tasting high-nutrient concoction, she was released, as the medic humorously put it, "under her own recognizance." Forcing unsteady legs to carry her in the direction of the bridge, her steps echoing hollowly along the silent corridors of the nearly empty ship, Gia finally entered inhabited territory in the deck immediately below the cavernous space vessel's humming Control Center.

Suddenly she was startled by a pair of strong arms and a hug. "Vic!" she said, astonished.

Galvic Hagan slackened his hold and grinned. "Welcome to the land of the living."

"Where . . . how . . . ?"

He chucked her under the chin. "Came aboard right after they turned you into a corpsicle, dear." His grin broadened. "By the way, the difference between our ages has narrowed a couple of years. Care to take me on?"

Placing both hands on his chest, she pushed herself away. "Boring couple of years, huh?"

"Not so much. I'm returning home to go back to school. Done a lot of studying."

"Subject?"

"Planetology."

"A good choice," Gia said approvingly. "You already have the field experience, so you should have no trouble—"

"Bless my soul, she's awake!" Beaming, Endart Grimes trotted over and grasped Gia's hand. "Galvic my boy, why didn't you tell me?"

"You didn't ask," the younger man sighed.

"And you, young lady. How do you feel after your second long rest in four years?"

Gia noted the fat man's apparent good health. "Not as up to it as you, I suspect. How do you do it?"

Grimes chuckled. "No miracle. There is still much work to do on the equipment, so I had myself revived several weeks ago." He patted his stomach. "I have had time to catch up."

"But between meals he is always in his workshop," Vic said. "Gia, you should see it. I bet he could build a phase converter if he wanted to!"

Grimes blushed. "Please. I am just a mechanic performing a few modest modifications." He added sadly, "unfortunately, there is still no way I can repair a sour module."

"Don't be so bashful, man. You're an artist!" The fresh voice was that of a large, middle-aged man with a lined face and twinkling blue eyes. He went directly to Gia and kissed her soundly. "You look well, Ms. Mayland."

"And so do you, captain," Gia returned fondly. It was no secret they were old friends, though Captain Joel Greshom's personal relationships were matters he normally did not discuss with his professional associates. Firmly holding her arm, he steered Gia across the deck to the door which led to his private quarters. Once inside, he sat her in the most comfortable chair. Then he called up the steward and ordered a light meal.

As she relaxed, she looked around the big room. At the simulated antiques, old leather-backed books, the handsome Turner reproduction above the realistic stone fireplace. "If the colonists had known about this—"

He laughed. "Girl, you're barking up the wrong tree. Many have supped here, and without exception they all felt sorry for me. I remember one farmer solemnly informing me that a few creature comforts are no substitute for a wide landscape under the open sky. He was right, too."

"You haven't been planetside since my mother died, have you?"

For a moment the captain looked bleak. "Never felt like it." He went to a trophy case, and from among the memorabilia of a dozen worlds lifted out a glittering cylinder. "Here. Forget about my past and concentrate on your own. A little something to refresh your memory."

It was like a tonic. Gia felt a restoring glow as she held it up to the light and examined the delicate structure contained within. "It's not a matter of memory. For me, it was yesterday when I brought this on board. Anyway, why isn't it in the safe? I don't think you realize its importance."

Again the big man laughed. "What would be the point? The person in charge of the safe also happens to be a loyal employee and shareholder of the outfit which is apparently the prime suspect behind your troubles. So why would I go to the trouble of protecting that bauble from Transtar's evil machinations—whose loyal employee and shareholder is me? Hmm?"

He was, of course, making fun of her. But the point was well taken, though Gia did not immediately abandon her concern. "So everyone knows about this? What it means and where it is kept?"

"I suppose. My officers of course, who often visit me here. And young Hagan. And certainly Endart Grimes."

"Oh yes. Endart Grimes." Gia reluctantly replaced the tiny AA in the trophy case and closed the door.

The captain eyed her curiously. "Don't you like the man?"

She shrugged. "I hardly know him."

"Which is the problem, I suspect. He acts like a fond uncle and you resent it. Right?"

"You are very discerning."

"Not really. I just know you too well. Anyway, he's not such a bad fellow. A little lonely perhaps, but he has his work to keep him company. He is very dedicated to what he does, you know."

"So are we all," Gia said moodily, reflecting on the fact that in her own job it was going to be difficult to sustain the interest and excitement of the Shouter assignment. When Jenny had suggested she belonged with the crystal-enclosed artifact right through to its hoped-for solution on Earth, it had made a lot of sense at the time. But in the cold light of reason, it was more likely the harried A.R.A. had had better things to do than invent work for an expediter who was better at detecting than expediting.

"Penny for your thoughts," the captain said.

"Nothing important," Gia lied. She forced a smile. "I think I need to resume an interrupted holiday."

She was serious about the holiday. A few days of relaxation might do much to revive her flagging spirts, especially while the artifact was being examined in Expediter's labs. But thoughts of sun and sand were put firmly aside by the first ground-to-orbit call to the huge starship. "I want you down on the first shuttle," Peter Digonness told her, his four-years-older screen image tight with suppressed anticipation. "If what you have is what I hope it is, then from now on you can select your own assignments with my blessing. If it is not, then you and I will probably end up sharing the same terminal in the computer pool."

Gia nodded. She knew the Deputy Director was not exaggerating the consequences of failure. "I am not really worried," she said. "The artifact was placed where it had to be found, so it has to have a purpose."

Digonness agreed soberly. "Perhaps. We do know that so far the Phuili have accomplished nothing with their unit. So it is just possible that bringing ours to Earth is the right approach. After all these years, I wonder—"

They were separated by millions of kilometers, their images relayed via a communications net encompassing ground and space. Yet suddenly the two shared a rapport far beyond the linking ability of lasers and microwaves. Gia had felt it before, she welcomed it gladly and then felt a sense of loss as it faded as abruptly as it came. Digonness's astonishment was replaced by a dawning realization, and then by an introspective calm. He said softly,

"It seems, my dear Gia, there is somewhat more to communicating than I realized."

It turned out that the first shuttle was not designed to carry passengers. The space below the flight deck was cramped, with Gia, Galvic Hagan and Endart Grimes squeezed into a space not as wide as a standard ground car. Behind them, most of the thirty-meter cargo bay was filled with two disassembled life suspension chambers and four unused modules, all destined for modifications at the P.L.S. plant in Seattle.

The artifact had been stowed in a compartment next to her seat, and as soon as the maneuvers of separation and retrofire were complete, Gia retrieved the crystal-enclosed model and turned it over in her hands.

"Some souvenir," Vic commented seriously.

"True," Gia agreed, peering at the delicate miniature within. Somehow her enthusiasm was diminished, making her wonder if she was a victim of overload—too much, too fast. Subjectively the rapid pace of events on the Shouter had happened only yesterday, and not even twenty-six months in stasis could relieve the effects of accumulated stress. Yet it had been only hours ago in real time that the feel of this ice-silk surface had kindled within her a soaring sense of accomplishment. There had been no doubt, no doubt at all, that the dream of Earthgate was finally on the verge of realization.

Now, she felt nothing. The dream was dormant.

Suddenly Gia stopped rotating the model. She upended it and peered along the bottom edge of the crystal cylinder. She carefully traced her thumb along the edge and then looked again. "This is not it," she whispered.

"It isn't what?" Galvic asked curiously.

She turned to him. The young man flinched at the shock in her eyes. "My God Gia, what—?"

"It's a fake," the expediter said. Abruptly she grasped his hand and dragged it, palm-wise, across the cylinder's edge. "Look. Is it bleeding?"

He pulled his hand free and glanced at the fading impression on the skin.

"No, it's not bleeding. Should it be?"

"You would have been sliced to the bone if this was the genuine artifact! See the little nick on the edge? Not even a diamond should be able to do that. Compared to the original, this is putty!" Gia looked across at the other passenger, "Isn't that right, Endart?"

The fat man, who had apparently been dozing, half roused himself. ". . . ah . . . I beg your pardon?"

"When did you make the substitution, Endart?"

"Now just a minute!" Astonished, Vic looked from one to the other. "Gia, what are you getting at? What substitution?"

"Ask him!" she flashed. Leaning forward, Gia met Grimes' heavy-lidded gaze. "Endart, what is your actual connection with P.L.S.?"

Grimes lowered his head modestly. "Founder, Director of Research and Chairman of the Board." He looked up. His face was still jovial, but the pale eyes had become aware. And cold. "Endart Penders Grimes. That is my full name, you see."

"Oh my lord." Galvic Hagan shook his head in disbelief. "Move over, Transtar."

"You'd better believe it," Gia said. "P.L.S. is a small one-specialty outfit heavily dependent on government grants to improve a product which Earthgate will make obsolete overnight. Now *that* is a motive! The woman once masculinely known as Jophrem Genese was working for Grimes all along. It was no accident she blew herself to kingdom-come when she pressed the button which was supposed to blow us out of the sky. One insignificant blob of denzonite, tuned to the same frequency as the denzonite Genese herself had concealed aboard our aircraft, and Grimes almost had it all. No us, no witnesses, hopefully no Earthgate, and no hired killer. Do I have it right, Mr. Gimes?"

The Chairman of Penders Life Support Systems was regarding his accuser thoughtfully. "Very ingenious. But, of course, absolute nonsense. For instance, why would I substitute for something which never existed in the first place?" He pointed at the artifact. "Where was it really made, Ms. Mayland? In the workshops of PERU perhaps? It seems to me that your scheme to save your own reputation at the expense of a poor fat man who has never done you harm is most reprehensible. I am sorry, but after we land I intend to report this whole sordid matter to the proper authorities."

It was an amazing performance. Despite herself, Gia felt a reluctant admiration for the mental agility contained within that polished skull. But Grimes was clearly on the defensive, so she determinedly pressed her advantage. "Go ahead. Report. Meanwhile, I am sure an analysis of material samples from your workshop will find something with an interesting similarity to material from this." Gia held up the artifact. "Or don't you think so?"

Grimes was unimpressed. "I use common enough substances. So make your analysis. It won't prove anything."

"It won't get us Earthgate either!" Vic said angrily, swiveling in his seat and grabbing the front of a voluminous tunic. "Tell us what you did with the original, you bastard, or by heaven I'll . . . *oof!*"

He gasped and released his grip as Gia thumped him between the shoulder blades. "Vic, you are a jackass," she said coldly. Her voice softened. "The artifact is indestructible, so he has to have concealed it somewhere. Probably, I suspect, aboard the *Farway*. We'll simply make sure nothing is shipped to ground until the ship is searched. Even if it takes weeks."

"Or years?" Grimes asked slyly as he straightened his rumpled tunic. "So the charade continues, eh, Ms. Mayland?" He smiled. "You will find nothing, of course. But we both know that, don't we?"

And he's probably right, was Gia's gloomy realization as she thought of the enormous volume contained within the living decks and storage spaces of the three hundred meter star ship. But whatever the outcome of the search, one thing was certain. Grimes had to pay for what he had done. If she could not see him put away in one of the orbital prisons, Gia was sure she could filter enough evidence through to the P.L.S. stockholders to exclude firmly the stout executive from any of the financial fruits of his crimes. Which would certainly damage his pride, as well as his bank account.

Damn him!

All the punishment in the world could not compensate for the loss of Earthgate. Staring miserably in front of her, Gia barely noticed the flare of a steering jet through the side window, and then the dropping away of Earth's horizon as the shuttle's nose came up for reentry. She heard a slight thrumming as the thick wings began to bite atmosphere, felt a gradual increase of weight as deceleration pressed her into her chair. As the shuttle slid down its narrow track of safety towards denser air, the thrumming increased and became a vibration. Reacting to computer commands, control surfaces extended from their housings. There was a coughing roar as ram-jets fired up. . . .

"Explosion aboard!"

Even from the lower deck they heard the pilot's shout as the shuttle shuddered and then began to break apart.

"Emergency separation!"

There was a bang and then breath was gasped out of their lungs as something shoved with enormous force against the rear bulkhead. Looking like a larger version of an ancient Apollo capsule, the separated nose section immediately flipped over to re-entry attitude, and for a moment Gia saw the crumpling shuttle fall away behind them. Haloed with a flickering blue light, the discarded stub-winged craft was falling in on itself.

It's imploding!

The moment was barely enough for astonished uncomprehension before there was another jolt as the drogue chute snapped out behind them and steadied the jarring motion of their fall. Somewhere a relay closed and the huge main canopy shot out after the drogue, again ramming their bodies deep into restraining cushions as the shroud lines snapped, stretched, and then held.

"Is everyone OK down there?" the pilot shouted. Apparently the intercom was gone, along with just about everything else.

"I think so!" Vic shouted back. "What the hell happened?"

"Something cut loose in the cargo bay, that's all we know. Thank God this is an old prototype model with capsule separation. Otherwise we'd be part of the mess back there. Anyway, brace yourselves. We're going to hit!''

They did, violently. After the first bounce the capsule hit again, tilted, then rolled completely over until it stopped with a shuddering jarr and a screech of riven metal. It took only a moment to trigger the latches of the escape hatch, and not much longer for the three passengers and two crewmen to scramble out of their dented confinement. They found themselves on a sandy slope with sparce patches of coarse grass struggling for existence amid eroded rock outcroppings. The sun was low, the sky clear, and the air cool. For a minute or so it was good to relax, to breathe deeply and to marvel at the fact they had all come through the experience with nothing more serious than a few scrapes and bruises. Even Endart Grimes, despite being older and overweight, looked almost content as he surveyed the scene. ''Where are we?''

The pilot noted the position of the sun, then looked at his watch. ''It's mid-afternoon and we were approaching Kennedy along a polar orbit. So I would say sixty degrees north or thereabouts.''

''Canada,'' Vic said. ''Some landing pad, huh?''

A wind began to blow up the slope and it seemed the sky was darkening. Gia thought she heard distant thunder. ''Hope we're not in for a drenching,'' she commented as she and Vic climbed up to the top of the slope. Already the wind was fiercer, so they crouched low until they reached the edge of a cliff which overlooked a very stormy sea. Winded, Gia sank down on her knees. ''If we had come down in that—''

''—we would not be breathing now,'' Galvic said, his face pale as he realized how close they had been to eternity.

There was a crunching of feet as the others joined them. By this time the wind was so strong everyone had to shout to be understood. Gusts of stinging sand beat on exposed flesh and sea birds squawked alarm as they flapped laboriously inland toward safety.

It was a strange kind of storm and it was becoming stranger. A few kilometers out from the shore, a roiling dark cloud seemed suspended over the water. Lightning flickered in and around the cloud and thunder rumbled incessantly. The wind had increased to a frenzy, forcing the five to flatten themselves prone on the ground. Gia thought the assistant pilot shouted something, but his words were swept away in the roaring cacophony.

What is it out there?

The question was obvious, the answer was not. For the first time in her life Gia felt a genuine fear of the unknown, like a child abruptly abandoned in a dark room. The wind whipped and howled toward the thing over the water, toward the frothing column that had reared up into the base of the cloud like a liquid pedestal. Within the cloud itself there was something shadowy, a vagueness that slowly rose upward until, just below the summit of the cloud, it began spreading into a gigantic T.

"It can't be," Gia whispered. "It just can't be."

But it can be, a voice mocked in her mind. *It is!*

Along with realization came a sound of laughter, high pitched and with more than a hint of hysteria. The wind was beginning to subside, enough so that Endart Grimes, between paroxysms of mirth, was able to gasp, "Don't you see, girl? Don't you see? I've given you Earthgate!"

"He has what?" Vic asked with astonishment, trying to look both at the cloud and at the wheezing executive. "What is the man blathering about?"

"I think it is pretty obvious," Gia replied stonily, her eyes fixed on the now unmistakable shape within its stormy cocoon.

"I didn't want even the slightest chance of it being found," Grimes went on hoarsely. Hands clutched against his stomach, he was rocking back and forth as if he was in pain. "So I hid it in one of the P.L.S. suspension chambers, just before the equipment was dismantled and loaded aboard the shuttle, I mean, how could I know it wanted Earth's atmosphere to feed on? That it was, in fact, nothing more than a template?" The fat man gave way to another wracking paroxysm of laughter. "Just think about it! If what you had with you in the cabin had been the real thing, we would not be here now, would we?" Wheezing horribly, he pointed shakily at the thing over the sea. "Instead, we'd be part of—"

He did not finish the sentence. Eyes bulging, Endart Penders Grimes toppled slowly on his side, quivered once and lay still. After a moment, Gia checked his pulse.

There wasn't any.

*   *   *

The place was Akimiski, a large island in James Bay. North of the island, James Bay widened into Hudson Bay, the ocean in a continent's heart. Ten kilometers off Akimiski's shore, a *seed* had reached for, and found, millions of tons of matter. Starting with a couple hundred tons of space-going machinery called a cargo shuttle, it then began absorbing from the gas-liquid interface at the planet's surface. Like a mini black hole it was impartial; along with air and water it took in huge numbers of fish and birds, a few seals, a couple of beluga whales, and one polar bear. It would have made no difference wherever it landed; ocean or desert, mountain top or city, it only needed matter. Unlike a black hole, however, the *seed* was not insatiable. It was, as a dying man pointed out, merely a template, a means to recreate itself on an incredibly larger scale.

Which it did.

Exactly two hours and thirteen minutes after the implosion began in the shuttle's cargo bay, the process of transformation was complete and a new AA towered over the shallow waters of James Bay. The vortex was no more; air and sea were calm, and a rescue heli-wing accomplished a smooth landing near the four survivors.

At plus two hours and thirty-two minutes, even as the heli-wing was climbing away from Akimiski, a huge sphere of flickering light suddenly appeared above the AA. There was no accompanying heat or noise, and the air remained calm.

At plus thirty hours and three minutes, a broad-winged aircraft appeared from the south and quietly vanished into the light. Roughly a tenth of a second later, *real time*, the same aircraft emerged above an AA locally known as "6093" and shortly thereafter alighted on the dusty surface of a hurriedly prepared runway. Six hundred light years had been traversed in less time than it takes to draw a breath.

Two passengers emerged from the aircraft. One, a young woman, held back as her older male companion walked hesitatingly toward a mixed group of humans and aliens who were waiting nearby. One of the group, a human, came forward and met the man halfway. They clasped hands and studied each other. Finally, a smile.

"Welcome home, Peter," Genevieve Hagan said softly.

ON THE DREAM CHANNEL PANEL

by Ian Watson

*Speculation on the future of advertising goes
way back to H.G. Wells's* When the Sleeper
Wakes *and probably earlier. Here's the latest
twist on that fine art as dreamed up by the
author of* The Book of the River *and* The
Embedding.

I had always regarded myself as a vivid dreamer, but even
I was amazed when my dreams were interrupted by the
advertisements.

I was climbing by rope ladder up the outside of a lighthouse to catch an airship due to depart from the top—all in
my dream, of course—when the scene suddenly blanked out
and cans of food were dancing round me to jolly musical
accompaniment, mainly percussion.

The labels showed some peculiar fruit or vegetable, which
at first I took to be maize but then decided looked more like a
hairy banana; and a moment later the tops of the cans ripped
off of their own accord, and the contents emptied out, *steaming*, on to floating plates—so those must have been self-
heating cans, only no one had put self-heating cans on the
market just yet. Stripped of their hairy yellow skins, the
insides of the "fruits" seemed more like frankfurters.

A choir of disembodied voices sang out gaily, "*Pop a can
of kallopies!*" And there was I back on the rope ladder again.
The dream continued . . .

* * *

"Have you ever heard of a tropical fruit called a *kallopie*?"
I asked Phyllis when I got to school the next morning. Phyllis
teaches Geography.

"You can get all sorts of imports at the Third World Food
Centre," she said. "Okra, yams, breadfruit. Maybe you can
get whatever it is there."

"But have you ever heard of them?"

"No," she admitted. "What are they? Where are they
from?"

Not from the Third World, I thought; just from the world
of my dreams. But since when did dreams have commercial
breaks in them?

I pursued this line of thought. It so happened that the
commercial TV networks had been blacked out by strikes for
the past week; and while I hardly regarded myself as the kind
of TV addict likely to suffer from withdrawal symptoms,
maybe without knowing it *I was*. Were we not all condi-
tioned, to a greater or lesser degree, by advertising? Wasn't it
a sad fact that commercials were often better made than the
programmes? Hence my subconscious felt obliged to offer a
substitute . . .

Admittedly this was a far-out hypothesis, but it led on to
the thought that if *I*, a fairly selective viewer, was hallucinating advertisements in my dreams, how much more so must
many of the school kids (TV addicts all of them) be feeling
the strain?

My second class that day was Current Affairs; so I decided
that we would discuss the role of the mass media. Who
knows, maybe I was the first adult to notice this quaint
phenomenon, of advertising-dreams?

After a while I asked the class, "Do any of you ever *dream*
about watching TV? For instance, how about last night?
Think back!"

Alas, no one could recall anything. Still, that wasn't at all
unusual. So I set my class a simple project: to keep pencil
and paper by their beds and note down the first thought in
their minds when they woke up. For this is an infallible way
of remembering dreams. However absurd or random, and
eminently forgettable, that first thought might seem to be,
nevertheless once capture and fix it, and like a string of silk
scarves emerging by magic from a conjuror's sleeve, in its

wake dream after dream would spill forth from amnesia into the light of day.

My own dreams were broken into again that night. As I lay abed in my little bachelor flat, enjoying some wonderfully Byzantine spy story of my unconscious mind's devising, suddenly there came a commercial for *koozels*—which were apparently a crunchy snack wondrous to the taste buds.

The next morning I was supposed to be teaching that same class the history of the French Revolution; but I checked up on the assignment first.

About half of the class had done as I'd asked, probably because of the novelty value; so I put it to them, "Did any of you have a dream interrupted by some sort of advertisement— like a commercial on TV?"

And the jailbait of the group, sexy fifteen-year-old Mitzi Hayes, stuck her hand up. She alone.

"A voice was trying to sell me something crunchy and delicious."

"Called what, Mitzi?"

"A noodle."

General hilarity erupted; the rest of the class were sure she was japing me.

"Think, Mitzi."

"No, a *koozel*: that's what it was!"

"Anyone else?"

"No one else."

So I quickly switched over to the topic of Robespierre, determined to avoid the teacher's trap of asking young Mitzi, when school was out, to a coffee bar to discuss her sleeping activities . . .

What I did instead was place a small ad in the local newspaper: "*Koozels or kallopies? Anyone who dreams of these please reply Box 17 in confidence.*"

And for good measure, digging deeper into my pocket, I placed similar small ads in four national newspapers.

Within a week I had eleven replies. Remarkably, most were from Appleby itself; and none was from further away than twenty miles.

So the twelve of us—discreetly excluding Mitzi—got together at my flat one evening the following week.

We were a retired dentist, an antiquarian bookseller, a ladies' hairdresser, a butcher, a hamburger cook, a shop assistant, a secretary, an unemployed plumber, a garage mechanic, a middle-aged lady medium, a postman, and a teacher (myself). So we constituted ourselves the "Dream Channel Panel," with myself as Chairman, and tried to puzzle out what the explanation was, and who we could complain to.

Max Edmunds was our dentist; and in his opinion some scientific laboratory in this very average—and thus ideal—town of Appleby had been funded by big advertising money to build a prototype dream-transmitter which could interfere with the brain waves of sleeping people and insert messages. He pointed to the restricted radius of replies I'd received, as evidence of a local source. At prsent only mock advertisements for imaginary products were being broadcast as tests; but soon it would be the real—and dangerously invasive—thing.

To date, by the way, another half a dozen products had paraded themselves before us in our nightly fantasies, besides repetitions of kallopies and koozels; and these had all been exotic and implausible foodstuffs; such as *kalakiko*, a powder which when sprinkled on a slice of bread promptly sprouted lucious brown mushrooms; *humbish*, an oily liquid which seemingly congealed a pint of water into lobster in aspic; and *ampathuse*, sparkling golden wine in self-chilling flasks . . . But why go on? The TV dispute was over by now; the dream-advertising wasn't.

Mary Gallagher, our medium, had originally been of the opinion that the commercials were mischievous spirit messages "from the other side." But when Elsie Levin, our cook at the new MacDonald's in town, suggested, "Perhaps it isn't *really* advertising? Perhaps it's a Government thing? Maybe it's an experiment in mind-control!" Mary threw the fat in the fire by saying, "And maybe one of *us* is actually one of *them*? If it's people, not spirits, who are doing it—why then, they could have read your small ads as easily as we could, Mr. Peck."

It took the best part of the next half hour to try to prove our *bona fides* to each other; and it was Glenda Scott, our hairdresser, who finally hauled us back on course.

"Maybe there isn't any dream-transmitter," she said. "Not in Appleby, anyway—not in *our* world. What if there's another world alongside ours; one where the people really do

eat such things? What if they know how to broadcast dreams
as entertainment—with commercials on the different dream-
channels? And somehow we've picked these up. One of our
hair driers used to pick up radio paging at the hospital.
'Doctor Muhammed to Emergency!' ''

Max Edmunds nodded. "A tooth filling sometimes picks
up radio shows."

Glenda beamed at this confirmation. "So we're intercept-
ing dream broadcasts from the other world. But not," she
added for the benefit of Mary, "*your* 'other world.' ''

"So where is it?" asked Tom Pimm, our butcher. "I don't
see it."

"Of course not. How could you? You're awake, and in our
world."

Max snapped his fingers. "Ah. You might have a point
there! It's a well-known fact that if you keep somebody
awake for long enough, they'll start hallucinating. People
have to dream, and if they can't get any sleep to do it in,
they'll do it wide awake. Might I suggest that one of us
volunteer to stay awake for several days—while the rest of us
form a rota to *keep* him awake? To see what happens."

Jon Rhys Jones, our unemployed plumber, raised his hand.
"I suppose I'd better be the volunteer. Got nothing better to
do, have I? And the wife's away visiting her mother."

"Over to you, Brian," Max said to me, as Chairman.
"We'll only need one person on duty to start with, but after
the first couple of days we'd better have several in attendance."

I took a vote on the proposal; but we were in general
agreement, so I drew up a rota then and there.

"Room's swimming," mumbled Jon, five days later, as
Glenda and Rog (our postman) marched him to and fro across
the lounge in his house. "Can't stand up."

So they steered him to the sofa, where Max checked his
pulse; then Glenda sat beside him, and periodically slapped
him on the cheek like a glamorous interrogator, varying this
by pinching and shaking him.

It was late Saturday night. Besides Glenda, Rog and Max,
I was there, and Mary Gallagher and Tom Pimm. Empty
lager cans lay about on the carpet, though we weren't allowing our volunteer to consume any alcohol in case this helped
him to pass out. The TV was on, and in the kitchen a radio

was playing pop music. All to keep us lively. At twelve o'clock the night shift was due to arrive.

And all week long the dream-commercials had continued to besiege us—though not Jon—most recently with outstanding claims for *sklesh*, a jar of violet paste to be spread on kallopies, as a relish.

It was eleven-thirty when it happened.

Suddenly part of the ceiling glowed—and it was as if a cornucopia opened. Or as if a jackpot had paid off in actual fruits. From nowhere, cans and jars and tins and phials fell through, bouncing on the carpet. One can hit Mary on the toe, and she squealed. We all retreated to the walls for a while, dragging Jon with us.

In fact the shower of produce probably lasted for less than a minute, but by then the middle of the room was ankle-deep in kallopies and sklesh, kalakiko and humbish and other things—enough to fill half a dozen hampers. As soon as the shower ceased Max rushed forward, grabbed up a can of kallopies and popped it open. Immediately, with a little cry, he set it down again and blew on his fingers. Then he hastened to the kitchen and returned with plates and forks. Soon we were all picnicking on the sizzling sausage-fruits— all except for poor Jon, who had staggered back to the sofa and fallen fast asleep. Goodness, kallopies on their own tasted delicious enough; but spread with sklesh they were bliss.

"Have to give it to them," admitted Tom Pimm, kissing his fingers. "First rate. Beats any sausage I've ever made."

And Glenda winked at Mary. "Our first delivery from the other world, eh?"

The doorbell rang just then. The night shift had arrived, in time to join in the feast. But there was plenty left over afterwards.

The rota was a time-consuming business, though, and as for volunteering to be the one who stayed awake, only a few of us could spare several days at a stretch. The bookseller Don Thwaite was next; then Glenda who took a week's leave from the salon; then Mary Gallagher. By this time we had a fair stack of foodstuffs in my flat, where we had decided to centralise everything and hold all subsequent "wakes," with me keeping strict inventory. But we were all feeling frayed and exhausted when the whole of the Dream Channel Panel met on that fourth weekend for a stocktaking. Besides, there were several domestic crises brewing, due to all the hours that some members of the panel were absenting themselves mysteriously from home. Though the dream-commercials still continued, teasing us with even more fabulous luxuries.

Mary stifled a yawn. "Surely there must be a better way! I'm quite black and blue from my stint."

"But how else can we get the stuff to materialise?" asked Rog.

Mary looked around our circle; most of us were seated on the floor. "Twelve of us," she mused. "If only there were thirteen."

"That's unlucky," objected Elsie.

"Why thirteen?" Tom asked.

"The number of a coven," said Don Thwaite. "That's what you're driving at, isn't it?" He chuckled fastidiously. "However, I don't happen to be a witch."

"And neither am I!" snapped Mary, indignant. "A medium is no witch."

"She might have been," said Max, "in the Middle Ages."

"As far as I'm concerned," said Don, "a medium isn't anything at all. Mary certainly didn't conjure up the food; and it isn't made of ectoplasm. I doubt if it comes from Fairyland—*or* the Inferno."

"All I'm saying," said Mary, "is that we tried one strange idea already—Mr. Edmunds' notion—and it worked. But that doesn't mean it's the only way, or the best. There must be *something* about the number thirteen . . ."

I hesitated; and then confessed. "Actually, there *are* thirteen of us. There's a girl at my school who's been picking up the commercials too."

"Well, why didn't you *say*?" demanded Tom Pimm. "Good grief, if there's any easier way to get our hands on the stuff!"

"I thought she was too young to be involved."

"How old is she?"

"Fifteen."

"Just the age," said Don Thwaite wisely, "when children are supposed to produce poltergeist effects. Thanks to all the strains of adolescence, and the sexual volcano stoking up . . ."

"Well, you'd better involve her now," declared Tom.

"And so say all of us." Rog, who had dark rings under his eyes, nodded.

"But I can't do that! I'm her teacher. How can I possibly invite a girl pupil along to what'll look like a coven?"

"Quite easily," said Glenda, juggling with a jar of sklesh. "She'll be flattered."

"I refuse. It's too risky."

However, the Dream Channel Panel voted me down.

"This is Mitzi," said I, leading her into my crowded flat the following Saturday.

I had kept my invitation as low-key as I could, while still asking her to tell no one; and had stressed that it was to meet friends of mine who were interested in her dreams. But Mitzi turned up at the door wearing a brief skirt and cheesecloth blouse, with her hair done in a pert ponytail and perfume subtly applied.

Whatever disappointment may have overcome her when she discovered the Dream Channel Panel in full session promptly vanished as soon as she tasted kallopies with sklesh and crunched some koozels—while I explained what had been happening during the past few weeks.

"So what do I do?" she asked us, posing in the center of the room.

"Ah now, that's just it, isn't it?" said Mary. "In my opinion we all ought to join hands and close our eyes."

"If she's supposed to be some sort of virgin witch," said Rog, eyeing Mitzi hopefully, "don't we need an altar—a table'll do—and candlesticks and a hen? And shouldn't she take her clothes off?"

"That'll do," said I sternly. "We'll try Mary's suggestion. And we'll all chant 'Pop a can of kallopies,' and the rest of the songs."

Soon, feeling faintly absurd as though we had been translated back to childhood to games of Ring-o-Rosies, we were all shuffling round in a circle singing jingles. This was hardly the picture of a coven of warlock shoplifters. But before long something tribal and primitive seemed to grip us and wash away our embarrassment, and we really swung into the spirit of it . . .

And part of the ceiling glowed.

No kallopies or koozels rained down, though.

Instead, what I can only call a "ladder of light" descended. Its siderails and spokes were fluorescent tubes, but minus the glass.

"Oh," gasped Elsie Levin. "Oh."

For a moment this seemed the best comment that any of us could make; but then Mary said, "*Thirteen* rungs; count them."

We did, and she was right.

"What is it, then: Jacob's Ladder?" asked Jon Rhys Jones in wonder.

"I don't notice many angels ascending and descending," said Don Thwaite.

"Since nothing's coming down," Tom Pimm suggested, "how about one of us nipping up to see?"

All eyes turned to him. But he shuffled evasively.

"Bit on the heavy side, aren't I? Looks fragile to me." With a professional glance he weighed Mitzi up. "The girl's the lightest."

"And it *is* my ladder, isn't it?" Heedless of whether the light might burn or electrocute her, she gripped hold. Quickly she climbed up, pausing once to smooth her skirt, not that this hid much, and vanished through the glow.

A minute later her hand reached back for balance and her face peered through. She regarded us upside-down.

"Hey, there's a real feast waiting!" Come on, the lot of you." Back out of sight she popped.

"I don't know about *all* of us," mused Jon Rhys Jones. "I read this book about mysterious disappearances, see . . . and, well, maybe one of us ought to hang on down below. If Tom's bothered about his weight . . ."

However, a hungry look had come over Tom Pimm's countenance. So in the end, it was our shop assistant Sandra—a shy creature—and Bob the mechanic who stayed below.

As Chairman, I was the first to follow Mitzi up. A moment later I was emerging through a similar glow in the floor of a simple open-air building: a circle of white columns supporting a cupola. Steps led on to a greensward, with woodland a few hundred yards distant. Twin fountains were spouting and plashing back into alabaster basins. Birdsong filled the air, though I didn't notice any birds. What I did observe was a whirling kaleidoscope of colours midway between the foun-

tains. At first I took this to be simply rainbows in the
spray-drift, since the sun was shining brightly; but really the
kaleidoscope was far too busy and vivid. The air smelled of
lilies and honeysuckle, though I couldn't see any flowers
either, only neat lawn.

Other seductive aromas floated from a long *alfresco* table
spread with gourmet goodies—which Mitzi was already
sampling.

As were we all, before long.

"But where are we?" wondered Glenda as she nibbled a
wafer spread with humbish.

Tom Pimm grandly waved an open flask of ampathuse, and
was perhaps about to offer an opinion . . . when a chime
sounded through the glade. About a hundred yards away the
air began to glow, and an Aladdin's palace—somewhere
between the Taj Mahal and a Chinese pagoda—emerged from
nowhere into solid substance, like a Polaroid picture develop-
ing. A band of people wearing skimpy tunics flocked out of it,
barefoot, and headed gleefully for our rotunda and the waiting feast. Noticing us, they straggled to a halt.

Only one man and one young woman continued. She was
the image of the young Brigitte Bardot; he was Cary Grant in
his middle years.

As for the others: Omar Sharif, Greta Garbo, Sophia Lo-
ren, all looking their very best . . . I gave up.

"Golly!" cried Mitzi. She was the only one of us dressed
like them. Which must have been why Bardot addressed her
first.

"How here?"

"We climbed up this ladder out of Mr Peck's flat—"
began Mitzi.

"Flat?"

"Fixed homes in heaps," commented Cary Grant. "Twentieth, twenty-first. Favourite era. Must be ex past-time.
Weirdest."

"There was this glow on the ceiling. And it's in there
too." Mitzi pointed at the rotunda.

Bardot skipped away and mounted the steps. Meanwhile I
began explaining to Cary Grant about our dreams of kallopies
and koozels; but Bardot returned before I'd quite done.

"True. Looked down. Surprise for two below!"

"Do you people have to talk like crossword puzzle clues?" grumbled Don Thwaite.

"Cross word?" Bardot looked mildly puzzled. "No, no anger. Psycho-physical weak spot detected. Maybe excessive reality alteration?"

Cary Grant nudged her. "Time travellers lured by Dream-food. Great endorsement!"

"I don't know whether I'm dreaming or awake," said Mitzi.

Cary Grant touched the palm of his hand to her forehead, as if to feel whether she was fevered.

"Frustration level seven," he told Bardot. "Desire level twelve! Phantasy level ten. Figures!"

"A hole in time," said Bardot. "Troublesome."

"Nonsense. Harmless. Imagine summoning great pre-Dream humans. From era of sleep and hard reality. Spearshaker, for instance. 'Imagination bodies forth the forms of things unknown, turns them to shapes, gives to airy nothing a local habitation,' eh? Erase memory afterwards. Safe."

"Remind you: cannot erase subconscious memory. Besides, more likely summon black-dreamers than white. Wizards, witches, wildfolk. Recall: number thirteen."

"Just what *has* the number thirteen got to do with all this?" I interrupted them.

"Easy," said Bardot. "Thirteen-sided resonance crystals implanted here," and she touched her own forehead. "Help us tap the Power. Of Reality Flow. Energy into matter; matter into energy. Whole universe oscillates in and out of reality at every moment, as though all is but a dream in the cosmic mind. So catch it on the hop; alter bits as you wish. Change self-form. Cook up dreamfood, as could never be otherwise. Whole thing highly—commercial, of course. Big Comp-brain co-ordinates all minds through crystals. Dream-patterns patented and licensed. Otherwise anarchy."

"Do you mean you can change reality at will? You can make imaginary things real?"

Bardot nodded. "World is all a dream. Science of it thus . . ."

And she explained, but I couldn't understand a word of her explanation. She was just getting on to the economics of it all—mental market forces, psychophysical supply and demand—when Cary Grant took pity. He clapped me on the shoulder.

"Eat, drink, be merry." He waved to the rest of the people who had turned themselves into film stars of our era.

"Hang on," Max Edmunds said, "if this is a world of dreams made real, then what does the world *really* look like?"

"Underneath? Under layer on layer of dream? Like geological deposits pressing down?" Cary Grant shrugged. "Who knows? Maybe it's a fossil. Dead stone."

But already Garbo and company were flooding past to the banquet, and tugging us along with them.

Tom Pimm slapped his belly.

"Full up," he announced tipsily.

"Time for Aphros, then," said Bardot.

"Afters? I couldn't eat another crumb."

"*Aphros*. Aphrodisiacs." She whistled a sequence of notes, and out of the busy kaleidoscope between the fountains, clouds of heady vapour began to spray.

I must draw a discreet cloak over what took place on the greensward next. Suffice it to say that we were quite weary by the time those future people escorted us back inside the rotunda, to the glow.

Escorted? *Marched* us, almost.

"What century is this, anyway?" Max Edmunds thought to ask as they were popping him down the hole; but Bardot only patted him on the head and thrust him out of sight.

Tom Pimm licked his lips. "Do you always finish your meals like that?" Bardot winked, and down he went too.

Next was Mitzi, but Cary Grant felt her forehead first. "Frustration level zero. Desire level one," he told Bardot.

She laughed. "Better go last. Hole might close early."

One by one we were hastily popped through the glow. Down in my flat it turned out that Bob and shy Sandra were hurriedly pulling on their clothes in some embarrassment, with their backs turned. Aphro-gas must have drifted through . . .

Last of all came Mitzi. As her feet touched the carpet the ladder began to fade, and the ceiling darkened over. Soon there was only painted plaster above.

Tom Pimm rubbed his hands. "Right! Next Saturday, everyone?"

But during the next week, I dreamed nothing memorable, and on the Saturday I found that this was true of the others too.

The thirteen of us still linked hands, danced round the room and sang jingles. But no glow appeared. No food fell. No ladder descended. In the end we had to give up.

"It's Mitzi's fault," declared Mary Gallagher. "She should have stayed pure. A virgin. It's like Mr. Edmunds said a while back . . . What did they call her up there? A sexus, was it?"

"A nexus. A connecting force." Max Edmunds nodded authoritatively. "It's all a question of adolescent libido and psychic energy. She was the paranormal channel into our dreams, and to the future Dreamworld. She was the sexual volcano—and now she's blown off steam."

"And whose fault is *that*?" Tom rounded on me accusingly. "I saw you and her, after the meal."

I defended myself. Hotly. Not least because a week had gone by and normal behaviour ruled again. "Don't blame me! Bardot arranged that deliberately—to fix the weak spot."

"And now we'll never eat as well again. All thanks to you. None of the rest of us would have touched Mitzi." Tom flushed with moral indignation.

"You were too busy with Greta Garbo," I pointed out. But I appeared to be in a weak position. For Glenda spoke out vindictively.

"What was all that about 'desire level twelve' beforehand, and 'desire level one' afterwards? What a mess you must have made of it. But what can one expect from a professional bachelor? You probably turned the poor girl off for life."

I turned to Mitzi, but she was staring away out of the window. I'd been wondering why she was wearing a shapeless sweater and old jeans; but surely that couldn't have anything to do with it.

"We'd better divvy up the takings," said Tom, just as though he was the Chairman; and no one disagreed. So he headed for my larder, to rifle it.

"Couldn't we," said I, "try a different approach?"

Jon Rhys Jones fairly glared at me. "It's all over, **boy**, don't you see?" I particularly resented the "boy."

But it wasn't all over.

Two months later Mitzi discovered that she was pregnant. She didn't tell me, though. The first I knew of it was when two police officers called. Because, of course, Mitzi was under the legal age for sexual relations. There was even a vague hint of unwillingness on her part. A whiff of rape rather than seduction. But I think this was just the police trying to get me to confess to something more serious, which might look better on their records.

Naturally I explained the events leading up to this awkward outcome; and referred the two officers to Glenda, Don, Max and the others for confirmation. By this date, alas, I hadn't any dreamfood left and had tossed the empties away. But I assured the officers that various cans, tubes and flasks would be buried in the garbage in-fill outside town. They might even still be lying on the surface. A search ought to turn them up. . . .

"So," said officer number one, ignoring this helpful advice as he scribbled in his notebook, "you freely admit that you had sexual intercourse with Mitzi Hayes here in your flat."

"No, no; up there." I pointed.

"On the *ceiling*? Like a fly?"

"Above."

"In the *loft*?"

"No, in the future . . . And it spoiled everything."

"I'll say it did," agreed number two sourly.

Still, they were quite formal and polite, merely arresting me and promising to corroborate my story with the others— and with Mitzi, who apparently had said nothing of the sort when they interviewed her. Well, that was understandable.

I also referred them for good measure to the small ads I'd placed a few months earlier. Why do such a thing, if this wasn't all gospel truth? They promised to check that out too.

Would you believe it, *not one* of the former members of the Dream Channel Panel backed my story up? A few conceded that they knew me casually by sight; the others swore blind that they had never met me in their lives.

While I was out on bail pending prosecution for sexual offences against a minor—and out of my job too, pending the outcome—Jon Rhys Jones slipped round furtively to my flat one night.

"We're awfully sorry, boy," was the gist of what he had to say. "You know how it is with us who have families to think about. And family businesses, such as butcher's shops. I mean, getting ourselves involved in an orgy! Good thing young Mitzi had the sense to confide in a man of experience like Tom . . ."

So that was it.

The really ironic thing was that I might have got off with a few months in jail, or even a suspended sentence. But not in view of what I'd said. This ensured that I was referred for a psychiatric report.

I had read about cases like mine before. Somebody commits a trivial offense, and next thing the poor sod is detained indefinitely at the pleasure of the overworked psychiatrists of our prison service. Because he's considered "mad" he can spend five years inside. Or ten.

Hastily swallowing my pride, I swore that I'd been lying.

And no one believed me.

Because of the newspaper ads. Which was particularly galling, as I need never have mentioned those.

Except that I had to, to explain how the Dream Channel Panel got together.

Except that it never did, according to the others—whose names I must have picked out of the phone book or a street directory, they supposed.

There was one small consolation in all this. I wasn't considered a violent sort of looney. So I wasn't sent to a high security lockup for the criminally insane miles from nowhere on some windswept moor. Instead I was despatched to a permissive prison for mild cases, where we inmates could weave baskets and grow cabbages for the Governor, and perform other useful intelligent forms of therapy.

It's been six months now, and as feared my case hasn't come up for review.

Prison food is ghastly, after you've tasted sklesh on kallopies.

Boiled cabbage, mashed potatoes, stringy stew: it's enough to drive any self-respecting gourmet round the bend.

But I'm making progress.

Because we're considered low risk in my group, the male nurses sometimes leave us in the workshop unsupervised. And I seize the opportunity to tell my fellow inmates tales of the dreamfood of the future. Not forgetting the orgy that followed.

And then I choose twelve disciples to dance round with me in a circle, singing:

"Can't refuse
"Ampathuse!"

and:

"We wish
"Humbish!"

There's no Mitzi here, of course. Women are kept apart from us. But consider: three of my group are under twenty. Morris, Martin and Paul. Morris is in here for exposing himself to little girls. Martin is a Peeping Tom. Paul stole ladies' underwear off washing lines. In their own way they're volcanoes of sexuality, and bound to be virgins too.

And all our dreams are troubled, now that I've persuaded my disciples to spit out their nightly doses of largactil and chlorpromazine, as soon as the nurses' backs are turned.

Troubled: though not quite yet by advertisements for kallopies and koozels. But if I plug away at my own propaganda, and if the prison kitchen keeps on dishing up such soggy cabbage, it's inevitable.

Consider: Frustration level ten. Desire level ten. Phantasy level ten!

We nearly did it this afternoon, too.

Thirteen of us were dancing round the workshop floor amidst neglected baskets. Morris was sweating with more than mere exertion. Paul was positively drooling. Martin looked goggle-eyed.

And a little circle upon the ceiling glowed. It wasn't only a patch of sunlight. It was the Glow.

"Keep it up!" I cried. "Pop a can of kallopies! Pop a can, pop a can! What do we wish? Humbish!"

At this point my lookout at the keyhole, Sparky Jones, an alcoholic, spotted male nurse Turner approaching at speed down the corridor. So, alas, we had to break ranks. The glow promptly faded out.

But tomorrow we'll do it. Or the week after. Now that the Dream Channel Panel is back in session again.

Food of the future, how I yearn for you!

THE GODS OF MARS
by Gardner Dozois, Jack Dann, and Michael Swanwick

Percival Lowell was one of the sharpest-eyed astronomers of his day, and his book Mars As the Abode of Life *was surely the inspiration for a generation of marvelous Mars tales, including, we feel sure, those of Edgar Rice Burroughs. Alas, the probes of seventy years later turned out to be grimly different . . . and, from the viewpoint of science fiction dreamers, disappointing. Still, one goes on hoping—and this tale by three writers all born long after Lowell's time, proves this.*

They were outside, unlashing the Mars lander, when the storm blew up.

With Johnboy and Woody crowded against his shoulders, Thomas snipped the last lashing. In careful cadence, the others straightened, lifting the ends free of the lander. At Thomas's command, they let go. The metal lashing soared away, flashing in the harsh sunlight, twisting like a wounded snake, dwindling as it fell below and behind their orbit. The lander floated free, tied to the *Plowshare* by a single, slim umbilicus. Johnboy wrapped a spanner around a hex-bolt over the top strut of a landing leg and gave it a spin. Like a slow, graceful spider leg, it unfolded away from the lander's body. He slapped his spanner down on the next bolt and yanked. But he hadn't braced himself properly, and his feet went out from under him in a slow somersault. He spun away, laughing, to the end of his umbilicus. The spanner went skimming back towrd the *Plowshare*, struck its metal skin, and sailed off into space.

"You meatballs!" Thomas shouted over the open intercom. The radio was sharp and peppery with sun static, but he could hear Woody and Johnboy laughing. "Cut it out! No skylarking! Let's get this done!"

"Everything okay out there?" asked Commander Redenbaugh, from inside the *Plowshare*. The commander's voice had a slight edge to it, and Thomas grimaced. The last time the three of them had gone out on EVA, practicing this very maneuver, Johnboy had started to horse around and had accidentally sent a dropped lugnut smashing through the source-crystal housing, destroying the laser link to Earth. And hadn't the commander gotten on their asses about *that*; NASA had been really pissed, too—with the laser link gone, they would have to depend solely on the radio, which was vulnerable to static in an active sun year like this.

It was hard to blame the others too much for cutting up a little on EVA, after long, claustrophobic months of being jammed together in the *Plowshare*, but the responsibility for things going smoothly was his. Out here, *he* was supposed to be in command. That made him feel lonely and isolated, but after all, it was what he had sweated and strived for since the earliest days of flight training. The landing party was his command, his chance for glory, and he wasn't going to let anybody or anything ruin it.

"Everything's okay, Commander," Thomas said. "We've got the lander unshipped, and we're almost ready to go. I estimate about twenty minutes to separation." He spoke in the calm, matter-of-fact voice that tradition demanded, but inside he felt the excitement building again and hoped his pulse rate wasn't climbing too noticeably on the readouts. In only a few minutes, they were going to be making the first manned landing on Mars! Within the hour, he'd be down there, where he'd dreamed of being ever since he was a boy. On *Mars*.

And *he* would be in command. *How about that, Pop,* Thomas thought, with a flash of irony. *That good enough for you? Finally?*

Johnboy had pulled himself back to the *Plowshare*.

"Okay, then," Thomas said dryly. "If you're ready, let's

get back to work. You and Woody get that junk out of the lander. I'll stay out here and mind the store."

"Yes, *sir*, sir," Johnboy said with amiable irony, and Thomas sighed. Johnboy was okay but a bit of a flake—you had to sit on him a little from time to time. Woody and Johnboy began pulling boxes out of the lander; it had been used as storage space for supplies they'd need on the return voyage, to save room in *Plowshare*. There were jokes cracked about how they ought to let some of the crates of flash-frozen glop that NASA straight-facedly called food escape into space, but at last, burdened with boxes, the two space-suited figures lumbered to the air lock and disappeared inside.

Thomas was alone, floating in space.

You really were alone out here, too, with nothing but the gaping immensity of the universe surrounding you on all sides. It was a little scary but at the same time something to savor after long months of being packed into the *Plowshare* with three other men. There was precious little privacy aboard ship—out here, alone, there was nothing *but* privacy. Just you, the stars, the void . . . and, of course, Mars.

Thomas relaxed at the end of his tether, floating comfortably, and watched as Mars, immense and ruddy, turned below him like some huge, slow-spinning, rusty-red top. Mars! Lazily, he let his eyes trace the familiar landmarks. The ancient dead-river valley of Kasei Vallis, impact craters puckering its floor . . . the reddish brown and gray of haze and frost in Noctis Labyrinthus, the Labyrinth of Night . . . the immense scar of the Vallis Marineris, greatest of canyons, stretching two thirds of the way around the equator . . . the great volcanic constructs in Tharsis . . . and there, the Chryse Basin, where soon they would be walking.

Mars was as familiar to him as the streets of his hometown—*more* so, since his family had spent so much time moving from place to place when he was a kid. Mars had stayed a constant, though. Throughout his boyhood, he had been obsessed with space and with Mars in particular . . . as if he'd somehow always known that one day he'd be here, hanging disembodied like some ancient god over the slowly spinning red planet below. In high school he had done a paper on Martian plate tectonics. When he was only a gangly grade-school kid, ten or eleven, maybe, he had memorized every available map of Mars, learned every crater and valley and mountain range.

Drowsily, his thoughts drifted even further back, to that day in the attic of the old house in Wrightstown, near McGuire Air Force Base—the sound of jets taking off mingling with the lazy Saturday afternoon sounds of kids playing baseball and yelling, dogs barking, lawn mowers whirring, the rusty smell of pollen coming in the window on the mild, spring air—when he'd discovered an old, dog-eared copy of Edgar Rice Burroughs's *A Princess of Mars*.

He'd stayed up there for hours reading it, while the day passed unnoticed around him, until the light got so bad that he couldn't see the type anymore. And that night he'd surreptitiously read it in bed, under the covers with a pencil flashlight, until he'd finally fallen asleep, his dreams reeling with giant, four-armed green men, thoats, zitidars, long-sword-swinging heroes, and beautiful princesses . . . the Twin Cities of Helium . . . the dead sea bottoms lit by the opalescent light of the two hurtling moons . . . the nomad caverns of the Tharks, the barbaric riders draped with glittering jewels and rich riding silks. For an instant, staring down at Mars, he felt a childish disappointment that all of that really wasn't waiting down there for him after all, and then he smiled wryly at himself. Never doubt that those childhood dreams had power— after all, one way or another, they'd *gotten* him here, hadn't they?

Right at that moment the sandstorm began to blow up.

It blew up from the hard-pan deserts and plains and as Thomas watched in dismay, began to creep slowly across the planet like a tarp being pulled over a work site. Down there, winds moving at hundreds of kilometers per hour were racing across the Martian surface, filling the sky with churning, yellow-white clouds of sand. A curtain storm.

"You see that, Thomas?" the commander's voice asked in Thomas's ears.

"Yeah," Thomas said glumly. "I see it."

"Looks like a bad one."

Even as they watched, the storm slowly and relentlessly blotted out the entire visible surface of the planet. The lesser features went first, the scarps and rills and stone fields, then the greater ones. The polar caps went. Finally even the top of

Olympus Mons—the tallest mountain in the solar system—disappeared.

"Well, that's it," the commander said sadly. "Socked in. No landing today."

"Son of a *bitch*!" Thomas exploded, feeling his stomach twist with disappointment and sudden rage. He'd been so *close*.

"Watch your language, Thomas," the commander warned. "This is an open channel." Meaning that we mustn't shock the Vast Listening Audience Back Home. Oh, horrors, certainly *not*.

"If it'd just waited a couple more hours, we would have been able to get *down* there—"

"You ought to be glad it didn't," the commander said mildly. "Then you'd have been sitting on your hands down there with all that sand piling up around your ears. The wind can hit one hundred forty miles an hour during one of those storms. *I'd* hate to have to try to sit one out on the ground. Relax, Thomas. We've got plenty of time. As soon as the weather clears, you'll go down. It can't last forever."

Five weeks later, the storm finally died.

Those were hard weeks for Thomas, who was as full of useless energy as a caged tiger. He had become overaware of his surroundings, of the pervasive, sour human smell, of the faintly metallic taste of the air. It was like living in a jungle-gym factory, all twisting pipes and narrow, cluttered passages, enclosed by metal walls that were never out of sight. For the first time during the long months of the mission, he began to feel seriously claustrophobic.

But the real enemy was time. Thomas was acutely aware that the inexorable clock of celestial mechanics was ticking relentlessly away . . . that soon the optimal launch window for the return journey to Earth would open and that they *must* shape for Earth then or never get home at all. Whether the storm had lifted yet or not, whether they had landed on Mars or not, whether Thomas had finally gotten a chance to show off his own particular righteous stuff or *not*, when the launch window opened, they had to go.

They had less than a week left in Mars orbit now, and still the sandstorm raged.

The waiting got on everyone's nerves. Thomas found Johnboy's manic energy particularly hard to take. Increasingly, he found himself snapping at Johnboy during meals and "happy hour," until eventually the commander had to take him aside and tell him to loosen up. Thomas muttered something apologetic, and the commander studied him shrewdly and said, "Plenty of time left, old buddy. Don't worry. We'll get you down there yet!" The two men found themselves grinning at each other. Commander Redenbaugh was a good officer, a quiet, pragmatic New Englander who seemed to become ever more phlegmatic and unflappable as the tension mounted and everyone else's nerves frayed. Johnboy habitually called him Captain Ahab. The commander seemed rather to enjoy the nickname, which was one of the few things that suggested that there might actually be a sense of humor lurking somewhere behind his deadpan facade.

The commander gave Thomas's arm an encouraging squeeze, then launched himself toward the communications console. Thomas watched him go, biting back a sudden bitter surge of words that he knew he'd never say . . . not up here, anyway, where the walls literally had ears. Ever since *Skylab*, astronauts had flown with the tacit knowledge that everything they said in the ship was being eavesdropped on and evaluated by NASA. Probably before the day was out somebody back in Houston would be making a black mark next to his name in a psychological-fitness dossier, just because he'd let the waiting get on his nerves to the point where the commander had had to speak to him about it. But damn it, it was *easier* for the rest—they didn't have the responsibility of being NASA's token Nigger in the Sky, with all the white folks back home waiting and watching to see how you were going to fuck up. He'd felt like a third wheel on the way out here—Woody and the commander could easily fly the ship themselves and even take care of most of the routine schedule of experiments—but the landing party was supposed to be *his* command, his chance to finally do something other than be the obligatory black face in the NASA photos of Our Brave Astronauts. He remembered his demanding, domineering, hard-driving father saying to him, hundreds of times in his adolescent years, "It's a white man's world out there. If you're going to make it, you got to show that you're *better* than any of them. You got to force yourself down their throats, *make* them need you. You got to be twice as good as any of them. . . . *Yeah, Pop,* Thomas thought, *you bet, Pop* . . . thinking, as he always did, of the one and only time he'd ever seen his father stinking, slobbering, falling-down drunk, the night the old man had been passed over for promotion to brigadier general for the third time, forcing him into mandatory retirement. *First they got to give you the chance, Pop*, he thought, remembering, again as he always did, a cartoon by Ron Cobb that he had seen when he was a kid and that had haunted him ever since: a cartoon showing black men in space suits on the moon—sweeping up around the Apollo 58 campsite.

"We're losing Houston again," Woody said. "I jes cain't keep the signal." He turned a dial, and the voice of Mission Control came into the cabin, chopped up and nearly obliterated by a hissing static that sounded like dozens of eggs frying in a huge iron skillet. ". . . read? . . . not read you . . . *Plowshare* . . . losing . . ." Sunspot activity had been unusually high for weeks, and just a few hours before, NASA had warned them about an enormous solar flare that was about to flood half the solar system with radio noise. Even as they listened, the voice was completely drowned out by static; the hissing noise kept getting louder and louder. "Weh-ayl," Woody said glumly, "that does it. That solar flare's screwing *every*thing up. If we still had the laser link" —here he flashed a sour look at Johnboy, who had the grace to look embarrassed—"we'd be okay, I guess, but with*out* it . . . weh-ayl, shit, it could be days before reception clears up. *Weeks*, maybe."

Irritably, Woody flipped a switch, and the hissing static noise stopped. All four men were silent for a moment, feeling their suddenly increased isolation. For months, their only remaining contact with Earth had been a faint voice on the radio, and now, abruptly, even that link was severed. It made them feel lonelier than ever and somehow farther away from home.

Thomas turned away from the communications console and automatically glanced out the big observation window at Mars. It took him a while to notice that there was something different about the view. Then he realized that the uniform, dirty yellow-white cloud cover was breaking up and becoming streaky, turning the planet into a giant, mottled Easter egg, allowing tantalizing glimpses of the surface. "Hey!" Thomas said, and at the same time Johnboy crowed, "Well, *well*, lookie there! Guess who's back, boys!"

They all crowded around the observation window, eagerly jostling one another.

As they watched, the storm died all at once, with the suddenness of a conjuring trick, and the surface was visible again. Johnboy let out an ear-splitting rebel yell. Everyone cheered. They were all laughing and joking and slapping one another's shoulders, and then, one by one, they fell silent.

Something was wrong. Thomas could feel the short hairs prickling erect along his back and arms, feel the muscles of his gut tightening. Something was *wrong*. What was it? What . . . ? He heard the commander gasp, and at the same time realization broke through into his conscious mind, and he felt the blood draining from his face.

Woody was the first to speak.

"But . . ." Woody said, in a puzzled almost petulant voice, like a bewildered child. "But . . . *that's not Mars.*"

The air is thin on Mars. So thin it won't hold up dust in suspension unless the wind is traveling at enormous speeds. When the wind dies, the dust falls like pebbles, fast and all at once.

After five weeks of storm, the wind died. The dust fell.

Revealing entirely the wrong planet.

The surface was still predominantly a muddy reddish orange, but now there were large mottled patches of green and grayish ocher. The surface seemed softer now, smoother, with much less rugged relief. It took a moment to realize why. The craters—so very like those on the moon both in shape and distribution—were gone, and so were most of the mountains, the scarps and rills, the giant volcanic constructs. In their place were dozens of fine, perfectly straight blue lines. They were bordered by bands of green and extended across the entire planet in an elaborate crisscrossing pattern, from polar icecap to polar icecap.

"I cain't *find* anything," Woody was saying exasperatedly. "What *happened* to everything? I cain't even see Olympus Mons, for Christsake! The biggest fucking volcano in the solar system! Where is it? And what the fuck are those lines?"

Again Thomas felt an incredible burst of realization well up inside him. He gaped at the planet below, unable to speak, unable to answer, but Johnboy did it for him.

Johnboy had been leaning close to the window, his jaw slack with amazement, but now an odd, dreamy look was stealing over his face, and when he spoke, it was in a matter-of-fact, almost languid voice. "They're canals," he said.

"Canals, my ass!" the commander barked, losing control of his temper for the first time on the mission. "There aren't any canals on Mars! That idea went out with Schiaparelli and Lowell."

Johnboy shrugged. "Then what are *those*?" he asked mildly, jerking his thumb toward the planet, and Thomas felt a chill feather up along his spine.

A quick visual search turned up no recognizable surface features, none of the landmarks familiar to them all from the *Mariner 9* and Viking orbiter photomaps—although Johnboy annoyed the commander by pointing out that the major named canals that Percival Lowell had described and mapped in the nineteenth century—Strymon, Charontis, Erebus, Orcus, Dis— *were* there, just as Lowell had said that they were.

"It's *got* to be the sandstorm that did it," Thomas said, grasping desperately for some rational explanation. "The wind moving the sand around from one place to another, maybe, covering up one set of surface features while at the same time exposing *another* set. . . ."

He faltered to a stop, seeing the holes in that argument even as Johnboy snorted and said. "Real good, sport, *real* good. But Olympus Mons just isn't *there*, a mountain three times higher than Mount Everest! Even if you could cover it up with sand, then what you'd have would be a fucking *sand dune* three times higher than Everest . . . but there don't seem to be any big mountains down there at all anymore."

"I know what happened," Woody said before Thomas could reply.

His voice sounded so strange that they all turned to look at him. He had been scanning the surface with the small optical telescope for the Mars-Sat experiments, but now he was leaning on the telescope mounting and staring at them instead. His eyes were feverish and unfocused and bright and seemed to have sunken into his head. He was trembling slightly, and his face had become waxen and pale.

He's scared, Thomas realized, *he's just plain scared right out of his skull.* . . .

"This has all happened before," Woody said hoarsely.

"What in the world are you talking about?" Thomas asked.

"Haven't you read your history?" Woody asked. He was a reticent man, slow voiced and deliberate, like most computer hackers, but now the words rushed from his mouth in a steadily accelerating stream, almost tumbling over one another in their anxiety to get out. His voice was higher than usual, and it held the ragged overtones of hysteria in it. "The *Mariner 9* mission, the robot probe. Back in 1971. Remember? Jes as the probe reached Mars orbit, before it could start sending back any photos, a great big curtain storm came up, jes like this one. Great *big* bastard. Covered *everything*. Socked the whole planet for weeks. No surface visibility at all. Had the scientists back home pulling their hair out. But when the storm finally did lift, and the photos did start coming in, everybody was jes flatout *amazed*. None of the Lowellian features, no canals, *nothing*—jes craters and rills and volcanoes, all the stuff we expected to see *this* time around." He gave a shaky laugh.

"So everybody jes shrugged and said Lowell had been wrong—poor visibility, selector bias, he jes *thought* he'd seen canals. Connected up existing surface features with imaginary lines, maybe. He'd seen what he wanted to see." Woody paused, licking at his lips, and then began talking faster and shriller than ever. "But that wasn't *true*, was it? We *know* better, don't we, boys? We can see the proof right out that window! My crazy ol' uncle Barry, *he* had the right of it from the start, and everybody else was *wrong*. He tole me what happened, but I was jes too dumb to believe him! It was the *space* people, the UFO people! The Martians! *They* saw the probe coming, and they whomped that storm up, to keep us from seeing the surface, and then they changed everything. Under the cover of the sandstorm, they changed the whole damn planet to fool us, to keep us from finding out *they* were there! This *proves* it! They changed it *back*! They're out there right *now*, the flying saucer people! They're *out* there—"

"Bullshit!" the commander said. His voice was harsh and loud and cracked like a whip, but it was the unprecedented use of obscenity that startled them more than anything else.

They turned to look at him, where he floated near the command console. Even Woody, who had just seemed on the verge of a breakdown, gasped and fell silent.

When he was sure he had everyone's attention, the commander smiled coldly and said, "While you were all going through your little psychodrama, I've been doing a little elementary checking. Here's the telemetry data, and you know what? *Every*thing shows up the same as it did before the sandstorm. Exactly . . . the . . . same. Deep radar, infrared, everything." He tapped the command console. "It's just the same as it ever was, no breathable air, low atmospheric pressure, subzero temperatures, nothing but sand and a bunch of goddamn rusty-red rocks. No vegetation, no surface water, *no canals*." He switched the view from the ship's exterior cameras onto the cabin monitor, and there for everyone to see was the familiar Mars of the Mariner and Viking probes, rocky, rugged, cratered, lifeless. No green oases. No canals.

Everyone was silent, mesmerized by the two contradictory images.

"I don't know what's causing this strange visual hallucination we're all seeing," the commander said, gesturing at the window and speaking slowly and deliberately. "But I do know that it *is* a hallucination. It doesn't show up on the cameras, it doesn't show up in the telemetry. It's just not real."

They adjourned the argument to the bar. Doofus the Moose—an orange inflatable toy out of Johnboy's personal kit—smiled benignly down on them as they sipped from bags of reconstituted citrus juice (NASA did not believe that they could be trusted with a ration of alcohol, and the hip flask Woody had smuggled aboard had been polished off long before) and went around and around the issue without reaching any kind of consensus. The "explanations" became more and more farfetched, until at last the commander uttered the classic phrase *mass hypnosis*, causing Johnboy to start whooping in derision.

There was a long, humming silence. Then Johnboy, his mood altering, said very quietly, "It doesn't matter anyway. We're never going to find out anything more about what's happening from up here." He looked soberly around at the others. "There's really only one decision we've got to make. Do we go on down, or not? Do we land?"

Even the commander was startled. "After all this—you still want to land?"

Johnboy shrugged. "Why not? It's what we came all the way out here for, isn't it?"

"It's too dangerous. We don't even know what's happening here."

"I thought it was only mass hypnosis," Johnboy said slyly.

"I think it is," the commander said stoutly, unperturbed by Johnboy's sarcasm. "But even if it is, we still don't know *why* we're having these hallucinations, do we? It could be a sign of organic deterioration or dysfunction of some sort, caused by who *knows* what. Maybe there's some kind of intense electromagnetic field out there that we haven't detected that's disrupting the electrical pathways of our nervous systems; maybe there's an unforeseen flaw in the recycling system that's causing some kind of toxic buildup that affects brain chemistry. . . . The point is, we're not *functioning* right; we're seeing things that aren't there!"

"None of that stuff matters," Johnboy said. He leaned forward, speaking now with great urgency and passion. No one had ever seen him so serious or so ferociously intent. "We have to land. Whatever the risk. It was hard enough funding *this* mission. If we fuck up out here, there may never be another one. NASA itself might not survive." He stared around at his crewmates. "How do *you* think it's going to look, Woody? We run into the greatest mystery the human race has ever encountered, and we immediately go scurrying home with our tails tucked between our legs without even investigating it? That sound good to you?"

Woody grunted and shook his head. "Sure doesn't, ol' buddy," he said. He glanced around the table and then coolly said, "Let's get on *down* there." Now that he was apparently no longer envisioning the imminent arrival of UFO-riding astronaut mutilators, Woody seemed determined to be as cool and unflappable and ultramacho as possible, as if to prove that he hadn't really been frightened after all.

There was another silence, and slowly Thomas became aware that everyone else was staring at him.

It all came down to him now. The deciding vote would be *his*: Thomas locked eyes with Johnboy, and Johnboy stared back at him with unwavering intensity. The question didn't

even need to be voiced; it hung in the air between them and
charged the lingering silence with tension. Thomas moved
uneasily under the weight of all those watching eyes. How *did*
he feel? He didn't really know—strange, that was about the
closest he could come to it . . . hung up between fear and
some other slowly stirring emotion he couldn't identify and
didn't really want to think about. But there was one thing he
was suddenly certain about. They weren't going to abandon
his part of the mission, not after he'd come this far! Certainly
he was never going to get another chance to get into the
history books. Probably that was Johnboy's real motive, too,
above and beyond the jazz about the survival of NASA.
Johnboy was a cool enough head to realize that if they came
home without landing, they'd be laughingstocks, wimps instead of heroes, and somebody *else* on some future mission
would get all the glory. Johnboy's ego was much too big to
allow him to take a chance on *that*. And he was right!
Thomas had even more reason to be afraid of being passed
over, passed by: When you were black, opportunities like this
certainly didn't knock more than once.

"We've still got almost three days until the launch window
opens," Thomas said, speaking slowly and deliberately. "I
think we should make maximum use of that time by going
down there and finding out as much as we can." He raised his
eyes and stared directly at the commander. "I say we *land*."

Commander Redenbaugh insisted on referring the issue to
Houston for a final decision, but after several hours of
trying, it became clear that he was not going to be able to
get through to Earth. For once, the buck was refusing to be
passed.

The commander sighed and ran his fingers wearily through
his hair. He felt old and tired and ineffectual. He knew what
Houston would probably have said, anyway. With the exception of the commander himself (who had been too well-
known *not* to be chosen), de facto policy for this mission had
been to select unmarried men with no close personal or
family ties back home. That alone spoke volumes. They were
supposed to be taking risks out here. That was what they
were here for. It was part of their job.

At dawn over Chryse, they went down.

* * *

As commander of the landing party, Thomas was first out of the lander. Awkward in his suit, he climbed backward out of the hatch and down the exterior ladder. He caught reeling flashes of the Martian sky, and it was orange, it should be. His first, instinctive reaction was relief, followed by an intense stab of perverse disappointment, which surprised him. As he hung from the ladder, one foot almost touching the ground, he paused to reel off the words that some P.R. man at NASA had composed for the occasion. "In the name of all humanity, we dedicate the planet of war to peace. May God grant us this." He put his foot down, then looked down from the ladder, twisting around to get a look at the spot he was standing on.

"Jesus *Christ*," he muttered reverently. Orange sky or not, there were *plants* of some kind growing here. He was standing almost knee-deep in them, a close-knit, springy mat of grayish-ocher vegetation. He knelt down and gingerly touched it.

"It looks like some kind of moss," he reported. "It's pliant and giving to the touch, springs slowly back up again. I can break it off in my hand."

The transmission from the *Plowshare* crackled and buzzed with static. "Thomas," said the commander's voice in his ear, "what are you *talking* about? Are you okay?"

Thomas straightened up and took his first long, slow look around. The ocher-colored moss stretched out to the orange horizon in all directions, covering both the flat plains immediately around them and a range of gently rolling hills in the middle distance to the north. Here and there the moss was punctuated by tight clusters of spiny, misshapen shrubs, usually brown or glossy black or muddy purple, and even occasionally by a lone tree. The trees were crimson, about ten feet high, the trunks glistened with the color of fresh, wet blood, and their flat, glassy leaves glittered like sheets of amethyst. Thomas dubbed them flametrees.

The lander was resting only several hundred yards away from a canal.

It was wide, the canal, and its still, perfectly clear waters reflected the sky as dark as wine, as red as blood. Small yellow flowers trailed delicate tentacles into the water from the edging walls, which were old and crumbling and carved with strange geometrical patterns of swirls and curlicues that might, just possibly, be runes.

It can't possibly be real, Thomas thought dazedly.

Johnboy and Woody were clambering down the ladder, clumsy and troll-like in their hulking suits, and Thoams moved over to make room for them.

"Mother dog!" Woody breathed, looking around him, the wonder clear in his voice. "This is really something, ain't it?" He laid a gloved hand on Thomas's shoulder. "*This* is what we saw from up there."

"But it's impossible," Thomas said.

Woody shrugged. "If it's a hallucination, then it's sure as hell a *beautiful* one."

Johnboy had walked on ahead without a word, until he was several yards away from the ship; now he came to a stop and stood staring out across the moss-covered plain to the distant hills. "It's like being born again," he whispered.

The commander cut in again, his voice popping and crackling with static. "Report in! What's going on down there?"

Thomas shook his head. "Commander, I wish I knew."

He unlashed the exterior camera from the lander, set it up on its tripod, removed the lens cover. "Tell me what you see."

"I see sand, dust, rocks . . . what else do you *expect* me to see?"

"No canals?" Thomas asked sadly. "No trees? No moss?"

"Christ, you're hallucinating again, aren't you?" the commander said. "This is what I was afraid of. All of you, listen to me! Listen good! There aren't any goddamn canals down there. Maybe there's water down a few dozen meters as permafrost. But the surface is as dry as the moon."

"But there's some sort of moss growing all over the place," Thomas said. "Kind of grayish-ocher color, about a foot and a half high. There's clumps of bushes. There's even *trees* of some kind. Can't you see any of that?"

"You're hallucinating," the commander said. "Believe me, the camera shows nothing but sand and rock down there. You're standing in a goddamn lunar desert and babbling to me about trees, for Christ's sake! That's enough for me. I want everybody back up here, right *now*. I shouldn't have let you talk me into this in the first place. We'll let Houston unravel all this. It's no longer our problem. Woody, come back here! Stick together, dammit!''

Johnboy was still standing where he had stopped, as if entranced, but Woody was wandering toward the canal, poking around, exploring.

"Listen up!" the commander said. "I want everybody back in the lander, right now. I'm going to get you out of there before somebody gets hurt. Everybody back *now*. That's an order! That's a direct order!''

Woody turned reluctantly and began bounding slowly toward the lander, pausing every few yards to look back over his shoulder at the canal.

Thomas sighed, not sure whether he was relieved to be getting out of here or heartbroken to be going so soon.

"Okay, Commander," Thomas said. "We read you. We're coming up. Right away." He took a few light, buoyant steps forward—fighting a tendency to bounce kangaroolike off the ground—and tapped Johnboy gently on the arm. "Come on. We've got to go back up."

Johnboy turned slowly around. "Do we?" he said. "Do we *really*?''

"Orders," Thomas said uneasily, feeling something begin to stir and turn over ponderously in the deep backwaters of his own soul. "I don't want to go yet, either, but the commander's right. If we're hallucinating . . .''

"Don't give me that shit!" Johnboy said passionately. "Hallucinating, my ass! You *touched* the moss, didn't you? You *felt* it. This isn't a hallucination, or mass hypnosis, or any of that other crap. This is a *world*, a new world, and it's *ours*!''

"Johnboy, get in the lander right now!" the commander broke in. "That's an order!''

"Fuck you, Ahab!" Johnboy said. "And fuck your orders, too!''

Thomas was shocked—and at the same time felt a stab of glee at the insubordination, an emotion that surprised him and that he hurried uneasily to deny, saying, "You're out of line, Johnboy, I want you to listen to me, now—''

"No, you listen to *me*," Johnboy said fiercely. "Look around you! I know you've read Burroughs. You *know* where you are! A dead sea bottom, covered with ocher-colored moss. Rolling hills. A *canal*.''

"Those are the very reasons why it can't be real," Thomas said uneasily.

"It's real if we *want* it to be real," Johnboy said. "It's here *because* of us. It's made *for* us. It's made *out* of us."

"Stop gabbing and get in the lander!" the commander shouted. "Move! Get your asses in gear!"

Woody had come up to join them. "Maybe we'd better—" he started to say, but Johnboy cut in with:

"Listen to me! I knew what was happening the moment I looked out and saw the Mars of Schiaparelli and Lowell, the *old* Mars. Woody, you said that Lowell saw what he wanted to see. That's *right*, but in a different way than you meant it. You know, other contemporary astronomers looked at Mars at the same time as Lowell, with the same kind of instruments, and saw no canals at all. You ever hear of consensual reality? Because Lowell wanted to see it, it existed for him! Just as it exists for us—because we want it to exist! We don't have to accept the gray reality of Ahab here and all the other gray little men back at NASA. They *want* it to be rocks and dust and dead, drab desert; they *like* it that way—"

"For God's sake!" the commander said. "Somebody get that nut in the lander."

"—but we don't like it! Deep down inside of us—Thomas, Woody—we don't *believe* in that Mars. We believe in this one—the *real* one. That's why it's here for us! That's why it's the way it is—it's made of our dreams. Who knows what's over those hills: bone-white faerie cities? four-armed green men? beautiful princesses? the Twin Cities of Helium? There could be *anything* out there!"

"Thomas!" the commander snapped. "Get Johnboy in the lander *now*. Use force if necessary, but *get him in there*. Johnboy! You're emotionally unstable. I want you to consider yourself under house arrest!"

"I've been under house arrest all my life," Johnboy said. "Now I'm *free*."

Moving deliberately, he reached up and unsnapped his helmet.

Thomas started forward with an inarticulate cry of horror, trying to stop him, but it was too late. Johnboy had his helmet completely off now, and was shaking his head to free his shaggy, blond hair, which rippled slightly in the breeze. He took a deep breath, another, and then grinned at Thomas.

"The air smells *great*," he said. "And, my God, is it clean!"

"Johnboy?" Thomas said hesitantly. "Are you *okay*?"

"Christ!" the commander was muttering. "Christ! Oh my God! Oh my sweet God!"

"I'm fine," Johnboy said. "In fact, I'm *terrific*." He smiled brilliantly at them, then sniffed at the inside of his helmet and made a face. "Phew! Smells like an armpit in there!" He started to strip off his suit.

"Thomas, Woody," the commander said leadenly. "Put Johnboy's body into the lander, and then get in there yourselves, fast, before we lose somebody else."

"But . . ." Thomas said, "there's nothing wrong with Johnboy. We're *talking* to him."

"God damn it, *look at your med readouts*."

Thomas glanced at the chin strap readout board, which was reflected into a tiny square on the right side of his faceplate. There was a tiny red light flashing on Johnboy's readout. "Christ!" Thomas whispered.

"He's *dead*, Thomas, he's *dead*. I can see his body. He fell over like he'd been poleaxed right after he opened his helmet and hemorrhaged his lungs out into the sand. *Listen* to me! Johnny's *dead*—anything else is a hallucination!"

Johnboy grinned at them, kicking free of his suit. "I may be dead, kids," he told them quizzically, "but let me tell *you*, dead or not, I feel one-hundred-percent better now that I'm out of that crummy suit, believe it. The air's a little bit cool, but it feels *wonderful*." He raised his arms and stretched lazily, like a cat.

"Johnboy—?" Woody said, tentatively.

"*Listen*," the commander raged. "You're hallucinating! You're talking to yourselves! Get in the lander! That's an *order*."

"Yes, *sir*, sir," Johnboy said mockingly, sketching a salute at the sky. "Are you actually going to *listen* to that asshole?" He stepped forward and took each of them by the arm and shook them angrily. "Do I *feel* dead to you, schmucks?"

Thomas *felt* the fingers close over his arm, and an odd, deep thrill shot through him—part incredulity, part supernatural dread, part a sudden, strange exhilaration. "I can *feel* him," Woody was saying wonderingly, patting Johnboy with his gloved hands. "He's solid. He's *there*. I'll be a son of a *bitch*—"

"Be one?" Johnboy said, grinning. "Ol' buddy, you already *are* one."

Woody laughed. "No hallucination's *that* corny," Woody said to Thomas. "He's real, all right."

"But the readout—" Thomas began.

"Obviously wrong. There's got to be some kind of mistake—"

Woody started to unfasten his helmet.

"No!" the commander screamed, and at the same time Thomas darted forward shouting, "Woody! Stop!" and tried to grab him, but Woody twisted aside and bounded limberly away, out of reach.

Cautiously, Woody took his helmet off. He sniffed suspiciously, his lean, leathery face stiff with tension, then he relaxed, and then he began to smile. "Hoo*ie*," he said in awe.

"Get his helmet back on, quick!" the commander was shouting. But Woody's medical readout was already flashing orange, and even as the commander spoke, it turned red.

"Too late!" the commander moaned. "Oh God, too *late*. . ."

Woody looked into his helmet at his own flashing readout. His face registered surprise for an instant, and then he began to laugh. "Weh-ayl," Woody drawled, "now that I'm officially a corpse, I guess I don't need *this* anymore." He threw his helmet aside; it bounced and rolled over the spongy moss. "Thomas," Woody said, "*you* do what you want, but I've been locked up in a smelly ol' tin can for months, and what *I'm* going to do is *wash my face* in some honest-to-God, unrecycled water!" He grinned at Thomas and began walking away toward the canal. "I might even take me a *swim*."

"Thomas . . ." the commander said brokenly. "Don't worry about the bodies. Don't worry about *anything* else. Just get in the lander. As soon as you're inside I'm going to trigger the launch sequence."

Johnboy was staring at him quizzically, compassionately—waiting.

"Johnboy . . ." Thomas said. "Johnboy, how can I tell which is real?"

"You choose what's real," Johnboy said quietly. "We all do."

"*Listen* to me, Thomas," the commander pleaded; there was an edge of panic in his voice. "You're talking to yourself again. Whatever you think you're seeing, or hearing, or even *touching*, it just *isn't real*. There can be tactile hallucinations, too, you know. It's not *real*."

"Old Ahab up there has made his choice, too," Johnboy said. "For him, in his own conceptual universe, Woody and I *are* dead. And that's real, too—for *him*. But you don't have to choose that reality. You can choose *this* one."

"I don't know," Thomas mumbled. "I just don't *know*."

Woody hit the water in an explosion of foam. He swam a few strokes, whooping, then turned to float on his back. "C'mon in, you guys!" he shouted.

Johnboy smiled, then turned to bring his face close to Thomas's helmet, peering in through the faceplate. Johnboy was still wearing that strange, dreamy look, so unlike his usual animated expression, and his eyes were clear and compassionate and calm. "It calls for an act of faith, Thomas. Maybe that's how every world begins." He grinned at Thomas. "Meanwhile, I think I'm going to take a swim, too." He strolled off toward the canal, bouncing a little at each step.

Thomas stood unmoving, the two red lights flashing on his chinstrap readout.

"They're both going swimming now," Thomas said dully.

"Thomas! Can you hear me, Thomas?"

"I hear you," Thomas mumbled.

They were having *fun* in their new world—he could see that. The kind of fun that kids had . . . that every child took for granted. The joy of discovery, of everything being *new* . . . the joy that seemed to get lost in the gray shuffle to adulthood, given up bit by incremental bit. . . .

"You're just going to have to trust me, Thomas. *Trust me*. Take my word for it that I know what I'm talking about. You're going to have to take that on faith. Now *listen* to me. No matter what you think is going on down there, *don't take your helmet off*."

His father used to lecture him in that same tone of voice, demanding, domineering . . . and at the same time condescending. Scornful. Daddy knows best. Listen to me, boy, I *know* what I'm talking about! Do what I *tell* you to do!

"Do you hear me? Do *not* take your helmet off! Under any circumstances at all. That's an *order*."

Thomas nodded, before he could stop himself. Here he was, good boy little Tommy, standing on the fringes again, taking orders, doing what he was told. Getting passed over *again*. And for what?

Something flew by in the distance, headed toward the hills. It looked to be about the size of a large bird, but like a dragonfly, it had six long, filmy gossamer wings, which it swirled around in a complexly interweaving pattern, as if it were rowing itself through the air.

"Get to the lander, Thomas, and close the hatch."

Never did have any fun. Have to be twice as good as *any* of them, have to bust your goddamn ass—

"That's a direct order, Thomas!"

You've got to make the bastards respect you, you've got to *earn* their respect. His father had said that a million times. And how little time it had taken him to waste away and die, once he'd stopped trying, once he realized that you can't earn what people aren't willing to sell.

A red and yellow lizard ran over his boot, as quick and silent as a tickle. It had six legs.

One by one, he began to undog the latches of his helmet.

"No! Listen to me! If you take off your helmet, you'll *die*. Don't do it! For God's sake, don't do it!"

The last latch. It was sticky, but he tugged at it purposefully.

"You're killing yourself! Stop it! *Please. Stop! You goddamn stupid nigger! Stop*—"

Thomas smiled, oddly enough feeling closer to the commander in that moment than he ever had before. "Too late," he said cheerfully.

Thomas twisted his helmet a quarter turn and lifted it off his head.

When the third red light winked on, Commander Redenbaugh slumped against the board and started to cry. He wept openly and loudly, for they had been good men, and he had failed all of them, even Thomas, the best and steadiest of the lot. He hadn't been able to save a goddamned one of them!

At last he was able to pull himself together. He forced himself to look again at the monitor, which showed three

space-suited bodies sprawled out lifelessly on the rusty-red
sand.

He folded his hands, bent his head, and prayed for the
souls of his dead companions. Then he switched the monitor
off.

It was time to make plans. Since the *Plowshare* would be
carrying a much lighter-than-anticipated return cargo, he had
enough excess fuel to allow him to leave a bit early, if he
wanted to, and he *did* want to. He began to punch figures into
the computer, smiling bitterly at the irony. Yesterday he had
been regretting that they had so little time left in Mars orbit.
Now, suddenly, he was in a hurry to get home . . . but no
matter how many corners he shaved, he'd still be several
long, grueling months in transit—with quite probably a court-
martial waiting for him when he got back.

For an instant, even the commander's spirit quailed at the
thought of that dreadful return journey. But he soon got
himself under control again. It would be a difficult and
unpleasant trip, right enough, but a determined man could
always manage to do what needed to be done.

Even if he had to do it alone.

When the *Plowshare*'s plasma drive was switched on, it
created a daytime star in the Martian sky. It was like a
shooting star in reverse, starting out at its brightest and
dimming rapidly as it moved up and away.

Thomas saw it leave. He was leaning against his makeshift
spear—flametree wood, with a fire-hardened tip—and watching Johnboy preparing to skin the dead hyena-leopard, when
he chanced to glance up. "Look," he said.

Johnboy followed Thomas's eyes and saw it, too. He
smiled sardonically and lifted the animal's limp paw, making
it wave bye-bye. "So long, Ahab," Johnboy said. "Good
luck." He went back to skinning the beast. The hyena-
leopard—a little bit larger than a wildcat, six-legged, saber-
tusked, its fur a muddy purple with rusty-orange spots—had
attacked without warning and fought savagely; it had taken all
three of them to kill it.

Woody looked up from where he was lashing a makeshift
flametree-wood raft together with lengths of wiring from the
lander. "I'm sure he'll make it okay," Woody said quietly.

Thomas sighed. "Yeah," he said, and then, more briskly,

"Let me give you a hand with that raft. If we snap it up, we ought to be ready to leave by morning."

Last night, climbing the highest of the rolling hills to the north, they had seen the lights of a distant city, glinting silver and yellow and orange on the far horizon, gleaming far away across the black midnight expanse of the dead sea bottom like an ornate and intricate piece of jewelry set against ink-black velvet.

Thomas was still not sure if he hoped there would be aristocratic red men there, and giant four-armed green Tharks, and beautiful Martian princesses. . . .

THE JAGUAR HUNTER

by Lucius Shepard

> *Lucius Shepard is the fastest rising new star in the short story field—and many of his tales show high familiarity with Latin America, its people and their way of life. This story is no exception. But is it fantasy or an other-dimensional conjecture? Your editors decided on the latter probability.*

It was his wife's debt to Onofrio Esteves, the appliance dealer, that brought Esteban Caax to town for the first time in almost a year. By nature he was a man who enjoyed the sweetness of the countryside above all else; the placid measures of a farmer's day invigorated him, and he took great pleasure in nights spent joking and telling stories around a fire, or lying beside his wife, Incarnación. Puerto Morada, with its fruit company imperatives and sullen dogs and cantinas that blared American music, was a place he avoided like the plague: indeed, from his home atop the mountain whose slopes formed the northernmost enclosure of Bahía Onda, the rusted tin roofs ringing the bay resembled a dried crust of blood such as might appear upon the lips of a dying man.

On this particular morning, however, he had no choice but to visit the town. Incarnación had—without his knowledge—purchased a battery-operated television set on credit from Onofrio, and he was threatening to seize Esteban's three milk cows in lieu of the eight hundred lempiras that was owed; he refused to accept the return of the television, but had sent word that he was willing to discuss an alternate method of payment. Should Esteban lose the cows, his income would drop below a subsistence level, and he would be forced to take up his old occupation, an occupation far more onerous than farming.

As he walked down the mountain, past huts of thatch and brushwood poles identical to his own, following a trail that wound through sun-browned thickets lorded over by banana trees, he was not thinking of Onofrio but of Incarnación. It was in her nature to be frivolous, and he had known this when he had married her; yet the television was emblematic of the differences that had developed between them since their children had reached maturity. She had begun to put on sophisticated airs, to laugh at Esteban's country ways, and she had become the doyenne of a group of older women, mostly widows, all of whom aspired to sophistication. Each night they would huddle around the television and strive to outdo one another in making sagacious comments about the American detective shows they watched; and each night Esteban would sit outside the hut and gloomily ponder the state of his marriage. He believed Incarnación's association with the widows was her manner of telling him that she looked forward to adopting the black skirt and shawl, that—having served his purpose as a father—he was now an impediment to her. Thought she was only forty-one, younger by three years than Esteban, she was withdrawing from the life of the senses, they rarely made love anymore, and he was certain that this partially embodied her resentment of the fact that the years had been kind to him. He had the look of one of the Old Patuca—tall, with chiseled features and wide-set eyes; his coppery skin was relatively unlined and his hair jet black. Incarnación's hair was streaked with gray, and the clean beauty of her limbs had dissolved beneath layers of fat. He had not expected her to remain beautiful, and he had tried to assure her that he loved the woman she was and not merely the girl she had been. But that woman was dying, infected by the same disease that had infected Puerto Morada, and perhaps his love for her was dying, too.

The dusty street on which the appliance store was situated ran in back of the movie theater and the Hotel Circo Del Mar, and from the inland side of the street Esteban could see the bell towers of Santa María del Onda rising above the hotel roof like the horns of a great stone snail. As a young man, obeying his mother's wish that he become a priest, he had spent three years cloistered beneath those towers, preparing for the seminary under the tutelage of old Father Gonsalvo. It was the part of his life he most regretted, because the academic disciplines he had mastered seemed to have stranded him between the world of the Indian and that of contemporary society; in his heart he held to his father's teachings—the principles of magic, the history of the tribe, the lore of nature—and yet he could never escape the feeling that such wisdom was either superstitious or simply unimportant. The shadows of the towers lay upon his soul as surely as they did upon the cobbled square in front of the church, and the sight of them caused him to pick up his pace and lower his eyes.

Farther along the street was the Cantina Atomica, a gathering place for the well-to-do youth of the town, and across from it was the appliance store, a one-story building of yellow stucco with corrugated metal doors that were lowered at night. Its facade was decorated by a mural that supposedly represented the merchandise within: sparkling refrigerators and televisions and washing machines, all given the impression of enormity by the tiny men and women painted below them, their hands upflung in awe. The actual merchandise was much less imposing, consisting mainly of radios and used kitchen equipment. Few people in Puerto Morada could afford more, and those who could generally bought elsewere. The majority of Onofrio's clientele were poor, hard-pressed to meet his schedule of payments, and to a large degree his wealth derived from selling repossessed appliances over and over.

Raimundo Esteves, a pale young man with puffy cheeks and heavily lidded eyes and a petulant mouth, was leaning against the counter when Esteban entered; Raimundo smirked and let out a piercing whistle, and a few seconds later his father emerged from the back room: a huge slug of a man, even paler than Raimundo. Filaments of gray hair were slicked down across his mottled scalp, and his belly stretched the front of a starched *guayabera*. He beamed and extended a hand.

"How good to see you," he said. "Raimundo! Bring us coffee and two chairs."

Much as he disliked Onofrio, Esteban was in no position to

be uncivil; he accepted the handshake. Raimundo spilled coffee in the saucers and clattered the chairs and glowered, angry at being forced to serve an Indian.

"Why will you not let me return the television?" asked Esteban after taking a seat; and then, unable to bite back the words, he added, "Is it no longer your policy to swindle my people?"

Onofrio sighed, as if it were exhausting to explain things to a fool such as Esteban. "I do not swindle your people. I go beyond the letter of the contracts in allowing them to make returns rather than pursuing matters through the courts. In your case, however, I have devised a way whereby you can keep the television without any further payments and yet settle the account. Is this a swindle?"

It was pointless to argue with a man whose logic was as facile and self-serving as Onofrio's. "Tell me what you want," said Esteban.

Onofrio wetted his lips, which were the color of raw sausage. "I want you to kill the jaguar of Barrio Carolina."

"I no longer hunt," said Esteban.

"The Indian is afraid," said Raimundo, moving up behind Onofrio's shoulder. "I told you."

Onofrio waved him away and said to Esteban, "That is unreasonable. If I take the cows, you will once again be hunting jaguars. But if you do this, you will have to hunt only one jaguar."

"One that has killed eight hunters." Esteban set down his coffee cup and stood. "It is no ordinary jaguar."

Raimundo laughed disparagingly, and Esteban skewered him with a stare.

"Ah!" said Onofrio, smiling a flatterer's smile. "But none of the eight used your method."

"Your pardon, *don* Onofrio," said Esteban with mock formality. "I have other business to attend."

"I will pay you five hundred lempiras in addition to erasing the debt," said Onofrio.

"Why?" asked Esteban. "Forgive me, but I cannot believe it is due to a concern for the public welfare."

Onofrio's fat throat pulsed, his face darkened.

"Never mind," said Esteban. "It is not enough."

"Very well. A thousand." Onofrio's casual manner could not conceal the anxiety in his voice.

Intrigued, curious to learn the extent of Onofrio's anxiety, Esteban plucked a figure from the air. "Ten thousand," he said. "And in advance."

"Ridiculous! I could hire ten hunters for this much! Twenty!"

Esteban shrugged. "But none with my method."

For a moment Onofrio sat with his hands enlaced, twisting them, as if struggling with some pious conception. "All right," he said, the words squeezed out of him. "Ten thousand!"

The reason for Onofrio's interest in Barrio Carolina suddenly dawned on Esteban, and he understood that the profits involved would make his fee seem pitifully small. But he was possessed by the thought of what ten thousand lempiras could mean: a herd of cows, a small truck to haul produce, or—and as he thought it, he realized this was the happiest possibility—the little stucco house in Barrio Clarín that Incarnación had set her heart on. Perhaps owning it would soften her toward him. He noticed Raimundo staring at him, his expression a knowing smirk; and even Onofrio, though still outraged by the fee, was beginning to show signs of satisfaction, adjusting the fit of his *guayabera*, slicking down his already-slicked-down hair. Esteban felt debased by their capacity to buy him, and to preserve a last shred of dignity, he turned and walked to the door.

"I will consider it," he tossed back over his shoulder. "And I will give you my answer in the morning."

"Murder Squad of New York," starring a bald American actor, was the featured attraction on Incarnación's television that night, and the widows sat cross-legged on the floor, filling the hut so completely that the charcoal stove and the sleeping hammock had been moved outside in order to provide good viewing angles for the latecomers. To Esteban, standing in the doorway, it seemed his home had been invaded by a covey of large black birds with cowled heads, who were receiving evil instruction from the core of a flickering gray jewel. Reluctantly, he pushed between them and made his way to the shelves mounted on the wall behind the set; he reached up to the top shelf and pulled down a long bundle wrapped in oil-stained newspapers. Out of the corner of his eye, he saw Incarnación watching him, her lips thinned, curved in a smile, and that cicatrix of a smile branded its mark on Esteban's heart. She knew what he was about, and she was delighted! Not in the least worried! Perhaps she had known of Onofrio's plan to kill the jaguar, perhaps she had schemed with Onofrio to entrap him. Infuriated, he barged through the widows, setting them to gabbling, and walked out into his banana grove and sat on a stone amidst it. The night was cloudy, and only a handful of stars showed between the tattered dark shapes of the leaves; the wind sent the leaves slithering together, and he heard one of his cows snorting and smelled the ripe odor of the corral. It was as if the solidity of his life had been reduced to this isolated perspective, and he bitterly felt the isolation. Though he would admit to fault in the marriage, he could think of nothing he had done that could have bred Incarnación's hateful smile.

After a while, he unwrapped the bundle of newspapers and drew out a thin-bladed machete of the sort used to chop banana stalks, but which he used to kill jaguars. Just holding it renewed his confidence and gave him a feeling of strength. It had been four years since he had hunted, yet he knew he had not lost the skill. Once he had been proclaimed the greatest hunter in the province of Neuva Esperanza, as had his father before him, and he had not retired from hunting because of age or infirmity, but because the jaguars were beautiful, and their beauty had begun to outweigh the reasons he had for killing them. He had no better reason to kill the jaguar of Barrio Carolina. It menaced no one other than those who hunted it, who sought to invade its territory, and its death would profit only a dishonorable man and a shrewish wife, and would spread the contamination of Puerto Morada. And besides, it was a black jaguar.

"Black jaguars," his father had told him, "are creatures of the moon. They have other forms and magical purposes with which we must not interfere. Never hunt them!"

His father had not said that the black jaguars lived on the moon, simply that they utilized its power; but as a child, Esteban had dreamed about a moon of ivory forests and silver meadows through which the jaguars flowed as swiftly as black water; and when he had told his father of the dreams, his father had said that such dreams were representations of a truth, and that sooner or later he would discover the truth underlying them. Esteban had never stopped believing in the dreams, not even in the face of the rocky, airless place depicted by the science programs on Incarnación's television: that moon, its mystery explained, was merely a less enlightening kind of dream, a statement of fact that reduced reality to the knowable.

But as he thought this, Esteban suddenly realized that killing the jaguar might be the solution to his problems, that by going against his father's teaching, that by killing his dreams, his Indian conception of the world, he might be able to find accord with his wife's; he had been standing halfway between the two conceptions for too long, and it was time for him to choose. And there was no real choice. It was this world he inhabited, not that of the jaguars; if it took the death of a magical creature to permit him to embrace as joys the television and trips to the movies and a stucco house in Barrio Clarín, well, he had faith in this method. He swung the machete, slicing the dark air, and laughed. Incarnación's frivolousness, his skill at hunting, Onofrio's greed, the jaguar, the television . . . all these things were neatly woven together like the elements of a spell, one whose products would be a denial of magic and a furthering of the unmagical doctrines that had corrupted Puerto Morada. He laughed again, but a second later he chided himself: it was exactly this sort of thinking he was preparing to root out.

Esteban waked Incarnación early the next morning and forced her to accompany him to the appliance store. His machete swung by his side in a leather sheath, and he carried a burlap sack containing food and the herbs he would need for the hunt. Incarnación trotted along beside him, silent, her face hidden by a shawl. When they reached the store, Esteban had Onofrio stamp the bill PAID IN FULL, then he handed the bill and the money to Incarnación.

"If I kill the jaguar or if it kills me," he said harshly, "this will be yours. Should I fail to return within a week, you may assume that I will never return."

She retreated a step, her face registering alarm, as if she had seen him in a new light and understood the consequences of her actions, but she made no move to stop him as he walked out the door.

Across the street, Raimundo Esteves was leaning against the wall of the Cantina Atomica, talking to two girls wearing jeans and frilly blouses; the girls were fluttering their hands and dancing to the music that issued from the cantina, and to Esteban they seemed more alien than the creature he was to hunt. Raimundo spotted him and whispered to the girls; they peeked over their shoulders and laughed. Already angry at Incarnación, Esteban was washed over by a cold fury. He crossed the street to them, rested his hand on the hilt of the machete, and stared at Raimundo; he had never before noticed how soft he was, how empty of presence. A crop of pimples straggled along his jaw, the flesh beneath his eyes was pocked by tiny indentations like those made by a silversmith's hammer, and, unequal to the stare, his eyes darted back and forth between the two girls.

Esteban's anger dissolved into revulsion. "I am Esteban Caax," he said. "I have built my own house, tilled my soil, and brought four children into the world. This day I am going to hunt the jaguar of Barrio Carolina in order to make you and your father even fatter than you are." He ran his gaze up and down Raimundo's body and, letting his voice fill with disgust, he asked, "Who are you?"

Raimundo's puffy face cinched in a knot of hatred, but he offered no response. The girls tittered and skipped through the door of the cantina; Esteban could hear them describing the incident, laughter, and he continued to stare at Raimundo. Several other girls poked their heads out the door, giggling and whispering. After a moment, Esteban spun on his heel and walked away. Behind him there was a chorus of unrestrained laughter, and a girl's voice called mockingly, "Raimundo! Who are you?" Other voices joined in, and it soon became a chant.

Barrio Carolina was not truly a barrio of Puerto Morada; it lay beyond Punta Manabique, the southernmost enclosure of the bay, and was fronted by a palm hammock and the loveliest stretch of beach in all the province, a curving slice of white sand giving way to jade-green shallows. Forty years before, it had been the headquarters of the fruit company's experimental farm, a project of such vast scope that a small town had been built on the site: rows of white frame houses with shingle roofs and screen porches, the kind you might see in a magazine illustration of rural America. The company had touted the project as being the keystone of the country's

future, and had promised to develop high-yield crops that
would banish starvation; but in 1947 a cholera epidemic had
ravaged the coast and the town had been abandoned. By the
time the cholera scare had died down, the company had
become well-entrenched in national politics and no longer
needed to maintain a benevolent image; the project had been
dropped and the property abandoned until—in the same year
that Esteban had retired from hunting—developers had bought
it, planning to build a major resort. It was then the jaguar had
appeared. Though it had not killed any of the workmen, it had
terrorized them to the point that they had refused to begin the
job. Hunters had been sent, and these the jaguar *had* killed.
The last party of hunters had been equipped with automatic
rifles, all manner of technological aids; but the jaguar had
picked them off one by one, and this project, too, had been
abandoned. Rumor had it that the land had recently been
resold (now Esteban knew to whom), and that the idea of a
resort was once more under consideration.

The walk from Puerto Morada was hot and tiring, and upon
arrival Esteban sat beneath a palm and ate a lunch of cold
banana fritters. Combers as white as toothpaste broke on the
shore, and there was no human litter, just dead fronds and
driftwood and coconuts. All but four of the houses had been
swallowed by the jungle, and only sections of those four
remained visible, embedded like moldering gates in a black-
ish green wall of vegetation. Even under the bright sunlight,
they were haunted-looking; their screens ripped, boards weathered gray, vines cascading over their facades. A mango tree
had sprouted from one of the porches, and wild parrots were
eating its fruit. He had not visited the barrio since childhood:
the ruins had frightened him then, but now he found them
appealing, testifying to the dominion of natural law. It distressed him that he would transform it all into a place where
the parrots would be chained to perches and the jaguars
would be designs on tablecloths, a place of swimming pools
and tourists sipping from coconut shells. Nonetheless, after
he had finished lunch, he set out to explore the jungle and
soon discovered a trail used by the jaguar: a narrow path that
wound between the vine-matted shells of the houses for about
a half mile and ended at the Rio Dulce. The river was a
murkier green than the sea, curving away through the jungle
walls; the jaguar's tracks were everywhere along the bank,

especially thick upon a tussocky rise some five or six feet above the water. This baffled Esteban. The jaguar could not drink from the rise, and it certainly would not sleep there. He puzzled over it awhile, but eventually shrugged it off, returned to the beach, and, because he planned to keep watch that night, took a nap beneath the palms.

Some hours later, around midafternoon, he was startled from his nap by a voice hailing him. A tall, slim, copper-skinned woman was walking toward him, wearing a dress of dark green—almost the exact color of the jungle walls—that exposed the swell of her breasts. As she drew near, he saw that though her features had a Patucan cast, they were of a lapidary fineness uncommon to the tribe; it was as if they had been refined into a lovely mask: cheeks planed into subtle hollows, lips sculpted full, stylized feathers of ebony inlaid for eyebrows, eyes of jet and white onyx, and all this given a human gloss. A sheen of sweat covered her breasts, and a single curl of black hair lay over her collarbone, so artful-seeming it appeared to have been placed there by design. She knelt beside him, gazing at him impassively, and Esteban was flustered by her heated air of sensuality. The sea breeze bore her scent to him, a sweet musk that reminded him of mangoes left ripening in the sun.

"My name is Esteban Caax," he said, painfully aware of his own sweaty odor.

"I have heard of you," she said. "The jaguar hunter. Have you come to kill the jaguar of the barrio?"

"Yes," he said, and felt shame at admitting it.

She picked up a handful of sand and watched it sift through her fingers.

"What is your name?" he asked.

"If we become friends, I will tell you my name," she said. "Why must you kill the jaguar?"

He told her about the television set, and then, to his surprise, he found himself describing his problems with Incarnación, explaining how he intended to adapt to her ways. These were not proper subjects to discuss with a stranger, yet he was lured to intimacy; he thought he sensed an affinity between them, and that prompted him to portray his marriage as more dismal than it was, for though he had never once been unfaithful to Incarnación, he would have welcomed the chance to do so now.

"This is a black jaguar," she said. "Surely you know they are not ordinary animals, that they have purposes with which we must not interfere?"

Esteban was startled to hear his father's words from her mouth, but he dismissed it as coincidence and replied, "Perhaps. But they are not mine."

"Truly, they are," she said. "You have simply chosen to ignore them." She scooped up another handful of sand. "How will you do it? You have no gun. Only a machete."

"I have this as well," he said, and from his sack he pulled out a small parcel of herbs and handed it to her.

She opened it and sniffed the contents. "Herbs? Ah! You plan to drug the jaguar."

"Not the jaguar. Myself." He took back the parcel. "The herbs slow the heart and give the body a semblance of death. They induce a trance, but one that can be thrown off at a moment's notice. After I chew them, I will lie down in a place that the jaguar must pass on its nightly hunt. It will think I am dead, but it will not feed unless it is sure that the spirit has left the flesh, and to determine this, it will sit on the body so it can feel the spirit rise up. As soon as it starts to settle, I will throw off the trance and stab it between the ribs. If my hand is steady, it will die instantly."

"And if your hand is unsteady?"

"I have killed nearly fifty jaguars," he said. "I no longer fear unsteadiness. The method comes down through my family from the Old Patuca, and it has never failed, to my knowledge."

"But a black jaguar . . ."

"Black or spotted, it makes no difference. Jaguars are creatures of instinct, and one is like another when it comes to feeding."

"Well," she said, "I cannot wish you luck, but neither do I wish you ill." She came to her feet, brushing the sand from her dress.

He wanted to ask her to stay, but pride prevented him, and she laughed as if she knew his mind.

"Perhaps we will talk again, Esteban," she said. "It would be a pity if we did not, for more lies between us than we have spoken of this day."

She walked swiftly down the beach, becoming a diminutive black figure that was rippled away by the heat haze.

* * *

That evening, needing a place from which to keep watch, Esteban pried open the screen door of one of the houses facing the beach and went onto the porch. Chameleons skittered into the corners, and an iguana slithered off a rusted lawn chair sheathed in spiderweb and vanished through a gap in the floor. The interior of the house was dark and forbidding, except for the bathroom, the roof of which was missing, webbed over by vines that admitted a gray-green infusion of twilight. The cracked toilet was full of rainwater and dead insects. Uneasy, Esteban returned to the porch, cleaned the lawn chair, and sat.

Out on the horizon the sea and sky were blending in a haze of silver and gray; the wind had died, and the palms were as still as sculpture; a string of pelicans flying low above the waves seemed to be spelling a sentence of cryptic black syllables. But the eerie beauty of the scene was lost on him. He could not stop thinking of the woman. The memory of her hips rolling beneath the fabric of her dress as she walked away was repeated over and over in his thoughts, and whenever he tried to turn his attention to the matter at hand, the memory became more compelling. He imagined her naked, the play of muscles rippling her haunches, and this so enflamed him that he started to pace, unmindful of the fact that the creaking boards were signaling his presence. He could not understand her effect upon him. Perhaps, he thought, it was her defense of the jaguar, her calling to mind of all he was putting behind him . . . and then a realization settled over him like an icy shroud.

It was commonly held among the Patuca that a man about to suffer a solitary and unexpected death would be visited by an envoy of death, who—standing in for family and friends—would prepare him to face the event; and Esteban was now very sure that the woman had been such an envoy, that her allure had been specifically designed to attract his soul to its imminent fate. He sat back down in the lawn chair, numb with the realization. Her knowledge of his father's words, the odd flavor of her conversation, her intimation that more lay between them: it all accorded perfectly with the traditional wisdom. The moon rose three-quarters full, silvering the sands of the barrio, and still he sat there, rooted to the spot by his fear of death.

He had been watching the jaguar for several seconds before
he registered its presence. It seemed at first that a scrap of
night sky had fallen onto the sand and was being blown by a
fitful breeze; but soon he saw that it was the jaguar, that it
was inching along as if stalking some prey. Then it leaped
high into the air, twisting and turning, and began to race up
and down the beach: a ribbon of black water flowing across
the silver sands. He had never before seen a jaguar at play,
and this alone was cause for wonder; but most of all, he
wondered at the fact that here were his childhood dreams
come to life. He might have been peering out onto a silvery
meadow of the moon, spying on one of its magical creatures.
His fear was eroded by the sight, and like a child he pressed
his nose to the screen, trying not to blink, anxious that he
might not miss a single moment.

At length the jaguar left off its play and came prowling up
the beach toward the jungle. By the set of its ears and the
purposeful sway of its walk, Esteban recognized that it was
hunting. It stopped beneath a palm about twenty feet from the
house, lifted its head, and tested the air. Moonlight frayed
down through the fronds, applying liquid gleams to its haunches;
its eyes, glinting yellow-green, were like peepholes into a lurid
dimension of fire. The jaguar's beauty was heartstopping—the
embodiment of a flawless principle—and Esteban, contrasting
this beauty with the pallid ugliness of his employer, with the
ugly principle that had led to his hiring, doubted that he could
ever bring himself to kill it.

All the following day he debated the question. He had
hoped the woman would return, because he had rejected the
idea that she was death's envoy—that perception, he thought,
must have been induced by the mysterious atmosphere of the
barrio—and he felt that if she were to argue the jaguar's
cause again, he would let himself be persuaded. But she did
not put in an appearance, and as he sat upon the beach,
watching the evening sun decline through strata of dusky
orange and lavender clouds, casting wild glitters over the sea,
he understood once more that he had no choice. Whether or
not the jaguar was beautiful, whether or not the woman had
been on a supernatural errand, he must treat these things as if
they had no substance. The point of the hunt had been to
deny mysteries of this sort, and he had lost sight of it under
the influence of old dreams.

He waited until moonrise to take the herbs, and then lay down beneath the palm tree where the jaguar had paused the previous night. Lizards whispered past in the grasses, sand fleas hopped onto his face: he hardly felt them, sinking deeper into the languor of the herbs. The fronds overhead showed an ashen green in the moonlight, lifting, rustling; and the stars between their feathered edges flickered crazily as if the breeze were fanning their flames. He became immersed in the landscape, savoring the smells of brine and rotting foliage that were blowing across the beach, drifting with them; but when he heard the pad of the jaguar's step, he came alert. Through narrowed eyes he saw it sitting a dozen feet away, a bulky shadow craning its neck toward him, investigating his scent. After a moment it began to circle him, each circle a bit tighter than the one before, and whenever it passed out of view, he had to repress a trickle of fear. Then, as it passed close on the seaward side, he caught a whiff of its odor.

A sweet, musky odor that reminded him of mangoes left ripening in the sun.

Fear welled up in him, and he tried to banish it, to tell himself that the odor could not possibly be what he thought. The jaguar snarled, a razor stroke of sound that slit the peaceful mesh of wind and surf, and realizing it had scented his fear, he sprang to his feet, waving his machete. In a whirl of vision, he saw the jaguar leap back, he shouted at it, waved the machete again, and sprinted for the house where he had kept watch. He slipped through the door and went staggering into the front room. There was a crash behind him, and turning, he had a glimpse of a huge black shape struggling to extricate itself from a moonlit tangle of vines and ripped screen. He darted into the bathroom, sat with his back against the toilet bowl, and braced the door shut with his feet.

The sound of the jaguar's struggles subsided, and for a moment he thought it had given up. Sweat left cold trails down his sides, his heart pounded. He held his breath, listening, and it seemed the whole world was holding its breath as well. The noises of wind and surf and insects were a faint seething; moonlight shed a sickly white radiance through the enlaced vines overhead, and a chameleon was frozen among peels of wallpaper beside the door. He let out a sigh and wiped the sweat from his eyes. He swallowed.

Then the top panel of the door exploded, shattered by a

black paw. Splinters of rotten wood flew into his face, and he screamed. The sleek wedge of the jaguar's head thrust through the hole, roaring. A gateway of gleaming fangs guarding a plush red throat. Half-paralyzed, Esteban jabbed weakly with the machete. The jaguar withdrew, reached in with its paw, and clawed at his leg. More by accident than design, he managed to slice the jaguar, and the paw, too, was withdrawn, He heard it rumbling in the front room, and then, seconds later, a heavy thump against the wall behind him. The jaguar's head appeared above the edge of the wall; it was hanging by its forepaws, trying to gain a perch from which to leap down into the room. Esteban scrambled to his feet and slashed wildly, severing vines. The jaguar fell back, yowling. For a while it prowled along the wall, fuming to itself. Finally there was silence.

When sunlight began to filter through the vines, Esteban walked out of the house and headed down the beach to Puerto Morada. He went with his head lowered, desolate, thinking of the grim future that awaited him after he returned the money to Onofrio: a life of trying to please an increasingly shrewish Incarnación, of killing lesser jaguars for much less money. He was so mired in depression that he did not notice the woman until she called to him. She was leaning against a palm about thirty feet away, wearing a filmy white dress through which he could see the dark jut of her nipples. He drew his machete and backed off a pace.

"Why do you fear me, Esteban?" she called, walking toward him.

"You tricked me into revealing my method and tried to kill me," he said. "Is that not reason for fear?"

"I did not know you or your method in that form. I knew only that you were hunting me. But now the hunt has ended, and we can be as man and woman."

He kept his machete at point. "What are you?" he asked.

She smiled. "My name is Miranda. I am Patuca."

"Patucas do not have black fur and fangs."

"I am of the Old Patuca," she said. "We have this power."

"Keep away!" He lifted the machete as if to strike, and she stopped just beyond his reach.

"You can kill me if that is your wish, Esteban." She spread her arms, and her breasts thrust forward against the fabric of her dress. "You are stronger than I, now. But listen to me first."

He did not lower the machete, but his fear and anger were being overridden by a sweeter emotion.

"Long ago," she said, "there was a great healer who foresaw that one day the Patuca would lose their place in the world, and so, with the help of the gods, he opened a door into another world where the tribe could flourish. But many of the tribe were afraid and would not follow him. Since then, the door has been left open for those who would come after." She waved at the ruined houses. "Barrio Carolina is the site of the door, and the jaguar is its guardian. But soon the fevers of this world will sweep over the barrio, and the door will close forever. For though our hunt has ended, there is no end to hunters or to greed." She came a step nearer. "If you listen to the sounding of your heart, you will know this is the truth."

He half-believed her, yet he also believed her words masked a more poignant truth, one that fitted inside the other the way his machete fitted into its sheath.

"What is it?" she asked. "What troubles you?"

"I think you have come to prepare me for death," he said, "and that your door leads only to death."

"Then why do you not run from me?" She pointed toward Puerto Morada. "That is death, Esteban. The cries of the gulls are death, and when the hearts of lovers stop at the moment of greatest pleasure, that, too, is death. This world is no more than a thin covering of life drawn over a foundation of death, like a scum of algae upon a rock. Perhaps you are right, perhaps my world lies beyond death. The two ideas are not opposed. But if I am death to you, Esteban, then it is death you love."

He turned his eyes to the sea, not wanting her to see his face. "I do not love you," he said.

"Love awaits us," she said. "And someday you will join me in my world."

He looked back to her, ready with a denial, but was shocked to silence. Her dress had fallen to the sand, and she was smiling. The litheness and purity of the jaguar were reflected in every line of her body; her secret hair was so absolute a black that it seemed an absence in her flesh. She moved close, pushing aside the machete. The tips of her breasts brushed against him, warm through the coarse cloth of his shirt; her hands cupped his face, and he was drowning in her heated scent, weakened by both fear and desire.

"We are of one soul, you and I," she said. "One blood and one truth. You cannot reject me."

Days passed, though Esteban was unclear as to how many. Night and day were unimportant incidences of his relationship with Miranda, serving only to color their lovemaking with a spectral or a sunny mood; and each time they made love, it was as if a thousand new colors were being added to his senses. He had never been so content. Sometimes, gazing at the haunted facades of the barrio, he believed that they might well conceal shadowy avenues leading to another world; however, whenever Miranda tried to convince him to leave with her, he refused: he could not overcome his fear and would never admit—even to himself—that he loved her. He attempted to fix his thoughts on Incarnación, hoping this would undermine his fixation with Miranda and free him to return to Puerto Morada; but he found that he could not picture his wife except as a black bird hunched before a flickering gray jewel. Miranda, however, seemed equally unreal at times. Once as they sat on the bank of the Rio Dulce, watching the reflection of the moon—almost full—floating upon the water, she pointed to it, and said, "My world is that near, Esteban. That touchable. You may think the moon above is real and this is only a reflection, but the thing most real, that most illustrates the real, is the surface that permits the illusion of reflection. Passing through this surface is what you fear, and yet it is so insubstantial, you would scarcely notice the passage."

"You sound like the old priest who taught me philosophy," said Esteban. "His world—his heaven—was also philosophy. Is that what your world is? The idea of a place? Or are there birds and jungles and rivers?"

Her expression was in partial eclipse, half-moonlit, half-shadowed, and her voice revealed nothing of her mood. "No more than there are here," she said.

"What does that mean?" he said angrily. "Why will you not give me a clear answer?"

"If I were to describe my world, you would simply think me a clever liar." She rested her head on his shoulder.

"Sooner or later you will understand. We did not find each other merely to have the pain of being parted."

In that moment her beauty—like her words—seemed a kind of evasion, obscuring a dark and frightening beauty beneath; and yet he knew that she was right, that no proof of hers could persuade him contrary to his fear.

One afternoon, an afternoon of such brightness that it was impossible to look at the sea without squinting, they swam out to a sandbar that showed as a thin curving island of white against the green water. Esteban floundered and splashed, but Miranda swam as if born to the element; she darted beneath him, tickling him, pulling at his feet, eeling away before he could catch her. They walked along the sand, turning over starfish with their toes, collecting whelks to boil for their dinner, and then Esteban spotted a dark stain hundreds of yards wide that was moving below the water beyond the bar; a great school of king mackerel.

"It is too bad we have no boat," he said. "Mackerel would taste better than whelks."

"We need no boat," she said. "I will show you an old way of catching fish."

She traced a complicated design in the sand, and when she had done, she led him into the shallows and had him stand facing her a few feet away.

"Look down at the water between us," she said. "Do not look up, and keep perfectly still until I tell you."

She began to sing with a faltering rhythm, a rhythm that put him in mind of the ragged breezes of the season. Most of the words were unfamiliar, but others he recognized as Patuca. After a minute he experienced a wave of dizziness, as if his legs had grown long and spindly, and he was now looking down from a great height, breathing rarefied air. Then a tiny dark stain materialized below the expanse of water between him and Miranda. He remembered his grandfather's stories of the Old Patuca, how—with the help of the gods—they had been able to shrink the world, to bring enemies close and cross vast distances in a matter of moments. But the gods were dead, their powers gone from the world. He wanted to glance back to shore and see if he and Miranda had become coppery giants taller than the palms.

"Now," she said, breaking off her song, "you must put your hand into the water on the seaward side of the school and gently wiggle your fingers. Very gently! Be sure not to disturb the surface.''

But when Esteban made to do as he was told, he slipped and caused a splash. Miranda cried out. Looking up, he saw a wall of jade-green water bearing down on them, its face thickly studded with the fleeting dark shapes of the mackerel. Before he could move, the wave swept over the sandbar and carried him under, dragging him along the bottom and finally casting him onto shore. The beach was littered with flopping mackerel; Miranda lay in the shallows, laughing at him. Esteban laughed, too, but only to cover up his rekindled fear of this woman who drew upon the powers of dead gods. He had no wish to hear her explanation; he was certain she would tell him that the gods lived on in her world, and this would only confuse him further.

Later that day as Esteban was cleaning the fish, while Miranda was off picking bananas to cook with them—the sweet little ones that grew along the riverbank—a Land-Rover came jouncing up the beach from Puerto Morada, an orange fire of the setting sun dancing on its windshield. It pulled up beside him, and Onofrio climbed out the passenger side. A hectic flush dappled his cheeks, and he was dabbing his sweaty brow with a handkerchief. Raimundo climbed out the driver's side and leaned against the door, staring hatefully at Esteban.

"Nine days and not a word," said Onofrio gruffly. "We thought you were dead. How goes the hunt?"

Esteban set down the fish he had been scaling and stood. "I have failed," he said, "I will give you back the money."

Raimundo chuckled—a dull, cluttered sound—and Onofrio grunted with amusement. "Impossible," he said. "Incarnación has spent the money on a house in Barrio Clarín. You must kill the jaguar."

"I cannot," said Esteban. "I will repay you, somehow."

"The Indian has lost his nerve, Father." Raimundo spat in the sand. "Let my friends and I hunt the jaguar."

The idea of Raimundo and his loutish friends thrashing through the jungle was so ludicrous that Esteban could not restrain a laugh.

"Be careful, Indian," Raimundo banged the flat of his hand on the roof of the car.

"It is you who should be careful," said Esteban. "Most

likely the jaguar will be hunting you." Esteban picked up his machete. "And whoever hunts this jaguar will answer to me as well."

Raimundo reached for something in the driver's seat and walked around in front of the hood. In his hand was a silvered automatic. "I await your answer," he said.

"Put that away!" Onofrio's tone was that of a man addressing a child whose menace was inconsequential, but the intent surfacing in Raimundo's face was not childish. A tic marred the plump curve of his cheek, the ligature of his neck was cabled, and his lips were drawn back in a joyless grin. It was thought Esteban—strangely fascinated by the transformation—like watching a demon dissolve its false shape: the true lean features melting up from the illusion of the soft.

"This son of a whore insulted me in front of Julia!" Raimundo's gun hand was shaking.

"Your personal differences can wait," said Onofrio. "This is a business matter." He held out his hand. "Give me the gun."

"If he is not going to kill the jaguar, what use is he?" said Raimundo.

"Perhaps we can convince him to change his mind." Onofrio beamed at Esteban. "What do you say? Shall I let my son collect his debt of honor, or will you fulfill our contract?"

"Father!" complained Raimundo; his eyes flicked sideways. "He . . ."

Esteban broke for the jungle. The gun roared, a white-hot claw swiped at his side, and he went flying. For an instant he did not know where he was; but then, one by one, his impressions began to sort themselves. He was lying on his injured side, and it was throbbing fiercely. Sand crusted his mouth and eyelids. He was curled up around his machete, which was still clutched in his hand. Voices above him, sand fleas hopping on his face. He resisted the urge to brush them off and lay without moving. The throb of his wound and his hatred had the same red force behind them.

". . . carry him to the river," Raimundo was saying, his voice atremble with excitement. "Everyone will think the jaguar killed him!"

"Fool!" said Onofrio. "He might have killed the jaguar, and you could have had a sweeter revenge. His wife . . ."

"This was sweet enough," said Raimundo.

A shadow fell over Esteban, and he held his breath. He needed no herbs to deceive this pale, flabby jaguar who was bending to him, turning him onto his back.

"Watch out!" cried Onofrio.

Esteban let himself be turned and lashed out with the machete. His contempt for Onofrio and Incarnación, as well as his hatred for Raimundo, was involved in the blow, and the blade lodged deep in Raimundo's side, grating on bone. Raimundo shrieked and would have fallen, but the blade helped to keep him upright; his hands fluttered around the machete as if he wanted to adjust it to a more comfortable position, and his eyes were wide with disbelief. A shudder vibrated the hilt of the machete—it seemed sensual, the spasm of a spent passion—and Raimundo sank to his knees. Blood spilled from his mouth, adding tragic lines to the corners of his lips. He pitched forward, not falling flat but remaining kneeling, his face pressed into the sand; the attitude of an Arab at prayer.

Esteban wrenched the machete free, fearful of an attack by Onofrio, but the appliance dealer was squirming into the Land-Rover. The engine caught, the wheels spun, and the car lurched off, turning through the edge of the surf and heading for Puerto Morada. An orange dazzle flared on the rear window, as if the spirit who had lured it to the bario was now harrying it away.

Unsteadily, Esteban got to his feet. He peeled his shirt back from the bullet wound. There was a lot of blood, but it was only a crease. He avoided looking at Raimundo and walked down to the water and stood gazing out at the waves; his thoughts rolled in with them, less thoughts than tidal sweeps of emotion.

It was twilight by the time Miranda returned, her arms full of bananas and wild figs. She had not heard the shot. He told her what had happened as she dressed his wounds with a poultice of herbs and banana leaves. "It will mend," she said of the wound. "But this"—she gestured at Raimundo—"this will not. You must come with me, Esteban. The soldiers will kill you."

"No," he said. "They will come, but they are Patuca . . . except for the captain, who is a drunkard, a shell of a man. I doubt he will even be notified. They will listen to my story, and we will reach an accommodation. No matter what lies Onofrio tells, his word will not stand against theirs.''

''And then?''

''I may have to go to jail for a while, or I may have to leave the province. But I will not be killed.''

She sat for a minute without speaking, the whites of her eyes glowing in the half-light. Finally she stood and walked off along the beach.

''Where are you going?'' he called.

She turned back. ''You speak so casually of losing me . . .'' she began.

''It is not casual!''

''No!'' She laughed bitterly. ''I suppose not. You are so afraid of life, you call it death and would prefer jail or exile to living it. That is hardly casual.'' She stared at him, her expression a cypher at that distance. ''I will not lose you, Esteban,'' she said. She walked away again, and this time when he called she did not turn.

Twilight deepened to dusk, a slow fill of shadow graying the world into negative, and Esteban felt himself graying along with it, his thoughts reduced to echoing the dull wash of the receding tide. The dusk lingered, and he had the idea that night would never fall, that the act of violence had driven a nail through the substance of his irresolute life, pinned him forever to this ashen moment and deserted shore. As a child he had been terrified by the possibility of such magical isolations, but now the prospect seemed a consolation for Miranda's absence, a remembrance of her magic. Despite her parting words, he did not think she would be back—there had been sadness and finality in her voice—and this roused in him feelings of both relief and desolation, feelings that set him to pacing up and down the tidal margin of the shore.

The full moon rose, the sands of the barrio burned silver, and shortly thereafter four soldiers came in a jeep from Puerto Morada. They were gnomish, copper-skinned men, and their uniforms were the dark blue of the night sky, bearing no device or decoration. Though they were not close friends, he knew them each by name. Sebastian, Amador, Carlito, and Ramón. In their headlights Raimundo's corpse—startlingly pale, the blood on his face dried into intricate whorls—looked like an exotic creature cast up by the sea, and their inspection of it smacked more of curiosity than of a search for evidence. Amador unearthed Raimundo's gun, sighted along it toward the jungle, and asked Ramón how much he thought it was worth.

"Perhaps Onofrio will give you a good price," said Ramón, and the others laughed.

They built a fire of driftwood and coconut shells, and sat around it while Esteban told his story; he did not mention either Miranda or her relation to the jaguar, because these men—estranged from the tribe by their government service—had grown conservative in their judgments, and he did not want them to consider him irrational. They listened without comment; the firelight burnished their skins to reddish gold and glinted on their rifle barrels.

"Onofrio will take his charge to the capital if we do nothing," said Amador after Esteban had finished.

"He may in any case," said Carlito. "And then it will go hard with Esteban."

"And," said Sebastian, "if an agent is sent to Puerto Morada and sees how things are with Captain Portales, they will surely replace him and it will go hard with us."

They stared into the flames, mulling over the problem, and Esteban chose the moment to ask Amador, who lived near him on the mountain, if he had seen Incarnación.

"She will be amazed to learn you are alive," said Amador. "I saw her yesterday in the dressmaker's shop. She was admiring the fit of a new black skirt in the mirror."

It was as if a black swath of Incarnación's skirt had folded around Esteban's thoughts. He lowered his head and carved lines in the sand with the point of his machete.

"I have it," said Ramón. "A boycott!"

The others expressed confusion.

"If we do not buy from Onofrio, who will?" said Ramón. "He will lose his business. Threatened with this, he will not dare involve the government. He will allow Esteban to plead self-defense."

"But Raimundo was his only son," said Amador. "It may be that grief will count more than greed in this instance."

Again they fell silent. It mattered little to Esteban what was decided. He was coming to understand that without Miranda, his future held nothing but uninteresting choices; he turned his gaze to the sky and noticed that the stars and the fire were flickering with the same rhythm, and he imagined each of them ringed by a group of gnomish, copper-skinned men, debating the question of his fate.

"Aha!" said Carlito. "I know what to do. We will occupy Barrio Carolina— the entire company—and *we* will kill the jaguar. Onofrio's greed cannot withstand this temptation."

"That you must not do," said Esteban.

"But why?" asked Amador. "We may not kill the jaguar, but with so many men we will certainly drive it away."

Before Esteban could answer, the jaguar roared. It was prowling down the beach toward the fire, like a black flame itself shifting over the glowing sand. Its ears were laid back, and silver drops of moonlight gleamed in its eyes. Amador grabbed his rifle, came to one knee, and fired: the bullet sprayed sand a dozen feet to the left of the jaguar.

"Wait!" cried Esteban, pushing him down.

But the rest had begun to fire, and the jaguar was hit. It leaped high as it had that first night while playing, but this time it landed in a heap, snarling, snapping at its shoulder; it regained its feet and limped toward the jungle, favoring its right foreleg. Excited by their success, the soldiers ran a few paces after it and stopped to fire again. Carlito dropped to one knee, taking careful aim.

"No!" shouted Esteban, and as he hurled his machete at Carlito, desperate to prevent further harm to Miranda, he recognized the trap that had been sprung and the consequences he would face.

The blade sliced across Carlito's thigh, knocking him onto his side. He screamed, and Amador, seeing what had happened, fired wildly at Esteban and called to the others. Esteban ran toward the jungle, making for the jaguar's path. A fusilade of shots rang out behind him, bullets whipped past his ears. Each time his feet slipped in the soft sand, the moonstruck facades of the barrio appeared to lurch sideways as if trying to block his way. And then, as he reached the verge of the jungle, he was hit.

The bullet seemed to throw him forward, to increase his speed, but somehow he managed to keep his feet. He careened along the path, arms waving, breath shrieking in his throat. Palmetto fronds swatted his face, vines tangled his legs. He felt no pain, only a peculiar numbness that pulsed low in his back; he pictured the wound opening and closing

like the mouth of an anemone. The soldiers were shouting his
name. They would follow, but cautiously, afraid of the jaguar, and he thought he might be able to cross the river before
they could catch up. But when he came to the river, he found
the jaguar waiting.

It was crouched on the tussocky rise, its neck craned over
the water, and below, half a dozen feet from the bank, floated
the reflection of the full moon, huge and silvery, an unblem-
ished circle of light. Blood glistened scarlet on the jaguar's
shoulder, like a fresh rose pinned in place, and this made it
look even more an embodiment of principle: the shape a god
might choose, that some universal constant might assume. It
gazed calmly at Esteban, growled low in its throat, and dove
into the river, cleaving and shattering the moon's reflection,
vanishing beneath the surface. The ripples subsided, the image of the moon reformed. And there, silhouetted against it,
Esteban saw the figure of a woman swimming, each stroke
causing her to grow smaller and smaller until she seemed no
more than a character incised upon a silver plate. It was not
only Miranda he saw, but all mystery and beauty receding
from him, and he realized how blind he had been not to
perceive the truth sheathed inside the truth of death that had
been sheathed inside her truth of another world. It was clear
to him now. It sang to him from his wound, every syllable a
heartbeat. It was written by the dying ripples, it swayed in the
banana leaves, it sighed on the wind. It was everywhere, and
he had always known it: If you deny mystery—even in the
guise of death—then you deny life, and you will walk like a
ghost through your days, never knowing the secrets of the
extremes. The deep sorrows, the absolute joys.

He drew a breath of the rank jungle air, and with it drew a
breath of a world no longer his, of the girl Incarnación, of
friends and children and country nights . . . all his lost
sweetness. His chest tightened as with the onset of tears, but
the sensation quickly abated, and he understood that the
sweetness of the past had been subsumed by a scent of
mangoes, that nine magical days—a magical number of days,
the number it takes to sing the soul to rest—lay between him
and tears. Freed of those associations, he felt as if he were
undergoing a subtle refinement of form, a winnowing, and he
remembered having felt much the same on the day when he
had run out the door of Santa María del Onda, putting behind

him its dark geometries and cobwebbed catechisms and generations of swallows that had never flown beyond the walls, casting off his acolyte's robe and racing across the square toward the mountain and Incarnación; it had been she who had lured him then, just as his mother had lured him to the church and as Miranda was luring him now, and he laughed at seeing how easily these three women had diverted the flow of his life, how like other men he was in this.

The strange bloom of painlessness in his back was sending out tendrils into his arms and legs, and the cries of the soldiers had grown louder. Miranda was a tiny speck shrinking against a silver immensity. For a moment he hesitated, experiencing a resurgence of fear; then Miranda's face materialized in his mind's eye, and all the emotion he had suppressed for nine days poured through him, washing away the fear. It was a silvery, flawless emotion, and he was giddy with it, light with it; it was like thunder and fire fused into one element and boiling up inside him, and he was overwhelmed by a need to express it, to mold it into a form that would reflect its power and purity. But he was no singer, no poet. There was but a single mode of expression open to him. Hoping he was not too late, that Miranda's door had not shut forever, Esteban dove into the river, cleaving the image of the full moon; and—his eyes still closed from the shock of the splash—with the last of his mortal strength, he swam hard down after her.

SAILING TO BYZANTIUM
by Robert Silverberg

Here's a possible classic which may seem at first to be a fantasy, but eventually you will see that it is indeed science fiction. Silverberg, a remarkable literary stylist, goes here on the principle that what was yesterday's magic could just be today's science. Add to that his expertise on ancient cultures (his most recent Gilgamesh the King) and we have something very unusual to savor.

At dawn he arose and stepped out onto the patio for his first look at Alexandria, the one city he had not yet seen. That year the five cities were Chang-an, Asgard, New Chicago, Timbuctoo, Alexandria: the usual mix of eras, cultures, realities. He and Gioia, making the long flight from Asgard in the distant north the night before, had arrived late, well after sundown, and had gone straight to bed. Now, by the gentle apricot-hued morning light, the fierce spires and battlements of Asgard seemed merely something he had dreamed.

The rumor was that Asgard's moment was finished, anyway. In a little while, he had heard, they were going to tear it down and replace it, elsewhere, with Mohenjo-daro. Though there were never more than five cities, they changed constantly. He could remember a time when they had had Rome of the Caesars instead of Chang-an, and Rio de Janeiro rather than Alexandria. These people saw no point in keeping anything very long.

It was not easy for him to adjust to the sultry intensity of Alexandria after the frozen splendors of Asgard. The wind, coming off the water, was brisk and torrid both at once. Soft turquoise wavelets lapped at the jetties. Strong presences assailed his senses: the hot heavy sky, the stinging scent of the red lowland sand borne on the breeze, the sullen swampy aroma of the nearby sea. Everything trembled and glimmered in the early light. Their hotel was beautifully situated, high on the northern slope of the huge artificial mound known as the Paneium that was sacred to the goat-footed god. From here they had a total view of the city; the wide noble boulevards, the soaring obelisks and monuments, the palace of Hadrian just below the hill, the stately and awesome Library, the temple of Poseidon, the teeming marketplace, the royal lodge that Mark Antony had built after his defeat at Actium. And of course the Lighthouse, the wondrous many-windowed Lighthouse, the seventh wonder of the world, that immense pile of marble and limestone and reddish-purple Aswan granite rising in majesty at the end of its mile-long causeway. Black smoke from the beacon-fire at its summit curled lazily into the sky. The city was awakening. Some temporaries in short white kilts appeared and began to trim the dense dark hedges that bordered the great public buildings. A few citizens wearing loose robes of vaguely Grecian style were strolling in the streets.

There were ghosts and chimeras and phantasies everywhere about. Two slim elegant centaurs, a male and a female, grazed on the hillside. A burly thick-thighed swordsman appeared on the porch of the temple of Poseidon holding a Gorgon's severed head; he waved it in a wide arc, grinning broadly. In the street below the hotel gate three small pink sphinxes, no bigger than housecats, stretched and yawned and began to prowl the curbside. A larger one, lion-sized, watched warily from an alleyway; their mother, surely. Even at this distance he could hear her loud purring.

Shading his eyes, he peered far out past the Lighthouse and across the water. He hoped to see the dim shores of Crete or Cyprus to the north, or perhaps the great dark curve of Anatolia. *Carry me toward that great Byzantium*, he thought. *Where all is ancient, singing at the oars.* But he beheld only the endless empty sea, sun-bright and blinding though the morning was just beginning. Nothing was ever where he expected it to be. The continents did not seem to be in their proper places any longer. Gioia, taking him aloft long ago in her little flitterflitter, had shown him that. The tip of South America was canted far out into the Pacific; Africa was weirdly foreshortened; a broad tongue of ocean separated Europe and Asia. Australia did not appear to exist at all. Perhaps they had dug it up and used it for other things. There was no trace of the world he once had known. This was the fiftieth century. "The fiftieth century after *what*?" he had asked several times, but no one seemed to know, or else they did not care to say.

"Is Alexandria very beautiful?" Gioia called from within.

"Come out and see."

Naked and sleepy-looking, she padded out onto the white-tiled patio and nestled up beside him. She fit neatly under his arm. "Oh, yes, yes!" she said softly. "So very beautiful, isn't it? Look, there, the palaces, the Library, the Lighthouse! Where will we go first? The Lighthouse, I think. Yes? And then the marketplace—I want to see the Egyptian magicians— and the stadium, the races—will they be having races today, do you think? Oh, Charles, I want to see everything!"

"Everything? All on the first day?"

"All on the first day, yes," she said. "Everything."

"But we have plenty of time, Gioia."

"Do we?"

He smiled and drew her tight against his side.

"Time enough," he said gently.

He loved her for her impatience, for her bright bubbling eagerness. Gioia was not much like the rest in that regard, though she seemed identical in all other ways. She was short, supple, slender, dark-eyed, olive-skinned, narrow-hipped, with wide shoulders and flat muscles. They were all like that, each one indistinguishable from the rest, like a horde of millions of brothers and sisters—a world of small, lithe, child-like Mediterraneans, built for juggling, for bull-dancing, for sweet white wine at midday and rough red wine at night. They had the same slim bodies, the same broad mouths, the same great glossy eyes. He had never seen anyone who appeared to be younger than twelve or older than twenty. Gioia was somehow a little different, although he did not quite know how; but he knew that it was for that imperceptible but significant difference that he loved her. And probably that was why she loved him also.

He let his gaze drift from west to east, from the Gate of the Moon down broad Canopus Street and out to the harbor, and off to the tomb of Cleopatra at the tip of long slender Cape Lochias. Everything was here and all of it perfect, the obelisks, the statues and marble colonnades, the courtyards and shrines and groves, great Alexander himself in his coffin of crystal and gold: a splendid gleaming pagan city. But there were oddities—an unmistakable mosque near the public gardens, and what seemed to be a Christian church not far from the Library. And those ships in the harbor, with all those red sails and bristling masts—surely they were medieval, and late medieval at that. He had seen such anachronisms in other places before. Doubtless these people found them amusing. Life was a game for them. They played at it unceasingly. Rome, Alexandria, Timbuctoo—why not? Create an Asgard of translucent bridges and shimmering ice-girt palaces, then grow weary of it and take it away? Replace it with Mohenjo-daro? Why not? It seemed to him a great pity to destroy those lofty Nordic feasting-halls for the sake of building a squat, brutal, sun-baked city of brown brick; but these people did not look at things the way he did. Their cities were only temporary. Someone in Asgard had said that Timbuctoo would be the next to go, with Byzantium rising in its place. Well, why not? Why not? They could have anything they liked. This was the fiftieth century, after all. The only rule was that there could be no more than five cities at once. "Limits," Gioia had informed him solemnly when they first began to travel together, "are very important." But she did not know why, or did not care to say.

He stared out once more toward the sea.

He imagined a newborn city congealing suddenly out of mists, far across the water: shining towers, great domed palaces, golden mosaics. That would be no great effort for them. They could just summon it forth whole out of time, the Emperor on his throne and the Emperor's drunken soldiery roistering in the streets, the brazen clangor of the cathedral gong rolling through the Grand Bazaar, dolphins leaping beyond the shoreside pavilions. Why not? They had Timbuctoo. They had Alexandria: Do you crave Constantinople? Then behold Constantinople! Or Avalon, or Lyonesse, or Atlantis.

They could have anything they liked. It is pure Schopenhauer here: the world as will and imagination. Yes! These slender dark-eyed people journeying tirelessly from miracle to miracle. Why not Byzantium next? Yes! Why not? *That is no country for old men,* he thought. *The young in one another's arms, the birds in the trees*—yes! Yes! Anything they liked. They even had him. Suddenly he felt frightened. Questions he had not asked for a long time burst through into his consciousness. *Who am I? Why am I here? Who is this woman beside me?*

"You're so quiet all of a sudden, Charles," said Gioia, who could not abide silence for very long. "Will you talk to me? I want you to talk to me. Tell me what you're looking for out there."

He shrugged. "Nothing."

"Nothing?"

"Nothing in particular."

"I could see you seeing something."

"Byzantium," he said. "I was imagining that I could look straight across the water to Byzantium. I was trying to get a glimpse of the walls of Constantinople."

"Oh, but you wouldn't be able to see as far as that from here. Not really."

"I know."

"And anyway Byzantium doesn't exist."

"Not yet. But it will. Its time comes later on."

"Does it?" she said. "Do you know that for a fact?"

"On good authority. I heard it in Asgard," he told her. "But even if I hadn't, Byzantium would be inevitable, don't you think? Its time would have to come. How could we not do Byzantium, Gioia? We certainly will do Byzantium, sooner or later. I know we will. It's only a matter of time. And we have all the time in the world."

A shadow crossed her face. "Do we? Do we?"

He knew very little about himself, but he knew that he was not one of them. That he knew. He knew that his name was Charles Phillips and that before he had come to live among these people he had lived in the year 1984, when there had been such things as computers and television sets and baseball and jet planes, and the world was full of cities, not merely five but thousands of them, New York and London

and Johannesburg and Paris and Liverpool and Bangkok and
San Francisco and Buenos Aires and a multitude of others, all
at the same time. There had been four and a half billion
people in the world then; now he doubted that there were as
many as four and a half millon. Nearly everything had changed
beyond comprehension. The moon still seemed the same, and
the sun; but at night he searched in vain for familiar constella-
tions. He had no idea how they had brought him from then to
now, or why. It did no good to ask. No one had any answers
for him; no one so much as appeared to understand what it
was that he was trying to learn. After a time he had stopped
asking; after a time he had almost entirely ceased wanting to
know.

He and Gioia were climbing the Lighthouse. She scampered ahead, in a hurry as always, and he came along behind
her in his more stolid fashion. Scores of other tourists, mostly
in groups of two or three, were making their way up the wide
flagstone ramps, laughing, calling to one another. Some of
them, seeing him, stopped a moment, stared, pointed. He
was used to that. He was so much taller than any of them; he
was plainly not one of them. When they pointed at him he
smiled. Sometimes he nodded a little acknowledgment.

He could not find much of interest in the lowest level, a
massive square structure two hundred feet high built of huge
marble blocks: within its cool musty arcades were hundreds
of small dark rooms, the offices of the Lighthouse's keepers
and mechanics, the barracks of the garrison, the stables for
the three hundred donkeys that carried the fuel to the lantern
far above. None of that appeared inviting to him. He forged
onward without halting until he emerged on the balcony that
led to the next level. Here the Lighthouse grew narrower and
became octagonal: its face, granite now and handsomely
fluted, rose in a stunning sweep above him.

Gioia was waiting for him there. "This is for you," she
said, holding out a nugget of meat on a wooden skewer.
"Roast lamb. Absolutely delicious. I had one while I was
waiting for you." She gave him a cup of some cool green
sherbet also, and darted off to buy a pomegranate. Dozens of
temporaries were roaming the balcony, selling refreshments
of all kinds.

He nibbled at the meat. It was charred outside, nicely pink
and moist within. While he ate, one of the temporaries came

up to him and peered blandly into his face. It was a stocky swarthy male wearing nothing but a strip of red and yellow cloth about its waist. "I sell meat," it said. "Very fine roast lamb, only five drachmas."

Phillips indicated the piece he was eating. "I already have some," he said.

"It is excellent meat, very tender. It has been soaked for three days in the juices of—"

"Please," Phillips said. "I don't want to buy any meat. Do you mind moving along?"

The temporaries had confused and baffled him at first, and there was still much about them that was unclear to him. They were not machines—they looked like creatures of flesh and blood—but they did not seem to be human beings, either, and no one treated them as if they were. He supposed they were artificial constructs, products of a technology so consummate that it was invisible. Some appeared to be more intelligent than others, but all of them behaved as if they had no more autonomy than characters in a play, which was essentially what they were. There were untold numbers of them in each of the five cities, playing all manner of roles: shepherds and swineherds, street-sweepers, merchants, boatmen, vendors of grilled meats and cool drinks, hagglers in the marketplace, schoolchildren, charioteers, policemen, grooms, gladiators, monks, artisans, whores and cutpurses, sailors— whatever was needed to sustain the illusion of a thriving, populous urban center. The dark-eyed people, Gioia's people, never performed work. There were not enough of them to keep a city's functions going, and in any case they were strictly tourists, wandering with the wind, moving from city to city as the whim took them, Chang-an to New Chicago, New Chicago to Timbuctoo, Timbuctoo to Asgard, Asgard to Alexandria, onward, ever onward.

The temporary would not leave him alone. Phillips walked away and it followed him, cornering him against the balcony wall. When Gioia returned a few minutes later, lips prettily stained with pomegranate juice, the temporary was still hovering about him, trying with lunatic persistence to sell him a skewer of lamb. It stood much too close to him, almost nose to nose, great sad cowlike eyes peering intently into his as it extolled with mournful mooing urgency the quality of its wares. It seemed to him that he had had trouble like this with

temporaries on one or two earlier occasions. Gioia touched
the creature's elbow lightly and said, in a short sharp tone
Phillips had never heard her use before, "He isn't interested.
Get away from him." It went at once. To Phillips she said,
"You have to be firm with them."

"I was trying. It wouldn't listen to me."

"You ordered it to go away, and it refused?"

"I asked it to go away. Politely. Too politely, maybe."

"Even so," she said. "It should have obeyed a human,
regardless."

"Maybe it didn't think I was human," Phillips suggested.
"Because of the way I look. My height, the color of my
eyes. It might have thought I was some kind of temporary
myself."

"No," Gioia said, frowning. "A temporary won't solicit
another temporary. But it won't ever disobey a citizen, either.
There's a very clear boundary. There isn't ever any confusion. I can't understand why it went on bothering you." He
was surprised at how troubled she seemed: far more so, he
thought, than the incident warranted. A stupid device, perhaps miscalibrated in some way, overenthusiastically pushing
its wares—what of it? What of it? Gioia, after a moment,
appeared to come to the same conclusion. Shrugging, she
said, "It's defective, I suppose. Probably such things are
more common than we suspect, don't you think?" There was
something forced about her tone that bothered him. She
smiled and handed him her pomegranate. "Here. Have a bite,
Charles. It's wonderfully sweet. They used to be extinct, you
know. Shall we go on upward?"

The octagonal midsection of the Lighthouse must have
been several hundred feet in height, a grim claustrophobic
tube almost entirely filled by the two broad spiraling ramps
that wound around the huge building's central well. The
ascent was slow: a donkey team was a little way ahead of
them on the ramp, plodding along laden with bundles of
kindling for the lantern. But at last, just as Phillips was
growing winded and dizzy, he and Gioia came out onto the
second balcony, the one marking the transition between the
octagonal section and the Lighthouse's uppermost storey,
which was cylindrical and very slender.

She leaned far out over the balustrade. "Oh, Charles, look
at the view! Look at it!"

It was amazing. From one side they could see the entire city, and swampy Lake Mareotis and the dusty Egyptian plain beyond it, and from the other they peered far out into the gray and choppy Mediterranean. He gestured toward the innumerable reefs and shallows that infested the waters leading to the harbor entrance. "No wonder they needed a lighthouse here," he said. "Without some kind of gigantic landmark they'd never have found their way in from the open sea."

A blast of sound, a ferocious snort, erupted just above him. He looked up, startled. Immense statues of trumpet-wielding Tritons jutted from the corners of the Lighthouse at this level; that great blurting sound had come from the nearest of them. A signal, he thought. A warning to the ships negotiating that troubled passage. The sound was produced by some kind of steam-powered mechanism, he realized, operated by teams of sweating temporaries clustered about bonfires at the base of each Triton.

Once again he found himself swept by admiration for the clever way these people carried out their reproductions of antiquity. Or *were* they reproductions, he wondered? He still did not understand how they brought their cities into being. For all he knew, this place was the authentic Alexandria itself, pulled forward out of its proper time just as he himself had been. Perhaps this was the true and original Lighthouse, and not a copy. He had no idea which was the case, nor which would be the greater miracle.

"How do we get to the top?" Gioia asked.

"Over there, I think. That doorway."

The spiraling donkey-ramps ended here. The loads of lantern fuel went higher via a dumb-waiter in the central shaft. Visitors continued by way of a cramped staircase, so narrow at its upper end that it was impossible to turn around while climbing. Gioia, tireless, sprinted ahead. He clung to the rail and labored up and up, keeping count of the tiny window-slits to ease the boredom of the ascent. The count was nearing a hundred when finally he stumbled into the vestibule of the beacon chamber. A dozen or so visitors were crowded into it. Gioia was at the far side, by the wall that was open to the sea.

It seemed to him he could feel the building swaying in the winds, up here. How high were they? Five hundred feet, six hundred, seven? The beacon chamber was tall and narrow, divided by a catwalk into upper and lower sections. Down

below, relays of temporaries carried wood from the dumb-
waiter and tossed it on the blazing fire. He felt its intense heat
from where he stood, at the rim of the platform on which the
giant mirror of polished metal was hung. Tongues of flames
leaped upward and danced before the mirror, which hurled its
dazzling beam far out to sea. Smoke rose through a vent. At
the very top was a colossal statue of Poseidon, austere, ferocious, looming above the lantern.

Gioia sidled along the catwalk until she was at his side.
"The guide was talking before you came," she said, pointing. "Do you see that place over there, under the mirror?
Someone standing there and looking into the mirror gets a
view of ships at sea that can't be seen from here by the
naked eye. The mirror magnifies things."

"Do you believe that?"

She nodded toward the guide. "It said so. And it also told
us that if you look in a certain way, you can see right across
the water into the city of Constantinople."

She is like a child, he thought. They all are. He said,
"You told me yourself this very morning that it isn't possible
to see that far. Besides, Constantinople doesn't exist right
now."

"It will," she replied. "*You* said that to me, this very
morning. And when it does, it'll be reflected in the Lighthouse mirror. That's the truth. I'm absolutely certain of it."
She swung about abruptly toward the entrance of the beacon
chamber. "Oh, look, Charles! Here come Nissandra and
Aramayne! And there's Hawk! There's Stengard!" Gioia
laughed and waved and called out names. "Oh, everyone's
here! *Everyone!*"

They came jostling into the room, so many newcomers that
some of those who had been there were forced to scramble
down the steps on the far side. Gioia moved among them,
hugging, kissing. Phillips could scarcely tell one from
another—it was hard for him even to tell which were the men
and which the women, dressed as they all were in the same
sort of loose robes—but he recognized some of the names.
These were her special friends, her set, with whom she had
journeyed from city to city on an endless round of gaiety in
the old days before he had come into her life. He had met a
few of them before, in Asgard, in Rio, in Rome. The beacon-
chamber guide, a squat wide-shouldered old Temporary wear-

ing a laurel wreath on its bald head, reappeared and began its
potted speech, but no one listened to it; they were all too busy
greeting one another, embracing, giggling. Some of them
edged their way over to Phillips and reached up, standing on
tiptoes, to touch their fingertips to his cheek in that odd hello
of theirs. "Charles," they said gravely, making two syllables
out of the name, as these people often did. "So good to see
you again. Such a pleasure. You and Gioia—such a handsome couple. So well suited to each other."

Was that so? He supposed it was.

The chamber hummed with chatter. The guide could not be
heard at all. Stengard and Nissandra had visited New Chicago
for the waterdancing—Aramayne bore tales of a feast in
Chang-an that had gone on for *days*—Hawk and Hekna had
been to Timbuctoo to see the arrival of the salt caravan, and
were going back there soon—a final party soon to celebrate
the end of Asgard that absolutely should not be missed—the
plans for the new city, Mohenjo-daro—we have reservations
for the opening, we wouldn't pass it up for anything—and,
yes, they were definitely going to do Constantinople after
that, the planners were already deep into their Byzantium
research—so good to see you, you look so beautiful all the
time—have you been to the Library yet? The zoo? To the
temple of Serapis?—

To Phillips they said, "What do you think of our Alexandria, Charles? Of course you must have known it well in your
day. Does it look the way you remember it?" They were
always asking things like that. They did not seem to comprehend that the Alexandria of the Lighthouse and the Library
was long lost and legendary by his time. To them, he suspected, all the places they had brought back into existence
were more or less contemporary. Rome of the Caesars, Alexandria of the Ptolemies, Venice of the Doges, Chang-an of
the T'angs, Asgard of the Aesir, none any less real than the
next nor any less unreal, each one simply a facet of the
distant past, the fantastic immemorial past, a plum plucked
from that dark backward and abysm of time. They had no
contexts for separating one era from another. To them all the
past was one borderless timeless realm. Why then should he
not have seen the Lighthouse before, he who had leaped into
this era from the New York of 1984? He had never been able
to explain it to them. Julius Caesar and Hannibal, Helen of

Troy and Charlemagne, Rome of the gladiators and New York of the Yankees and Mets, Gilgamesh and Tristan and Othello and Robin Hood and George Washington and Queen Victoria—to them, all equally real and unreal, none of them any more than bright figures moving about on a painted canvas. The past, the past, the elusive and fluid past—to them it was a single place of infinite accessibility and infinite connectivity. Of course they would think he had seen the Lighthouse before. He knew better than to try again to explain things. "No," he said simply. "This is my first time in Alexandria."

They stayed there all winter long, and possibly some of the spring. Alexandria was not a place where one was sharply aware of the change of seasons, nor did the passage of time itself make itself very evident when one was living one's entire life as a tourist.

During the day there was always something new to see. The zoological garden, for instance: a wondrous park, miraculously green and lush in this hot dry climate, where astounding animals roamed in enclosures so generous that they did not seem like enclosures at all. Here were camels, rhinoceroses, gazelles, ostriches, lions, wild asses; and here too, casually adjacent to those familiar African beasts, were hippogriffs, unicorns, basilisks, and fire-snorting dragons with rainbow scales. Had the original zoo of Alexandria had dragons and unicorns? Phillips doubted it. But this one did; evidently it was no harder for the backstage craftsmen to manufacture mythic beasts than it was for them to turn out camels and gazelles. To Gioia and her friends all of them were equally mythical, anyway. They were just as awed by the rhinoceros as by the hippogriff. One was no more strange—nor any less—than the other. So far as Phillips had been able to discover, none of the mammals or birds of his era had survived into this one except for a few cats and dogs, though many had been reconstructed.

And then the Library! All those lost treasures, reclaimed from the jaws of time! Stupendous columned marble walls, airy high-vaulted reading-rooms, dark coiling stacks stretching away to infinity. The ivory handles of seven hundred thousand papyrus scrolls bristling on the shelves. Scholars and librarians gliding quietly about, smiling faint scholarly smiles

but plainly preoccupied with serious matters of the mind.
They were all temporaries, Phillips realized. Mere props, part
of the illusion. But were the scrolls illusions too? "Here we
have the complete dramas of Sophocles," said the guide with
a blithe wave of its hand, indicating shelf upon shelf of texts.
Only seven of his hundred twenty-three plays had survived
the successive burnings of the library in ancient times by
Romans, Christians, Arabs: were the lost ones here, the
Triptolemus, the *Nausicaa*, the *Jason*, and all the rest? And
would he find here too, miraculously restored to being, the
other vanished treasures of ancient literature—the memoirs of
Odysseus, Cato's history of Rome, Thucydides' life of Pericles,
the missing volumes of Livy? But when he asked if he might
explore the stacks, the guide smiled apologetically and said
that all the librarians were busy just now. Another time,
perhaps? Perhaps, said the guide. It made no difference,
Phillips decided. Even if these people somehow had brought
back those lost masterpieces of antiquity, how would he read
them? He knew no Greek.

The life of the city buzzed and throbbed about him. It was
a dazzlingly beautiful place: the vast bay thick with sails, the
great avenues running rigidly east-west, north-south, the sunlight rebounding almost audibly from the bright walls of the
palaces of kings and gods. They have done this very well,
Phillips thought: very well indeed. In the marketplace hard-
eyed traders squabbled in half a dozen mysterious languages
over the price of ebony, Arabian incense, jade, panther-skins.
Gioia bought a dram of pale musky Egyptian perfume in a
delicate tapering glass flask. Magicians and jugglers and
scribes called out stridently to passersby, begging for a few
moments of attention and a handful of coins for their labor.
Strapping slaves, black and tawny and some that might have
been Chinese, were put up for auction, made to flex their
muscles, to bare their teeth, to bare their breasts and thighs to
prospective buyers. In the gymnasium naked athletes hurled
javelins and discuses, and wrestled with terrifying zeal.Gioia's
friend Stengard came rushing up with a gift for her, a golden
necklace that would not have embarrassed Cleopatra. An hour
later she had lost it, or perhaps had given it away while
Phillips was looking elsewhere. She bought another, even
finer, the next day. Anyone could have all the money he

wanted, simply by asking: it was as easy to come by as air, for these people.

Being here was much like going to the movies, Phillips told himself. A different show every day: not much plot, but the special effects were magnificent and the detail-work could hardly have been surpassed. A megamovie, a vast entertainment that went on all the time and was being played out by the whole population of Earth. And it was all so effortless, so spontaneous: just as when he had gone to a movie he had never troubled to think about the myriad technicians behind the scenes, the cameramen and the costume designers and the set-builders and the electricians and the model-makers and the boom operators, so too here he chose not to question the means by which Alexandria had been set before him. It felt real. It *was* real. When he drank the strong red wine it gave him a pleasant buzz. If he leaped fron the beacon chamber of the Lighthouse he suspected he would die, though perhaps he would not stay dead for long: doubtless they had some way of restoring him as often as was necessary. Death did not seem to be a factor in these people's lives.

By day they saw sights. By night he and Gioia went to parties, in their hotel, in seaside villas, in the palaces of the high nobility. The usual people were there all the time, Hawk and Hekna, Aramayne, Stengard and Shelimir, Nissandra, Asoka, Afonso, Protay. At the parties there were five or ten temporaries for every citizen, some as mere servants, others as entertainers or even surrogate guests, mingling freely and a little daringly. But everyone knew, all the time, who was a citizen and who just a temporary. Phillips began to think his own status lay somewhere between. Certainly they treated him with a courtesy that no one ever would give a temporary, and yet there was a condescension to their manner that told him not simply that he was not one of them but that he was someone or something of an altogether different order of existence. That he was Gioia's lover gave him some standing in their eyes, but not a great deal: obviously he was always going to be an outsider, a primitive, ancient and quaint. For that matter he noticed that Gioia herself, though unquestionably a member of the set, seemed to be regarded as something of an outsider, like a tradesman's great-granddaughter in a gathering of Plantagenets. She did not always find out about the best parties in time to attend; her friends did not always reciprocate her effusive greetings with the same degree of warmth; sometimes he noticed her straining to hear some bit of gossip that was not quite being shared with her. Was it because she had taken him for her lover? Or was it the other way around: that she had chosen to be his lover precisely because she was *not* a full member of their caste?

Being a primitive gave him, at least; something to talk about at their parties. "Tell us about war," they said. "Tell us about elections. About money. About disease." They wanted to know everything, though they did not seem to pay close attention: their eyes were quick to glaze. Still, they asked. He described traffic jams to them, and politics, and deodorants, and vitamin pills. He told them about cigarettes, newspapers, subways, telephone directories, credit cards, and basketball.

"Which was your city?" they asked. New York, he told them. "And when was it? The seventh century, did you say?" The twentieth, he told them. They exchanged glances and nodded. "We will have to do it," they said. "The World Trade Center, the Empire State Building, the Citicorp Center, the Cathedral of St. John the Divine: how fascinating! Yankee Stadium. The Verrazzano Bridge. We will do it all. But first must come Mohenjo-daro. And then, I think, Constantinople. Did your city have many people?" Seven million, he said. Just in the five boroughs alone. They nodded, smiling amiably, unfazed by the number.

Seven million, seventy million—it was all the same to them, he sensed. They would just bring forth the temporaries in whatever quantity was required. He wondered how well they would carry the job off. He was no real judge of Alexandrias and Asgards, after all. Here they could have unicorns and hippogriffs in the zoo, and live sphinxes prowling in the gutters, and it did not trouble him. Their fanciful Alexandria was as good as history's, or better. But how sad, how disillusioning it would be, if the New York that they conjured had Greenwich Village uptown and Times Square in the Bronx, and the New Yorkers, gentle and polite, spoke with the honeyed accents of Savannah or New Orleans. Well, that was nothing he needed to brood about just now. Very likely they were only being courteous when they spoke of doing his New York. They had all the vastness of the past to choose from: Nineveh, Memphis of the Pharaohs, the London of Victoria or Shakespeare or Richard the Third, Florence of the Medici, the Paris of Abelard and Heloise or the Paris of Louis XIV, Moctezuma's Tenochtitlan and Atahuallpa's Cuzco; Damascus, St. Petersburg, Babylon, Troy. And then there were all the cities like New Chicago, out of time that was time yet unborn to him but ancient history to them. In such richness, such an infinity of choices, even mighty New York might have to wait a long while for its turn. Would he still be among them by the time they got around to it? By then, perhaps, they might have become bored with him and returned him to his own proper era. Or possibly he would simply have grown old and died. Even here, he supposed, he would eventually die, though no one else ever seemed to. He did not know. He realized that in fact he did not know anything.

The north wind blew all day long. Vast flocks of ibises appeared over the city, fleeing the heat of the interior, and screeched across the sky with their black necks and scrawny legs extended. The sacred birds, descending by the thousands, scuttered about in every crossroad, pouncing on spiders and beetles, on mice, on the debris of the meat-shops and the bakeries. They were beautiful but annoyingly ubiquitous, and they splashed their dung over the marble buildings; each morning squadrons of temporaries carefully washed it off. Gioia said little to him now. She seemed cool, withdrawn, depressed; and there was something almost intangible about her, as though she were gradually becoming transparent. He felt it would be an intrusion upon her privacy to ask her what was wrong. Perhaps it was only restlessness. She became religious, and presented costly offerings at the temples of Serapis, Isis, Poseidon, Pan. She went to the necropolis west of the city to lay wreaths on the tombs in the catacombs. In a single day she climbed the Lighthouse three times without any sign of fatigue. One afternoon he returned from a visit to the Library and found her naked on the patio; she had anointed herself all over with some aromatic green salve. Abruptly she said, "I think it's time to leave Alexandria, don't you?"

She wanted to go to Mohenjo-daro, but Mohenjo-daro was not yet ready for visitors. Instead they flew eastward to Chang-an, which they had not seen in years. It was Phillips' suggestion: he hoped that the cosmopolitan gaudiness of the old T'ang capital would lift her mood.

They were to be guests of the Emperor this time: an unusual privilege, which ordinarily had to be applied for far in advance, but Phillips had told some of Gioia's highly placed friends that she was unhappy, and they had quickly arranged everything. Three endless bowing functionaries in flowing yellow robes and purple sashes met them at the Gate of Brilliant Virtue in the city's south wall and conducted them to their pavilion, close by the imperial palace and the Forbidden Garden. It was a light, airy place, thin walls of plastered brick braced by graceful columns of some dark, aromatic wood. Fountains played on the roof of green and yellow tiles, creating an unending cool rainfall of recirculating water. The balustrades were of carved marble, the door-fittings were of gold.

There was a suite of private rooms for him, and another for her, though they would share the handsome damask-draped bedroom at the heart of the pavilion. As soon as they arrived Gioia announced that she must go to her rooms to bathe and dress. "There will be a formal reception for us at the palace tonight," she said. "They say the imperial receptions are splendid beyond anything you could imagine. I want to be at my best." The Emperor and all his ministers, she told him, would receive them in the Hall of the Supreme Ultimate; there would be a banquet for a thousand people; Persian dancers would perform, and the celebrated jugglers of Chungnan. Afterward everyone would be conducted into the fantastic landscape of the Forbidden Garden to view the dragon-races and the fireworks.

He went to his own rooms. Two delicate little maid-servants undressed him and bathed him with fragrant sponges. The pavilion came equipped with eleven temporaries who were to be their servants: soft-voiced unobtrusive cat-like Chinese, done with perfect verisimilitude, straight black hair, glowing skin, epicanthic folds. Phillips often wondered what happened to a city's temporaries when the city's time was over. Were the towering Norse heroes of Asgard being recycled at this moment into wiry dark-skinned Dravidians for Mohenjo-daro? When Timbuctoo's day was done, would its brightly robed black warriors be converted into supple Byzantines to stock the arcades of Constantinople? Or did they simply discard the old temporaries like so many excess props, stash them in warehouses somewhere, and turn out the appropriate quantities of the new model? He did not know; and once when he had asked Gioia about it she had grown uncomfortable and vague. She did not like him to probe for information, and he suspected it was because she had very little to give. These people did not seem to question the workings of their own world; his curiosities were very twentieth-century of him, he was frequently told, in that gently patronizing way of theirs. As his two little maids patted him with their sponges he thought of asking them where they had served before Chang-an. Rio? Rome? Haroun al-Raschid's Baghdad? But these fragile girls, he knew, would only giggle and retreat if he tried to question them. Interrogating temporaries was not only improper, but pointless: it was like interrogating one's luggage.

When he was bathed, and robed in rich red silks he wandered the pavilion for a little while, admiring the tinkling pendants of green jade dangling on the portico, the lustrous auburn pillars, the rainbow hues of the intricately interwoven girders and brackets that supported the roof. Then, weary of his solitude, he approached the bamboo curtain at the entrance to Gioia's suite. A porter and one of the maids stood just within. They indicated that he should not enter; but he scowled at them and they melted from him like snowflakes. A trail of incense led him through the pavilion to Gioia's innermost dressing-room. There he halted, just outside the door.

Gioia sat naked with her back to him at an ornate dressing-table of some rare flame-colored wood inlaid with bands of orange and green porcelain. She was studying herself intently in a mirror of polished bronze held by one of her maids: picking through her scalp with her fingernails, as a woman might do who was searching out her gray hairs.

But that seemed strange. Gray hair, on Gioia? On a citizen? A temporary might display some appearance of aging, perhaps, but surely not a citizen. Citizens remained forever young. Gioia looked like a girl. Her face was smooth and unlined, her flesh was firm, her hair was dark: that was true of all of them, every citizen he had ever seen. And yet there was no mistaking what Gioia was doing. She found a hair, frowned, drew it taut, nodded, plucked it. Another. Another.

She pressed the tip of her finger to her cheek as if testing it for resilience. She tugged at the skin below her eyes, pulling it downward. Such familiar little gestures of vanity; but so odd here, he thought, in this world of the perpetually young. Gioia, worried about growing old? Had he simply failed to notice the signs of age on her? Or was it that she worked hard behind his back at concealing them? Perhaps that was it. Was he wrong about the citizens, then? Did they age even as the people of less blessed eras had always done, but simply have better ways of hiding it? How old was she, anyway? Thirty? Sixty? Three hundred?

Gioia appeared satisfied now. She waved the mirror away; she rose; she beckoned for her banquet robes. Phillips, still standing unnoticed by the door, studied her with admiration: the small round buttocks, almost but not quite boyish, the elegant line of her spine, the surprising breadth of her shoulders. No, he thought, she is not aging at all. Her body is still like a girl's. She looks as young as on the day they first had met, however long ago that was—he could not say; it was hard to keep track of time here; but he was sure some years had passed since they had come together. Those gray hairs, those wrinkles and sags for which she had searched just now with such desperate intensity, must all be imaginary, mere artifacts of vanity. Even in this remote future epoch, then, vanity was not extinct. He wondered why she was so concerned with the fear of aging. An affectation? Did all these timeless people take some perverse pleasure in fretting over the possibility that they might be growing old? Or was it some private fear of Gioia's, another symptom of the mysterious depression that had come over her in Alexandria?

Not wanting her to think that he had been spying on her, when all he had really intended was to pay her a visit, he slipped silently away to dress for the evening. She came to him an hour later, gorgeously robed, swaddled from chin to ankles in a brocade of brilliant colors shot through with threads of gold, face painted, hair drawn up tightly and fastened with ivory combs: very much the lady of the court. His servants had made him splendid also, a lustrous black surplice embroidered with golden dragons over a sweeping floor-length gown of shining white silk, a necklace and pendant of red coral, a five-cornered gray felt hat that rose in tower upon tower like a ziggurat. Gioia, grinning, touched her fingertips to his cheek. "You look marvelous!" she told him. "Like a grand mandarin!"

"And you like an empress," he said. "Of some distant land: Persia, India. Here to pay a ceremonial visit on the Son of Heaven." An excess of love suffused his spirit, and catching her lightly by the wrist, he drew her toward him, as close as he could manage it considering how elaborate their costumes were. But as he bent forward and downward, meaning to brush his lips lightly and affectionately against the tip of her nose, he perceived an unexpected strangeness, an anomaly: the coating of white paint that was her makeup seemed oddly to magnify rather than mask the contours of her skin, highlighting and revealing details he had never observed before. He saw a pattern of fine lines radiating from the corners of her eyes, and the unmistakable beginning of a quirk-mark in her cheek just to the left of her mouth, and perhaps the faint indentation of frown-lines in her flawless forehead. A shiver traveled along the nape of his neck. So it was not affectation, then, that had had her studying her mirror so fiercely. Age was in truth beginning to stake its claim on her, despite all that he had come to believe about these people's agelessness. But a moment later he was not so sure. Gioia turned and slid gently half a step back from him—she must have found his stare disturbing—and the lines he had thought he had seen were gone. He searched for them and saw only girlish smoothness once again. A trick of the light? A figment of an overwrought imagination? He was baffled.

"Come," she said. "We mustn't keep the Emperor waiting."

Five mustachioed warriors in armor of white quilting and seven musicians playing cymbals and pipes escorted them to the Hall of the Supreme Ultimate. There they found the full court arrayed: princes and ministers, high officials, yellow-robed monks, a swarm of imperial concubines. In a place of honor to the right of the royal thrones, which rose like gilded scaffolds high above all else, was a little group of stern-faced men in foreign costumes, the ambassadors of Rome and Byzantium, of Arabia and Syria, of Korea, Japan, Tibet, Turkestan. Incense smouldered in enameled braziers. A poet sang a delicate twanging melody, accompanying himself on a small harp. Then the Emperor and Empress entered: two tiny aged people, like waxen images, moving with infinite slowness, taking steps no greater than a child's. There was the sound of trumpets as they ascended their thrones. When the little Emperor was seated—he looked like a doll up there, ancient, faded, shrunken, yet still somehow a figure of extraordinary power—he stretched forth both his hands, and enormous gongs began to sound. It was a scene of astonishing splendor, grand and overpowering.

These are all temporaries, Phillips realized suddenly. He saw only a handful of citizens—eight, ten, possibly as many as a dozen—scattered here and there about the vast room. He knew them by their eyes, dark, liquid, knowing. They were watching not only the imperial spectacle but also Gioia and him; and Gioia, smiling secretly, nodding almost imperceptibly to them, was acknowledging their presence and their interest. But those few were the only ones in here who were autonomous living beings. All the rest—the entire splendid court, the great mandarins and paladins, the officials, the giggling concubines, the haughty and resplendent ambassadors, the aged Emperor and Empress themselves, were simply part of the scenery. Had the world ever seen entertainment on so grand a scale before? All this pomp, all this pageantry, conjured up each night for the amusement of a dozen or so viewers?

At the banquet the little group of citizens sat together at a table apart, a round onyx slab draped with translucent green silk. There turned out to be seventeen of them in all, including Gioia; Gioia appeared to know all of them, though none, so far as he could tell, was a member of her set that he had met before. She did not attempt introductions. Nor was conversation at all possible during the meal: there was a constant astounding roaring din in the room. Three orchestras played at once and there were troupes of strolling musicians also, and a steady stream of monks and their attendants marched back and forth between the tables loudly chanting sutras and waving censers to the deafening accompaniment of drums and gongs. The Emperor did not descend from his throne to join the banquet; he seemed to be asleep, though now and then he waved his hand in time to the music. Gigantic half-naked brown slaves with broad cheekbones and mouths like gaping pockets brought forth the food, peacock tongues and breasts of phoenix heaped on mounds of glowing saffron-colored rice, served on frail alabaster plates. For chopsticks they were given slender rods of dark jade. The wine, served in glistening crystal beakers, was thick and sweet, with an aftertaste of raisins, and no beaker was allowed to remain empty for more than a moment.

Phillips felt himself growing dizzy: when the Persian dancers emerged he could not tell whether there were five of them or fifty, and as they performed their intricate whirling routines it seemed to him that their slender muslin-veiled forms were blurring and merging one into another. He felt frightened by their proficiency, and wanted to look away, but he could not. The Chung-nan jugglers that followed them were equally skillful, equally alarming, filling the air with scythes, flaming torches, live animals, rare porcelain vases, pink jade hatchets, silver bells, gilded cups, wagon-wheels, bronze vessels, and never missing a catch. The citizens applauded politely but did not seem impressed. After the jugglers, the dancers returned, performing this time on stilts; the waiters brought platters of steaming meat of a pale lavender color, unfamiliar in taste and texture: filet of camel, perhaps, or haunch of hippopotamus, or possibly some choice chop from a young dragon. There was more wine. Feebly Phillips tried to wave it away, but the servitors were implacable. This was a drier sort, greenish-gold, austere, sharp on the tongue. With it came a silver dish, chilled to a polar coldness, that held shaved ice flavored with some potent smoky-flavored brandy. The jugglers were doing a second turn, he noticed. He thought he was going to be ill. He looked helplessly toward Gioia, who seemed sober but fiercely animated, almost manic, her eyes blazing like rubies. She touched his cheek fondly.

A cool draft blew through the hall: they had opened one entire wall, revealing the garden, the night, the stars. Just outside was a colossal wheel of oiled paper stretched on wooden struts. They must have erected it in the past hour: it stood a hundred fifty feet high or even more, and on it hung lanterns by the thousands, glimmering like giant fireflies. The guests began to leave the hall. Phillips let himself be swept along into the garden, where under a yellow moon strange crook-armed trees with dense black needles loomed ominously. Gioia slipped her arm through his. They went down to a lake of bubbling crimson fluid and watched scarlet flamingo-like birds ten feet tall fastidiously spearing angry-eyed turquoise eels. They stood in awe before a fat-bellied Buddha of gleaming blue tilework, seventy feet high. A horse with a golden mane came prancing by, striking showers of brilliant red sparks wherever its hooves touched the ground. In a grove of lemon trees that seemed to have the power to wave their slender limbs about, Phillips came upon the Emperor, standing by himself and rocking gently back and forth. The old man seized Phillips by the hand and pressed something into his palm, closing his fingers tight about it; when he opened his fist a few moments later he found his palm full of gray irregular pearls. Gioia took them from him and cast them into the air, and they burst like exploding firecrackers, giving off splashes of colored light. A little later, Phillips realized that he was no longer wearing his surplice or his white silken undergown. Gioia was naked too, and she drew him gently down into a carpet of moist blue moss, where they made love until dawn, fiercely at first, then slowly, languidly, dreamily. At sunrise he looked at her tenderly and saw that something was wrong.

"Gioia?" he said doubtfully.

She smiled. "Ah, no. Gioia is with Fenimon tonight. I am Belilala."

"With—Fenimon?"

"They are old friends. She had not seen him in years."

"Ah. I see. And you are—?"

"Belilala," she said again, touching her fingertips to his cheek.

It was not unusual, Belilala said. It happened all the time; the only unusual thing was that it had not happened to him before now. Couples formed, traveled together for a while, drifted apart, eventually reunited. It did not mean that Gioia had left him forever. It meant only that just now she chose to be with Fenimon. Gioia would return. In the meanwhile he would not be alone. "You and I met in New Chicago," Belilala told him. "And then we saw each other again in Timbuctoo. Have you forgotten? Oh, yes, I see that you have forgotten!" She laughed prettily; she did not seem at all offended.

She looked enough like Gioia to be her sister. But, then, all the citizens looked more or less alike to him. And apart from their physical resemblance, so he quickly came to realize, Belilala and Gioia were not really very similar. There was a calmness, a deep reservoir of serenity, in Belilala that

Gioia, eager and volatile and ever impatient, did not seem to have. Strolling the swarming streets of Chang-an with Belilala, he did not perceive in her any of Gioia's restless feverish need always to know what lay beyond, and beyond, and beyond even that. When they toured the Hsing-ch'ing Palace, Belilala did not after five minutes begin—as Gioia surely would have done—to seek directions to the Fountain of Hsuan-tsung or the Wild Goose Pagoda. Curiosity did not consume Belilala as it did Gioia. Plainly she believed that there would always be enough time for her to see everything she cared to see. There were some days when Belilala chose not to go out at all, but was content merely to remain at their pavilion playing a solitary game with flat porcelain counters, or viewing the flowers of the garden.

He found, oddly, that he enjoyed the respite from Gioia's intense world-swallowing appetites; and yet he longed for her to return. Belilala—beautiful, gentle, tranquil, patient—was too perfect for him. She seemed unreal in her gleaming impeccability, much like one of those Sung celadon vases that appear too flawless to have been thrown and glazed by human hands. There was something a little soulless about her: an immaculate finish outside, emptiness within. Belilala might almost have been a temporary, he thought, though he knew she was not. He could explore the pavilions and palaces of Chang-an with her, he could make graceful conversation with her while they dined, he could certainly enjoy coupling with her; but he could not love her or even contemplate the possibility. It was hard to imagine Belilala worriedly studying herself in a mirror for wrinkles and gray hairs. Belilala would never be any older than she was at this moment; nor could Belilala ever have been any younger. Perfection does not move along an axis of time. But the perfection of Belilala's glossy surface made her inner being impenetrable to him. Gioia was more vulnerable, more obviously flawed—her restlessness, her moodiness, her vanity, her fears—and therefore she was more accessible to his own highly imperfect twentieth-century sensibility.

Occasionally he saw Gioia as he roamed the city, or thought he did. He had a glimpse of her among the miracle-vendors in the Persian Bazaar, and outside the Zoroastrian temple, and again by the goldfish pond in the Serpentine Park. But he was never quite sure that the woman he saw was really Gioia, and he never could get close enough to her to be certain: she had a way of vanishing as he approached, like some mysterious Lorelei luring him onward and onward in a hopeless chase. After a while he came to realize that he was not going to find her until she was ready to be found.

He lost track of time. Weeks, months, years? He had no idea. In this city of exotic luxury, mystery, and magic all was in constant flux and transition and the days had a fitful, unstable quality. Buildings and even whole streets were torn down of an afternoon and re-erected, within days, far away. Grand new pagodas sprouted like toadstools in the night. Citizens came in from Asgard, Alexandria, Timbuctoo, New Chicago, stayed for a time, disappeared, returned. There was a constant round of court receptions, banquets, theatrical events, each one much like the one before. The festivals in honor of past emperors and empresses might have given some form to the year, but they seemed to occur in a random way, the ceremony marking the death of T'ai Tsung coming around twice the same year, so it seemed to him, once in a season of snow and again in high summer, and the one honoring the ascension of the Empress Wu being held twice in a single season. Perhaps he had misunderstood something. But he knew it was no use asking anyone.

One day Belilala said unexpectedly, "Shall we go to Mohenjo-daro?"

"I didn't know it was ready for visitors," he replied.

"Oh, yes. For quite some time now."

He hesitated. This had caught him unprepared. Cautiously he said, "Gioia and I were going to go there together, you know."

Belilala smiled amiably, as though the topic under discussion were nothing more than the choice of that evening's restaurant.

"Were you?" she asked.

"It was all arranged while we were still in Alexandria. To go with you instead—I don't know what to tell you, Belilala." Phillips sensed that he was growing terribly flustered. "You know that I'd like to go. With you. But on the other hand I can't help feeling that I shouldn't go there until I'm back with Gioia again. If I ever am." How foolish this sounds, he thought. How clumsy, how adolescent. He found that he was having trouble looking straight at her. Uneasily he said, with a kind of desperation in his voice, "I did promise her—there was a commitment, you understand—a firm agreement that we would go to Mohenjo-daro together—"

"Oh, but Gioia's already there!" said Belilala in the most casual way.

He gaped as though she had punched him.

"What?"

"She was one of the first to go, after it opened. Months and months ago. You didn't know?" she asked, sounding surprised, but not very. "You really didn't know?"

That astonished him. He felt bewildered, betrayed, furious. His cheeks grew hot, his mouth gaped. He shook his head again and again, trying to clear it of confusion. It was a moment before he could speak. "Already there?" he said at last. "Without waiting for me? After we had talked about going there together—after we had agreed—"

Belilala laughed. "But how could she resist seeing the newest city? You know how impatient Gioia is!"

"Yes. Yes."

He was stunned. He could barely think.

"Just like all short-timers," Belilala said. "She rushes here, she rushes there. She must have it all, now, now, right away, at once, instantly. You ought never expect her to wait for you for anything for very long: the fit seizes her, and off she goes. Surely you must know that about her by now."

"A short-timer?" He had not heard that term before.

"Yes. You knew that. You must have known that." Belilala flashed her sweetest smile. She showed no sign of comprehending his distress. With a brisk wave of her hand she said, "Well, then, shall we go, you and I? To Mohenjo-daro?"

"Of course," Phillips said bleakly.

"When would you like to leave?"

"Tonight," he said. He paused a moment. "What's a short-timer, Belilala?"

Color came to her cheeks. "Isn't it obvious?" she asked.

Had there ever been a more hideous place on the face of the earth than the city of Mohenjo-daro? Phillips found it difficult to imagine one. Nor could he understand why, out of all the cities that had ever been, these people had chosen to restore this one to existence. More than ever they seemed alien to him, unfathomable, incomprehensible.

From the terrace atop the many-towered citadel he peered down into grim claustrophobic Mohenjo-daro and shivered. The stark, bleak city looked like nothing so much as some prehistoric prison colony. In the manner of an uneasy tortoise it huddled, squat and compact, against the gray monotonous Indus River plain: miles of dark burnt-brick walls enclosing miles of terrifyingly orderly streets, laid out in an awesome, monstrous gridiron pattern of maniacal ridigity. The houses themselves were dismal and forbidding too, clusters of brick cells gathered about small airless courtyards. There were no windows, only small doors that opened not onto the main boulevards but onto the tiny mysterious lanes that ran between the buildings. Who had designed this horrifying metropolis? What harsh, sour souls they must have had, these frightening and frightened folk, creating for themselves in the lush fertile plains of India such a Supreme Soviet of a city!

"How lovely it is," Belilala murmured. "How fascinating!"

He stared at her in amazement.

"Fascinating? Yes," he said. "I suppose so. The same way that the smile of a cobra is fascinating."

"What's a cobra?"

"Poisonous predatory serpent," Phillips told her. "Probably extinct. Or formerly extinct, more likely. It wouldn't surprise me if you people had re-created a few and turned them loose in Mohenjo to make things livelier."

"You sound angry, Charles."

"Do I? That's not how I feel."

"How do you feel, then?"

"I don't know," he said after a long moment's pause. He shrugged. "Lost, I suppose. Very far from home."

"Poor Charles."

"Standing here in this ghastly barracks of a city, listening to you tell me how beautiful it is, I've never felt more alone in my life."

"You miss Gioia very much, don't you?"

He gave her another startled look.

"Gioia has nothing to do with it. She's probably been having ecstasies over the loveliness of Mohenjo just like you. Just like all of you. I suppose I'm the only one who can't find the beauty, the charm. I'm the only one who looks out there and sees only horror, and then wonders why nobody else sees it, why in fact people would set up a place like this for *entertainment*, for *pleasure*—''

Her eyes were gleaming. ''Oh, you are angry! You really are!''

''Does that fascinate you too?'' he snapped. ''A demonstration of genuine primitive emotion? A typical quaint twentieth-century outburst?'' He paced the rampart in short quick anguished steps. ''Ah. Ah. I think I understand it now, Belilala. Of course: I'm part of your circus, the star of the sideshow. I'm the first experiment in setting up the next stage of it, in fact.'' Her eyes were wide. The sudden harshness and violence in his voice seemed to be alarming and exciting her at the same time. That angered him even more. Fiercely he went on, ''Bringing whole cities back out of time was fun for a while, but it lacks a certain authenticity, eh? For some reason you couldn't bring the inhabitants too; you couldn't just grab a few million prehistorics out of Egypt or Greece or India and dump them down in this era. I suppose because you might have too much trouble controlling them, or because you'd have the problem of disposing of them once you were bored with them. So you had to settle for creating temporaries to populate your ancient cities. But now you've got me. I'm something more real than a temporary, and that's a terrific novelty for you, and novelty is the thing you people crave more than anything else: maybe the *only* thing you crave. And here I am, complicated, unpredictable, edgy, capable of anger, fear, sadness, love, and all those other formerly extinct things. Why settle for picturesque architecture when you can observe picturesque emotion, too? What fun I must be for all of you! And if you decide that I was really interesting, maybe you'll ship me back where I came from and check out a few other ancient types—a Roman gladiator, maybe, or a Renaissance pope, or even a Neanderthal or two—

''Charles,'' she said tenderly. ''Oh, Charles, Charles, Charles, how lonely you must be, how lost, how troubled! Will you ever forgive me? Will you ever forgive us all?''

Once more he was astounded by her. She sounded entirely sincere, altogether sympathetic. Was she? Was she, really? He was not sure he had ever had a sign of genuine caring from any of them before, not even Gioia. Nor could he bring himself to trust Belilala now. He was afraid of her, afraid of all of them, of their brittleness, their slyness, their elegance. He wished he could go to her and have her take him in her arms; but he felt too much the shaggy prehistoric just now to be able to risk asking that comfort of her.

He turned away and began to walk around the rim of the citadel's massive wall.

"Charles?"

"Let me alone for a little while," he said.

He walked on. His forehead throbbed and there was a pounding in his chest. All stress systems going full blast, he thought: secret glands dumping gallons of inflammatory substances into his bloodstream. The heat, the inner confusion, the repellent look of this place—

Try to understand, he thought. Relax. Look about you. Try to enjoy your holiday in Mohenjo-daro.

He leaned warily outward, over the edge of the wall. He had never seen a wall like this; it must be forty feet thick at the base, he guessed, perhaps even more, and every brick perfectly shaped, meticulously set. Beyond the great rampart, marshes ran almost to the edge of the city, although close by the wall the swamps had been dammed and drained for agriculture. He saw lithe brown farmers down there, busy with their wheat and barley and peas. Cattle and buffaloes grazed a little farther out. The air was heavy, dank, humid. All was still. From somewhere close at hand came the sound of a droning, whining stringed instrument and a steady insistent chanting.

Gradually a sort of peace pervaded him. His anger subsided. He felt himself beginning to grow calm again. He looked back at the city, the rigid interlocking streets, the maze of inner lanes, the millions of courses of precise brickwork.

It is a miracle, he told himself, that this city is here in this place and at this time. And it is a miracle that I am here to see it.

Caught for a moment by the magic within the bleakness, he thought he began to understand Belilala's awe and delight, and he wished now that he had not spoken to her so sharply. The city was alive. Whether it was the actual Mohenjo-daro of thousands upon thousands of years ago, ripped from the past by some wondrous hook, or simply a cunning reproduction, did not matter at all. Real or not, this was the true

Mohenjo-daro. It had been dead and now, for the moment, it was alive again. These people, these *citizens*, might be trivial, but reconstructing Mohenjo-daro was no trivial achievement. And that the city that had been reconstructed was oppressive and sinister-looking was unimportant. No one was compelled to live in Mohenjo-daro any more. Its time had come and gone, long ago; those little dark-skinned peasants and craftsmen and merchants down there were mere temporaries, mere inanimate things, conjured up like zombies to enhance the illusion. They did not need his pity. Nor did he need to pity himself. He knew that he should be grateful for the chance to behold these things. Some day, when this dream had ended and his hosts had returned him to the world of subways and computers and income tax and television networks, he would think of Mohenjo-daro as he had once beheld it, lofty walls of tightly woven dark brick under a heavy sky, and he would remember only its beauty.

Glancing back, he searched for Belilala and could not for a moment find her. Then he caught sight of her carefully descending a narrow staircase that angled down the inner face of the citadel wall.

"Belilala!" he called.

She paused and looked his way, shading her eyes from the sun with her hand. "Are you all right?"

"Where are you going?"

"To the baths," she said. "Do you want to come?"

He nodded. "Yes. Wait for me, will you? I'll be right there." He began to run toward her along the top of the wall.

The baths were attached to the citadel: a great open tank the size of a large swimming pool, lined with bricks set on edge in gypsum mortar and waterproofed with asphalt, and eight smaller tanks just north of it in a kind of covered arcade. He supposed that in ancient times the whole complex had had some ritual purpose, the large tank used by common folk and the small chambers set aside for the private ablutions of priests or nobles. Now the baths were maintained, it seemed, entirely for the pleasure of visiting citizens. As Phillips came up the passageway that led to the main bath he saw fifteen or twenty of them lolling in the water or padding languidly about, while temporaries of the dark-skinned Mohenjo-daro type served them drinks and pungent little morsels of spiced meat as though this were some sort of luxury resort. Which was, he realized, exactly what it was. The temporaries wore white cotton loincloths; the citizens were naked. In his former life he had encountered that sort of casual public nudity a few times on visits to California and the south of France, and it had made him mildly uneasy. But he was growing accustomed to it here.

The changing-rooms were tiny brick cubicles connected by rows of closely placed steps to the courtyard that surrounded the central tank. They entered one and Belilala swiftly slipped out of the loose cotton robe that she had worn since their arrival that morning. With arms folded she stood leaning against the wall, waiting for him. After a moment he dropped his own robe and followed her outside. He felt a little giddy, sauntering around naked in the open like this.

On the way to the main bathing area they passed the private baths. None of them seemed to be occupied. They were elegantly constructed chambers, with finely jointed brick floors and carefully designed runnels to drain excess water into the passageway that led to the primary drain. Phillips was struck with admiration for the cleverness of the prehistoric engineers. He peered into this chamber and that to see how the conduits and ventilating ducts were arranged, and when he came to the last room in the sequence he was surprised and embarrassed to discover that it was in use. A brawny grinning man, big-muscled, deep-chested, with exuberantly flowing shoulder-length red hair and a flamboyant, sharply tapering beard, was thrashing about merrily with two women in the small tank. Phillips had a quick glimpse of a lively tangle of arms, legs, breasts, buttocks.

"Sorry," he muttered. His cheeks reddened. Quickly he ducked out, blurting apologies as he went. "Didn't realize the room was occupied—no wish to intrude—"

Belilala had proceeded on down the passageway. Phillips hurried after her. From behind him came peals of cheerful raucous booming laughter and high-pitched giggling and the sound of splashing water. Probably they had not even noticed him.

He paused a moment, puzzled, playing back in his mind that one startling glimpse. Something was not right. Those women, he was fairly sure, were citizens: little slender elfin dark-haired girlish creatures, the standard model. But the man? That great curling sweep of red hair? Not a citizen. Citizens did not affect shoulder-length hair. And *red*? Nor had he ever seen a citizen so burly, so powerfully muscular. Or one with a beard. But he could hardly be a temporary, either. Phillips could conceive no reason why there would be so Anglo-Saxon-looking a temporary at Mohenjo-daro; and it was unthinkable for a temporary to be frolicking like that with citizens, anyway.

"Charles?"

He looked up ahead. Belilala stood at the end of the passageway, outlined in a nimbus of brilliant sunlight. "Charles?" she said again. "Did you lose your way?"

"I'm right here behind you," he said. "I'm coming."

"Who did you meet in there?"

"A man with a beard."

"With a what?"

"A beard," he said. "Red hair growing on his face. I wonder who he is."

"Nobody I know," said Belilala. "The only one I know with hair on his face is you. And yours is black, and you shave it off every day." She laughed. "Come along, now! I see some friends by the pool!"

He caught up with her and they went hand in hand out into the courtyard. Immediately a waiter glided up to them, an obsequious little temporary with a tray of drinks. Phillips waved it away and headed for the pool. He felt terribly exposed: he imagined that the citizens disporting themselves here were staring intently at him, studying his hairy primitive body as though he were some mythical creature, a Minotaur, a werewolf, summoned up for their amusement. Belilala drifted off to talk to someone and he slipped into the water, grateful for the concealment it offered. It was deep, warm, comforting. With swift powerful strokes he breast-stroked from one end to the other.

A citizen perched elegantly on the pool's rim smiled at him. "Ah, so you've come at last, Charles!" Char-less. Two syllables. Someone from Gioia's set: Stengard, Hawk, Aramayne? He could not remember which one. They were all so much alike.

Phillips returned the man's smile in a half-hearted, tentative way. He searched for something to say and finally asked, "Have you been here long?"

"Weeks. Perhaps months. What a splendid achievement this city is, eh, Charles? Such utter unity of mood—such a total statement of a uniquely single-minded esthetic—"

"Yes. Single-minded is the word," Phillips said drily.

"Gioia's word, actually. Gioia's phrase. I was merely quoting."

Gioia. He felt as if he had been stabbed.

"You've spoken to Gioia lately?" he said.

"Actually, no. It was Hekna who saw her. You do remember Hekna, eh?" He nodded toward two naked women standing on the brick platform that bordered the pool, chatting, delicately nibbling morsels of meat. They could have been twins. "There is Hekna, with your Belilala." Hekna, yes. So this must be Hawk, Phillips thought, unless there has been some recent shift of couples. "How sweet she is, your Belilala," Hawk said. "Gioia chose very wisely when she picked her for you."

Another stab: a much deeper one. "Is that how it was?" he said. "Gioia *picked* Belilala for me?"

"Why, of course!" Hawk seemed surprised. It went without saying, evidently. "What did you think? That Gioia would merely go off and leave you to fend for yourself?"

"Hardly. Not Gioia."

"She's very tender, very gentle, isn't she?"

"You mean Belilala? Yes, very," said Phillips carefully. "A dear woman, a wonderful woman. But of course I hope to get together with Gioia again soon." He paused. "They say she's been in Mohenjo-daro almost since it opened."

"She was here, yes."

"*Was?*"

"Oh, you know Gioia," Hawk said lightly. "She's moved along by now, naturally."

Phillips leaned forward. "Naturally," he said. Tension thickened his voice. "Where has she gone this time?"

"Timbuctoo, I think. Or New Chicago. I forget which one it was. She was telling us that she hoped to be in Timbuctoo for the closing-down party. But then Fenimon had some pressing reason for going to New Chicago. I can't remember what they decided to do." Hawk gestured sadly. "Either way, a pity that she left Mohenjo before the new visitor came. She had such a rewarding time with you, after all: I'm sure she'd have found much to learn from him also."

The unfamiliar term twanged an alarm deep in Phillips' consciousness. *"Visitor?"* he said, angling his head sharply toward Hawk. "What visitor do you mean?"

"You haven't met him yet? Oh, of course, you've only just arrived."

Phillips moistened his lips. "I think I may have seen him. Long red hair? Beard like this?"

"That's the one! Willoughby, he's called. He's—what?—a Viking, a pirate, something like that. Tremendous vigor and force. Remarkable person. We should have more visitors, I think. They're far superior to temporaries, everyone agrees. Talking with a temporary is a little like talking to one's self, wouldn't you say? They give you no significant illumination. But a visitor— someone like this Willoughby—or like you, Charles—a visitor can be truly enlightening, a visitor can transform one's view of reality—"

"Excuse me," Phillips said. A throbbing began behind his forehead. "Perhaps we can continue this conversation later, yes?" He put the flats of his hands against the hot brick of the platform and hoisted himself swiftly from the pool. "At dinner, maybe—or afterward—yes? All right?" He set off at a quick half-trot back toward the passageway that led to the private baths.

As he entered the roofed part of the structure his throat grew dry, his breath suddenly came short. He padded quickly up the hall and peered into the little bath-chamber. The bearded man was still there, sitting up in the tank, breast-high above the water, with one arm around each of the women. His eyes gleamed with fiery intensity in the dimness. He was grinning in marvelous self-satisfaction; he seemed to brim with intensity, confidence, gusto.

Let him be what I think he is, Phillips prayed. I have been alone among these people long enough.

"May I come in?" he asked.

"Aye, fellow!" cried the man in the tub thunderously. "By my troth, come ye in, and bring your lass as well! God's teeth, I wot there's room aplenty for more folk in this tub than we!"

At that great uproarious outcry Phillips felt a powerful surge of joy. What a joyous rowdy voice! How rich, how lusty, how totally uncitizenlike!

And those oddly archaic words! *God's teeth? By my Troth?* What sort of talk was that? What else but the good pure sonorous Elizabethan diction! Certainly it had something of the roll and fervor of Shakespeare about it. And spoken with—an Irish brogue, was it? No, not quite: it was English, but English spoken in no matter Phillips had ever heard.

Citizens did not speak that way. But a *visitor* might.

So it was true. Relief flooded Phillips' soul. Not alone, then! Another relict of a former age—another wanderer—a companion in chaos, a brother in adversity—a fellow voyager, tossed even farther than he had been by the tempests of time—

The bearded man grinned heartily and beckoned to Phillips with a toss of his head. "Well, join us, join us, man! 'Tis good to see an English face again, amidst all these Moors and rogue Portugals! But what have ye done with thy lass? One can never have enough wenches, d'ye not agree?"

The force and vigor of him were extraordinary: almost too much so. He roared, he bellowed, he boomed. He was so very much what he ought to be that he seemed more a character out of some old pirate movie than anything else, so blustering, so real, that he seemed unreal. A stage-Elizabethan, larger than life, a boisterous young Falstaff without the belly.

Hoarsely, Phillips said, "Who are you?"

"Why, Ned Willoughby's son Francis am I, of Plymouth. Late of the service of Her Most Protestant Majesty, but most foully abducted by the powers of darkness and cast away among these blackamoor Hindus, or whatever they be. And thyself?"

"Charles Phillips." After a moment's uncertainty he added. "I'm from New York."

"*New* York? What place is that? In faith, man, I know it not!"

"A city in America."

"A city in America, forsooth! What a fine fancy that is! In America, you say, and not on the Moon, or perchance underneath the sea?" To the women Willoughby said, "D'ye hear him? He comes from a city in America! With the face of an Englishman, though not the manner of one, and not quite the proper sort of speech. A city in America! A *city*. God's blood, what will I hear next?"

Phillips trembled. Awe was beginning to take hold of him.

This man had walked the streets of Shakespeare's London, perhaps. He had clinked canisters with Marlowe or Essex or Walter Raleigh; he had watched the ships of the Armada wallowing in the Channel. It strained Phillips' spirit to think of it. This strange dream in which he found himself was compounding its strangeness now. He felt like a weary swimmer assailed by heavy surf, winded, dazed. The hot close atmosphere of the baths was driving him toward vertigo. There could be no doubt of it any longer. He was not the only primitive—the only *visitor*—who was wandering loose in this fiftieth century. They were conducting other experiments as well. He gripped the sides of the door to steady himself and said, "When you speak of Her Most Protestant Majesty, it's Elizabeth the First you mean, is that not so?"

"Elizabeth, aye! As to the First, that is true enough, but why trouble to name her thus? There is but one. First and Last, I do trow, and God save her, there is no other!"

Phillips studied the other man warily. He knew that he must proceed with care. A misstep at this point and he would forfeit any chance that Willoughby would take him seriously. How much metaphysical bewilderment, after all, could this man absorb? What did he know, what had anyone of his time known, of past and present and future and the notion that one might somehow move from one to the other as readily as one would go from Surrey to Kent? That was a twentieth-century idea, late nineteenth, at best, a fantastical speculation that very likely no one had even considered before Wells had sent his time traveler off to stare at the reddened sun of the earth's last twilight. Willoughby's world was a world of Protestants and Catholics, of kings and queens, of tiny sailing vessels, of swords at the hip and ox-carts on the road: that world seemed to Phillips far more alien and distant than was this world of citizens and temporaries. The risk that Willoughby would not begin to understand him was great.

But this man and he were natural allies against a world they had never made. Phillips chose to take the risk.

"Elizabeth the First is the queen you serve," he said. "There will be another of her name in England, in due time. Had already been, in fact."

Willoughby shook his head like a puzzled lion. "Another Elizabeth, d'ye say?"

"A second one, and not much like the first. Long after

your Virgin Queen, this one. She will reign in what you think of as the days to come. That I know without doubt."

The Englishman peered at him and frowned. "You see the future? Are you a soothsayer, then? A necromancer, mayhap? Or one of the very demons that brought me to this place?"

"Not at all," Phillips said gently. "Only a lost soul, like yourself." He stepped into the little room and crouched by the side of the tank. The two citizen-women were staring at him in bland fascination. He ignored them. To Willoughby he said, "Do you have any idea where you are?"

The Englishman had guessed, rightly enough, that he was in India: "I do believe these little brown Moorish folk are of the Hindu sort," he said. But that was as far as his comprehension of what had befallen him could go.

It had not occurred to him that he was no longer living in the sixteenth century. And of course he did not begin to suspect that this strange and somber brick city in which he found himself was a wanderer out of an era even more remote than his own. Was there any way, Phillips wondered, of explaining that to him?

He had been here only three days. He thought it was devils that had carried him off. "While I slept did they come for me," he said. "Mephistophilis Sathanas his henchmen seized me—God alone can say why—and swept me in a moment out to this torrid realm from England, where I had reposed among friends and family. For I was between one voyage and the next, you must understand, awaiting Drake and his ship—you know Drake, the glorious Francis? God's blood, there's a mariner for ye! We were to go to the Main again, he and I, but instead here I be in this other place—" Willoughby leaned close and said, "I ask you, soothsayer, how can it be, that a man go to sleep in Plymouth and wake up in India? It is passing strange, is it not?"

"That it is," Phillips said.

"But he that is in the dance must needs dance on, though he do but hop, eh? So do I believe." He gestured toward the two citizen-women. "And therefore to console myself in this pagan land I have found me some sport among these little Portugal women—"

"Portugal?" said Phillips.

"Why, what else can they be, but Portugals? Is it not the

Portugals who control all these coasts of India? See, the people are of two sorts here, the blackamoors and the others, the fair-skinned ones, the lords and masters who lie here in these baths. If they be not Hindus, and I think they are not, then Portugals is what they must be.'' He laughed and pulled the women against himself and rubbed his hands over their breasts as though they were fruits on a vine. ''Is that not what you are, you little naked shameless Papist wenches? A pair of Portugals, eh?''

They giggled, but did not answer.

''No,'' Phillips said. ''This is India, but not the India you think you know. And these women are not Portuguese.''

''Not Portuguese?'' Willoughby said, baffled.

''No more so than you. I'm quite certain of that.''

Willoughby stroked his beard. ''I do admit I found them very odd, for Portugals. I have heard not a syllable of their Portugee speech on their lips. And it is strange also that they run naked as Adam and Eve in these baths, and allow me free plunder of their women, which is not the way of Portugals at home, God wot. But I thought me, this is India, they choose to live in another fashion here—''

''No,'' Phillips said. ''I tell you, these are not Portuguese, nor any other people of Europe who are known to you.''

''Prithee, who are they, then?''

Do it delicately, now, Phillips warned himself. *Delicately.*

He said, ''It is not far wrong to think of them as spirits of some kind—demons, even. Or sorcerers who have magicked us out of our proper places in the world.'' He paused, groping for some means to share with Willoughby, in a way that Willoughby might grasp, this mystery that had enfolded them. He drew a deep breath. ''They've taken us not only across the sea,'' he said, ''but across the years as well. We have both been hauled, you and I, far into the days that are to come.''

Willoughby gave him a look of blank bewilderment.

''Days that are to come? Times yet unborn, d'ye mean? Why, I comprehend none of that!''

''Try to understand. We're both castaways in the same boat, man! But there's no way we can help each other if I can't make you see—''

Shaking his head, Willoughby muttered, ''In faith, good friend, I find your words the merest folly. Today is today, and tomorrow is tomorrow, and how can a man step from one to t'other until tomorrow be turned into today?''

"I have no idea," said Phillips. Struggle was apparent on Willoughby's face; but plainly he could perceive no more than the haziest outline of what Phillips was driving at, if that much. "But this I know," he went on, "that your world and all that was in it is dead and gone. And so is mine, though I was born four hundred years after you, in the time of the second Elizabeth.''

Willoughby snorted scornfully. "Four hundred—"

"You must believe me!"

"Nay! Nay!"

"It's the truth. Your time is only history to me. And mine and yours are history to *them*—ancient history. They call us visitors, but what we are is captives.'' Phillips felt himself quivering in the intensity of his effort. He was aware how insane this must sound to Willoughby. It was beginning to sound insane to him. "They've stolen us out of our proper times—seizing us like gypsies in the night—"

"Fie, man! You rave with lunacy!"

Phillips shook his head. He reached out and seized Willoughby tightly by the wrist. "I beg you, listen to me!" The citizen-women were watching closely, whispering to one another behind their hands, laughing. "Ask them!" Phillips cried. "Make them tell you what century this is! The sixteenth, do you think? Ask them!''

"What century could it be, but the sixteenth of our Lord?"

"They will tell you it is the fiftieth."

Willoughby looked at him pityingly. "Man, man, what a sorry thing thou art! The fiftieth, indeed!" He laughed. "Fellow, listen to me, now. There is but one Elizabeth, safe upon her throne in Westminster. This is India. The year is Anno 1591. Come, let us you and I steal a ship from these Portugals, and make our way back to England, and peradventure you may get from there to your America—"

"There is no England."

"Ah, can you say that and not be mad?"

"The cities and nations we knew are gone. These people live like magicians, Francis.'' There was no use holding anything back now, Phillips thought leadenly. He knew that he had lost. "They conjure up places of long ago, and build them here and there to suit their fancy, and when they are bored with them they destroy them, and start anew. There is no England. Europe is empty, featureless, void. Do you know what cities there are? There are only five in all the world. There is Alexandria of Egypt. There is Timbuctoo in Africa. There is New Chicago in America. There is a great city in China—in Cathay, I suppose you would say. And there is this place, which they call Mohenjo-daro, and which is far more ancient than Greece, than Rome, than Babylon.''

Quietly Willoughby said, "Nay. This is mere absurdity. You say we are in some far tomorrow, and then you tell me we are dwelling in some city of long ago.''

"A conjuration, only,'' Phillips said in desperation. "A likeness of that city. Which these folk have fashioned some-how for their own amusement. Just as we are here, you and I: to amuse them. Only to amuse them.''

"You are completely mad.''

"Come with me, then. Talk with the citizens by the great pool. Ask them what year this is; ask them about England; ask them how you come to be here.'' Once again Phillips grasped Willoughby's wrist. "We should be allies. If we work together, perhaps we can discover some way to get ourselves out of this place, and—''

"Let me be, fellow.''

"Please—''

"Let me be!'' roared Willoughby, and pulled his arm free. His eyes were stark with rage. Rising in the tank, he looked about furiously as though searching for a weapon. The citizen-women shrank back away from him, though at the same time they seemed captivated by the big man's fierce outburst. "Go to, get you to Bedlam! Let me be, madman! Let me be!''

Dismally Phillips roamed the dusty unpaved streets of Mohenjo-daro alone for hours. His failure with Willoughby had left him bleak-spirited and somber: he had hoped to stand back to back with the Elizabethan against the citizens, but he saw now that that was not to be. He had bungled things; or, more likely, it had been impossible ever to bring Willoughby to see the truth of their predicament.

In the stifling heat he went at random through the confus-ing congested lanes of flat-roofed, windowless houses and blank, featureless walls until he emerged into a broad market-place. The life of the city swirled madly around him: the pseudo-life, rather, the intricate interactions of the thousands of temporaries who were nothing more than wind-up dolls set in motion to provide the illusion that pre-Vedic India was still a going concern. Here vendors sold beautiful little carved stone seals portraying tigers and monkeys and strange humped cattle, and women bargained vociferously with craftsmen for ornaments of ivory, gold, copper, and bronze. Weary-looking women squatted behind immense mounds of newly made pottery, pinkish-red with black designs. No one paid any attention to him. He was the outsider here, neither citizen nor temporary. They belonged.

He went on, passing the huge granaries where workmen ceaselessly unloaded carts of wheat and others pounded grain on great circular brick platforms. He drifted into a public restaurant thronging with joyless silent people standing elbow to elbow at small brick counters, and was given a flat round piece of bread, a sort of tortilla or chapatti, in which was stuffed some spiced mincemeat that stung his lips like fire. Then he moved onward, down a wide, shallow, timbered staircase into the lower part of the city, where the peasantry lived in cell-like rooms packed together as though in hives.

It was an oppressive city, but not a squalid one. The intensity of the concern with sanitation amazed him: wells and fountains and public privies everywhere, and brick drains running from each building, leading to covered cesspools. There was none of the open sewage and pestilent gutters that he knew still could be found in the India of his own time. He wondered whether ancient Mohenjo-daro had in truth been so fastidious. Perhaps the citizens had redesigned the city to suit their own ideals of cleanliness. No: most likely what he saw was authentic, he decided, a function of the same obsessive discipline that had given the city its rigidity of form. If Mohenjo-daro had been a verminous filthy hole, the citizens probably would have re-created it in just that way, and loved it for its fascinating, reeking filth.

Not that he had ever noticed an excessive concern with authenticity on the part of the citizens; and Mohenjo-daro, like all the other restored cities he had visited, was full of the usual casual anachronisms. Phillips saw images of Shiva and Krishna here and there on the walls of buildings he took to be temples, and the benign face of the mother-goddess Kali loomed in the plazas. Surely those deities had arisen in India long after the collapse of the Mohenjo-daro civilization. Were the citizens indifferent to such matters of chronology? Or did they take a certain naughty pleasure in mixing the eras—a mosque and a church in Greek Alexandria, Hindu gods in prehistoric Mohenjo-daro? Perhaps their records of the past had become contaminated with errors over the thousands of years. He would not have been surprised to see banners bearing portraits of Gandhi and Nehru being carried in procession through the streets. And there were phantasms and chimeras at large here again too, as if the citizens were untroubled by the boundary between history and myth: little fat elephant-headed Ganeshas blithely plunging their trunks into water-fountains, a six-armed, three-headed woman sunning herself on a brick terrace. Why not? Surely that was the motto of these people: *Why not, why not, why not?* They could do as they pleased, and they did. Yet Gioia had said to him, long ago, "Limits are very important." In what, Phillips wondered, did they limit themselves, other than the number of their cities? Was there a quota, perhaps, on the number of "visitors" they allowed themselves to kidnap from the past? Until today he had thought he was the only one; now he knew there was at least one other; possibly there were more elsewhere, a step or two ahead or behind him, making the circuit with the citizens who traveled endlessly from New Chicago to Chang-an to Alexandria. We should join forces, he thought, and compel them to send us back to our rightful eras. *Compel?* How? File a class-action suit, maybe? Demonstrate in the streets? Sadly he thought of his failure to make common cause with Willoughby. We are natural allies, he thought. Together perhaps we might have won some compassion from these people. But to Willoughby it must be literally unthinkable that Good Queen Bess and her subjects were sealed away on the far side of a barrier hundreds of centuries thick. He would prefer to believe that England was just a few months' voyage away around the Cape of Good Hope, and that all he need do was commandeer a ship and set sail for home. Poor Willoughby: probably he would never see his home again.

The thought came to Phillips suddenly:
Neither will you.
And then, after it:
If you could go home, would you really want to?

One of the first things he had realized here was that he knew almost nothing substantial about his former existence. His mind was well stocked with details on life in twentieth-century New York, to be sure; but of himself he could say not much more than that he was Charles Phillips and had come from 1984. Profession? Age? Parents' names? Did he have a wife? Children? A cat, a dog, hobbies? No data: none. Possibly the citizens had stripped such things from him when they brought him here, to spare him from the pain of separation. They might be capable of that kindness. Knowing so little of what he had lost, could he truly say that he yearned for it? Willoughby seemed to remember much more of his former life, and longed for it all the more. He was spared that. Why not stay here, and go on and on from city to city, sightseeing all of time past as the citizens conjured it back into being? Why not? Why not? The chances were that he had no choice about it, anyway.

He made his way back up toward the citadel and to the baths once more. He felt a little like a ghost, haunting a city of ghosts.

Belilala seemed unaware that he had been gone for most of the day. She sat by herself on the terrace of the baths, placidly sipping some thick milky beverage that had been sprinkled with a dark spice. He shook his head when she offered him some.

"Do you remember I mentioned that I saw a man with red hair and a beard this morning?" Phillips said. "He's a visitor. Hawk told me that."

"Is he?" Belilala asked.

"From a time about four hundred years before mine. I talked with him. He thinks he was brought here by demons." Phillips gave her a searching look. "I'm a visitor too, isn't that so?"

"Of course, love."

"And how was *I* brought here? By demons also?"

Belilala smiled indifferently. "You'd have to ask someone else. Hawk, perhaps. I haven't looked into these things very deeply."

"I see. Are there many visitors here, do you know?"

A languid shrug. "Not many, no, not really. I've only heard of three or four besides you. There may be others by now, I suppose.'' She rested her hand lightly on his. "Are you having a good time in Mohenjo, Charles?''

He let her question pass as though he had not heard it.

"I asked Hawk about Gioia,'' he said.

"Oh?''

"He told me that she's no longer here, that she's gone on to Timbuctoo or New Chicago, he wasn't sure which.''

"That's quite likely. As everybody knows, Gioia rarely stays in the same place very long.''

Phillips nodded. "You said the other day that Gioia is a short-timer. That means she's going to grow old and die, doesn't it?''

"I thought you understood that, Charles.''

"Whereas you will not age? Nor Hawk, nor Stengard, nor any of the rest of your set?''

"We will live as long as we wish,'' she said. "But we will not age, no.''

"What makes a person a short-timer?''

"They're born that way, I think. Some missing gene, some extra gene—I don't actually know. It's extremely uncommon. Nothing can be done to help them. It's very slow, the aging. But it can't be halted.''

Phillips nodded. "That must be very disagreeable,'' he said. "To find yourself one of the few people growing old in a world where everyone stays young. No wonder Gioia is so impatient. No wonder she runs around from place to place. No wonder she attached herself so quickly to the barbaric hairy visitor from the twentieth century, who comes from a time when *everybody* was a short-timer. She and I have something in common, wouldn't you say?''

"In a manner of speaking, yes.''

"We understand aging. We understand death. Tell me: is Gioia likely to die very soon, Belilala?''

"Soon? Soon?'' She gave him a wide-eyed child-like stare. "What is soon? How can I say? What you think of as soon and what I think of as soon are not the same things, Charles.'' Then her manner changed: she seemed to be hearing what he was saying for the first time. Softly she said, "No, no, Charles. I don't think she will die very soon.''

"When she left me in Chang-an, was it because she had become bored with me?''

Belilala shook her head. "She was simply restless. It had nothing to do with you. She was never bored with you."

"Then I'm going to go looking for her. Wherever she may be, Timbuctoo, New Chicago, I'll find her. Gioia and I belong together."

"Perhaps you do," said Belilala. "Yes. Yes, I think you really do." She sounded altogether unperturbed, unrejected, unbereft. "By all means, Charles. Go to her. Follow her. Find her. Wherever she may be."

They had already begun dismantling Timbuctoo when Phillips got there. While he was still high overhead, his flitterflitter hovering above the dusty tawny plain where the River Niger met the sands of the Sahara, a surge of keen excitement rose in him as he looked down at the square gray flat-roofed mud brick buildings of the great desert capital. But when he landed he found gleaming metal-skinned robots swarming everywhere, a horde of them scuttling about like giant shining insects, pulling the place apart.

He had not known about the robots before. So that was how all these miracles were carried out, Phillips realized: an army of obliging machines. He imagined them bustling up out of the earth whenever their services were needed, emerging from some sterile subterranean storehouse to put together Venice or Thebes or Knossos or Houston or whatever place was required, down to the finest detail, and then at some later time returning to undo everything that they had fashioned. He watched them now, diligently pulling down the adobe walls, demolishing the heavy metal-studded gates, bulldozing the amazing labyrinth of alleyways and thoroughfares, sweeping away the market. On his last visit to Timbuctoo that market had been crowded with a horde of veiled Tuaregs and swaggering Moors, black Sudanese, shrewd-faced Syrian traders, all of them busily dickering for camels, horses, donkeys, slabs of salt, huge green melons, silver bracelets, splendid vellum Korans. They were all gone now, that picturesque crowd of swarthy temporaries. Nor were there any citizens to be seen. The dust of destruction choked the air. One of the robots came up to Phillips and said in a dry-crackling insect-voice, "You ought not to be here. This city is closed."

He stared at the flashing, buzzing band of scanners and sensors across the creature's glittering tapered snout. "I'm trying to find someone, a citizen who may have been here recently. Her name is—''

"This city is closed," the robot repeated inexorably.

They would not let him stay as much as an hour. There is no food here, the robot said, no water, no shelter. This is not a place any longer. You may not stay. You may not stay. You may not stay.

This is not a place any longer.

Perhaps he could find her in New Chicago, then. He took to the air again, soaring northward and westward over the vast emptiness. The land below him curved away into the hazy horizon, bare, sterile. What had they done with the vestiges of the world that had gone before? Had they turned their gleaming metal beetles loose to clean everything away? Were there no ruins of genuine antiquity anywhere? No scrap of Rome, no shard of Jerusalem, no stump of Fifth Avenue? It was all so barren down there: an empty stage, waiting for its next set to be built. He flew on a great arc across the jutting hump of Africa and on into what he supposed was southern Europe: the little vehicle did all the work, leaving him to doze or stare as he wished. Now and again he saw another flitterflitter pass by, far away, a dark distant winged teardrop outlined against the hard clarity of the sky. He wished there was some way of making radio contact with them, but he had no idea how to go about it. Not that he had anything he wanted to say; he wanted only to hear a human voice. He was utterly isolated. He might just as well have been the last living man on Earth. He closed his eyes and thought of Gioia.

"Like this?" Phillips asked. In an ivory-paneled oval room sixty stories above the softly glowing streets of New Chicago he touched a small cool plastic canister to his upper lip and pressed the stud at its base. He heard a foaming sound; and then blue vapor rose to his nostrils.

"Yes," Cantilena said. "That's right."

He detected a faint aroma of cinnamon, cloves, and something that might almost have been broiled lobster. Then a spasm of dizziness hit him and visions rushed through his head: Gothic cathedrals, the Pyramids, Central Park under fresh snow, the harsh brick warrens of Mohenjo-daro, and fifty thousand other places all at once, a wild rollercoaster ride through space and time. It seemed to go on for centuries. But finally his head cleared and he looked about, blinking, realizing that the whole thing had taken only a moment. Cantilena still stood at his elbow. The other citizens in the room—fifteen, twenty of them—had scarcely moved. The strange little man with the celadon skin over by the far wall continued to stare at him.

"Well?" Cantilena asked. "What did you think?"

"Incredible."

"And very authentic. It's an actual New Chicagoan drug. The exact formula. Would you like another?"

"Not just yet," Phillips said uneasily. He swayed and had to struggle for his balance. Sniffing that stuff might not have been such a wise idea, he thought.

He had been in New Chicago a week, or perhaps it was two, and he was still suffering from the peculiar disorientation that that city always aroused in him. This was the fourth time that he had come here, and it had been the same every time. New Chicago was the only one of the reconstructed cities of this world that in its original incarnation had existed *after* his own era. To him it was an outpost of the incomprehensible future; to the citizens it was a quaint simulacrum of the archaeological past. That paradox left him aswirl with impossible confusions and tensions.

What had happened to *old* Chicago was of course impossible for him to discover. Vanished without a trace, that was clear: no Water Tower, no Marina City, no Hancock Center, no Tribune building, not a fragment, not an atom. But it was hopeless to ask any of the million-plus inhabitants of New Chicago about their city's predecessor. They were only temporaries; they knew no more than they had to know, and all that they had to know was how to go through the motions of whatever it was that they did by way of creating the illusion that this was a real city. They had no need of knowing ancient history.

Nor was he likely to find out anything from a citizen, of course. Citizens did not seem to bother much about scholarly matters. Phillips had no reason to think that the world was anything other than an amusement park to them. Somewhere, certainly, there had to be those who specialized in the serious study of the lost civilizations of the past—for how, otherwise, would these uncanny reconstructed cities be brought into

being? "The planners," he had once heard Nissandra or
Aramayne say, "are already deep into their Byzantium research." But who were the planners? He had no idea. For all
he knew, they were the robots. Perhaps the robots were the
real masters of this whole era, who created the cities not
primarily for the sake of amusing the citizens but in their own
diligent attempt to comprehend the life of the world that had
passed away. A wild speculation, yes; but not without some
plausibility, he thought.

He felt oppressed by the party gaiety all about him. "I
need some air," he said to Cantilena, and headed toward the
window. It was the merest crescent, but a breeze came through.
He looked out at the strange city below.

New Chicago had nothing in common with the old one but
its name. They had built it, at least, along the western shore
of a large inland lake that might even be Lake Michigan,
although when he had flown over it had seemed broader and
less elongated than the lake he remembered. The city itself
was a lacy fantasy of slender pastel-hued buildings rising at odd
angles and linked by a webwork of gently undulating aerial
bridges. The streets were long parentheses that touched the
lake at their northern and southern ends and arched gracefully
westward in the middle. Between each of the great boulevards ran a track for public transportation—sleek aquamarine
bubble-vehicles gliding on soundless wheels—and flanking
each of the tracks were lush strips of park. It was beautiful,
astonishingly so, but insubstantial. The whole thing seemed
to have been contrived from sunbeams and silk.

A soft voice beside him said, "Are you becoming ill?"

Phillips glanced around. The celadon man stood beside
him: a compact, precise person, vaguely Oriental in appearance. His skin was of a curious gray-green hue like no skin
Phillips had ever seen, and it was extraordinarily smooth in
texture, as though he were made of fine porcelain.

He shook his head. "Just a little queasy," he said. "This
city always scrambles me."

"I suppose it can be disconcerting," the little man replied.
His tone was furry and veiled, the inflection strange. There
was something feline about him. He seemed sinewy, unyield-
ing, almost menacing. "Visitor, are you?"

Phillips studied him a moment. "Yes," he said.

"So am I, of course."

"Are you?"

"Indeed." The little man smiled. "What's your locus? Twentieth century? Twenty-first at the latest, I'd say."

"I'm from 1984. 1984 A.D."

Another smile, a self-satisfied one. "Not a bad guess, then." A brisk tilt of the head. "Y'ang-Yeovil."

"Pardon me?" Phillips said.

"Y'ang-Yeovil. It is my name. Formerly Colonel Y'ang-Yeovil of the Third Septentriad."

"Is that on some other planet?" asked Phillips, feeling a bit dazed.

"Oh, no, not at all," Y'ang-Yeovil said pleasantly. "This very world, I assure you. I am quite of human origin. Citizen of the Republic of Upper Han, native of the city of Port Ssu. And you—forgive me—your name—?"

"I'm sorry. Phillips. Charles Phillips. From New York City, once up a time."

"Ah, New York!" Y'ang-Yeovil's face lit with a glimmer of recognition quickly faded. "New York—New York—it was very famous, that I know—"

This is very strange, Phillips thought. He felt greater compassion for poor bewildered Francis Willoughby now. This man comes from a time so far beyond my own that he barely knows of New York—he must be a contemporary of the real New Chicago, in fact; I wonder whether he finds this version authentic—and yet to the citizens this Y'ang-Yeovil too is just a primitive, a curio out of antiquity—

"New York was the largest city of the United States of America," Phillips said.

"Of course. Yes. Very famous."

"But virtually forgotten by the time the Republic of Upper Han came into existence, I gather."

Y'ang-Yeovil said, looking uncomfortable, "There were disturbances between your time and mine. But by no means should you take from my words the impression that your city was—"

Sudden laughter resounded across the room. Five or six newcomers had arrived at the party. Phillips stared, gasped, gaped. Surely that was Stengard—and Aramayne beside him—and that other woman, half-hidden behind them—

"If you'll pardon me a moment—" Phillips said, turning abruptly away from Y'ang-Yeovil. "Please excuse me. Someone just coming in—a person I've been trying to find ever since—''

He hurried toward her.

"Gioia?'' he called. "Gioia, it's me! Wait! Wait!''

Stengard was in the way. Aramayne, turning to take a handful of the little vapor-sniffers from Cantilena, blocked him also. Phillips pushed through them as though they were not there. Gioia, halfway out the door, halted and looked toward him like a frightened deer.

"Don't go,'' he said. He took her hand in his.

He was startled by her appearance. How long had it been since their strange parting on that night of mysteries in Chang-an? A year? A year and a half? So he believed. Or had he lost all track of time? Were his perceptions of the passing of the months in this world that unreliable? She seemed at least ten or fifteen years older. Maybe she really was; maybe the years had been passing for him here as in a dream, and he had never known it. She looked strained, faded, worn. Out of a thinner and strangely altered face her eyes blazed at him almost defiantly, as though saying, *See? See how ugly I have become?*

He said, "I've been hunting for you for—I don't know how long it's been, Gioia. In Mohenjo, in Timbuctoo, now here. I want to be with you again.''

"It isn't possible.''

"Belilala explained everything to me in Mohenjo. I know that you're a short-timer—I know what that means, Gioia. But what of it? So you're beginning to age a little. So what? So you'll only have three or four hundred years, instead of forever. Don't you think I know what it means to be a short-timer? I'm just a simple ancient man of the twentieth century, remember? Sixty, seventy, eighty years is all we would get. You and I suffer from the same malady, Gioia. That's what drew you to me in the first place. I'm certain of that. That's why we belong with each other now. However much time we have, we can spend the rest of it together, don't you see?''

"You're the one who doesn't see, Charles,'' she said softly.

"Maybe. Maybe I still don't understand a damned thing

about this place. Except that you and I—that I love you—that I think you love me—''

"I love you, yes. But you don't understand. It's precisely because I love you that you and I—you and I can't—''

With a despairing sigh she slid her hand free of his grasp. He reached for her again, but she shook him off and backed up quickly into the corridor.

"Gioia?''

"Please," she said. "No. I would never have come here if I knew you were here. Don't come after me. Please. Please."

She turned and fled.

He stood looking after her for a long moment. Cantilena and Aramayne appeared, and smiled at him as if nothing at all had happened. Cantilena offered him a vial of some sparkling amber fluid. He refused with a brusque gesture. Where do I go now, he wondered? What do I do? He wandered back into the party.

Y'ang-Yeovil glided to his side. "You are in great distress,'' the little man murmured.

Phillips glared. "Let me be.''

"Perhaps I could be of some help.''

"There's no help possible,'' said Phillips. He swung about and plucked one of the vials from a tray and gulped its contents. It made him feel as if there were two of him, standing on either side of Y'ang-Yeovil. He gulped another. Now there were four of him. "I'm in love with a citizen,'' he blurted. It seemed to him that he was speaking in chorus.

"Love. Ah. And does she love you?''

"So I thought. So I think. But she's a short-timer. Do you know what that means? She's not immortal like the others. She ages. She's beginning to look old. And so she's been running away from me. She doesn't want me to see her changing. She thinks it'll disgust me, I suppose. I tried to remind her just now that I'm not immortal either, that she and I could grow old together, but she—''

"Oh, no,'' Y'ang-Yeovil said quietly. "Why do you think you will age? Have you grown any older in all the time you have been here?''

Phillips was nonplussed. "Of course I have. I—I—''

"Have you? Y'ang-Yeovil smiled. "Here. Look at yourself.'' He did something intricate with his fingers and a shimmering zone of mirror-like light appeared between them.

Phillips stared at his reflection. A youthful face stared back at him. It was true, then. He had simply not thought about it. How many years had he spent in this world? The time had simply slipped by: a great deal of time, though he could not calculate how much. They did not seem to keep close count of it here, nor had he. But it must have been many years, he thought. All that endless travel up and down the globe—so many cities had come and gone—Rio, Rome, Asgard, those were the first three that came to mind—and there were others; he could hardly remember every one. Years. His face had not changed at all. Time had worked its harshness on Gioia, yes, but not on him.

"I don't understand," he said. "Why am I not aging?"

"Because you are not real," said Y'ang-Yeovil. "Are you unaware of that?"

Phillips blinked. "Not—real?"

"Did you think you were lifted bodily out of your own time?" the little man asked. "Ah, no, no, there is no way for them to do such a thing. We are not actual time travelers: not you, not I, not any of the visitors. I thought you were aware of that. But perhaps your era is too early for a proper understanding of these things. We are very cleverly done, my friend. We are ingenious constructs, marvelously stuffed with the thoughts and attitudes and events of our own times. We are their finest achievement, you know: far more complex even than one of these cities. We are a step beyond the temporaries—more than a step, a great deal more. They do only what they are instructed to do, and their range is very narrow. They are nothing but machines, really. Whereas we are autonomous. We move about by our own will; we think, we talk, we even, so it seems, fall in love. But we will not age. How could we age? We are not real. We are mere artificial webworks of mental responses. We are mere illusions, done so well that we deceive even ourselves. You did not know that? Indeed, you did not know?"

He was airborne, touching destination buttons at random. Somehow he found himself heading back toward Timbuctoo. *This city is closed. This is not a place any longer.* It did not matter to him. Why should anything matter?

Fury and a choking sense of despair rose within him. I am software, Phillips thought. I am nothing but software.

Not real. Very cleverly done. An ingenious construct. A mere illusion.

No trace of Timbuctoo was visible from the air. He landed anyway. The gray sandy earth was smooth, unturned, as though there had never been anything there. A few robots were still about, handling whatever final chores were required in the shutting-down of a city. Two of them scuttled up to him. Huge bland gleaming silver-skinned insects, not friendly.

"There is no city here," they said. "This is not a permissible place."

"Permissible by whom?"

"There is no reason for you to be here."

"There's no reason for me to be anywhere," Phillips said. The robots stirred, made uneasy humming sounds and ominous clicks, waved their antennae about. They seem troubled, he thought. They seem to dislike my attitude. Perhaps I run some risk of being taken off to the home for unruly software for debugging. "I'm leaving now," he told them. "Thank you. Thank you very much." He backed away from them and climbed into his flitterflitter. He touched more destination buttons.

We move about by our own will. We think, we talk, we even fall in love.

He landed in Chang-an. This time there was no reception committee waiting for him at the Gate of Brilliant Virtue. The city seemed larger and more resplendent: new pagodas, new palaces. It felt like winter: a chilly cutting wind was blowing. The sky was cloudless and dazzlingly bright. At the steps of the Silver Terrace he encountered Francis Willoughby, a great hulking figure in magnificent brocaded robes, with two dainty little temporaries, pretty as jade statuettes, engulfed in his arms. "Miracles and wonders! The silly lunatic fellow is here too!" Willoughby roared. "Look, look, we are come to far Cathay, you and I!"

We are nowhere, Phillips thought. *We are mere illusions, done so well that we deceive even ourselves.*

To Willoughby he said, "You look like an emperor in those robes, Francis."

"Aye, like Prester John!" Willoughby cried. "Like Tamburlaine himself! Aye, am I not majestic?" He slapped Phillips gaily on the shoulder, a rough playful poke that spun him halfway about, coughing and wheezing. "We flew in the air, as the eagles do, as the demons do, as the angels do! Soared like angels! Like angels!'' He came close, looming over Phillips. ''I would have gone to England, but the wench Belilala said there was an enchantment on me that would keep me from England just now; and so we voyaged to Cathay. Tell me this, fellow, will you go witness for me when we see England again? Swear that all that has befallen us did in truth befall? For I fear they will say I am as mad as Marco Polo, when I tell them of flying to Cathay.''

''One madman backing another?'' Phillips asked. ''What can I tell you? You still think you'll reach England, do you?'' Rage rose to the surface in him, bubbling hot. ''Ah, Francis, Francis, do you know your Shakespeare? Did you go to the plays? We aren't real. *We aren't real.* We are such stuff as dreams are made on, the two of us. That's all we are. O brave new world! What England? Where? There's no England. There's no Francis Willoughby. There's no Charles Phillips. What we are is—''

''Let him be, Charles,'' a cool voice cut in.

He turned. Belilala, in the robes of an empress, coming down the steps of the Silver Terrace.

''I know the truth,'' he said bitterly. ''Y'ang-Yeovil told me. The visitor from the twenty-fifth century. I saw him in New Chicago.''

''Did you see Gioia there too?'' Belilala asked.

''Briefly. She looks much older.''

''Yes. I know. She was here recently.''

''And has gone on, I suppose?''

''To Mohenjo again, yes. Go after her, Charles. Leave poor Francis alone. I told her to wait for you. I told her that she needs you, and you need her.''

''Very kind of you. But what good is it, Belilala? I don't even exist. And she's going to die.''

''You exist. How can you doubt that you exist? You feel, don't you? You suffer. You love. You love Gioia: is that not so? And you are loved by Gioia. Would Gioia love what is not real?''

''You think she loves me?''

''I know she does. Go to her, Charles. Go. I told her to wait for you in Mohenjo.''

Phillips nodded numbly. What was there to lose?

''Go to her,'' said Belilala again. ''Now.''

"Yes," Phillips said. "I'll go now." He turned to Willoughby. "If ever we meet in London, friend, I'll testify for you. Fear nothing. All will be well, Francis."

He left them and set his course for Mohenjo-daro, half expecting to find the robots already tearing it down. Mohenjo-daro was still there, no lovelier than before. He went to the baths, thinking he might find Gioia there. She was not; but he came upon Nissandra, Stengard, Fenimon. "She has gone to Alexandria," Fenimon told him. "She wants to see it one last time, before they close it."

"They're almost ready to open Constantinople," Stengard explained. "The capital of Byzantium, you know, the great city by the Golden Horn. They'll take Alexandria away, you understand, when Byzantium opens. They say it's going to be marvelous. We'll see you there for the opening, naturally?"

"Naturally," Phillips said.

He flew to Alexandria. He felt lost and weary. All this is hopeless folly, he told himself. I am nothing but a puppet jerking about on its strings. But somewhere above the shining breast of the Arabian Sea the deeper implications of something that Belilala had said to him started to sink in, and he felt his bitterness, his rage, his despair, all suddenly beginning to leave him. *You exist. How can you doubt that you exist? Would Gioia love what is not real?* Of course. Of course. Y'ang-Yeovil had been wrong: visitors were something more than mere illusions. Indeed Y'ang-Yeovil had voiced the truth of their condition without understanding what he was really saying: *We think, we talk, we fall in love.* Yes. That was the heart of the situation. The visitors might be artificial, but they were not unreal. Belilala had been trying to tell him that just the other night. *You suffer. You love. You love Gioia. Would Gioia love what is not real?* Surely he was real, or at any rate real enough. What he was was something strange, something that would probably have been all but incomprehensible to the twentieth-century people whom he had been designed to simulate. But that did not mean that he was unreal. Did one have to be of woman born to be real? No. No. No. His kind of reality was a sufficient reality. He had no need to be ashamed of it. And, understanding that, he understood that Gioia did not need to grow old and die. There was a way by which she could be saved, if only she would embrace it. If only she would.

When he landed in Alexandria he went immediately to the hotel on the slopes of the Paneium where they had stayed on their first visit, so very long ago; and there she was, sitting quietly on a patio with a view of the harbor and Lighthouse. There was something calm and resigned about the way she sat. She had given up. She did not even have the strength to flee from him any longer.

"Gioia," he said gently.

She looked older than she had in New Chicago. Her face was drawn and sallow and her eyes seemed sunken; and she was not even bothering these days to deal with the white strands that stood out in stark contrast against the darkness of her hair. He sat down beside her and put his hand over hers, and looked out toward the obelisks, the palaces, the temples, the Lighthouse. At length he said, "I know what I really am, now."

"Do you, Charles?" She sounded very far away.

"In my era we called it software. All I am is a set of commands, responses, cross-references, operating some sort of artificial body. It's infinitely better software than we could have imagined. But we were only just beginning to learn how, after all. They pumped me full of twentieth-century reflexes. The right moods, the right appetites, the right irrationalities, the right sort of combativeness. Somebody knows a lot about what it was like to be a twentieth-century man. They did a good job with Willoughby, too, all that Elizabethan rhetoric and swagger. And I suppose they got Y'ang-Yeovil right. *He* seems to think so: who better to judge? The twenty-fifth century, the Republic of Upper Han, people with gray-green skin, half Chinese and half Martian for all I know. *Somebody* knows. Somebody here is very good at programming, Gioia."

She was not looking at him.

"I feel frightened, Charles," she said in that same distant way.

"Of me? Of the things I'm saying?"

"No, not of you. Don't you see what has happened to me?"

"I see you. There are changes."

"I lived a long time wondering when the changes would begin. I thought maybe they wouldn't, not really. Who wants to believe they'll get old? But it started when we were in Alexandria that first time. In Chang-an it got much worse. And now—now—"

He said abruptly, "Stengard tells me they'll be opening Constantinople very soon."

"So?"

"Don't you want to be there when it opens?"

"I'm becoming old and ugly, Charles."

"We'll go to Constantinople together. We'll leave tomorrow, eh? What do you say? We'll charter a boat. It's a quick little hop, right across the Mediterranean. Sailing to Byzantium! There was a poem, you know, in my time. Not forgotten, I guess, because they've programmed it into me. All these thousands of years, and someone still remembers old Yeats. *The young in one another's arms, birds in the trees.* Come with me to Byzantium, Gioia."

She shrugged. "Looking like this? Getting more hideous every hour? While *they* stay young forever? While *you*—" She faltered; her voice cracked; she fell silent.

"Finish the sentence, Gioia."

"Please. Let me alone."

"You were going to say, 'While *you* stay young forever too, Charles,' isn't that it? You knew all along that I was never going to change. I didn't know that, but you did."

"Yes. I knew. I pretended that it wasn't true—that as I aged, you'd age too. It was very foolish of me. In Chang-an, when I first began to see the real signs of it—that was when I realized I couldn't stay with you any longer. Because I'd look at you, always young, always remaining the same age, and I'd look at myself, and—" She gestured, palms upward. "So I gave you to Belilala and ran away."

"All so unnecessary, Gioia."

"I didn't think it was."

"But you don't have to grow old. Not if you don't want to!"

"Don't be cruel, Charles," she said tonelessly. "There's no way of escaping what I have."

"But there is," he said.

"You know nothing about these things."

"Not very much, no," he said. "But I see how it can be done. Maybe it's a primitive simple-minded twentieth-century sort of solution, but I think it ought to work. I've been playing with the idea ever since I left Mohenjo. Tell me this, Gioia: Why can't you go to them, to the programmers, to the artificers, the planners, whoever they are, the ones who create the cities and the temporaries and the visitors. And have yourself made into something like me!''

She looked up, startled. ''What are you saying?''

''They can cobble up a twentieth-century man out of nothing more than fragmentary records and make him plausible, can't they? Or an Elizabethan, or anyone else of any era at all, and he's authentic, he's convincing. So why couldn't they do an even better job with you? Produce a Gioia so real that even Gioia can't tell the difference? But a Gioia that will never age—a Gioia-construct, a Gioia-program, a visitor-Gioia! Why not? Tell me why not, Gioia.''

She was trembling. ''I've never heard of doing any such thing!''

''But don't you think it's possible?''

''How would I know?''

''Of course it's possible. If they can create visitors, they can take a citizen and duplicate her in such a way that—''

''It's never been done. I'm sure of it. I can't imagine any citizen agreeing to any such thing. To give up the body—to let yourself be turned into—into—''

She shook her head, but it seemed to be a gesture of astonishment as much as of negation.

He said, ''Sure. To give up the body. Your natural body, your aging, shrinking, deteriorating short-timer body. What's so awful about that?''

She was very pale. ''This is craziness, Charles. I don't want to talk about it any more.''

''It doesn't sound crazy to me.''

''You can't possibly understand.''

''Can't I? I can certainly understand being afraid to die. I don't have a lot of trouble understanding what it's like to be one of the few aging people in a world where nobody grows old. What I can't understand is why you aren't even willing to consider the possibility that—''

''No,'' she said. ''I tell you, it's crazy. They'd laugh at me.''

''Who?''

''All of my friends. Hawk, Stengard, Aramayne—'' Once again she would not look at him. ''They can be very cruel, without even realizing it. They despise anything that seems ungraceful to them, anything sweaty and desperate and cowardly. Citizens don't do sweaty things, Charles. And that's how this will seem. Assuming it can be done at all. They'll be terribly patronizing. Oh, they'll be sweet to me, yes, dear Gioia, how wonderful for you, Gioia, but when I turn my back they'll laugh. They'll say the most wicked things about me. I couldn't bear that.''

"They can afford to laugh," Phillips said. "It's easy to be brave and cool about dying when you know you're going to live forever. How very fine for them; but why should you be the only one to grow old and die? And they won't laugh, anyway. They're not as cruel as you think. Shallow, maybe, but not cruel. They'll be glad that you've found a way to save yourself. At the very least, they won't have to feel guilty about you any longer, and that's bound to please them. You can—''

"Stop it," she said.

She rose, walked to the railing of the patio, stared out toward the sea. He came up behind her. Red sails in the harbor, sunlight glittering along the sides of the Lighthouse, the palaces of the Ptolemies stark white against the sky. Lightly he rested his hand on her shoulder. She twitched as if to pull away from him, but remained where she was.

"Then I have another idea," he said quietly. "If you won't go to the planners, *I* will. Reprogram me, I'll say. Fix things so that I start to age at the same rate you do. It'll be more authentic, anyway, if I'm supposed to be playing the part of a twentieth-century man. Over the years I'll very gradually get some lines in my face, my hair will turn gray, I'll walk a little more slowly—we'll grow old together, Gioia. To hell with your lovely immortal friends. We'll have each other. We won't need them.''

She swung around. Her eyes were wide with horror.

"Are you serious, Charles?"

"Of course."

"No," she murmured. "No. Everything you've said to me today is monstrous nonsense. Don't you realize that?"

He reached for her hand and enclosed her fingertips in his. "All I'm trying to do is find some way for you and me to—''

"Don't say any more," she said. "Please." Quickly, as though drawing back from a suddenly flaring flame, she tugged her fingers free of his and put her hand behind her. Though his face was just inches from hers he felt an immense chasm opening between them. They stared at one another for a moment; then she moved deftly to his left, darted around him, and ran from the patio.

Stunned, he watched her go, down the long marble corridor and out of sight. It was folly to give pursuit, he thought. She was lost to him: that was clear, that was beyond any question. She was terrified of him. Why cause her even more anguish? But somehow he found himself running through the halls of the hotel, along the winding garden path, into the cool green groves of the Paneium. He thought he saw her on the portico of Hadrian's palace, but when he got there the echoing stone halls were empty. To a temporary that was sweeping the steps he said, "Did you see a woman come this way?" A blank sullen stare was his only answer.

Phillips cursed and turned away.

"Gioia?" he called. "Wait! Come back!"

Was that her, going into the Library? He rushed past the startled mumbling librarians and sped through the stacks, peering beyond the mounds of double-handled scrolls into the shadowy corridors. "Gioia? *Gioia!*" It was a desecration, bellowing like that in this quiet place. He scarcely cared.

Emerging by a side door, he loped down to the harbor. The Lighthouse! Terror enfolded him. She might already be a hundred steps up that ramp, heading for the parapet from which she meant to fling herself into the sea. Scattering citizens and temporaries as if they were straws, he ran within. Up he went, never pausing for breath, though his synthetic lungs were screaming for respite, his ingeniously designed heart was desperately pounding. On the first balcony he imagined he caught a glimpse of her, but he circled it without finding her. Onward, upward. He went to the top, to the beacon chamber itself: no Gioia. Had she jumped? Had she gone down one ramp while he was ascending the other? He clung to the rim and looked out, down, searching the base of the Lighthouse, the rocks offshore, the causeway. No Gioia. I will find her somewhere, he thought. I will keep going until I find her. He went running down the ramp, calling her name. He reached ground level and sprinted back toward the center of town. Where next? The temple of Poseidon? The tomb of Cleopatra?

He paused in the middle of Canopus Street, groggy and dazed.

"Charles?" she said.

"Where are you?"

"Right here. Beside you." She seemed to materialize from the air. Her face was unflushed, her robe bore no trace of perspiration. Had he been chasing a phantom through the city? She came to him and took his hand, and said softly, tenderly, "Were you really serious, about having them make you age?"

"If there's no other way, yes."

"The other way is so frightening, Charles."

"Is it?"

"You can't understand how much."

"More frightening than growing old? Than dying?"

"I don't know," she said. "I suppose not. The only thing I'm sure of is that I don't want you to get old, Charles."

"But I won't have to. Will I?" He stared at her.

"No," she said. "You won't have to. Neither of us will."

Phillips smiled. "We should get away from here," he said after a while. "Let's go across to Byzantium, yes, Gioia? We'll show up in Constantinople for the opening. Your friends will be there. We'll tell them what you've decided to do. They'll know how to arrange it. Someone will."

"It sounds so strange," said Gioia. "To turn myself into—into a visitor? A visitor in my own world?"

"That's what you've always been, though."

"I suppose. In a way. But at least I've been *real* up to now."

"Whereas I'm not?"

"Are you, Charles?"

"Yes. Just as real as you. I was angry at first, when I found out the truth about myself. But I came to accept it. Somewhere between Mohenjo and here, I came to see that it was all right to be what I am: that I perceive things, I form ideas, I draw conclusions. I am very well designed, Gioia. I can't tell the difference between being what I am and being completely alive, and to me that's being real enough. I think, I feel, I experience joy and pain. I'm as real as I need to be. And you will be too. You'll never stop being Gioia, you know. It's only your body that you'll cast away, the body that played such a terrible joke on you anyway." He brushed her cheek with his hand. "It was all said for us before, long ago:

Once out of nature I shall never take
My bodily form from any natural thing,
But such a form as Grecian goldsmiths make
Of hammered gold and gold enamelling
To keep a drowsy Emperor awake—"

"Is that the same poem?" she asked.

"The same poem, yes. The ancient poem that isn't quite forgotten yet."

"Finish it, Charles."

—"*Or set upon a golden bough to sing*
To lords and ladies of Byzantium
Of what is past, or passing, or to come."

"How beautiful. What does it mean?"

"That it isn't necessary to be mortal. That we can allow ourselves to be gathered into the artifice of eternity, that we can be transformed, that we can move on beyond the flesh. Yeats didn't mean it in quite the way I do—he wouldn't have begun to comprehend what we're talking about, not a word of it—and yet, and yet—the underlying truth is the same. Live, Gioia! With me!" He turned to her and saw color coming into her pallid cheeks. "It does make sense, what I'm suggesting, doesn't it? You'll attempt it, won't you? Whoever makes the visitors can be induced to remake you. Right? What do you think: can they, Gioia?"

She nodded in a barely perceptible way. "I think so," she said faintly. "It's very strange. But I think it ought to be possible. Why not, Charles? Why not?"

"Yes," he said. "Why not?"

In the morning they hired a vessel in the harbor, a low sleek pirogue with a blood-red sail, skippered by a rascally-looking temporary whose smile was irresistible. Phillips shaded his eyes and peered northward across the sea. He thought he could almost make out the shape of the great city sprawling on its seven hills, Constantine's New Rome beside the Golden Horn, the mighty dome of Hagia Sophia, the somber walls of the citadel, the palaces and churches, the Hippodrome, Christ

in glory rising above all else in brilliant mosaic streaming
with light.

"Byzantium," Phillips said. "Take us there the shortest
and quickest way."

"It is my pleasure," said the boatman with unexpected
grace.

Gioia smiled. He had not seen her looking so vibrantly
alive since the night of the imperial feast in Chang-an. He
reached for her hand—her slender fingers were quivering
lightly—and helped her into the boat.

WEBRIDER

by Jayge Carr

It may have been Edgar Rice Burroughs who invented what I think of as the "wish-fulfillment" technique of space flight on behalf of John Carter. Carl Sagan, in his new novel Contact, seems to have devised a variation of this, a sort of interstellar invisible subway system. In this unusual story there is yet another such system, the web that connects the worlds. Would that it were so!

The Eternal Second ended, and once again I had survived.

There was a reception committee at the terminus. Not for me, for what I carried.

"Left thigh," I said, as a dozen anxious-eyed humans converged on me before I could take a second step away from the terminus out of which I had just emerged. I turned so that my left side faced them, and three banged into each other to kneel. I pressed the under-the-skin control at my waist, and my left thigh split neatly and painlessly open. Impatient fingers probed the organi-synthetic-lined cavity revealed. What they wanted was there, of course; the thigh carry is *safe*, if blighted uncomfortable for the carrier.

If Whatever-they-wanted had been smaller, I'd've used my mouth. I'm one of those who can keep their mouths shut while riding.

Then they had the four unbreakable vials out and were hasting away with them. What was left of the reception

committee was shaking my hands and trying to shove beakers
full of unknown swizzles and platters of equally exotic eatments
at me, while gabbling out thank-yous at a kilometer-a-
second rate.

I'm left-handed, so it was my right arm I stuck out.
"*High*-nutri. Now." My third and fourth words on this world
I had never seen before and would probably never see again
once I'd been called off of it.

They'd been briefed. A medico—a short but swishious fem
with come-hither-and-enjoy eyes—clamped a dingus of a type
I'd never seen before around my arm. I felt something physically digging in, invading my body-integral space to insert
the nutri. But primitive as the method was, it worked *fast*. I
could feel the dizziness wearing off, a contented glow spreading outward from my arm.

"Thanks," I told her. "Good stuff."

"Any time, honored Webrider. I'm Medico Miyoshi Alnasr.
If, during your stay on our world, you should again require
my services—" She pressed a head-only mini-holo of herself,
no bigger than my thumbnail, against the back of my wrist,
where it adhered neatly. "—just peel the outer layer to
activate the summoner. I answer," her voice dropped, "twenty-
eight hours a day. . . ."

Groupie, I thought, but I didn't jerk off the summoner.
Odds were I would need her professional services at some
point; turista is a chronic disease among webriders. But as for
anything else . . . no mistaking the look in her eyes, in all
their eyes. Until what I carried did what they needed it to do,
I could have asked for half their world—and gotten it.

There was more in her eyes, though. An avidity I saw far
too often. This one liked the glamor and notoriety of succor-
ing a webrider, the more the better—and the how of it didn't
matter a rotted bean to her.

Webriders learn to live with that, and the envy. Webriders are
never allowed to forget that they are the true elite, those very,
very few who can step in a terminus on one world and step out—
alive!—on another. For the rest, it can only be slower-than-light
wombships, taking months and years—even at the compressed
time of relativistic velocity—from one world to another.

We have not only the freedom of the stars, but the un-
speakable glory of riding the web. The Eternal Second. The
ultimate experience.

Webriding. Flowing through stars, points of flame running through hands that aren't hands, the psychic You bound up in the physical You that's just a pattern sliding along the web, held together and existing only by the strength of will of the webrider. Sailing on evanescent wings of mind through the energy/matter currents of space, down one fragile strand of the web and up another. Feeling torn apart, as the pattern that is You is spread over parsecs, smeared across the stars; and yet, godlike, knowing those stars, sensing with psychic "eyes" the entire spectrum of space/time, so that the beat of the pulsars is like the universe's throbbing heart. . . .

We have our glory, and one of the prices we pay for it is the groupies.

Not that I was worried about the medico; she was one of the safe kind of groupie. The only kind the locals would and should let near a webrider. The greedy but selfish kind, wanting close but not *too* close, snatching a rubbed-off glamor. But never for a second considering risking her own precious hide for the real thing.

It's the other kind of groupie who is so dangerous, the *real* groupie. The one who will do anything to get on the web. Infinitely dangerous to a rider, to a rider's peace of mind, so necessary for safe webriding. They try to sneak up close to a rider, and then. . . .

Oh, groupies are necessary. Where else would we get our recruits?

But they have to be kept away from the riders, because it hurts too much, to lose someone you've grown close to. A double hurt for me, because I and my sister were once groupies ourselves. I am a rider now, but our tree lost us both. She, as like me as a holo image, is now atoms scattered across half a galaxy. I relive that loss with every would-be rider that dies—and so many of them do die.

Another price we pay. And they, the world-dwellers, try to make it up to us, forgetting that what's infinitely precious on one world may be common as oxy on another. Not that I could take any of it with me. What is desperately needed, I take in the thigh, or use the mouth carry. But for myself—never.

There are other rewards besides those which can be carried. In the crowd surrounding me, eagerly talking or humbly waiting for me to express my opinion, were at least four citizens obviously put there for me to choose from. An ultra brawn, one of the prettiest boychicks I'd ever seen, a super-swishious fem that eclipsed the medico by several orders of magnitude, and an adorable nymphet. All choice, but by this world's standards. Which meant, short, broad, tailless, blue-tinted skin, and pale, almost colorless hair that grew in little tufts over every bit of exposed skin I could see—plenty! —except around eyes and mouths. I'd seen weirder, lots, and I probably looked just as odd to them, if not odder.

I'm a straight fem, myself, and the brawn seemed well endowed with what a brawn should have—his costume left little to my fertile imagination—so I wasted no time in putting a possessive hand on his arm and asking him to stick around, while I politely implied to the other three that if that was the way my tastes went, they'd certainly have been my choice.

The nymphet pouted, but the brawn was looking me up and down in a very unprofessional way, part smugness at being chosen, but mostly yum-*yum!* *I'm* gonna *enjoy* this!

I was no little complimented.

Mother Leaf, how that crowd around me talked and talked. A rider needs two things to restore physical/psychic energy after a ride, and I'd only had one. When my knees began to buckle, I let them. He caught me easily, and lifted me into a comfortable baby-carry, though I was a head taller than he. I wrapped my tail around his waist.

"Medico Alnasr," he called, voice shot through with worry.

"You," I said, and smiled. He got the message, prehensile tails have their uses, after all. He strode through the mob, my weight nothing, like a feeding black hole through a galaxy's heart. Which suited me just fine.

There was one odd incident. A fem—older, if wrinkles and missing tufts of hair meant what such signs usually mean—caught sight of my brawn's face and her own went pure blue. "Malachi," she hissed, but my brawn never missed stride. I shrugged mentally; relative, lover, or whatever, she'd have him back as soon as I left.

All my energies were most satisfactorily restored.

He was a pleasant conversationalist, too, easily talking about his exotic—to me—world of shallow seas and endless island chains. Not his fault, either, when a careless mention of his own family, his own sister, reminded me once again of the one I had lost. Sensing my inner withdrawal, he laughed and changed the subject, refusing to let me brood over a childhood spent in the crests of giant trees and a lost more-than-sister. Still talking, he led me out onto a transparent floored balcony, cantilevered over a crystal water lagoon, filled with living rainbows darting through equally living though grotesque mazes.

His name was (he had quickly confirmed this) Malachi; and I sensed his curiosity growing about mine. I would have told him freely, except—

I have no name.

A twig may not choose a name until he/she has pollinated or budded. (Old habits die hard; we give birth as any other humans, except always clutches of identicals. But we identify with our trees. For example—) I am—or was—a twig of the tree called Tamarisk, of the 243rd generation born under Her shading leaves. But I was unbudded when I came to the web—too young—and unbudded I must stay until I die, or am thrown off the web for whatever reason, which is almost the same things. A budding fem can't ride, and I am a rider, I must ride.

On the rolls of the web I am carried as "Twig Tamarisk of Sequoia Upper." But that is for others' convenience. I have never chosen a name for myself, now I never will.

I told him to call me "Twig" and he looked me up and down and stifled laughter. I supposed to one as broad as he, I did look like a walking twig.

He gestured upward, that I might admire the gauzy dayring while he controlled his face. There was a rustle behind us; I caught my lip. We were supposed to be alone, but there are fanatics on many worlds. Twisted minds. Haters, who strike out at the handiest—or most prominent—targets.

I said nothing. Malachi could have been in on it, whatever it was. I simply moved a little away, as though to follow better Malachi's pointing finger. Until he heard the sounds, too—

The intruder hadn't a chance. Unarmed, the unfilled muscles and flesh of a youthful growth spurt, he was surprised by Malachi's savage attack.

In seconds, Malachi had his opponent face down on the deck, hands caught behind his back, and was looking about for something to tie his wrists together with. The stranger squirmed desperately but futilely, until he managed to twist his head around so that his gaze met mine, his face younger even than the still growing body, blue-rimmed eyes rawly swollen, the irises scarcely darker than the blue-tinted whites. "Webrider, *please*," he begged.

I knew the look in those eyes, all webriders see it over and over.

"Let him up, Malachi."

"But he shouldn't be here. He may have come to attack—" Which showed that some on this world had heard certain tales, too.

"No, Malachi, he's a groupie. Aren't you, bud?"

Sullenly. "I don't know what a groupie is."

"Do you want to ride the web yourself—or just hear about other worlds and webriding?"

Each tuft of his hair was tied with a different colored ribbon. His mouth dropped open, revealing black (painted?) teeth—and I knew I had guessed right. "How did you know—"

I laughed. "Did you think you were the only one, then?" I stretched out one hand to Malachi, the other to the boy, to help them to their feet. "Come on, relax, get comfortable. What's your—" Out of old habit I started to say tree, but remembered in time. "—name, bud?"

Malachi let him up but continued to glare suspiciously at him; the boy glared back, sour and silent.

"Well," I perched on a railing, and a crisp breeze rippled playfully over my skin, "shall we call you Incognit, then, bud?"

"Incog—what?"

"Incognit. It means 'unknown' in one of the Austere systems' tongues. It's one of their planets, actually, that's how I heard of it. Awkward place, for a stranger, the land looks firm, but if you're fool enough to step on it, you'd sink in up to your eyebrows—or a little more. All the land—at least all near the terminus—is like that. I guess that sandy patch of yours," I gestured with my head toward the golden sweep surrounded by rippling blue, "reminded me of Incognit, put the word in my head."

"You mean," his eyes were huge, hypnotic in their intensity, "that there's a settled world with no solid land at all?"

"Affirm." I was being a fool, and knew it. But ah, the wistful adulation, the fearful hope in those shades-of-blue eyes. Surely, if I emphasized the negative strongly enough. . . . "More than one, in fact. Sink worlds like Incognit, and worlds that are covered with water. One I was on was all water, but it had so many buildings, their foundations on pilings sunk into bedrock, that you couldn't tell it unless you went down, oh, hundreds of levels. And there are worlds where there are no real boundaries at all, just a slow gradient, a gradual increase of pressure as you sink down, until you reach the core. And that's only solid if you consider ultracompressed matter, no crystalline structure at all, as solid. And there are worlds—''

"How can people live on a world like that, with no solid anywhere?"

"Floaters," I had a persistent itch between my shoulder-blades, just to the left of my mane, and I swung my tail around to scratch it with the prehensile's tip. "Big ones and little ones, all with lifepods dangling beneath." I grinned, remembering. "Scared the sap out of my hosts on that world, I did. Inside the pods could have been anywhere, except for the swaying motion. But outside—the vanes and ropes and controls reminded me of the vines and limbs of the treecrest where I was born and grew up. A little higher, of course . . . I was never on the floor of anything until I entered training. Only animals live on the rootfloor of my world, it's dark all the time, and well, I hadn't realized how I missed crestdriving and vineswinging and everything else until I hit that world. Had to stop, though; I was afraid I'd give somebody a heart attack. Quite a sight it was, great mats of those floaters all roped together; never found out what they were, the floaters. Artificial, or animals, or made from dead animals. . . .''

I kept talking, trying to guess from his reactions whether he was just a listener—or a would-be rider.

I should have known, though. Anybody with nerve to break in the way he had was no mere listener.

While I talked, I hooked into webmind, that almost living totality of all information fed into all the terminuses of the web. Nobody knows why all successful riders can hook into webmind, sooner or later if not immediately. I could, from my very first ride, just by wanting to, with no more effort than remembering the way the leaves uncurled on my home treecrest every spring, or the shimmering colors of Under-the-Falls on a planet called Niagara Ultimate.

My question for webmind was a simple one: what percentage of successes this world enjoyed.

Blight! No successes, never; the training school had been closed down long ago, all native attempts at webriding made illegal. (Yet they were willing to use the web, so long as others took the risks!) A few fanatics had continued to try, despite the illegality, the guards; all had failed.

I kept talking, and eventually the groupie asked the inevitable, revealing question, "What does it feel like to ride the web?"

What does it feel like to *live*?

Only riders know.

I tried to describe the indescribable. But always with the caveat. "Most people aren't strong enough. They try, but their psychic You can't hold their pattern together, and it begins to spread and spread, thinner and thinner, until it isn't a pattern at all, atom sundered from atom, the physical body only a new current among the nebulae, undetectible by the most sensitive instruments we have . . .

"Splattering, we call it.

"Nine out of ten, bud. Remember it. Repeat it to yourself. Nine out of ten. Nine out of ten, *trained*. Worse than nine out of ten, for the untrained."

He didn't believe me. He thought I was lying. And I was, but not the way he thought. It's not nine out of ten, it's ninety-nine out of a hundred. Yet if I'd told him the truth, that less than one percent survive their first ride, he certainly wouldn't have believed me.

I had to warn him, force him to recognize the risks, the odds against him. With luck, I might discourage him entirely. If he wanted the web, badly enough, nothing I or anyone could say or do would stop him (I knew!). But at least, he would have been warned.

Or so I told myself.

The path to Blight, they say, is leaved with good intentions.

I shooed him away, finally, his taste for adventure (I prayed!) sated for a good long while.

Afterwards, the reaction set in. Until a tentative hand brushed my shoulder. "Can I help?" Harsh breathing and a dark cloud of worry at my back.

I shook my head, still staring unseeing at blue on blue vistas. Until I realized that panic was about to explode behind me. "It hurts, that's all, Malachi. But it wasn't your fault. No one can keep determined enough groupies away, no matter what security measures they use. Only—try harder, your people must try *harder*. Keep groupies away from me, Malachi. Away!"

"You've privacy now, but they'll hear and obey, once you yourself break the privacy. But—" The hand on my shoulder trembled. "—I don't understand. You were—very kind, to that one youngster. Why deny others what they crave? Shutting yourself away to recuperate, that's understandable. But afterwards, a few simple words seem harmless enough—"

"Harmless!" I whirled, tail curling and uncurling in a manner that would have signaled attack-to-the-death in my home tree. "It hurts *me*, Malachi! It makes me remember, too many have died. And for *them*—don't you understand, are you blind—they want to *ride*. And for some, being close to a rider is the final encouragement. They see a rider, a successful rider, and they think they can be successful, too. So they try. And they die. They *die*, Malachi. You can't stop it entirely, no one can. But you can at least—discourage—"

He flushed blue and looked guilty as Blight. But it wasn't his fault, and he was a splendid brawn. I caught his arms, leaned my head against warm breadth of shoulder, firm with thick muscle, and sighed. "You'll never understand, will you, my solid, feet-on-the-trunk Malachi. You're happy with your life as it is, you've never been infected with a madness, wanted something so desperately you'd sell your soul, your tree, anything to have it. I know, I had it, never recovered, riders never do. But you—the joys of today, eh, brawn? Would *you* face almost certain death for the chance to become a webrider?"

He stiffened like a crestdweller bitten by a duasp, then his deep chuckles shook us both from top to toe. Until he showed me once again how joyous the joys of the present can be.

I was given the tour royale the next planetary days. My brawn Malachi disappeared as soon as we emerged from our little suite-over-the-water, but as soon as I asked for him, I got him back.

There was the Blightedest smug expression on his face, and an almost tastable current of disapproval from the others. But—I liked what I liked. If I had somehow offended against this world's mores—tough. I didn't bother to dip into webmind to search among this world's customs to see what, or if, I was doing wrong.

As many worlds as I've been to, there's always something new. A sight, a sport, and amusement. Malachi and I shared them all, sometimes he the master I the tyro, sometimes the two of us tyros together.

Yet it wasn't all lotus-eating. There are many ways a webrider, a webrider who can hook into webmind, can be useful.

Through work or play, whenever I was tired or sad or down for any reason, I could always reach behind myself to have my hand taken in a hard warm hand. Malachi was there when I needed him, never intruding unless I needed him. As though to remind me that there are everyday pleasures and everyday lives, and even some people to whom webriding is not the be-all and the end-all. I could only thank Mother Leaf for those whose lives were so filled to the brim that they didn't need the web. Live long and fully, Malachi, my sweet brawn. Live long and fully!

Oh, I was useful, my brawn an everpresent silent shadow. I knew how long it had been since they had called on web, webmind told me. They'd waited overlong, until a true almost-death emergency. I was sure they'd smile to see my back stepping into the terminus.

But I have my loyalty to web. I wanted them to be impressed with the advantages of web, and webriders. I couldn't stay too long, of course, a rider has to ride constantly to stay in tune. But I told webmind to keep me on low-priority unless there was a starprime emergency.

So I was still there when Incognit splattered.

They screamed for me, of course, but too late. I was physically away from the web, and it was all over in a second, anyway.

I knew what had happened, knew as soon as it happened, knew nothing could be done.

He'd splattered, in the Second, and that—was it.

I went, nonetheless, though it took me several standard hours to get to the terminus from where I'd been.

Besides the usual component of VIP's, technies, medicos, and curious, there was a furious female who rounded on me as I entered the outer door to the terminus hall and snarled, "Ausantr—get him!"

"I can't." I didn't know if she was mother, sister, or lover, but she was in an emotional state I wouldn't have thought these stolid heavies could achieve. She was shorter than I, but solid muscle. Her hand slammed around, and I went *up* and crashed into a wall so hard my teeth met in my lip before I crumpled down in a heap.

Six hands got in each other's way helping me up, and when I had my feet steady under me, Malachi and the female were rolling about, hands at each other's throats and snarling threats so laced with local dialect I couldn't understand them.

I wiped blood from my mouth as others managed to separate the combatants. Despite the hands holding her, she glared lasers at me. "You people—" It was sneer and curse.

"And yours. You called for a webrider. You wish the web to be kept open, the riders to ride. Over a hundred die, for each successful rider. One of those who died could have been me; I accepted the risk, so did the bud. And your people must share the responsibility, too, as long as they leave the web connected to your world."

I saw it sinking in. Then, "And it doesn't bother you . . . those hundred deaths?"

When one of them was my sister, my image, my other self?

She turned away, shoulders slumping.

"I need a medico, my lip is bleeding. It must be sealed before I try to ride."

Webmind had already told me that he hadn't made it to the first crossing, but I searched anyway, sweeping up one strand and down the next, diving at a junction and sliding up its strands, again and again.

I tried almost too long, then I was back—empty-handed.

"Remember, if you must remember, the happinesses he had, that you and he had together."

"You were only gone a second!"

The Eternal Second.

"I could have reached another Arm in that second, or gathered him back, if he were there to gather. There wasn't a flavor of another on the web." She raised her fist again—and believed. Her shoulders sagged, the fist dropped, and she walked away, out of the door, out of my life.

Malachi only waited for the high-nutri band to be placed around my arm before scooping me up and walking out with me.

After that, though his world held much to enjoy, I was only waiting for my Call.

Not that I wouldn't learn to live, in time, with Incognit's death, and my guilt. But not while I still walked his world, where every step I took reminded me that I'd slaughtered an innocent bud as surely as if I'd pushed him off a low-lying branch and watched him fall to the deadly floor below.

At last, the Call came. A nearby world to supply emergency multiprograms for a planet in a distant Arm. A short hop, and then a long, long ride. I said no goodbyes, riders never do. The odds are against returning to the same world a second time. We used cats' goodbyes. (I sometimes wondered which of the many animals called cats I've seen on various worlds is the cat the silent good-bye was named after.)

I would miss Malachi, though. There was more to him than the usual live-for-the-moment brawn. His life-choice mayn't've been mine, but I couldn't help admiring him, if for nothing more than the tenacity I sometimes sensed beneath the surface of bonhomie.

The terminus was warmed up, glowing as I approached. I stood, breathing deeply, one . . . three . . . and took the giant step.

I wasn't alone!

I could feel—him, Malachi!—*splattering*; and I grabbed instinctively, and clung tightly, with psychic arms I hadn't known I possessed. Past and present merged, we had joined hearts and minds and psyches in a dozen different ways, altered each other, grown close, laughed, cried, made love; now we sailed down the web—together.

The Eternal Second, space spread out within you, galaxies spinning like diadems, beating suns like beating hearts, the itch of nebulas, the sharp tang of holes, the gentle warmth of starwombs.

He was laughing and crying and spilling out delight as sweet as a new opened cupra blossom.

We were two in one, web wrapped around us yet riding down it, an endless tightrope stretched to infinity.

Until we erupted through the terminus, two separate entities again, no longer one. He was still laughing, falling helplessly to a glitterchrome deck, laughing, laughing, *laughing*. I wasn't much abler than he, but I was so furious I leaned over and slapped him so hard the shape of his teeth imprinted on my hand. "Don't you *ever* do that again."

Still laughing, he pulled me down and kissed me, and there it was, in his eyes, that hunger I'd seen in so many others.

So quiet he had stood, politely behind me while I told my tales, patiently listening, never interrupting—behind me so I couldn't see the greedy hunger in his eyes, too.

"You—sneak," I snarled, as soon as he let me go to breathe. "You slithering snake, you—" He laughed, and I understood, all of it. "You set the whole thing up, you planned this from the beginning, you—" His laughter was louder than a world's dying. "You—used—me!" I was really infuriated, which is no way to go on a webride. A puzzled technie was watching us, holding out the canister that would have to go in my thigh.

"You hold on to *that*—" I pointed to Malachi. "And you throw him down to the floor for the trogs to—you put him in the deepest, dryest dungeon hole you have, and don't you—"

"Webrider," he sat up, face still split by that triumphant grin, "you object because I used you to get what I always wanted. But you were willing—not willing—you expected, as a matter of right, to use *me*, or one like me, to be given whatever you wanted, whatever you asked for, just because you're a webrider. And yet you blame *me*, for using you."

I had to see the humor of it. "Is it kinder to pretend," I asked, "to arouse expectations I can't possibly fulfill. Or—do you expect riders to live celibate?"

"Never you," he blinked agreement. "As for expectations—I know the next leg of your trip is too far, too hard for a beginner. But I expect you to come back for me, as soon as you can."

"You conceited—I've had a hundred, more, better than you."

He stood, still shorter than me, still grinning. "You're not my first, either." I held still only because the medico was seaming my thigh. "You'll be back, rider. You see, I know your weakness."

"Do you?" I was already starting my deep breathing again.

"Yes, rider. I know your weakness. If you don't come back, you know I'll follow. And—your weakness—you have a conscience."

Riding angry is a good way to get splattered. I kept up my slow breathing, ran through calming mantras, readying myself. I knew he was right, but I wouldn't tell him so. Let him sweat—he wasn't all *that* sure, under his camouflage of certitude—for a while.

But I'd be back, not just because of any outmoded nonsense of conscience—though that was there, Blight take him!
—but because the web *owed* him now.

There had never been a successful paired ride before.
Never. So paired rides had been forbidden. Then why had we
succeeded now—had we simply that much more skill at
riding?

Or—could it be as simple as a strong bonded *mixed* pair
was necessary to balance on the web? In early days, riders
shared their homeworld prejudices. We have forgotten today
that different once meant despicable, that pariah—the womb-
shippers, those condemned to the slow death of space to help
hold the worlds together—was a term of contempt. In the
early days of the web, before Abednego Jones and the great
joining, paired riders would have been from a single world;
or worse, from different worlds, but assigned together, against
their own deepest inclinations, the prejudices there, at best
lightly concealed. Could it be that now, with prejudices
mostly forgotten with time, that all it took was a strong
bonding of unlikes?

And could it be—a novice bonded to an adept—must we
always and forever pay ninety-nine prices for the one?

Groupies had been kept fanatically away from riders up to
now. Speaking, light contact if it couldn't be avoided, but
never closeness. I wasn't the only rider with a conscience,
who couldn't bear to see someone he/she had been close to,
splatter. . . .

Now Malachi had proved it could be done. So—let the
groupies have their way, let them pair, emotionally, physically, however they could with an experienced rider. Maybe. . . .

Could we end that constant loneliness, the scourge of
riding. I'd felt it, marrow-deep, blade-sharp, until the temptation comes, the one last glorious ride, to the ends of the
universe and beyond . . . the infinite Eternal Second . . .
ending in death. . . .

I risked one look back before I stepped into the terminus.
He was surrounded by guards in moss-green but he was
smiling. . . .

He was right.

I'd be back.

For the next-to-the-last time, I rode the web—alone.

WITH VIRGIL ODDUM AT THE EAST POLE

by Harlan Ellison

Harlan Ellison has won enough Hugos to make a picket fence. Masterminding the revival of The Twilight Zone *TV series is an instance of his wider approach to the imagination. Though many of his more recent stories are fantastic, they are rarely hard-core science fiction. This story, one of the keystones of his experimental book* Medea, *is an exception—an interplanetary of high caliber.*

Dedicated to the genius of Sabotini Rodia

The day he crawled out of the dead cold Icelands, the glaciers creeping down the great cliff were sea-green: endless rivers of tinted, faceted emeralds lit from within. Memories of crippled chances shone in the ice. That was a day, and I remember this clearly, during which the purple sky of Hotlands was filled with the downdrifting balloon spores that had died rushing through the beams of the UV lamps in the peanut fields of the silver crescent. That was a day—remembering clearly—with Argo squatting on the horizon of Hotlands, an enormous inverted tureen of ruby glass.

He crawled toward me and the ancient fux I called Amos the Wise; crawled, literally crawled, up the land bridge of Westspit onto Meditation Island. Through the slush and sludge and amber mud of the Terminator's largest island.

His heat-envelope was filthy and already cracking, and he tore open the velcro mouthflap without regard for saving the garment as he crawled toward a rotting clump of spillweed.

When I realized that he intended to *eat* it, I moved to him quickly and crouched in front of him so he couldn't get to it.

"I wouldn't put that in your mouth," I said. "It'll kill you."

He didn't say anything, but he looked up at me from down there on his hands and knees with an expression that said it all. He was starving, and if I didn't come up with some immediate alternative to the spillweed, he was going to eat it anyhow, even if it killed him.

This was only one hundred and nineteen years after we had brought the wonders of the human race to Medea, and though I was serving a term of penitence on Meditation Island, I wasn't so sure I wanted to make friends with another human being. I was having a hard enough time just communicating with fuxes. I certainly didn't want to take charge of his life . . . even in as small a way as being responsible for saving it.

Funny the things that flash through your mind. I remember at that moment, with him looking at me so desperately, recalling a cartoon I'd once seen: it was one of those standard thirsty-man-crawling-out-of-the-desert cartoons, with a long line of crawl-marks stretching to the horizon behind an emaciated, bearded wanderer. And in the foreground is a man on a horse, looking down at this poor dying devil with one clawed hand lifted in a begging gesture, and the guy on the horse is smiling and saying to the thirsty man, "Peanut butter sandwich?"

I didn't think he'd find it too funny.

So I pulled up the spillweed, so he wouldn't go for it before I got back, and I trotted over to my wickyup and got him a ball of peanut cheese and a nip-off bulb of water, and came back and helped him sit up to eat.

It took him a while, and of course we were covered with pink and white spores by the time he finished. The smell was awful.

I helped him to his feet. Pretty unsteady. And he leaned on me walking back to the wickyup. I laid him down on my air-mattress and he closed his eyes and fell asleep immediately. Maybe he fainted, I don't know.

His name was Virgil Oddum; but I didn't know that, either, at the time.

I didn't ever know much about him. Not then, not later, not even now. It's funny how everybody knows *what* he did, but not why he did it, or even who he was; and until recently, not so much as his name, nothing.

In a way, I really resent it. The only reason anybody knows me is because I knew him, Virgil Oddum. But they don't care about me or what I was going through, just him, because of what he did. My name is Pogue. William Ronald Pogue, like *rogue*; and I'm important, too. You should know names.

Jason was chasing Theseus through the twilight sky directly over the Terminator when he woke up. The clouds of dead balloon spores had passed over and the sky was amber again, with bands of color washing across the bulk of Argo. I was trying to talk with Amos the Wise.

I was usually trying to talk with Amos the Wise.

The xenoanthropologists at the main station at Perdue Farm in the silver crescent call communication with the fuxes *ekstasis*—literally, "to stand outside oneself." A kind of enriched empathy that conveys concepts and emotional sets, but nothing like words or pictures. I would sit and stare at one of the fuxes, and he would crouch there on his hindquarters and stare back at me; and we'd both fill up with what the other was thinking. Sort of. More or less overcome with vague feelings, general tones of emotion . . . memories of when the fux had been a hunter; when he had had the extra hindquarters he'd dropped when he was female; the vision of a kilometer-high tidal wave once seen near the Seven Pillars on the Ring; chasing females and endlessly mating. It was all there, every moment of what was a long life for a fux: fifteen Medean years.

But it was all flat. Like a drama done with enormous expertise and no soul. The arrangement of thoughts was random, without continuity, without flow. There was no color, no interpretation, no sense of what it all meant for the dromids.

It was artless and graceless; it was merely data.

And so, trying to "talk" to Amos was like trying to get a computer to create original, deeply meaningful poetry. Sometimes I had the feeling he had been "assigned" to me, to humor me; to keep me busy.

At the moment the man came out of my wickyup, I was trying to get Amos to codify the visual nature of the fuxes' religious relationship to Caster C, the binary star that Amos and his race thought of as Maternal Grandfather and Paternal Grandfather. For the human colony they were Phrixus and Helle.

I was trying to get Amos to understand flow and the emotional load in changing colors when the double shadow fell between us and I looked up to see the man standing behind me. At the same moment I felt a lessening of the ekstasis between the fux and me. As though some other receiving station were leaching off power.

The man stood there, unsteadily, weaving and trying to keep his balance, staring at Amos. The fux was staring back. They were communicating, but what was passing between them I didn't know. Then Amos got up and walked away, with that liquid rolling gait old male fuxes affect after they've dropped their hindquarters. I got up with some difficulty: since coming to Medea I'd developed mild arthritis in my knees, and sitting cross-legged stiffened me.

As I stood up, he started to fall over, still too weak from crawling out of Icelands. He fell into my arms, and I confess my first thought was annoyance because now I *knew* he'd be another thing I'd have to worry about.

"Hey, hey," I said, "take it easy."

I helped him to the wickyup, and put him on his back on the air-mattress. "Listen, fellah," I said, "I don't want to be cold about this, but I'm out here all alone, paying my time. I don't get another shipment of rations for about four months and I can't keep you here."

He didn't say anything. Just stared at me.

"Who the hell are you? Where'd you come from?"

Watching me. I used to be able to read expression very accurately. Watching me, with hatred.

I didn't even know him. He didn't have any idea what was what, why I was out there on Meditation Island; there wasn't any reason he should hate me.

"How'd you get here?"

Watching. Not a word out of him.

"Listen, mister: here's the long and short of it. There isn't any way I can get in touch with anybody to come and get you. And I can't keep you here because there just isn't enough ration. And I'm not going to let you stay here and starve in front of me, because after a while you're sure as hell going to go for my food and I'm going to fight you for it, and one of us is going to get killed. And I am not about to have that kind of a situation, understand? Now I know this is chill, but you've got to go. Take a few days, get some strength. If you hike straight across Eastspit and keep going through Hotlands, you might get spotted by someone out spraying the fields. I doubt it, but maybe.''

Not a sound. Just watching me and hating me.

"Where'd you come from? Not out there in Icelands. Nothing can live out there. It's minus thirty Celsius. Out there." Silence. "Just glaciers. Out there."

Silence. I felt that uncontrollable anger rising in me.

"Look, jamook, I'm not having this. Understand me? I'm just not having any of it. You've got to go. I don't give a damn if you're the Count of Monte Crespo or the lost Dauphin of Threx: you're getting the hell out of here as soon as you can crawl." He stared up at me and I wanted to hit the bastard as hard as I could. I had to control myself. This was the kind of thing that had driven me to Meditation Island.

Instead, I squatted there watching him for a long time. He never blinked. Just watched me. Finally, I said, very softly, "What'd you say to the fux?"

A double shadow fell through the door and I looked up. It was Amos the Wise. He'd peeled back the entrance flap with his tail because his hands were full. Impaled on the three long, sinewy fingers of each hand were six freshly caught dartfish. He stood there in the doorway, bloody light from the sky forming a corona that lit his blue, furry shape; and he extended the skewered fish.

I'd been six months on Meditation Island. Every day of that time I'd tried to spear a dartfish. Flashfreeze and peanut cheese and box-ration, they can pall on you pretty fast. You want to gag at the sight of silvr wrap. I'd wanted fresh food. Every day for six months I'd tried to catch something live. They were too fast. That's why they weren't called slowfish. The fuxes had watched me. Not one had ever moved to show me how they did it. Now this old neuter Amos was offering me half a dozen. I knew what the guy had said to him.

"Who the hell are you?" I was about as skewed as I could be. I wanted to pound him out a little, delete that hateful look on his face, put him in a way so I wouldn't have to care for him. He didn't say a word, just kept looking at me; but the fux came inside the wickyup—first time he'd ever done *that*, damn his slanty eyes!—and he moved around between us, the dartfish extended.

This guy had some kind of *hold* over the aborigine! He didn't say a thing, but the fux knew enough to get between us and insist I take the fish. So I did it, cursing both of them under my breath.

As I pried off the six dartfish I felt the old fux pull me into a flow with him. Stronger than I'd ever been able to do it when we'd done ekstasis. Amos the Wise let me know this was a very holy creature, this thing that had crawled out of the Icelands, and I'd better treat him pretty fine, or else. There wasn't even a hint of a picture of what *or else* might be, but it was a strong flow, a *strong* flow.

So I took the fish and put them in the larder, and I let the fux know how grateful I was, and he didn't pay me enough attention to mesmerize a gnat; and the flow was gone; and he was doing ekstasis with my guest lying out as nice and comfy as you please; and then he turned and slid out of the wickyup and was gone.

I sat there through most of the night watching him. One moment he was staring at me, the next he was asleep; and I went on through that first night just sitting there looking at him gonked-in like that, where I would have been sleeping if he hadn't showed up. Even asleep he hated me. But he was too weak to stay awake and enjoy it.

So I looked at him, wondering who the hell he was, most of that night. Until I couldn't take it anymore, and near to morning I just beat the crap out of him.

They kept bringing food. Not just fish, but plants I'd never seen before, things that grew out there in Hotlands east of us, out there where it always stank like rotting garbage. Some of the plants needed to be cooked, and some of them were delicious just eaten raw. But I knew they'd never have shown me *any* of that if it hadn't been for him.

He never spoke to me, and he never told the fuxes that I'd beaten him the first night he was in camp; and his manner never changed. Oh, I knew he could talk all right, because when he slept he tossed and thrashed and shouted things in his sleep. I never understood any of it; some offworld language. But whatever it was, it made him feel sick to remember it. Even asleep he was in torment.

He was determined to stay. I knew that from the second day. I caught him pilfering stores.

No, that's not accurate. He was doing it openly. I didn't catch him. He was going through the stash in the transport sheds: mostly goods I wouldn't need for a while yet; items whose functions no longer related to my needs. He had already liberated some of those items when I discovered him burrowing through the stores: the neetskin tent I'd used before building the wickyup from storm-hewn fellner trees; the spare air-mattress; a hologram projector I'd used during the first month to keep me entertained with a selection of laser beads, mostly Nōh plays and conundramas. I'd grown bored with the diversions very quickly: they didn't seem to be a part of my life of penitence. He had commandeered the projector, but not the beads. Everything had been pulled out and stacked.

"What do you think you're doing?" I stood behind him, fists knotted, waiting for him to say something snappy.

He straightened with some difficulty, holding his ribs where I'd kicked him the night before. He turned and looked at me evenly. I was surprised: he didn't seem to hate me as much as he'd let it show the day before. He wasn't afraid of me, though I was larger and had already demonstrated that I could bash him if I wanted to bash him, or leave him alone if I chose to leave him alone. He just stared, waiting for me to get the message.

The message was that he was here for a while.

Like it or not.

"Just stay out of my way," I said. "I don't like you, and that's not going to change. I made a mistake pulling that spillweed, but I won't make any more mistakes. Keep out of my food stores, keep away from me, and don't get between me and the dromids. I've got a job to do, and you interfere . . . I'll weight you down, toss you in, and what the scuttlefish don't chew off is going to wash up at Icebox. You got that?"

I was just shooting off my mouth. And what was worse than my indulging in the same irrational behavior that had already ruined my life, was that he knew I was just making a breeze. He looked at me, waited long enough so I couldn't pretend to have had my dignity scarred, and he went back to searching through the junk. I went off looking for fuxes to interrogate, but they were avoiding us that day.

By that night he'd already set up his own residence.

And the next day Amos delivered two females to me, who unhinged themselves on their eight legs in a manner that was almost sitting. And the old neuter let me know these two—he used an ekstasis image that conveyed *nubile*—would join flow with me in an effort to explain their relationship to Maternal Grandfather. It was the first voluntary act of assistance the tribe had offered in six months.

So I knew my unwelcome guest was paying for his sparse accommodations.

And later that day I found wedged into one of the extensible struts I'd used in building the wickyup, the thorny branch of an emeraldberry bush. It was festooned with fruit. Where the aborigines had found it, out there in that shattered terrain, I don't know. The berries were going bad, but I pulled them off greedily, nicking my hands on the thorns, and squeezed their sea-green juice into my mouth.

So I knew my unwelcome guest was paying for his sparse accommodations.

And we went on that way, with him lurking about and sitting talking to Amos and his tribe for hours on end, and me stumping about trying to play Laird of the Manor and getting almost nowhere trying to impart philosophical concepts to a race of creatures that listened attentively and then gave me the distinct impression that I was retarded because I didn't understand Maternal Grandfather's hungers.

Then one day he was gone. It was early in the crossover season and the hard winds were rising from off the Hotlands. I came out of the wickyup and knew I was alone. But I went to his tent and looked inside. It was empty, as I'd expected it to be. On a rise nearby, two male fuxes and an old neuter were busy patting the ground, and I strolled to them and asked where the other man was. The hunters refused to join flow with me, and continued patting the ground in some sort of ritual. The old fux scratched at his deep blue fur and told me the holy creature had gone off into the Icelands. Again.

I walked to the edge of Westspit and stared off toward the glacial wasteland. It was warmer now, but that was pure desolation out there. I could see faint trails made by his skids, but I wasn't inclined to go after him. If he wanted to kill himself, that was his business.

I felt an irrational sense of loss.

It lasted about thirty seconds; then I smiled; and went back to the old fux and tried to start up a conversation.

Eight days later the man was back.

Now he was starting to scare me.

He'd patched the heat-envelope. It was still cracked and looked on the edge of unserviceability, but he came striding out of the distance with a strong motion, the skids on his boots carrying him boldly forward till he hit the mush. Then he bent and, almost without breaking stride, pulled them off, and kept coming. Straight in toward the base camp, up Westspit. His cowl was thrown back, and he was breathing deeply, not even exerting himself much, his long, horsey face flushed from his journey. He had nearly two weeks' growth of beard and so help me he looked like one of those soldiers of fortune you see smoking clay pipes and swilling up boar piss in the spacer bars around Port Medea. Heroic. An adventurer.

He sloughed in through the mud and the suckholes filled with sargasso, and he walked straight past me to his tent and went inside, and I didn't see him for the rest of the day. But that night, as I sat outside the wickyup, letting the hard wind tell me odor tales of the Hotlands close to Argo at the top of the world, I saw Amos the Wise and two other old dromids come over the rise and go down to his tent; and I stared at them until the heroic adventurer came out and squatted with them in a circle.

They didn't move, they didn't gesticulate, they didn't do a goddamned thing; they just joined flow and passed around the impressions like a vonge-coterie passing its dream-pipe.

And the next morning I was wakened by the sound of clattering, threw on my envelope and came out to see him snapping together the segments of a jerry-rigged sledge of some kind. He'd cannibalized boot skids and tray shelves from the transport sheds and every last one of those lash-up spiders the lading crews use to tighten down cargo. It was an ugly, rickety thing, but it looked as if it would slide across ice once he was out of the mush.

Then it dawned on me he was planning to take all that out there into the Icelands. "Hold it, mister," I said. He didn't stop working. I strode over and gave him a kick in the hip. "I said: hold it!"

With his right hand he reached out, grabbed my left ankle, and *lifted*. I half-turned, found myself off the ground, and when I looked up I was two meters away, the breath pulled out of me; on my back. He was still working, his back to me.

I got up and ran at him. I don't recall seeing him look up, but he must have, otherwise how could he have gauged my trajectory?

When I stopped gasping and spitting out dirt, I tried to turn over and sit up, but there was a foot in my back. I thought it was him, but when the pressure eased and I could look over my shoulder I saw the blue-furred shape of a hunter fux standing there, a spear in his sinewy left hand. It wasn't aimed at me, but it was held away in a direct line that led back to aiming at me. Don't mess with the holy man, that was the message.

An hour later he pulled the sledge with three spiders wrapped around his chest and dragged it off behind him, down the land-bridge and out into the mush. He was leaning forward, straining to keep the travois from sinking into the porridge till he could hit firmer ice. He was one of those old holograms you see of a coolie in the fields, pulling a plow by straps attached to a leather band around his head.

He went away and I wasn't stupid enough to think he was going for good and all. That was an *empty* sledge.

What would be on it when he came back?

It was a thick, segmented tube a meter and a half long. He'd chipped away most of the ice in which it had lain for twenty years, and I knew what it was, and where it had come from, which was more than I could say about him.

It was a core laser off the downed Daedalus power satellite whose orbit had decayed inexplicably two years after the Northcape Power District had tossed the satellite up. It had been designed to calve into bergs the glaciers that had gotten too close to coastal settlements; and then melt them. It had gone down in the Icelands of Phykos, somewhere between the East Pole and Icebox, almost exactly two decades ago. I'd flown over it when they'd hauled me in from Enrique and the bush pilot decided to give me a little scenic tour. We'd looked down on the wreckage, now part of a complex ice sculpture molded by wind and storm.

And this nameless skujge who'd invaded my privacy had gone out there, somehow chonked loose the beamer—and its power collector, if I was right about the fat package at the end of the tube—and dragged it back who knows how many kilometers . . . for why?

Two hours later I found him down one of the access hatches that led to the base camp's power station, a fusion plant, deuterium source; a tank that had to be replenished every sixteen months: I didn't have a refinery.

He was examining the power beamers that supplied heat and electricity to the camp. I couldn't figure out what he was trying to do, but I got skewed over it and yelled at him to get his carcass out of there before we both froze to death because of his stupidity.

After a while he came up and sealed the hatch and went off to tinker with his junk laser.

I tried to stay away from him in the weeks that followed. He worked over the laser, stealing bits and pieces of anything nonessential that he could find around the camp. It became obvious that though the lacy solar-collector screens had slowed the *Daedalus*'s fall as they'd been burned off, not even that had saved the beamer from serious damage. I had no idea why he was tinkering with it, but I fantasized that if he could get it working he might go off and not come back.

And that would leave me right where I'd started, alone with creatures who did not paint pictures or sing songs or devise dances or make idols; to whom the concept of art was unknown; who responded to my attempts to communicate on an esthetic level with the stolid indifference of grandchildren forced to humor a batty old aunt.

It was penitence indeed.

Then one day he was finished. He loaded it all on the sledge—the laser, some kind of makeshift energy receiver package he'd mated to the original tube, my hologram projector, and spider straps and harnesses, and a strut tripod— and he crawled down into the access hatch and stayed there for an hour. When he came back out he spoke to Amos, who had arrived as if silently summoned, and when he was done talking to him he got into his coolie rig and slowly dragged it all away. I started to follow, just to see where he was going, but Amos stopped me. He stepped in front of me and he had ekstasis with me and I was advised not to annoy the holy man and not to bother the new connections that had been made in the camp's power source.

None of that was said, of course. It was all vague feelings and imperfect images. Hunches, impressions, thin sugges- tions, intuitive urgings. But I got the message. I was all alone on Meditation Island, there by sufferance of the dromids. As long as I did not interfere with the holy adventurer who had come out of nowhere to fill me with the rage I'd fled across the stars to escape.

So I turned away from the Icelands, good riddance, and tried to make some sense out of the uselessness of my life. Whoever he had been, I knew he wasn't coming back, and I hated him for making me understand what a waste of time I was.

That night I had a frustrating conversation with a turquoise fux in its female mode. The next day I shaved off my beard and thought about going back.

He came and went eleven times in the next two years. Where and how he lived out there, I never knew. And each time he came back he looked thinner, wearier, but more ecstatic. As if he had found God out there. During the first year the fuxes began making the trek: out there in the shad- owed vastness of the Icelands they would travel to see him. They would be gone for days and then return to speak among themselves. I asked Amos what they did when they made their hegira, and he said, though ekstasis, "He must live, is that not so?" To which I responded, "I suppose so," though I wanted to say, "Not necessarily."

He returned once to obtain a new heat-envelope. I'd had supplies dropped in, and they'd sent me a latest model, so I didn't object when he took my old suit.

He returned once for the death ceremony of Amos the Wise, and seemed to be leading the service. I stood there in the circle and said nothing, because no one asked me to contribute.

He returned once to check the fusion plant connections.

But after two years he didn't return again.

And now the dromids were coming from what must have been far distances, to trek across Meditation Island, off the land-bridge, and into the Icelands. By the hundreds and finally thousands they came, passed me, and vanished into the eternal winterland. Until the day a group of them came to me; and their leader, whose name was Ben of Old Times, joined with me in the flow and said, "Come with us to the holy man." They'd always stopped me when I tried to go out there.

"Why? Why do you want me to go now? You never wanted me out there before." I could feel the acid boiling up in my anger, the tightening of my chest muscles, the clenching of my fists. They could burn in Argo before I'd visit that lousy skujge!

Then the old fux did something that astonished me. In three years they had done *nothing* astonishing except bring me food at the man's request. But now the aborigine extended a slim-fingered hand to his right; and one of the males, a big hunter with bright-blue fur, passed him his spear. Ben of the Old Times pointed it at the ground and, with a very few strokes, *drew two figures in the caked mud at my feet.*

It was a drawing of two humans standing side-by side, their hands linked. One of them had lines radiating out from his head, and above the figures the dromid drew a circle with comparable lines radiating outward.

It was the first piece of intentional art I had ever seen created by a Medean life form. The first, as far as I knew, that had ever *been* created by a native. And it had happened as I watched. My heart beat faster. I *had* done it! I had brought the concept of art to at least one of these creatures.

"I'll come with you to see him," I said.

Perhaps my time in purgatory was coming to an end. It was possible I'd bought some measure of redemption.

I checked the fusion plant that beamed energy to my heat-envelope, to keep me from freezing; and I got out my boot skids and Ba'al ice-claw; and I racked the ration dispenser in my pack full of silvr wrap; and I followed them out there. Where I had not been permitted to venture, lest I interfere with their holy man. Well, we'd see who was the more important of us two: a nameless intruder who came and went without ever a thank you, or William Ronald Pogue, the man who brought art to the Medeans!

For the first time in many years I felt light, airy, worthy. I'd sprayed fixative on that pictograph in the mud. It might be the most valuable exhibit in the Pogue Museum of Native Art. I chuckled at my foolishness, and followed the small band of fuxes deeper into the Icelands.

It was close on crossback season, and the winds were getting harder, the storms were getting nastier. Not as impossible as it would be a month hence, but bad enough.

We were beyond the first glacier that could be seen from Meditation Island, the spine of ice cartographers had named the Seurat. Now we were climbing through the NoName Cleft, the fuxes chinking out hand- and footholds with spears and claws, the Ba'al snarling and chewing pits for my own ascent. Green shadows swam down through the Cleft. One moment we were pulling ourselves up through twilight, and the next we could not see the shape before us. For an hour we lay flat against the ice-face as an hysterical wind raged down the Cleft, trying to tear us loose and fling us into the cut below.

The double shadows flickered and danced around us. Then everything went into the red, the wind died, and through now-bloody shadows we reached the crest of the ridge beyond the Seurats.

A long slope lay before us, rolling to a plain of ice and slush pools, very different from the fields of dry ice that lay farther west to the lifeless expanse of Farside. Sunday was rapidly moving into Darkday.

Across the plain, vision was impeded by a great wall of frigid fog that rose off the tundra. Vaguely, through the miasma, I could see the great glimmering bulk of the Rio de Luz, the immense kilometers-long ice mountain that was the final barrier between the Terminator lands and the frozen nothingness of Farside. The River of Light.

We hurried down the slope, some of the fuxes simply tucking two, four, or six of their legs under them and sliding down the expanse to the plain. Twice I fell, rolled, slid on my butt, tried to regain my feet, tumbled again and decided to use my pack as a toboggan. By the time we had gained the plain, it was nearly Darkday and fog had obscured the land.

We decided to camp till Dimday, hacked out sleeping pits in the tundra, and buried ourselves.

Overhead the raging aurora drained red and green and purple as I closed my eyes and let the heat of the envelope take me away. What could the "holy man" want from me after all this time?

We came through the curtain of fog, the Rio de Luz scintillating dimly beyond its mask of gray-green vapor. I estimated that we had come more than thirty kilometers from Meditation Island. It was appreciably colder now, and ice crystals glimmered like rubies and emeralds in the blue fux fur. And, oddly, a kind of breathless anticipation had come over the aborigines. They moved more rapidly, oblivious to the razor winds and the slush pools underfoot. They jostled one another in their need to go toward the River of Light and whatever the man out there needed me to assist with.

It was a long walk, and for much of that time I could see little more of the icewall than its cruel shape rising at least fifteen hundred meters above the tundra. But as the fog thinned, the closer we drew to the base of the ice mountain, the more I had to avert my eyes from what lay ahead: the permanent aurora lit the ice and threw off a coruscating glare that was impossible to bear.

And then the fuxes dashed on ahead and I was left alone, striding across the tundra toward the Rio de Luz.

I came out of the fog.

And I looked up and up at what rose above me, touching the angry sky and stretching as far away as I could see to left and right. It seemed hundreds of kilometers in length, but that was impossible.

I heard myself moaning.

But I could not look away, even if it burned out my eyes.

Lit by the ever-changing curtain of Medea's sky, the crash and downdripping of a thousand colors that washed the ice in patterns that altered from instant to instant, the Rio de Luz had been transformed. The man had spent three years melting and slicing and sculpting—I couldn't tell how many—kilometers of living ice into a work of high art.

Horses of liquid blood raced through valleys of silver light. The stars were born and breathed and died in one lacy spire. Shards of amber brilliance shattered against a diamond-faceted icewall through a thousand apertures cut in the facing column. Fairy towers too thin to exist rose from a shadowed hollow and changed color from meter to meter all up their length. Legions of rainbows rushed from peak to peak, like waterfalls of precious gems. Shapes and forms and spaces merged and grew and vanished as the eye was drawn on and on. In a cleft he had formed an intaglio that was black and ominous as the specter of death. But when light hit it suddenly, shattering and spilling down into the bowl beneath, it became a great bird of golden promise. And the sky was there, too. All of it, reflected back and new because it had been pulled down and captured. Argo and the far suns and Phrixus and Helle and Jason and Theseus and memories of suns that had dominated the empty places and were no longer even memories. I had a dream of times past as I stared at one pool of changing colors that bubbled and sang. My heart was filled with feelings I had not known since childhood. And it never stopped. The pinpoints of bright blue flame skittered across the undulating walls of sculpted ice, rushed toward certain destruction in the deeps of a runoff cut, paused momentarily at the brink, then flung themselves into green oblivion. I heard myself moaning and turned away, looking back toward the ridge across the fog and tundra; and I saw nothing, nothing! It was too painful not to see what he had done. I felt my throat tighten with fear of missing a moment of that great pageant unfolding on the ice tapestry. I turned back and it was all new, I was seeing it first and always as I had just minutes before . . . was it minutes . . . how long had I been staring into that dream pool . . . how many years had passed . . . and would I be fortunate enough to spend the remainder of my life just standing there breathing in the rampaging beauty I beheld? I couldn't think, pulled air into my lungs only when I had forgotten to breathe for too long a time.

Then I felt myself being pulled along and cried out against whatever force had me in its grip that would deprive me of a second of that towering narcotic.

But I was pulled away, and was brought down to the base of the River of Light, and it was Ben of the Old Times who had me. He forced me to sit, with my back to the mountain, and after a very long time in which I sobbed and fought for air, I was able to understand that I had almost been lost, that the dreamplace had taken me. But I felt no gratitude. My soul ached to rush out and stare up at beauty forever.

The fux flowed with me, and through ekstasis I felt myself ceasing to pitch and yaw. The colors dimmed in the grottos behind my eyes. He held me silently with a powerful flow until I was William Pogue again. Not just an instrument through which the ice mountain sang its song, but Pogue, once again Pogue.

And I looked up, and I saw the fuxes hunkered around the body of their "holy man," and they were making drawings in the ice with their claws. And I knew it was not I who had brought them to beauty.

He lay face-down on the ice, one hand still touching the laser tube. The hologram projector had been attached with a slipcard computer. Still glowing was an image of the total sculpture. Almost all of it was in red lines, flickering and fading and coming back in with power being fed from base camp; but one small section near the top of an impossibly-angled flying bridge and minaret section was in blue line.

I stared at it for a while. Then Ben said this was the reason I had been brought to that place. The holy man had died before he could complete the dreamplace. And in a rush of flow he showed me where, in the sculpture, they had first understood what beauty was, and what art was, and how they were one with the Grandparents in the sky. Then he created a clear, pure image. It was the man, flying to become one with Argo. It was the stick figure in the mud: it was the uninvited guest with the lines of radiance coming out of his head.

There was a pleading tone in the fux's ekstasis. Do this for us. Do what he did not have the time to do. Make it complete.

I stared at the laser lying there, with its unfinished hologram image blue and red and flickering. It was a bulky, heavy tube, a meter and a half long. And it was still on. He had fallen in the act.

I watched them scratching their first drawings, even the least of them, and I wept within myself; for Pogue who had come as far as he could, only to discover it was not far enough. And I hated him for doing what I could not do. And I knew he would have completed it and then walked off into the emptiness of Farside, to die quickly in the darkness, having done his penance . . . and more.

They stopped scratching, as if Ben had ordered them to pay

some belated attention to me. They looked at me with their
slanted vulpine eyes now filling with mischief and wonder. I
stared back at them. Why should I? Why the hell should I?
For what? Not for me, that's certain!

We sat there close and apart, for a long time, as the
universe sent its best light to pay homage to the dreamplace.

The body of the penitent lay at my feet.

From time to time I scuffed at the harness that would hold
the laser in position for cutting. There was blood on the
shoulder straps.

After a while I stood up and lifted the rig. It was much
heavier than I'd expected.

Now they come from everywhere to see it. Now they call it
Oddum's Tapestry, not the Rio de Luz. Now everyone speaks
of the magic. A long time ago he may have caused the death
of thousands in another place, but they say that wasn't intentional; what he brought to the Medeans was on purpose. So
it's probably right that everyone knows the name Virgil Oddum,
and what he created at the East Pole.

But they should know me, too. I was there! I did some of
the work.

My name is William Ronald Pogue, and I mattered. I'm
old, but I'm important, too. You should know names.

THE CURSE OF KINGS
by Connie Willis

The science of xeno-archaeology does not exist, primarily because there is simply at this time nothing to work on. That it will come into existence during the centuries to come is assured once we encounter evidence of intelligent life elsewhere in our galaxy. This remarkable and moving story is based upon such a premise—a new-found world with a history and a continuing society. How will the explorers from Earth, with our experience of our own past glories, handle something of that sort?

There was a curse. It lay on all of us, though we didn't know it. Anyway Lacau didn't. Standing there, reading the tomb seal out loud to me in my cage, he didn't have a clue who the warning was meant for. And the Sandalman, standing on the black ridge watching the bodies burn, had no idea he had already fallen victim to it.

The princess knew, leaning her head in hopelessness against the wall of her tomb ten thousand years ago. And Evelyn, eaten alive by it, she knew. She tried to tell me that last night on Colchis while we waited for this ship.

The electricity was off again, and Lacau had lit a photosene lamp and put it close to the translator so I could see the dials. Evelyn's voice had gotten so bad that the fix needed constant adjusting. The lamp's flame lit only the space around me. Lacau, bending over the hammock, was in total darkness.

Evelyn's bey sat by the lamp, watching the reddish flame, her mouth open and her black teeth shining in the light. I expected her to stick her hand in the flame any minute, but she didn't. The air was still and full of dust. The lamp flame didn't even flicker.

"Evie," Lacau said. "We don't have any time left. The Sandalman's soldiers will be here before morning. They'll never let us leave."

Evelyn said something, but the translator didn't pick it up.

"Move the mike closer," I said. "I didn't get that."

"Evie," he said again. "We need you to tell us what happened. Can you do that for us, Evie? Tell us what happened?"

She tried again. I had the volume dial kicked as high as it would go, and the translator picked it up this time, but only as static. Evelyn started to cough, a sharp, terrible sound that the translator turned into a scream.

"For God's sake, put her on the respirator," I said.

"I can't," he said. "The power pack is dead." And the other respirator has to be plugged in, I thought, and you've used up all the extension cords. But I didn't say it. Because if he put her on the respirator, he would have to unplug the refrigerator.

"Then get her a drink of water," I said.

He took the Coke bottle off the create by the hammock, put the straw in it, and leaned into the darkness to tilt Evelyn's head forward so she could drink. I turned the translator off. It was bad enough listening to her try to talk. I didn't think I could stand listening to her try to drink.

After what seemed like an hour, he set the Coke bottle down on the crate again. "Evelyn," he said. "Try to tell us what happened. Did you go in the tomb?"

I switched the translator back on and kept my finger ready on the record button. There was no point in recording the tortured sounds she was making.

"Curse," Evelyn said clearly, and I pushed the button down. "Don't open it. Don't open it." She stopped and tried to swallow. "Wuhdayuh?"

"What day is it?" the translator said.

She tried to swallow again, and Lacau reached for the

Coke bottle, pulled the straw out, and handed it to the bey. "Go get some more water." The little bey stood up, her black eyes still fixed on the flame, and took the bottle. "Hurry," Lacau said.

"Hurry," Evelyn said. "Before bey."

"Did you open the tomb when the bey went to get the Sandalman?"

"Oh, don't open it. Don't open it. Sorry. Didn't know."

"Didn't know what, Evelyn?" Lacau said.

The bey was still staring, fascinated, at the flame, her mouth open so that I could see her shiny black teeth. I looked at the thick green bottle she was holding in her dirty-looking hands. The straw in it was glass, too, thick and uneven and full of bubbles, probably made out at the bottling plant. Its sides were scored with long scratches. Evelyn had made those scratches when she sucked the water up through the straw. One more day and she'll have it cut to ribbons, I thought, and then remembered we didn't have one more day. Not unless Evelyn's bey suddenly pitched forward into the red flame, honeycombs sharpening on her dirty brown skin, inside her throat, inside her lungs.

"Hurry," Evelyn said into the hypnotic silence, and the little bey looked over at the hammock as if she had just woken up and hurried out of the room with the Coke bottle. "Hurry. What day is it? Have to save the treasure. He'll murder her."

"Who, Evelyn? Who'll murder her? Who will he murder?"

"We shouldn't have gone in," she said, and let her breath out in a sigh that sounded like sand scratching on glass. "Beware. Curse of kings."

"She's quoting what was on the door seal," Lacau said. He straightened up. "They did go in the tomb," he said. "I suppose you got that on your recorder."

"No," I said, and pushed "erase." "She still isn't down from the dilaudid. I'll start recording when she starts making sense."

"The Commission would have found for the Sandalman," Lacau said. "Howard swore they didn't go in, that they waited for the Sandalman."

"What difference does it make?" I said. "Evelyn won't be alive to testify at any Commission hearing and neither will we

if the Sandalman and his soldiers get here before the ship, so
what the hell difference does it make? There won't be any
treasure left either after the Commission gets through, so why
are we making this damned recording? By the time the Commission hears it, it'll be too late to save her."

"What if it *was* something in the tomb, after all? What if it
was a virus?"

"It wasn't," I said. "The Sandalman poisoned them. If it
was a virus, then why doesn't the bey have it? She was in the
tomb with them, wasn't she?"

"Hurry," somebody said, and I thought for a minute it
was Evelyn, but it was the bey. She came running into the
room, the Coke bottle splashing water everywhere.

"What is it?" Lacau said. "Is the ship here?"

She yanked at his hand. "Hurry," she said, and dragged
him down the long hall of packing crates.

"Hurry," Evelyn said softly, like an echo, and I got up
and went over to the hammock. I could hardly see her, which
made it a little easier. I unclenched my fists and said, "It's
me, Evelyn. It's Jack."

"Jack," she said. I could hardly hear her. Lacau had
clipped the mike to the plastic mesh that was pulled up to her
neck, but she was fading fast and starting to wheeze again.
She needed a shot of the morphate. It would ease her breathing, but this soon after the dilaudid it would put her out like a
light.

"I delivered the message to the Sandalman," I said, leaning over to catch what she would say. "What was in the
message, Evelyn?"

"Jack," she said. "What day is it?"

I had to think. It felt like I had been here years. "Wednes-
day," I said.

"Tomorrow," she said. She closed her eyes and seemed to
relax almost into sleep.

I was not going to get anything out of her. I sprayed on
plasticgloves, picked up the injection kit, and broke it open.
The morphate would put her out in minutes, but until then she
would be free from the pain and maybe coherent.

Her arm had fallen over the side of the hammock. I moved
the lamp a little closer and tried to find a place to give the
injection. Her whole arm was covered with a network of
honeycombed white ridges, some of them nearly two centi-

meters high now. They had softened and thickened since the first time I'd seen her. Then they had been thin and razor-sharp. There was no way I was going to be able to find a vein among them, but as I watched, the heat from the photosene flame softened a circle of skin on her forearm, and the five-sided ridges collapsed around it so I could get the hypo in.

I jabbed twice before blood pooled up the soft depression where the needle had gone in. It dripped onto the floor. I looked around, but there was nothing to wipe it up with. Lacau had used the last of the cotton this morning. I took a piece of paper off my notebook and blotted the blood with it.

The bey had come back in. She ducked under my elbow with a piece of plastic mesh held out flat. I folded the paper up and dropped it in the center of the plastic. The bey folded the plastic mesh over it and folded up the ends, making it into a kind of packet, careful not to touch the blood. I stood and looked at it.

"Jack," Evenlyn said. "She was murdered."

"Murdered?" I said and reached over to adjust the fix again. All I got was feedback. "Who was murdered, Evelyn?"

"The princess. They killed her. For the treasure." The morphate was taking effect. I could make her words out easily, though they didn't make sense. Nobody had murdered the princess. She had been dead ten thousand years. I leaned farther over her.

"Tell me what was in the message you gave me to take to the Sandalman, Evelyn," I said.

The lights came on. She put her hand over her face as if to hide it. "Murdered the Sandalman's bey. Had to. To save the treasure."

I looked at the little bey. She was still holding the packet of plastic, turning it over and over in her dirty-looking hands.

"Nobody murdered the bey," I said. "She's right here."

She didn't hear me. The shot was taking effect. Her hand relaxed and then slid down to her breast. Where it had pressed against her forehead and cheek, the fingers had left deep imprints in the wax-soft skin. The pressure of her fingers had flattened the honeycombed ridges at the ends of her fingers and pushed them back so that the ends of her bones were sticking out.

She opened her eyes. "Jack," she said clearly, and her

voice was so hopeless I reached over and turned the translator
off. "Too late."

Lacau pushed past me and lifted up the mesh drape. "What
did she say?" he demanded.

"Nothing," I said, peeling off the plasticgloves and throw-
ing them in the open packing crate we were using for the
things Evelyn had touched. The bey was still playing with the
plastic packet she had wrapped around the blood-soaked paper. I grabbed it away from her and put it in the box. "She's
delirious," I said. "I gave her her shot. Is the ship here?"

"No," he said, "but the Sandalman is."

"Curse," Evelyn said. But I didn't believe her.

I had been burning eight columns about a curse when I
intercepted the message from Lacau. I was halfway across
Colchis's endless desert continent with the Lisii team. I had
run out of stories on the team's incredible find, which con-
sisted of two clay pots and some black bones. Two pots was
more than Howard's team out at the Spine had come up with
in five years, and my hotline had been making noises about
pulling me off on the next circuit ship.

I didn't think they would as long as AP kept Bradstreet on
the planet. When and if anybody found the treasure they were
all looking for, the hotline that had somebody on Colchis
would be the one that got the scoop. And in the meantime
good stories would see to it that I was in the right place at the
right time when the story of the century finally broke, so I'd
hotfooted it up north to cover a two-bit suhundulim massacre
and then out here to Lisii. When the pots gave out I made up
a curse.

It wasn't much of a curse—no murders, no avalanches, no
mysterious fires—but every time somebody sprained an ankle
or got bitten by a kheper, I got at least four columns out of it.

After my first one, headered, "Curse of Kings Strikes Again,"
went out, Howard, over at the Spine, sent me a ground-to-
ground that read, "The curse has to be in the same place as
the treasure, Jackie-boy!"

I burned back, "If the treasure's over there, what am I
doing stuck out here? Find something so I can come back."

I didn't get an answer to that, and the Lisii team didn't
find any more bones, and the curse grew and grew. Six rocks
the size of my thumbnail rattled down a lava slope the Lisii

team had just walked down, and I headered my story, "Mysterious Rockfall Nearly Buries Archaeologists: Is King's Curse Responsible?" and was feeding it into the burner when I heard the sizzle I'd set up to alert me to the consul's transmissions. Hotline reporters weren't supposed to trespass on official transmissions, and Lacau, the consul over at the Spine, had double-cooked his to make sure we didn't, but burners have only so many firelines, and I'd had enough time on Lisii to try them all.

It was a ship-in-area request. He'd put, "Hurry," at the end of it. The circuit ship was only a month away, and he couldn't wait for it. They'd found something.

I burned the rest of my story. Then I hit ground-to-ground and sent Howard a copy of the header with the tag, "Found anything yet?" I didn't get an answer.

I went out and found the team and asked them if there was anything anybody needed from the base camp, one of my shock boards had gone bad and I was going to run in. I made a list of what they wanted, loaded my equipment in the jeep, and took off for the Spine.

I burned stories all the way, sending them ground-to-ground to the relay I kept in my tent back at Lisii, so it would look to Bradstreet like my stories were still coming from there. I had to stop the jeep every time and set up the burn equipment, but I didn't want him heading for the Spine. He was still up north, waiting for another massacre, but he had a Swallow that could get him to the Spine in a day and a half.

So I sent out a story headered, "Khepers Threaten Team's Life—Curse's Agents?" about the tick-like khepers, who sucked the blood out of anybody dumb enough to stick his hand down a hole. Since the Lisii team made their living doing just that, their arms were spotted with white circles of dead skin where the poison had entered their blood. The bites didn't heal, and your blood was toxic for a week or so, which prompted somebody to put up a sign on the barracks that read, "No Nibbling Allowed," with a skull-and-crossbones under it. I didn't say that in my story, of course. I made them out to be agents of the dead curse, wreaking vengeance on whoever dared disturb the sleep of Colchis's ancient kings.

The second day out I intercepted an answer from a ship. It was an Amenti freighter, and it was a long way away, but it was coming. It could make it in a week. Lacau's answer was only one word. "Hurry."

If I was going to beat the ship in, I couldn't waste any more time burning stories. I pulled out some back-up tapes I'd made, deliberately dateless, and sent those: a flattering piece on Lacau, the long-suffering consul who has to keep the peace and divide the treasure, interviews with Howard and Borchardt, a not-so-flattering piece on the local dictator-type, the Sandalman, a recap of the accidental discovery of the ransacked tombs in the Spine that had brought Howard and his gang here in the first place. I was taking a risk doing all these stories on the Spine, but I hoped Bradstreet would check the transmission-point and decide I was trying to throw him off. With luck he'd tear off to Lisii in his damned Swallow, convinced the team had struck pay dirt and I was trying to keep it a secret till I got my scoop.

I skidded into the Sandalman's village six days after I left Lisii. I was still a day and a half from the Spine, but with the ship due in two days they had to be here, where it would land, and not out at the Spine.

There was a deathly silence over the white clay settlement that reminded me of someplace else. It was a little after five. Afternoon nap time. Nobody would be up till at least six, but I knocked on the consul's door anyway. Nobody was home, and the place was locked up tight. I peeked in through the cloth blinds, but I couldn't see much. What I could see was that Lacau's burn equipment wasn't on the desk, and that worried me. There was nobody home in the low building the Spine team used as a barracks either, and where the hell was everybody? They wouldn't still be out at the Spine, not with a ship coming in tomorrow. Maybe the ship had come and gone two days ahead of schedule.

I hadn't burned a story since the day before yesterday. I'd run out of tapes and I hadn't dared risk taking the time to stop and set up the equipment when it might mean getting there too late. Over at Lisii I had been careful every once in a while to let my stories pile up for two or three days and then send them all at once so that Bradstreet wouldn't immediately jump to conclusions when I missed a deadline. He was going to catch on pretty soon, though, and I didn't have anything else to do. I wasn't going to go tearing off to the Spine until I'd talked to somebody and made sure that was where they were, and I couldn't go at night anyway, so I sat down on the low clay step of the barracks porch, set up my burn equipment, and ran a check on the ship. Still on its way. It would be here day after tomorrow. So where was the team? Curse Strikes Again? Team Disappears?

I couldn't do that story, so I whipped off a couple of columns on the one member of the Howard team I hadn't met—Evelyn Herbert. She'd joined the team right after I went north to cover the massacre, and I didn't know much about her. Bradstreet had said she was beautiful. Actually that wasn't what he'd said. He said she was the most beautiful woman he'd ever seen, but that was because we were stuck in Khamsin and had drunk a fifth of gin in endless bottles of Coke. "She has this face," he said, "like Helen of Troy's. A face that could launch . . ." The comparison had petered out since if there was anything on Colchis to launch neither of us was sober enough to think of it. "Even the Sandalman's crazy about her."

I had refused to believe that. "No, really," Bradstreet had protested sloppily, "he's given her presents, he even gave her her own bey, he wanted her to move into his private compound but she wouldn't. I tell you, you've got to see her. She's beautiful."

I still hadn't believed it, but it made a good story. I burned it as the romance of the century, and that took care of yesterday's story. But what about today's?

I went around and knocked on all the doors again. It was still awfully quiet, and I'd remembered what it reminded me of—Khamsin right after the massacre. What if Lacau's hysterical, "Hurry!" had had something to do with the Sandalman? What if the Sandalman had taken one look at the treasure and decided he wanted it all for himself? I sat back down, and burned a story on the Commission. Whenever there was a controversy over archaeological finds, the Commission on Antiquities came and sat on it until everybody was bored and ready to give up. Everyone took them far more seriously than they deserved to be taken. Once they'd even been called in to settle who owned a planet when a dig turned up proof that the so-called natives had really landed in a spaceship several thousand years before. The Commission took this on with a straight face, even if it was like the Neanderthals demanding Earth back, listened to evidence for something over four years, as if they were actually going to do something, and finally recessed to review the accumulated heaps of testimony and let the opposing sides fight it out for themselves. They were still in recess ten years later, but I didn't say that in the story. I wrote up the Commission as the arm of archaeological justice—fair but stern and woe to anybody who gets greedy. Maybe it would make the Sandalman think twice about massacreing Howard's team and taking all the treasure for himself, if he hadn't done that already.

There still weren't any signs of life, and what if that meant there weren't any signs of life? I went the round of the doors again, afraid one of them would swing open on a heap of bodies. But unlike Khamsin, there were no signs of destruction either. There hadn't been a massacre. They were probably all over at the Sandalman's divvying up the treasure.

There was no way to see into the high-walled compound. I rattled the fancy iron gate, and a bey I didn't recognize came out. She was carrying a photosene lantern, bringing it out to be lit before the sun went down, and I was not sure she'd heard me banging on the gate. She looked old.

It's hard to tell with beys, who never get bigger than twelve-year-olds. Their black hair doesn't turn gray and they don't usually lose their black teeth, but this one was wearing a black robe instead of a shift, which meant she had a high station in the Sandalman's household even though I didn't remember her, and her forearms were covered with kheper bites. Either she was exceptionally curious, even for a bey, or she'd been around awhile.

"Is the Sandalman here?" I said.

She didn't answer. She hung the lantern on a hook off to the inside of the gate and watched as the pool of photochemical liquid in its base caught fire.

"I need to see the Sandalman," I said more loudly. She must be hard of hearing.

"No one in," she said, her dished faced impassive. Did that mean the Sandalman wasn't there or that she wasn't supposed to let anybody in?

"Is the Sandalman here?" I said. "I want to see him."

"No one in," she repeated. The Sandalman's other bey had been a lot easier to get information out of. I had given her a pocket mirror and made a friend for life. The fact that she wasn't here probably meant the Sandalman wasn't either. But where had they gone?

"I'm a reporter," I said, and stuck my press card at her. "Show him this. I think he'll want to talk to me."

She looked at the card, rubbed her dirty-looking finger along the smooth plastic, and turned it over.

"Where is he? Out at the Spine?"

The bey turned the card back over to the front. She poked at the hotline's holo-banner with the same finger, as if she could stick it between the three-dimensional letters.

"Where's Lacau? Where's Howard? Where's the Sandalman?"

She held the card up sideways and peered along its edge. She flipped it over, looking at the letters, and turned it sideways again, slowly, watching the three-dimensional effect go flat.

"Look," I said. "You can keep the press card. It's a present. Just tell your boss I'm here."

She was trying to pry the 3-D letters up with the tip of her black fingernail. I should never have given her the press card.

I opened up my knapsack, got out a bottle of Coke, and held it out to her, just this side of the gate. She actually looked up from the press card long enough to grab for it. I took a step backward. "Where are the dig men?" I said, and then remembered it's the bey women who run things, if you could call running errands for the suhundulim and drinking Cokes running things, but at least they were up most of the day. The male beys slept, and the females ignored them and any other male who wasn't giving them a direct order, but they might notice a female. "Where's Evelyn Herbert?"

"Big cloud," she said.

Big cloud? What did that mean? This wasn't the season for the big desert-drenching thunderstorms. A fire? A ship?

"Where?" I said.

She reached for the Coke bottle. I let her almost get it. "Big cloud where?"

She pointed east to where the lava spills formed a low ridge. The flat basin beyond was where they landed the ships. What if some other ship had responded to Lacau's message? Some ship that had already been and gone, team and treasure with it?

"Ship?" I said.

"No," she said, and made a lunge through the bars for the Coke. "Big cloud."

I gave it to her. She retreated to the front steps of the main house and sat down. She took a swig of the Coke and turned the press card over and over in her other hand, making it flash in the sunlight.

"How long has it been there?" I said.

She didn't even act like she'd heard me.

On the way out to the ridge I convinced myself the bey had seen a dust devil. I didn't want to believe a ship had been and gone with the treasure and the team. Maybe if it was a ship, it was still there.

It wasn't. I could see the half-mile circle of scorched dirt where they always landed the ships even before I got to the top of the ridge, and it was empty, but I went on up. And there was the big cloud. A plastic-mesh geodome in the middle of the basin. The consul's landrover was parked on the far side of it and several crawlers that they must have used to bring the treasure down from the Spine.

I hid the jeep behind a hump of lava and then crept around behind the rocks until I could see in the front door. There were a couple of suhundulim guarding the tent, which was the best proof yet that there was a treasure. The Commission's only ruling said that the archaeologist's government got half of everything and the "natives" got the other half. The Sandalman would be making sure he got his half. I was surprised Howard hadn't posted a guard, too, since the ruling said any tampering with the treasure meant forfeiture of the whole thing by the offending party. At Lisii the guards had practically sat on those poor skeletons and clay shards to make sure nobody sneaked a shinbone in his pocket and hoping somebody would so they could claim the whole treasure by default.

I'd never get past the Sandalman's guards. If I wanted a story I'd have to go in the back door. I crept as far back as the jeep and then down the ridge, keeping as much rock between me and the guards as I could. I didn't take my burn equipment. I wasn't sure I could even get in, and I didn't want somebody confiscating it on the grounds that burning a story was tampering. Besides, the black lava was honeycombed with sharp-edged holes. I didn't want to risk dropping my equipment and breaking it.

I kept out of sight as long as I could and then ran across the open sand to the side of the dome away from the consul's landrover and ducked under the outer layer of mesh. The tent didn't have a back door. I hadn't expected it to. The Lisii team had a tent just like this for storing their clay pots, and the only way in was under the mesh at the bottom. But the sides of this "big cloud" were packed with boxes and equipment right up to the walls.

I edged along the side of the tent until I came to a place where the plastic gave a little, and slit it with my knife. I looked through the slit, saw nothing but more plastic mesh a few feet away, and squeezed through.

I scared the little bey who was standing there half to death. She flattened herself against one of the packing cases, clutching a Coke bottle with a straw in it.

She'd scared me, too. "Shh," I said, and put my finger to my lips, but she didn't scream. She hung onto the Coke bottle for dear life and started edging away from me.

"Hey," I said softly. "Don't be scared. You know me." Now I knew where the Sandalman had to be because here was his bey. The old one at the gate must have been left to guard the compound while they were out here. "Remember, I gave you the mirror?" I whispered. "Where's your boss? Where's the Sandalman?"

She stopped and looked at me, her big eyes wide. "Mirror," she said, and nodded, but she didn't come any closer and she let go of the Coke bottle.

"Where's the Sandalman?" I asked her again. No answer. "Where are dig men?" I said. Still no answer. "Where is Evelyn Herbert?"

"Evelyn," she said, and stretched out one dirty-looking arm to point in the direction of a plastic curtain. I ducked through it.

This area of the tent was draped on all sides with plastic mesh, making a kind of low-ceilinged room. The packing cases that were stacked against the side of the tent shut out most of the evening light, and I could hardly see. There was some kind of hammock affair near the wall, hung with more plastic. I could hear someone breathing heavily, unevenly.

"Evelyn?" I said.

The bey had followed me into the room. "Is there a light?" I said to her. She ducked past me and pulled on a string to light a single light bulb hanging from a tangle of cords. Then she backed over against the far wall. The breathing was coming from the hammock.

"Evelyn?" I said, and lifted up the plastic drape.

"Oh," I said, and it came out like a groan. I put my hand over my mouth as if I were trying to get out of a fire, choking on the smoke, smothering, and backed away from the hammock. I practically backed into the little bey, who was pressed so flat against the flimsy wall I thought she was going to go right through it.

"What's wrong with her?" I grabbed her by her bony little shoulders. "What happened?"

I was scaring her to death. There was no way she could answer me. I let go of her shoulders and she pressed herself into the plastic folds of the wall till she nearly disappeared.

"What's wrong with her?" I whispered, and knew my voice still sounded terrifying. "Is it some kind of virus?"

"Curse," the little bey said, and the lights went out.

I stood there in the dark, and I could hear Evelyn's ragged, tortured breathing and the rapid, frightened sound of my own, and for one minute I believed the bey. Then the light came on again, and I looked over at the plastic-draped hammock, and knew I was standing only a few feet away from the biggest story I was ever going to get.

"Curse," the little bey repeated, and I thought, "No, it's not a curse. It's my scoop."

I went over to the hammock again and lifted the plastic drape with two fingers and looked at what had been Evelyn Herbert. A padded mesh blanket was pulled up to her neck, and her hands were crossed over her chest. They were covered with a network of white ridges, even on the fingernails. In the depressions between the ridges the skin was so thin it was transparent. I could see the veins and the raw red tissue under them.

Whatever it was covered her face, too, even her eyelids and the inside of her open mouth. Over her cheekbones the white honeycombs were thicker and farther apart, and they looked so soft I thought her bones would poke through at any moment. My skin crawled at the thought that the plastic might be covered with the virus, that I might already have been infected when I came into the room.

She opened her eyes, and I gripped the plastic so hard I almost yanked it down. Tiny honeycombs, so fine they looked like spiderwebs, filmed her eyes. I don't know if she could see me or not.

"Evelyn," I said. "My name is Jack Merton. I'm a reporter. Can you talk?"

She made a strangled sound. I couldn't make it out. She shut her eyes and tried again, and this time I understood her.

"Help me," she said.

"What do you want me to do?" I said.

She made a series of sounds that had to be words but I had no idea what they were. I wished to God the translator was here instead of in the jeep.

She tried to raise herself up by the muscles in her shoulders and back, not even attempting to use her hands. She coughed, a hard, scraping sound, as if she were trying to clear her throat, and made a sound.

"I've got a machine that will make it easier for you to talk," I said. "A translator. Out in my jeep. I'll go get it."

She said clearly, "No," and then the same string of unintelligible sounds.

"I can't understand you," I said, and she reached out suddenly and took hold of my shirt. I backed away so fast I knocked into the lightbulb and sent it swinging. The little bey edged out from the wall to watch it.

"Treasure," Evelyn said, and took a long dragging breath. "Sandalman. Poy. Son."

"Poison?" I said. The light swung wildly over her. I looked at my shirt front. It was cut to pieces where she had grabbed it, slashed into long ribbons by those ridges on her hands. "Who poisoned you? The Sandalman?"

"Help me," she said.

"Was the treasure poisoned, Evelyn?"

She tried to shake her head.

"Take . . . message."

"Message? To who?"

"San . . . man," she said, and her muscles gave way and she sank back against the hammock, coughing and taking little rasping breaths in between.

I stepped back so her coughing couldn't reach me. "Why?

Are you trying to warn the Sandalman that somebody poisoned you? Why do you want me to take a message to the Sandalman?''

She had stopped coughing. She lay looking up at me. "Help me," she said.

"If I take your message to the Sandalman, will you tell me what happened?" I said. "Will you tell me who poisoned you?"

She tried to nod and started coughing again. The little bey sprang forward with a Coke bottle, stuck a glass straw in it, and tipped it forward so Evelyn could drink. Some of the water spilled onto her chin and into her mouth, and the bey wiped it away with the tail of her dirty-looking shift. Evelyn tried to raise herself up again, and the bey helped her, putting her arm around Evelyn's ridge-covered shoulders. The ridges there were as thick as those on her face, and they didn't seem to cut the bey. If anything, they seemed to flatten a little under the weight of the bey's arm. She stuck the straw in Evelyn's mouth. Evelyn choked and started coughing again. The bey waited, and then tried again, and this time Evelyn got a drink. She lay back.

"Yes," she said, more clearly than she had said anything so far. "Lamp."

I thought I had misunderstood her. "What's the message, Evelyn?" I said. "What do you want to tell him?"

"Lamp," she said again, and tried to gesture with her hand. I turned around and looked. A photosene lamp stood on an upturned plastic cargo carton. Next to it were two disposable injection kits, the kind you find in portable first aid kits, and a plastic packet. The bey handed it to me. I took it from her gingerly, hoping Evelyn hadn't touched the packet, that the bey had put the message inside for her. Then I looked at her hands again and my slashed shirt and knew the bey had not only had to put the message in the plastic envelope, she had probably had to write it out for her, too. I hoped it was readable.

I stuck it in the foil-lined pouch I used for my spare burn-charges and tried to fight the feeling that I needed to wash my hands. I went back over to the hammock. "Where is he? Is he here, in the dome?"

She tried to shake her head again. I was beginning to be able to understand her motions, but I wished again for the translator so I could be sure of what she was saying. "No," she said, and coughed. "Not here. Compound. Village."

"He's in the compound? Are you sure? I was there this afternoon. I didn't see anybody but one of his beys."

She sighed, a terrible sound like a candle guttering out in the wind. "Compound. Hurry."

"All right," I said. "I'll try to get back before dark."

"Hurry," she said, and started to cough again.

I ducked out the way I had come. On the way out I asked the bey if the Sandalman was really back at the compound.

"North," she said. "Soldiers." Which could mean any number of things.

"He's gone north?" I said. "He isn't at the compound?"

"Compound," she said. "Treasure."

"But he's not here, in the tent? Are you sure?"

"Compound," she said. "Soldiers."

I gave up. I glanced around the plastic-hung hall I was in, wondering if I should try to find Howard or Lacau or somebody before I went traipsing back to the compound to look for the Sandalman. There was hardly any light left. If I waited much longer, it would be dark, and I couldn't run the risk of being kept here by an indignant Lacau, with the message burning a hole in my pocket. At least if I went back to the jeep I could read the message, and that might give me a clue as to what in the hell was going on around here. I thought there was a good chance the Sandalman actually was in the compound. If he had gone north he wouldn't have left his bey behind.

I went back out through the slit I'd made and hotfooted it across the space of open plain to the safety of the ridge. Once there, I took my sticklight out and kept it trained on my feet so I wouldn't fall in a hole. I stopped halfway up in the shadow of a long black crevice, to catch my breath and read the messages. There wouldn't be enough light if I waited till I got up to the jeep. It was already dark enough that I was going to have to use the sticklight. I pulled the burn pouch out of my shirt and started to open it.

"Come back!" a voice shouted directly beneath me. I flattened myself into the crevice like Evelyn's bey. The sticklight skittered away and down a hole.

"Come back! You don't have to touch him! I'll do that!" I raised my head a little and looked down. It had been some freak of acoustics produced by the face of the lava ridge. Lacau was nowhere near me. He, and two stocky figures in white robes who had to be suhundulim, were on the other side of the tent, so far away I could hardly make them out in the deepening twilight, though Lacau's voice was coming through as clearly as if he were standing directly beneath me.

"I'll do the burying, for God's sake. All you have to do is dig the grave." Lacau turned and gestured toward the tent, and his voice cut off. Whose grave? I looked where he was gesturing and could make out a bluish-gray shape on the sand. A body wrapped in plastic. "The Sandalman sent you here to guard the treasure, and that includes doing what I tell you," Lacau said. "When he gets back, I'll . . ."

I didn't hear the rest of it, but whatever he had said had not convinced them. They continued to back away from him, and after a minute they turned and ran. I was glad it was nearly dark so I couldn't see them. The suhundulim have always given me the creeps. Bands of herniated muscle ripple under their skin, especially on their faces and their hands and feet. When Bradstreet burns stories about them, he describes them as looking like welts or rope burns, but he's crazy. They look like snakes. The Sandalman isn't too bad—he's got a lot on his feet, which Bradstreet said looked like sandals when he burned the story that gave the Sandalman his name, but hardly any on his face.

The Sandalman. He must be at the compound because Lacau had said, "When he gets back." None of them were looking my way, so I went up and over the ridge as quietly as I could in case the echo thing worked both ways.

There was still enough light in the west to drive by. I thought about stopping midway, switching on the headlights, and reading Evelyn's message in their beam, but I didn't want Lacau to see my lights and figure out where I'd been. I could read the message by one of the lights in the village before I got to the Sandalman's.

I didn't turn on my lights until I couldn't see my hand in front of my face, and when I did I saw I'd practically crashed into the village wall. There weren't any lights along the wall. I left my jeep lights on, wishing I could drive the jeep into the village.

As soon as I was inside the wall, I could see the lantern I'd watched the bey hang out. It was the only light in the whole place, and there was still that massacre-quiet. Maybe they'd found out what was lying in that hammock in the plastic-dome and had taken off like the suhundulim guards.

I went over to the Sandalman's gate and looked up at the lantern. It was just out of my reach or I would have lifted it off its hook and gone off to the shelter of an alley where I could read the message without anybody seeing me. Including the Sandalman. I didn't think he'd take kindly to somebody opening his mail. I huddled against the wall and pulled out the burn pouch.

"No one in," the bey said. She still had the press card in her hand. It looked gnawed around the edges. She must have been sitting on the steps ever since this afternoon, trying to get the holo-letters out.

"I have to see the Sandalman," I said. "Let me in. I have a message for him."

She was looking at the burn pouch curiously. I stuck it back in my pocket.

"Let me in," I said. "Go tell the Sandalman I'm here and I want to see him. Tell him I have a message for him."

"Message," the bey said, watching the pocket where the burn pouch had gone.

I gave up and pulled the pouch out of my shirt. I took the plastic packet out and showed it to her. "Message. For Sandalman. Let me in."

"No one in," she said. "I take." Her hand lunged through the iron gate.

I yanked the packet away from her. "Message not for you. For Sandalman. Take me to Sandalman. Now."

I had frightened her. She backed away from the gate toward the steps. "No one in," she said, and sat down. She began turning the press card over and over in her dirty-looking hands.

"I'll give you something," I said. "If you take the message to the Sandalman, I'll give you something. Better than the press card."

She came back to the gate, still looking suspicious. I had no idea what I had on me that she might like. I rummaged in my torn shirt pocket and came up with a pen that had holo-letters down its side. "I'll give you this," I said, holding it out in one hand. "You tell Sandalman I have message for him." I held the packet out, too, so she would understand. "Let me in," I said.

She was faster than a striking snake. One minute she was edging forward, looking at the pen. The next she had the packet. She grabbed the lantern off its hook and ran up the steps.

"Don't," I said. "Wait." The door shut behind her. I couldn't see a thing.

Great. The bey would make a nice meal of the message, I was no closer to a story than I had been, and Evelyn would probably be dead by the time I got back to the dome. I felt my way along the wall till I could see the jeep's lights. They were starting to dim. Great. Now the battery was going. I would not have been surprised to find Bradstreet sitting in the driver's seat, burning a story on my equipment.

I didn't have a prayer of finding my way back to the dome in the pitch black that was Colchis's night, so I left the lights on and hoped Lacau wouldn't see me coming. Even with them on, I high-centered the jeep twice and crashed into a chunk of lava that cast no shadow at all.

I took my shredded shirt off and left it in the jeep. It took me forever to get down the ridge in the dark, carrying the translator and my burn equipment, and the slit I had made in the tent wasn't big enough for me and the bulky boxes. I set them down, slipped through the slit backwards, and pulled the burn box through after me. I hefted the translator onto my shoulder.

"What took you so long, Jack?" Lacau said. "The Sandalman's guards have been gone a couple of hours. I knew I shouldn't have tried to get them to help me. Now they've run away and you've gotten in. Is Bradstreet here, too?"

I turned around. Lacau was standing there, looking like he hadn't slept in a week.

"Why don't you go right back out the way you came in and I'll pretend I never saw you?" he said.

"I'm here to get a story," I said. "You don't really think I'll leave till I get it, do you? I want to see Howard."

"No," Lacau said.

"Right to know," I said, and reached automatically for the press card the bey was probably chewing on right now. If she hadn't already started on Evelyn's message. "You can't deny a hotline reporter access to the principals in a story."

"He's dead," Lacau said. "I buried him this afternoon."

I tried to look like I had come to get a story about a treasure, like I'd never seen the horror that lay in the hammock down the hall, and I guess I did okay because Lacau didn't look suspicious. Maybe he had stopped looking and feeling shock and didn't expect it from me. Or maybe I looked just like I was supposed to.

"Dead?" I said, and tried to remember what he looked like, but all I could see was what was left of Evelyn's face, and her hands clutching my shirt, sharp as a razor and not even looking like a hand.

"What about Callender?"

"He's dead, too. They're all dead except Borchardt and Herbert, and they can't talk. You got here too late."

The strap of the translator was digging into my shoulder. I shifted to adjust it.

"What's that?" he said. "A translator? Can it do anything with distorted language? With somebody who can't talk because of . . . can it do that?"

"Yes," I said. "What's going on? What happened to Howard and the others?"

"I'm confiscating your burn equipment," he said. "And your translator."

"You can't do that," I said, and started to back away from him. "Hotline reporters have free access."

"Not in here they don't. Give me the translator."

"What do you need it for? I thought you said Borchardt and Herbert couldn't talk."

Lacau reached behind him. "Pick up the burn equipment and come this way," he said, and pulled out a photosene flamethrower made out of what looked like a Coke bottle and a mirror, one of the homemade jobs the suhundulim had massacred everybody with. Lacau tilted it so the mirror was under the light bulb hanging above us. I picked up the burn equipment.

He led me away from Evelyn, through a maze of cargo cartons and boxes to the center of the tent. Plastic mesh was draped over where I thought Borchardt might be lying in a hammock like Evelyn's. If he'd hoped to get me lost, it hadn't worked. I could find Evelyn easily. All I had to do was follow the web-like tangle of electrical cords.

The center area looked like a warehouse, piles of open crates everywhere, shovels and picks and sifters, all the archaeologists' equipment, stacked against them. Their packs and sleeping bags were over at one side in a tangled heap next to a pile of flattened cargo cartons. In the middle was a wire cage and facing it, directly under another mess of electrical cords and plugged into it, was a refrigerator. It was big, an ancient double-door commercial job, and I would have bet it came from the Coca-Cola bottling plant. No sign of the treasure, unless it was all already packed. Or in cold storage. I wondered what the cage was for.

"Put down the equipment," Lacau said, and started fiddling with the mirror again. "Get in the cage."

"Where's your burn equipment?" I said.

"None of your business."

"Look," I said. "You've got your job to do, and I've got mine. All I want is a story."

"A story?" Lacau said. He shoved me into the cage. "How about this for a story? You've just been exposed to a deadly virus. You're under quarantine," he said, and reached up and turned out the light.

Boy, I really knew how to get a story. First the Sandalman's bey and now Lacau, and I was no closer to knowing what was going on than when I was back at Lisii, and maybe only hours away from coming down with what was eating Evelyn. I rattled the wire mesh and yelled for Lacau awhile. Then I played with the lock and yelled some more, but I couldn't see anything or hear anything except the wheezing hum of the refrigerator. Its silence was the only way I could tell when the electricity went off, which it did at least four times during the night. After awhile I hunched against the corner of the cage and tried to sleep.

As soon as it was light, I took off my clothes and checked myself all over for honeycombs. I couldn't see any. I pulled my pants and shoes back on, scribbled a message on a page of my notebook and started banging on the cage again. The bey came in. She had a tray. It had a hard chunk of local bread, a harder one of cheese, and a bottle of Coke with a glass straw in it. It better not be the same one Evelyn had been drinking out of.

"Who else is here?" I asked the bey, but she looked skittish. I had really scared her last night.

I smiled at her. "You remember me, don't you? I gave you a mirror." She didn't smile back. "Are there other beys here?"

She set the tray down on a carton and poked the bread through at me a chunk at a time. "What other beys are here besides you?" I said.

She couldn't get the Coke bottle through the wire without its spilling all over. After a minute or two of her trying, I said, "Here, look, let's cooperate," and I leaned forward and sucked on the straw while she held the bottle.

When I straightened up, she said, "Only me. No beys. Only me."

"Look," I said. "I want you to take a message to Lacau."

She didn't answer, but at least she didn't back away. I pulled out my trusty holo-lettered pen and held it close to my body. I wasn't going to make the same mistake as last night. "I'll give you pen if you take message to Lacau."

She backed away and stood pressed against the refrigerator, her large black eyes fastened on the pen. I scribbled Lacau's name on the message with it, and put it back in my pocket, and her eyes followed it, fascinated. "I gave you mirror," I said. "I give you this." She darted forward to take the message I was holding out to her, and I finished my breakfast and took a nap and wondered what had happened to the message I had given the Sandalman's bey.

When I woke up again, it was fully light, and I could see a lot of things I'd missed last night. My burn equipment was still here, on the other side of the sleeping bags, but I couldn't see the translator anywhere. One of the packing crates, a little one, was right outside the cage. I wriggled my hand through a square of wire and pulled the box in close enough to pull the masking tape off. I wondered who had packed the treasure. Howard's team? Or had they started dropping like flies as soon as they found it? The crate looked like too good a job for the suhundulim to have done it. It looked almost like Lacau's style, but why would he pack it? His job was just to keep it from being stolen.

Masking tape and padded mesh and bubbles, all very neat.
I pushed my hand through the wire till it stuck, tipped the box
a little forward with my other hand, and was able to get a grip
on something. I pulled it out.

It was a vase of some kind. I was holding it by the long,
narrow neck. In it was a silver tube that was supposed to look
like a flower, a lily maybe, widening out and then narrowing
toward the open top. The sides of the tube were etched with
fine lines. The vase itself was made of some kind of blue
ceramic, as thin as eggshell. I wrapped it up in plastic mesh
and laid it back in the box. I rummaged in the bubbles some
more and came up with something that looked like a cross
between one of Lisii's clay pots and something a bey had
chewed on for a while and then spit out.

"That's the door seal," Lacau said. "According to
Borchardt, it says, 'Beware the curse of kings and keepers
that turn men's dreams to blood.'" He took the clay tablet
out of my hands.

"Did you get my message?" I said, trying to pull my
hands back through the cage wire. I scraped my wrist. It
started to bleed. "Well," I said, "did you get the message?"

He threw a chewed wad of paper at me. "More or less,"
he said. "Beys tend to be curious about anything you give
them. What was in the message?"

"I want to make a deal with you."

Lacau started to put the door seal back in the carton. "I
already know how to work the translator," he said. "And the
burn equipment."

"Nobody knows I'm here. I've been relaying stories back
to Lisii ground-to-ground for burning."

"What kind of stories?" he said. He had straightened up,
still holding the door seal.

"Fillers. The local wildlife, old interviews, the Commission. Human interest stuff."

"The Commission?" he said. He had made a sudden,
lurching movement as if he had almost dropped the door seal
and then caught it at the last instant. I wondered if he was
okay. He looked terrible.

"I've got a relay set up back in Lisii. My transmissions go
out through it, and Bradstreet thinks I'm still in Lisii. If I stop
burning stories, he'll know something's up. He's got a Swallow. He could be here as soon as tomorrow."

Lacau put the vase carefully in the carton and piled bubbles around it. He taped it shut and put down the masking tape. "What's your deal?"

"I start filing stories again that will convince Bradstreet I'm still in Lisii."

"And in return?"

"You tell me what's going on. You let me interview the team. You give me a scoop."

"Can you keep him away till day after tomorrow?"

"What happens tomorrow?"

"Can you?"

"Yes."

He thought about it. "The ship will be here tomorrow morning," he said slowly. "I'm going to need help loading the treasure."

"I'll help you," I said.

"No private interviews, no private access to the burn equipment. I get censorship of stories you file."

"Okay," I said.

"You don't file the story on this till we're off Colchis."

I would have agreed to anyting. This was not just a local bit of nastiness, minor potentate poisons a few strangers. There was a story here like no story I had ever had, and I would have agreed to kiss the Sandalman's snaky feet to get it.

"Deal," I said.

Lacau took a deep breath. "We found a treasure in the Spine," he said. "Three weeks ago. A princess's tomb. It's worth . . . I don't know. Most of the artifacts are made of silver, and their archaelogical value alone is beyond price.

"A week ago, two days after we'd finished clearing the tomb and bringing it down here where we could work on it, the team came down with . . . something. A virus of some kind. Just the team. Not the Sandalman's representative, not the bearers who brought the stuff down from the Spine. Nobody but the team. The Sandalman claims they opened the tomb themselves without waiting for local authorization." He stopped.

"And if they did, that would mean they forfeit and the Sandalman gets the whole thing. Convenient. Where was the Sandalman's rep while they were supposedly doing all this?"

"It was this bey. She went back to get the Sandalman. The

team stayed behind to guard the treasure. Howard swears, swore they didn't go in, that they waited until the Sandalman and his bearers got there. He says, said the team was poisoned.''

"Poy son," Evelyn had said. "Sandalman."

"The Sandalman claims it was some kind of guard poison put in the tomb by the ancients, that the team touched it when they opened the tomb illegally.''

"Who did Howard say poisoned them?" I said.

"He didn't. The . . . this thing they caught went into their throats. Howard couldn't talk at all after the first day. Evelyn Herbert is still able to talk, but she's very hard to understand. That's why I need the translator. I need to talk to Evelyn and find out how they were poisoned.''

I thought about what he had said. Some kind of guard poison in the tomb. I knew about that. I had burned stories about the poisons the ancients of all cultures put in their tombs to keep defilers from ransacking them, the contact poisons they put on the artifacts themselves. I had handled the door seal.

Lacau was watching me. He said, "I helped bring the treasure down from the Spine. So did the bearers. And I've been handling the bodies. I've been wearing plasticgloves, but that wouldn't protect me from airborne or droplet infection. Whatever it is, I don't think it's contagious.''

"Do you think it's a poison, like Howard said?" I asked.

"My official position is that it's a virus that was present in the tomb and that the entire party, including the Sandalman's representative, was exposed to it when the tomb was opened.''

"And the Sandalman.''

"The Sandalman's bey entered the tomb before he did. Then the team. Then the Sandalman. My official position is that the virus was erobic and that after the tomb had been open to the air a few minutes, it was no longer virulent.''

"But you don't believe that?"

"No.''

"Then why take that position? Why not accuse the Sandalman? If the treasure's what you want, that'll make sure you get it. The Commission . . .''

"The Commission will close the planet and investigate the charges.''

"And you don't want that?"

I wanted to ask why not, but I figured I'd better be out of the cage before I asked that. "But if it's a virus, what's your excuse for why the bey hasn't come down with it?" I said.

"Difference in body chemistry and size. I declared the quarantine, and the Sandalman went along with it, more or less. He agreed to give us an extension of a week to allow for the variation in incubation time of the virus in the bey before he files his complaint with the Commission. The week's up day after tomorrow. If the bey comes down with it in the next two days . . ."

Which explained why the Sandalman's bey was here, in quarantine with the archaeologists, when no one else, not even the Sandalman's guards, would set foot inside the tent. She was not Evelyn's nurse. She was the sole hope of the expedition.

And she was not going to catch anything. The Sandalman had agreed to the extension. He had been willing to leave her with the team. He would never have done that if he had thought there was even the slightest chance of her coming down with it. So there was not any chance. Unless Evelyn knew what the poison was. Unless she had threatened to poison the Sandalman's bey. Unless that was what was in the message.

"Why didn't he just kill the team right there in the tomb?" I said. "If all he wants is the treasure, why didn't he see to it they were buried by a rockfall or something and call it an accident?"

"There'd still have been an investigation. He couldn't risk that."

I was about to ask why he couldn't, but I'd thought of something more important. "Where is he anyway?"

"He's gone north to Khamsin to get an army," he said.

Khamsin. So the Sandalman wasn't at the compound after all, and the bey was probably making a nice meal of Evelyn's message by now. And when he arrived in Khamsin nothing I could say would convince Bradstreet something wasn't going on. I wondered if Lacau had figured that out yet.

He unlocked the cage. "I'm taking you to see Evelyn Herbert," he said. "But I want you to file a story first."

"Okay," I said. I had already decided what I was going to send. I wasn't going to be able to fool Bradstreet, but maybe

I could throw him off just long enough for me to get my scoop.

"I want a printout first," Lacau said.

"This burner doesn't use one," I said, "but you can put the message on hold and then delete whatever you want from the monitor before we burn it." I pointed to the hold button.

"All right," he said.

"I put it in lock," I said, but he kept his hand on the hold key through the whole message.

I typed in a private priority that read, "Big Doings at the Spine. Hold 12-column."

"You're trying to get him out to the Spine?" Lacau said. "That won't work. He'll see the dome. Anyway, he can't uncook an official message, can he?"

"Of course he can. How do you think I knew you had a ship coming in? But he also knows that I know he can and he won't trust this message. This is the one he'll believe." I tapped the code for ground transmission, fed in the message, and waited for the burner to tell me it wouldn't go through. It couldn't do that until Lacau let go of the hold key, and I didn't even have to ask him. He raised his hand and put it over his chin and watched the screen.

I waited the length of time it would have taken me to weigh odds that Bradstreet would ignore a local message if it weren't flagged with a priority and then decide to send it straight. "Coming back as fast as I can. Stall," I typed. I signed it, "Jackie."

"Who's this message going to?" Lacau said.

"Nobody. I've got a relay set up in my tent. I'll put the message in store and hold it. I'll file a story in the morning about the Spine. It'll be transmitted from here, which is a day's trip from the Spine."

"So he'll think you're doing just what you said. Heading for Lisii."

"Yes," I said. "Now do I get to see Evelyn Herbert?"

"Yes," he said, and started back along the maze of boxes and electrical cords with me following. Halfway there he stopped and said, as if he had just remembered, "This . . . thing they've come down with is pretty bad. They look . . . I want you to be prepared," he said.

"I'm a reporter," I said, so that if I didn't look horrified enough Lacau would think it was because I was used to seeing horrors, but I made the speech for nothing. I didn't have any trouble registering shock. Evelyn looked just as bad the second time.

Lacau had put some kind of contraption across her chest. It was plugged into the spiderweb of cords overhead. I set up the translator. There wasn't much I could really do until Evelyn did a fix for us but I fiddled with it anyway, and the bey watched me, all eyes. Lacau sprayed on plasticgloves and went over to the hammock to look at her.

"I gave her her shot half an hour ago," he said. "It'll be a few more minutes."

"What are you giving her?" I said.

"Dilaudid and sulfadine morphates. It was all there was in the first aid kit. There were IV packs, but they kept leaking."

He said that without emotion, as if he had not had the horror of trying to put an IV in an arm that could cut an IV pack to ribbons. He did not seem at all afraid of her.

"The dilaudid puts her out cold for about an hour, and then after that she's pretty lucid, but in a lot of pain. The morphates are better for pain, but they put her under after only a couple of minutes."

"If it's going to be awhile, I'm going to show the bey the translator, okay?" I said. "If I take it apart and explain everything, we decrease our chances of finding it taken apart tomorrow morning. Is that all right?"

He nodded and went over to look at Evelyn again.

I pulled the face off the box, motioned the bey over, and started my spiel. Every burn chip, every hold strip, every circuit. I pulled them all out and let her handle them, hold them up to the light, stick them in her mouth, and finally put them back in the way they belonged with her own dirty little hands. Halfway through the electricity went off again, and we sat for five full minutes in twilight, but Lacau made no move to get up or to light the photosene lamp.

"It's the respirator," he said. "I've got one on Borchardt, too. It keeps overloading the generator." I wished the lights would come back on so I could see his face more clearly. I was more than ready to believe the generator could overload. The one out at Lisii was off half the time without benefit of respirators, but I was still sure he was lying. It was that

double-door refrigerator next to my cage that was overloading
the generator and making the lights go out. And what was in
that refrigerator? Coca-Cola?

The lights came on. Lacau leaned over Evelyn, and the
little bey and I snapped the last burn chip in place and put the
face back on the translator. I gave the bey a burned-out hold
strip to keep, and she went off in a corner to examine it.

Lacau said, "Evelyn?" and she murmured something.

"I think we're about ready," he said. "What do you want
her to say?"

I handed him a clip mike to fasten on the plastic drape
above her head. "Refrigerator," I said, and knew I'd gone
too far. I was liable to find myself back in the cage. "Have
her say anything you want so I can get a fix. Her name.
Anything."

"Evie," he said, and his voice was surprisingly gentle. "We
have a machine here that can help you talk. I want you to say
your name."

She said something, but the box didn't pick it up. "The
mike's not close enough," I said.

Lacau pulled the plastic drape down a little, and she made
a sound again, and this time it came out of the box as static. I
twiddled dials to get an initial sound, but couldn't get it to
match.

"Have her try it again. I'm not getting anything," I said,
and punched hold so I could hang onto the sound and work
with it, but it was still noise, no matter what I did. I began to
wonder if the bey had put one of the tubes in backwards.

"Can you try it again?" Lacau said gently. "Evelyn?" and
this time he bent so far over her he was practically touching
her. Noise.

"There's something the matter with the box," I said.

"She's not saying, 'Evelyn,' " Lacau said.

"What's she saying then?"

Lacau straightened up and looked at me. "Message," he
said.

The lights went out again, just for a few seconds, and
while they were out I said, trying to sound a little impatient
and not at all nervous, "Okay, then, I'll get a fix on 'message.' Have her say it again."

The lights came back on, and then the centering lights on
the translator blinked on, and her voice, sounding like a

woman's voice now, said, "Message," and then, "Something to tell you."

There was a deadly silence. I was surprised the box wasn't picking up my heartbeat and making it into the word "caught." The lights went out again and stayed out. Evelyn started wheezing. The wheezing got rapidly worse.

"Can't you switch the respirator onto batteries?" I said.

"No," Lacau said. "I'll have to get the other one." He pulled out a sticklight and used it to light the photosene lamp. He picked the lamp up by its base and went out.

As soon as I couldn't see the wavering shadows along the hall of boxes anymore, I felt my way over to the bed. I nearly tripped over the bey, who was sitting cross-legged by the bed, sucking on the hold strip. "Get water," I said.

"Evelyn," I said, using the sound she was making to tell me where she was. "Evelyn, it's me, Jack. I was here before."

The wheezing stopped, just like that, as if she were holding her breath.

"I gave the message to the Sandalman," I said. "I handed it to him myself."

She said something, but I was too far away from the translator to pick it up. It sounded like "light."

"I went right away. As soon as I left you last night."

This time I made out the word. "Good," she said, and the lights went on.

"What was in the message, Evelyn?"

"What message?" Lacau said.

He set the respirator down beside the bed. I could see why he hadn't wanted to use it. It was the kind that fastened over the trachea and cut off all speech.

"What were you trying to say, Evie?" he said.

"Message," she said. "Sandalman. Good."

"She's not making any sense," I said. "Is she still under the morphates? Ask her something you know the answer to."

"Evelyn," he said. "Who was with you out on the Spine?"

"Howard. Callender. Borchardt." She stopped a minute as if she were trying to remember. "Bey."

"That's fine. You don't have to tell me the others. When you found the treasure, what did you do?"

"Waited. Sent bey. Waited Sandalman."

"Did you go in the tomb?" He had been over these questions before. I could tell by the way he asked them, but on the last question his tone changed, and I waited to hear her answer, too.

"No," she said, and the word came through absolutely clearly. "Waited Sandalman."

"What were you trying to tell me, Evelyn? Yesterday. You kept trying to tell me something, and I couldn't understand you. But now I've got a translator. What were you trying to tell me?"

What would she say to him? Never mind? I got somebody else to deliver it? It crossed my mind, then and later, that she could not tell us apart, that her ears were filled with honey-combs, too, and our voices bending over her sounded the same to her. That wasn't true, of course. She knew exactly who she was talking to until the very last. But right then I held my breath, my hand hovering over the switch, thinking that if I waited she might tell Lacau I'd been in here before. Thinking, too, that if I waited she would tell me what was in the message.

"Were you trying to tell me about the poison, Evelyn?"

"Too late," she said.

Lacau turned around. "I didn't catch that," he said. "What did she say?"

"I think she said, 'treasure.' "

"Treasure," she said. "Curse." Her breathing steadied. The translator stopped picking it up. Lacau stood up and let the drape down over her.

"She's asleep," he said. "She never lasts long on the morphates." He turned around and looked at me. The bey had been waiting for her chance. She grabbed the Coke bottle off the cargo carton and ducked past him. He turned and looked at her.

"Maybe she's right," he said tonelessly. "Maybe it is a curse."

I was watching the bey, too, as she stood there waiting for Evelyn to wake up so she could give her a drink, no taller than a ten-year-old, clutching the Coke bottle in one hand and the hold strip I had given her in the other. I tried to think what she would look like when the poison started working on her.

"I think sometimes I could almost do it," Lacau said.

"Do what?" I said.

"I think I could poison the Sandalman's bey to save the treasure if I knew what the poison was. That's a kind of curse, isn't it, wanting something so badly you'd kill somebody for it?"

"Yes," I said. The bey stuck the hold strip in her mouth.

"Every since I saw the treasure, I . . ."

I stood up. "You'd kill a harmless bey for a goddamned blue vase?" I said angrily. "When you'll get the treasure anyway? You can take blood samples. You can prove the team was poisoned. The Commission will award you the treasure."

"The Commission will close the planet."

"What difference will that make?"

"They will destroy the treasure," Lacau said, as if he'd forgotten I was there.

"What are you talking about? They won't let the Sandalman or his cronies anywhere near the treasure. They'll see to it nobody damages the merchandise. They'll take their own sweet time about it, but you'll get your treasure."

"You haven't seen the treasure," he said. "You . . ." He put up his hands in a gesture of despair. "You don't understand."

"Then maybe you'd better show me this wonderful treasure," I said.

His shoulders slumped. "All right," he said, and everything in me said Story.

He locked me in the cage again while he hooked the respirator back up to Borchardt. I didn't ask to go with him. I had known Borchardt almost as long as I had Howard, although I hadn't liked him as well. But I wouldn't have wished this on him. It was nearly noon. The sun was practically overhead and hot enough to burn a hole right through the plastic. Lacau came back in half an hour, looking worse than ever.

He sat down on a packing crate and put his hands up to his head. "Borchardt's dead," he said. "He died while we were in with Evelyn."

"Let me out of the cage," I said.

"Borchardt had a theory about the beys," Lacau said. "About their curiosity. He looked on it as a curse."

"Curse," Evelyn's bey had said, huddled against the wall.

"Let me out of the cage," I said.

"He thought that when the suhundulim came the beys were curious about them and the 'snakes underneath,' so curious they let them stay. And the suhundulim enslaved them. Borchardt maintained the beys were a great people with a highly developed civilization until the suhundulim came and took Colchis away from them."

"Let me out of the cage, Lacau."

He bent over and dug down into the packing case beside him. "This could never have been made by a suhundulim," he said, and pulled it out, spilling plastic bubbles everywhere. "It's spun silver strung with ceramic beads so tiny you can't see them except under a microscope. No suhundulim could make that."

"No," I said. It did not look like beads strung on a silver wire. It looked like a cloud, a majestic desert thunderhead. When Lacau turned it in the light coming through the plastic roof, it shaded into rose and lavender. It was beautiful.

"A suhundulim could make this, however," he said, and turned it around so I could see the other side. It was mashed flat, a dull gray mass. "One of the Sandalman's bearers dropped it bringing it out of the tomb."

He laid it carefully back in its nest of plastic bubbles and taped the box shut. He walked over and stood in front of the cage. "They will close the planet," he said. "Even if we could keep it out of the Sandalman's hands, the Commission will take a year, two years, to make a decision, maybe longer."

"Let me out," I said.

He turned and opened the double doors of the refrigerator and stepped back so I could see what was inside. "The electricity goes of all the time. Sometimes it stays off for days," he said.

From the moment I had intercepted Lacau's message, I had known it was the story of the century. I had felt it in my bones. And here it was.

It was a statue of a girl. A child, twelve maybe. No older than that. She sat on a block of solid beaten silver. She was wearing a white and blue dress with trailing fringes, and she was leaning against the side wall of the refrigerator, her hand and forearm flat against it and her head leaning on her hand, as if she were overcome by some great grief. I couldn't see her face.

Her black hair was bound in the same silver stuff the cloud had been made of, and around her neck was a collar of the blue faience etched in silver. One knee was slightly forward, and I could see her foot in a silver shoe. She was made of wax, as soft and white as skin, and I knew that if she could somehow turn her sorrowing face and look at me, it would be the face I had waited all my life to see. I clutched the wire of the cage and could not get my breath.

"The beys' civilization was very advanced," Lacau said. "Arts, science, embalming." He smiled at my uncomprehending frown. "She's not a statue. She's a bey princess.

"The embalming process turned the tissues to wax." He leaned over her. "The tomb was in a cave that was naturally refrigerated, but we had to bring her down from the Spine. Howard sent me back to try to find temp control equipment and coolants. This was all I could find. It was out at the bottling plant," Lacau said, and lifted the blue-and-white fringe of her trailing skirt. "We didn't try to move her till the last day. The Sandalman's bearers bumped her against the door of the tomb getting her out," he said.

The wax of her leg was flattened and pushed up. Nearly half of the black femur was exposed.

No wonder Evelyn's first word to me had been, "Hurry." No wonder Lacau had laughed when I told him the Commission would keep the treasure safe. The investigation would take a year or more, and she would sit here with electricity flickering on and off.

"We have to get her off the planet," I said, and my hands clutched the mesh so hard the wire cut nearly through to the bone.

"Yes," Lacau said, in a tone that told me what I should have known.

"The Sandalman won't let her off Colchis," I said. "He's afraid the Commission will try to take the planet away from him." And I had burned a story about the Commission to scare him. "They won't do anything. They're not going to give Colchis to a bunch of ten-year-olds who keep sticking things in their mouths, no matter who was here first."

"I know," Lacau said.

"He poisoned the team," I said, and turned to look at the

princess, her beautiful face that I could not see turned to the
wall in some ancient grief. He had killed the team, and when
he got back from the north with his army he would kill us.
And destroy the princess. "Where's your burn equipment?" I
said.

"The Sandalman has it."

"Then he knows when the ship will be here. We've got to
get her out of here."

"Yes," Lacau said. He let go of the blue-and-white fringe,
and it fell across her foot. He shut the door of the refrigerator.

"Let me out of the cage," I said. "I'll help you. Whatever
you're going to do, I'll help you."

He looked at me a long minute, as if he were trying to
decide whether he could trust me. "I'll let you out," he said
finally. "But not yet."

It was dark again before he came to get me. He had come
through the center area twice. The first time he got a shovel
from the jumble of equipment stacked against the cargo cartons.
The second time he opened the refrigerator again to get out an
injection kit for Evelyn's shot, and I stood in the cage and
stared at the princess, waiting for her to turn her head. Sitting
there afterwards, waiting for Lacau to finish doing whatever
it was he did not trust me to help him with, I was surprised
to see that the wire of the cage had not mashed and flattened
my hands like tallow.

It had been dark over an hour when Lacau came and let me
out. He had a coil of yellow extension cords with him, and
the shovel. He leaned it against the pile of flattened cartons,
dumped the cords on the floor beside it, and unlocked the
cage.

"We have to move the refrigerator," he said. "We'll put it
against the back wall of the tent so we can load it into the
ship as soon as it lands."

I went over to the heap of cords and began to untangle
them. I didn't ask him where he'd gotten them. One of them
looked like the cord to Evelyn's respirator. We plugged the
cords together, and then Lacau unplugged the refrigerator.
My grip on the cord tightened as he did it, even though I
knew he was going to plug it into the extension cord and
hook it up again and the whole process wasn't going to take
more than thirty seconds. He plugged it in carefully, as if he

were afraid the lights would go off when he did it, but they didn't even flicker.

They dimmed a little when we picked the refrigerator up between us, but it weighed less than I thought it would. As soon as we shuffled past the first row of packing crates, I saw what Lacau had been doing at least part of the day. He'd moved as many boxes as he could to the east side of the tent and up against the wall, leaving a passage wide enough for us to get through with the refrigerator and a space for it against the wall of the tent. He'd hooked a light up, too. The extension cord didn't quite reach, and we had to set the refrigerator down a few meters from the wall of the tent. It was still close enough. If the ship got here in time.

"Is the Sandalman here yet?" I said. Lacau was walking rapidly back to the center area, and I wasn't at all sure I should follow him. I wasn't going to let myself be locked in that cage for the Sandalman's soldiers to find. I stayed where I was.

"Do you have a recorder?" Lacau said. He stopped and looked at me. "Do you have a recorder?"

"No," I said.

"I want you to record Evelyn's testimony," he said. "We'll need it if the Commission is called in."

"I don't have a recorder," I said.

"I won't lock you in again," he said. He reached in his pocket and tossed me something. It was the handlock to the cage. "If you don't trust me, you can give it to Evelyn's bey."

"There's a record button on the translator," I said.

And we went in and interviewed Evelyn and she told me there was a curse and I didn't believe her. And the Sandalman came.

Lacau seemed unconcerned that the Sandalman was camped on the ridge above us. "I've unscrewed all the light bulbs," he said, "and they can't see into this room. I put a tarp on the roof this afternoon." He sat back down next to Evelyn. "They have lanterns, but they won't try coming down that ridge at night."

"What happens when the sun comes up?" I said.

"I think she's coming around," he said. "Turn the recorder on. Evelyn, we've got a recorder here. We need you to tell us what happened. Can you talk?''

"Last day," Evelyn said.

"Yes," Lacau said. "This is the last day. The ship will be here in the morning to take us home. We'll get you to a doctor."

"Last day," she said again. "In tomb. Loading princess. Cold."

"What was that last word?" Lacau said.

"It sounded like, 'cold,' " I said.

"It was cold in the tomb, wasn't it, Evie? Is that what you mean?"

She tried to shake her head. "Coke," she said. "Sandalman. Here. Must be thirsty. Coke."

"The Sandalman gave you a Coke? Was the poison in the Coke? Is that how he poisoned the team?"

"Yes," she said, and it came out like a sigh, as if that was what she had been trying to tell us all along.

"What kind of poison was it, Evelyn?"

"Blue."

Lacau jerked around to look at me. "Did she say, 'blood'?"

I shook my head. "Ask her again," I said.

"Blood," Evelyn said clearly. "Keep her."

"What's she talking about?" I said. "A kheper bite can't kill you. It doesn't even make you sick."

"No," Lacau said, "but enough kheper poison could. I should have seen the similarities, the replacement of the cell structure, the waxiness. The ancient beys used a concentrated distillation of kheper-infected blood for embalming. 'Beware the curse of kings and khepers.' How do you suppose the Sandalman figured it out?"

Maybe he hadn't had to, I thought. Maybe he'd had the poison all along. Maybe his ancestors, landing on Colchis, had been as curious as the beys they were going to steal a planet from. "Show us how your embalming process works," they might have said, and then, when they'd seen the obvious benefits, they'd said to the smartest of the beys, just like the Sandalman had said to Howard and Evelyn and the rest of the team, "Here. Have a Coke. You must be thirsty."

I thought of the beautiful princess, leaning against her hand. And Evelyn. And Evelyn's bey, sitting in front of the photosene flame, all unaware.

"Is it contagious?" I said for the last time. "Would Evelyn's blood be poisonous, too?"

Lacau blinked at me as if he could not make out what I was saying. "Only if you drank it, I think," he said after a minute. He looked down at Evelyn. "She was asking me to poison the bey," he said. "But I couldn't understand her. It was before you got here with the translator."

"You'd have done it, wouldn't you?" I said. "If you'd known what the poison was, that her blood was poisonous, you'd have killed the bey to save the treasure?"

He wasn't listening to me. He was looking up at the roof of the tent where the tarp didn't quite cover. "Is it getting light?" he said.

"Not for another hour," I said.

"No," he said, "I would have done almost anything for her." His voice was so full of longing it embarrassed me to listen to him. "But not that."

He gave Evelyn a second shot and blew out the lamp. After a few minutes he said, "There are three injection kits left. In the morning I'm going to give Evelyn all of them." I wondered if he was looking at me the way he had when I was in the cage, wondering if he could trust me to do what had to be done.

"Will it kill her?" I said.

"I hope so," he said. "There's no way we can move her."

"I know," I said, and we sat in the darkness for a long time.

"Two days," he said, and his voice was full of that same longing. "The incubation period was only two days."

And then we sat there not saying anything, waiting for the sun to come up.

When it did, Lacau took me into what had been Howard's room, where he had cut a flap-like window in the plastic wall that faced the ridge, and I saw what he had done. The Sandalman's soldiers lined the top of the ridge. They were too far away to be able to see the snakes rippling across their faces, but I knew they were looking down at the dome, and on the sand in front of us, laid end to end, were the bodies.

"How long have they been there?" I said.

"I put them out there yesterday afternoon. After Borchardt died."

"You dug Howard up?" I said. Howard was lying nearest us. He did not look as bad as I had imagined he would. He had almost no honeycombs, and although his skin looked waxy and soft like the skin over Evelyn's cheekbones, he looked almost like I remembered him. The sun had done that. He was melting out there in the sun.

"Yes," he said. "The Sandalman knows it's a poison, but the rest of the suhundulim don't. They'll never cross that line of bodies. They're afraid of catching the virus."

"He'll tell them," I said.

"Would you believe him?" he said. "Would you cross that line because he told you it wasn't a virus?"

"It's a good thing you left me in the cage," I said. "I wouldn't have helped you do this."

Light flashed from the ridge. "Are they firing at us?" I said.

"No," he said. "The Sandalman's head bey has something shiny in her hand that's reflecting the sunlight."

It was the bey from the compound. She had my press card and was moving it back and forth so it lashed sunlight.

"She wasn't there before," Lacau said. "The Sandalman must have brought her out to show his soldiers she hasn't caught the virus and they won't either."

"What?" I said. "Why would she catch it? I thought Evelyn's bey was the one who was with the team."

He was frowning at me. "Evelyn's bey never went anywhere near the Spine. She's a maidservant the Sandalman gave Evelyn. How did you get the idea she was the Sandalman's representative?" He looked at me in disbelief. "You don't think the Sandalman would let us anywhere near his bey after we'd negotiated for the extra days, do you? He wouldn't have trusted us not to poison her like he poisoned the team. He locked her up tight in his compound before he went north," he said bitterly.

"And Evelyn knew that," I said. "She knew the Sandalman had gone north. She knew he'd left his bey behind. Didn't she?"

Lacau didn't answer. He was watching the bey. The Sandalman offered her something, and she took it. It looked like a bucket. She had to stick the press card in her mouth to free both hands so she could lift it. The Sandalman said something to her, and she started down the ridge, spilling liquid from the bucket as she went. The Sandalman had left his bey behind at the compound, locked up, but the guards had run off like the guards at the dome, and a curious bey could open any lock.

"She doesn't seem to be sick, does she?" Lacau said bitterly. "And our week is up. The team caught it in two days."

"Two," I said. "Did Evelyn know the Sandalman left his bey behind?"

"Yes," Lacau said, watching the ridge. "I told her."

The little bey was down the ridge and onto the plain. The Sandalman yelled something at her, and she began to run. The bucket banged against her legs, and more liquid spilled out. As soon as she reached the line of bodies, she stopped and looked back at the ridge. The Sandalman yelled again. He was a long way away, but the ridge amplified his voice. I could hear him quite clearly.

"Pour," he said. "Pour fire," and the little bey tipped the bucket and started down the row.

"Photosene," Lacau said tonelessly. "The sunlight will ignite it."

A lot had spilled out of the bucket on the way down, none of it on the bey, for which I was thankful. There were only a few drops left to shake over Howard. The bey dropped the bucket and danced back. At the other end of the row, Callender's shirt took fire. I shut my eyes.

"Two lousy days," Lacau said. Callender's mustache was on fire. Borchardt smouldered and then flared up yellowly like a candle. Lacau didn't even see me leave.

I followed the electrical cords back to Evelyn's room, half-running. The bey wasn't there. I flipped on the translator and yanked the drape up and looked down at her. "What was in the message, Evelyn?" I said.

The sound of her breathing was so loud nothing was going to get through on the translator. Her eyes were closed.

"You knew the Sandalman had already gone north when you sent me back to the compound, didn't you?" The translator was picking up my own voice and echoing it back to me. "You knew I was lying when I told you I'd delivered the message to the Sandalman. But you didn't care. Because the message wasn't for him. It was for his bey.''

She said something. The translator couldn't do anything with it, but it didn't matter. I knew what it was. "Yes," she said, and I felt a sudden desire to hit her, to watch the honeycombed cheeks cave in under the force of my hand and mash against bone.

"You knew she'd put it in her mouth, didn't you?"

"Yes," she said, and opened her eyes. There was a dull roaring outside.

"You murdered her," I said.

"Had to. To save the treasure," she said. "Sorry. Curse."

"There isn't any curse," I said, clenching my hands at my sides so I wouldn't hit her. "That was just a story you made up to stall me till the poison could take effect, wasn't it?"

She started to cough. The bey darted in front of me with the Coke bottle. She put the straw in Evelyn's mouth, propped Evelyn's head up with her hand, and tilted her gently forward so she could drink.

"You'd have killed your own bey, too, if you had to, wouldn't you?" I said. "For the treasure. For the goddamned treasure!"

"Curse," Evelyn said.

"The ship's here," Lacau said behind me, "but we'll never make it. Howard's the only one left. They're sending the bey down with more photosene."

"We'll make it," I said, and switched the translator off. I took out my knife and slit the wall of the tent behind Evelyn's hammock. Evelyn's bey scampered to her feet and came over to where we were standing. The Sandalman's bey was half-way across the plain with the bucket. She was moving more slowly this time, and none of the photosene was splashing out. Above, on the ridge, the Sandalman's soldiers edged forward.

"We can load the treasure," I said. "Evelyn's seen to that."

The bey made it to the bodies. She started to tip the bucket onto Howard, then seemed to change her mind, and set the bucket down. The Sandalman yelled something at her. She took hold of the bucket, let go of it again, and fell over.

"You see," I said. "It was a virus after all."

There was a sound from above her like a stuttering sigh,

and the Sandalman's soldiers began to back away from the edge of the ridge.

A loading crew was there before we even had the back of the tent sliced open. Lacau pointed them at the nearest boxes, and they didn't even ask any questions. They just started carrying them out to the ship. Lacau and I picked up the refrigerator, gently, gently, so as not to bang the princess's shins, and carried her across the sand to the ship's loading bay.

The captain took one look at her and yelled for the rest of his crew to come and help load. "Hurry," he said after us. "They're bringing up some kind of weapon on the ridge there."

We hurried. We handed stuff out the back door, and the crew ran the boxes across the sand faster than Evelyn's bey getting a drink of water in a Coke bottle, and we still weren't fast enough. There was a soft whoosh and splat on the roof overhead, and liquid trickled down the plastic mesh over our heads.

"He's got a photosene cannon," Lacau said. "Is the blue vase out?"

"Where's Evelyn's bey?" I said, and took off for Evelyn's room. The mesh drape above the hammock was already melting, the fire slicing through it like a knife. The little bey was flattened against the inner wall where I had seen her that first night, watching the fire. I grabbed her up under my arm and dived for the center area.

I couldn't get through. The packing cases that lined the tent were a wall of roaring flame. I ducked back into Evelyn's room. I saw immediately that we could not get out that way either, and just as immediately I remembered the slit I'd made in the wall.

I clamped my hand over the bey's mouth so she wouldn't breathe in the fumes from the melting plastic, held my breath, and started past the hammock.

Evelyn was still alive.

I could not hear her wheezing above the fire, but I could see her chest rise and fall before it began to melt. She was lying with her face pressed against the side of the melting hammock, and she turned her face toward me as I stopped as if she had heard me. The honeycombs on her face widened and flattened, and then smoothed out with the heat, and for a minute I saw her as she must have looked when Bradstreet saw her and said that she was beautiful, as she must have looked when the Sandalman gave her his own bey. The face she turned to me was the face that I had waited all my life to see. And only saw too late.

She guttered out like a candle, and I stood there and watched her, and by the time she was dead the roof had caved in on Lacau and two of the crew. And the blue vase had already been broken in a mad dash to the ship with the last of the treasure.

But we saved the princess. And I got my story.

It is the story of the century. At least that's what Bradstreet's boss called it when he fired him. My boss is asking for forty columns a day. I give them to him.

They are great stories. In them Evelyn is a beautiful victim and Lacau is a hero. I am a hero, too. After all, I helped save the treasure. The stories I burn don't tell how Lacau dug up Howard and built a fort with him or how I got the Lisii team killed. In the stories I burn there is only one villain.

I send forty columns a day out over the burner and try to put the blue vase back together and in what time is left I write this story, which I will not send anywhere. The bey fiddles with the lights.

Our cabin has a system of air-current-sensitive highlights that dim and brighten automatically as you move. The bey cannot get enough of them. She does not even mess with the blue vase or try to put the pieces in her mouth.

I have figured out what the vase is, by the way. The etched lines on the silver straw that looks like a lily are scratches. I am piecing together a ten-thousand-year-old Coke bottle. Here. You must be thirsty. The beys may have had a wonderful civilization, but years before the Sandalman's grandparents even showed up, they were busy poisoning princesses. They murdered her, and she must have known it, and that's why she leans her head against her hand so hopelessly. They murdered her for what? For a treasure? For a planet? For a story? And didn't anybody try to save her?

The first thing Evelyn said to me was, "Help me." What if I had? What if I had said the hell with the story and called Bradstreet, sent him over to get the Lisii team's doctor and evacuate the rest of the team? What if, while he was still on the way, I had burned a message to the Sandalman that said, "You can have the princess if you'll let us off the planet?" and then plugged in that trachea respirator that wouldn't let her talk but might have kept her alive till we could get her onto a ship?

I like to think that I would have done that if I had known her, if it had not been, as she said, "Too late." But I don't know. The Sandalman, who was so enamoured of her that he gave her his own bey, stood in the tomb and offered her poison in a Coke bottle. And Lacau knew her, but what he went back for, what he died for, was not her but a blue vase.

"There was a curse," I say.

Evelyn's bey drifts slowly across the room, and the lights brighten and then dim again as she passes. "All," she says, and sits down on the bunk. The reading light at the end of the bed goes on.

"What?" I say, and wish I still had the translator.

"Curse everybody," she says. "You. Me. All." She crosses her dirty-looking hands over her breast and lies down on the bed. The lights go out. It is just like old times.

In a minute she'll get tired of it being dark and get up, and I'll go back to labeling the jigsawed pieces of the blue vase so a team of archaeologists who have not yet been killed by the curse can put it back together. But for now I have to sit in the dark.

"Curse everybody." Even the Lisii team. Because of the relay in my tent, the Sandalman thought they were helping me get the treasure off Colchis. He buried them alive in the cave they were excavating. He couldn't kill Bradstreet because he was halfway to the Spine with a broken-down Swallow, and by the time he got it fixed the Commission had landed, and he'd been fired and my boss had hired him to file stories on the hearings. They have the Sandalman in custody in a geodome like the one he burned down. The rest of the suhundulim sit in on the Commission's hearings, but the beys, according to Bradstreet, don't pay any attention to them. They are more interested in the Commission's judicial wigs. They have stolen four of them so far.

Evelyn's bey gets up and then flops back down on the bunk, trying to make the highlights flicker. She is not at all curious about this story I am writing, this tale of murder and poison and other curses men fall victim to. Maybe her people got enough of that in the good old days. Maybe Borchardt was wrong and the suhundulim didn't take Colchis away from them at all. Maybe the minute they landed, the beys said, "Here. Take it. Hurry."

She has fallen asleep. I can hear her quiet, even breathing. She is not under the curse, at least.

I saved her, and I saved the princess, even though I was a thousand years too late. So maybe I am not entirely in its clutches either. But in a few minutes I will go turn on a light and finish this story, and when I'm done with it I'll put it in a nice, safe place. Like a tomb. Or a refrigerator.

Why? Because having gotten this story at such great cost I am determined to tell it? Or because the curse of kings stands all around me like a cage, hangs overhead like a tangle of electrical cords?

"The curse of kings and keepers," I say, and my bey scrambles off the bunk and tears out of the cabin to fetch me a drink of water in a Coke bottle she must have been carrying when I dragged her on board, as if I were her new patient and lay under a drape of plasticmesh, already dying.

FERMI AND FROST
by Frederik Pohl

Frederik Pohl has become something of a world traveler, and a visit to the strange volcanic land of Iceland must have inspired this vision of nuclear disaster. This is not so much a story of imaginative projection as an attempt to depict accurately—without self-delusion—what may well happen.

On Timothy Clary's ninth birthday he got no cake. He spent all of it in a bay of the TWA terminal at John F. Kennedy airport in New York, sleeping fitfully, crying now and then from exhaustion or fear. All he had to eat was stale Danish pastries from the buffet wagon and not many of them, and he was fearfully embarrassed because he had wet his pants. Three times. Getting to the toilets over the packed refugee bodies was just about impossible. There were twenty-eight hundred people in a space designed for a fraction that many, and all of them with the same idea. Get away! Climb the highest mountain! Drop yourself splat, sprang, right in the middle of the widest desert! Run! Hide!—

And pray. Pray as hard as you can, because even the occasional planeload of refugees that managed to fight their way aboard and even take off had no sure hope of refuge when they got wherever the plane was going. Families parted. Mothers pushed their screaming children aboard a jet and melted back into the crowd before screaming, more quietly, themselves.

259

Because there had been no launch order yet, or none that the public had heard about anyway, there might still be time for escape. A little time. Time enough for the TWA terminal, and every other airport terminal everywhere, to jam up with terrified lemmings. There was no doubt that the missiles were poised to fly. The attempted Cuban coup had escalated wildly, and one nuclear sub had attacked another with a nuclear charge. That, everyone agreed, was the signal. The next event would be the final one.

Timothy knew little of this, but there would have been nothing he could have done about it—except perhaps cry, or have nightmares, or wet himself, and young Timothy was doing all of those anyway. He did not know where his father was. He didn't know where his mother was, either, except that she had gone somewhere to try to call his father, but then there had been a surge that could not be resisted when three 747s at once had announced boarding, and Timothy had been carried far from where he had been left. Worse than that. Wet as he was, with a cold already, he was beginning to be very sick. The young woman who had brought him the Danish pastries put a worried hand to his forehead and drew it away helplessly. The boy needed a doctor. But so did a hundred others, elderly heart patients and hungry babies and at least two women close to childbirth.

If the terror had passed and the frantic negotiations had succeeded, Timothy might have found his parents again in time to grow up and marry and give them grandchildren. If one side or the other had been able to preempt, and destroy the other, and save itself, Timothy forty years later might have been a graying, cynical colonel in the American military government of Leningrad. (Or body servant to a Russian one in Detroit.) Or if his mother had pushed just a little harder earlier on, he might have wound up in the plane of refugees that reached Pittsburgh just in time to become plasma. Or if the girl who was watching him had become just a little more scared, and a little more brave, and somehow managed to get him through the throng to the improvised clinics in the main terminal, he might have been given medicine, and found somebody to protect him, and take him to a refuge, and lived. . . .

But that is in fact what did happen!

*   *   *

Because Harry Malibert was on his way to a British Interplanetary Society seminar in Portsmouth, he was already sipping Beefeater Martinis in the terminal's Ambassador Club when the unnoticed TV at the bar suddenly made everybody notice it.

Those silly nuclear-attack communications systems that the radio station tested out every now and then, and nobody paid any attention to any more—why, this time it was real! They were serious! Because it was winter and snowing heavily Malibert's flight had been delayed anyway. Before its rescheduled departure time came, all flights had been embargoed. Nothing would leave Kennedy until some official somewhere decided to let them go.

Almost at once the terminal began to fill with would-be refugees. The Ambassador Club did not fill at once. For three hours the ground-crew stew at the desk resolutely turned away everyone who rang the bell who could not produce the little red card of admission; but when the food and drink in the main terminals began to run out the Chief of Operations summarily opened the club to everyone. It didn't help relieve the congestion outside, it only added to what was within. Almost at once a volunteer doctors' committee seized most of the club to treat the ill and injured from the thickening crowds, and people like Harry Malibert found themselves pushed into the bar area. It was one of the Operations staff, commandeering a gin and tonic at the bar for the sake of the calories more than the booze, who recognized him. "You're Harry Malibert. I heard you lecture once, at Northwestern."

Malibert nodded. Usually when someone said that to him he answered politely, "I hope you enjoyed it," but this time it did not seem appropriate to be normally polite. Or normal at all.

"You showed slides of Arecibo," the man said dreamily. "You said that radio telescope could send a message as far as the Great Nebula in Andromeda, two million light-years away—if only there was another radio telescope as good as that one there to receive it."

"You remember very well," said Malibert, surprised.

"You made a big impression, Dr. Malibert." The man glanced at his watch, debated, took another sip of his drink. "It really sounded wonderful, using the big telescopes to listen for messages from alien civilizations somewhere in space—maybe hearing some, maybe making contact, maybe not being alone in the universe any more. You made me wonder why we hadn't seen some of these people already, or anyway heard from them—but maybe,'' he finished, glancing bitterly at the ranked and guarded aircraft outside, ''maybe now we know why.''

Malibert watched him go, and his heart was leaden. The thing he had given his professional career to—SETI, the Search for Extra-Terrestrial Intelligence—no longer seemed to matter. If the bombs went off, as everyone said they must, then that was ended for a good long time, at least—

Gabble of voices at the end of the bar; Malibert turned, leaned over the mahogany, peered. The *Please Stand By* slide had vanished, and a young black woman with pomaded hair, voice trembling, was delivering a news bulletin:

''—the president has confirmed that a nuclear attack has begun against the United States. Missiles have been detected over the Arctic, and they are incoming. Everyone is ordered to seek shelter and remain there pending instructions—''

Yes. It was ended, thought Malibert, at least for a good long time.

The surprising thing was that the news that it had begun changed nothing. There were no screams, no hysteria. The order to seek shelter meant nothing at John F. Kennedy Airport, where there was no shelter any better than the building they were in. And that, no doubt, was not too good. Malibert remembered clearly the strange aerodynamic shape of the terminal's roof. Any blast anywhere nearby would tear that off and send it sailing over the bay to the Rockaways, and probably a lot of the people inside with it.

But there was nowhere else to go.

There were still camera crews at work, heaven knew why. The television set was showing crowds in Times Square and Newark, a clot of automobiles stagnating on the George Washington Bridge, their drivers abandoning them and running for the Jersey shore. A hundred people were peering around each other's heads to catch glimpses of the screen, but all that anyone said was to call out when he recognized a building or a street.

Orders rang out: ''You people will have to move back! We need the room! Look, some of you, give us a hand with these patients." Well, that seemed useful, at least. Malibert volunteered at once and was given the care of a young boy, teeth chattering, hot with fever. "He's had tetracyclin," said the doctor who turned the boy over to him. "Clean him up if you can, will you? He ought to be all right if—"

If any of them were, thought Malibert, not requiring her to finish the sentence. How did you clean a young boy up? The question answered itself when Malibert found the boy's trousers soggy and the smell told him what the moisture was. Carefully he laid the child on a leather love seat and removed the pants and sopping undershorts. Naturally the boy had not come with a change of clothes. Malibert solved that with a pair of his own jockey shorts out of his briefcase—far too big for the child, of course, but since they were meant to fit tightly and elastically they stayed in place when Malibert pulled them up to the waist. Then he found paper towels and pressed the blue jeans as dry as he could. It was not very dry. He grimaced, laid them over a bar stool and sat on them for a while, drying them with body heat. They were only faintly wet ten minutes later when he put them back on the child—

San Francisco, the television said, had ceased to transmit.

Malibert saw the Operations man working his way toward him and shook his head. "It's begun," Malibert said, and the man looked around. He put his face close to Malibert's.

"I can get you out of here," he whispered. "There's an Icelandic DC-8 loading right now. No announcement. They'd be rushed if they did. There's room for you, Dr. Malibert."

It was like an electric shock. Malibert trembled. Without knowing why he did it, he said, "Can I put the boy on instead?"

The Operations man looked annoyed. "Take him with you, of course," he said. "I didn't know you had a son."

"I don't," said Malibert. But not out loud. And when they were in the jet he held the boy in his lap as tenderly as though he were his own.

If there was no panic in the Ambassador Club at Kennedy there was plenty of it everywhere else in the world. What everyone in the superpower cities knew was that their lives were at stake. Whatever they did might be in vain, and yet they had to do something. Anything! Run, hide, dig, brace, stow . . . pray. The city people tried to desert the metropo-

lises for the open safety of the country, and the farmers and
the exurbanites sought the stronger, safer buildings of the
cities.

And the missiles fell.

The bombs that had seared Hiroshima and Nagasaki were
struck matches compared to the hydrogen-fusion flares that
ended eighty million lives in those first hours. Firestorms
fountained above a hundred cities. Winds of three hundred
kilometers an hour pulled in cars and debris and people, and
they all became ash that rose to the sky. Splatters of melted
rock and dust sprayed into the air.

The sky darkened.

Then it grew darker still.

When the Icelandic jet landed at Keflavik Airport Malibert
carried the boy down the passage to the little stand marked
Immigration. The line was long, for most of the passengers
had no passports at all, and the immigration woman was very
tired of making out temporary entrance permits by the time
Malibert reached her. "He's my son," Malibert lied. "My
wife has his passport, but I don't know where my wife is."

She nodded wearily. She pursed her lips, looked toward the
door beyond which her superior sat sweating and initialing
reports, then shrugged and let them through. Malibert took
the boy to a door marked *Snirtling,* which seemed to be the
Icelandic word for toilets, and was relieved to see that at least
Timothy was able to stand by himself while he urinated,
although his eyes stayed half closed. His head was very hot.
Malibert prayed for a doctor in Reykjavik.

In the bus the English-speaking tour guide in charge of
them—she had nothing else to do, for her tour would never
arrive—sat on the arm of a first-row seat with a microphone
in her hand and chatted vivaciously to the refugees. "Chicago? Ya, is gone, Chicago. And Detroit and Pitts-burrug—is
bad. New York? Certainly New York too!" she said severely,
and the big tears rolling down her cheek made Timothy cry
too.

Malibert hugged him. "Don't worry, Timmy," he said.
"No one would bother bombing Reykjavik." And no one
would have. But when the bus was ten miles farther along
there was a sudden glow in the clouds ahead of them that
made them squint. Someone in the USSR had decided that it

was time for neatening up loose threads. That someone, whoever remained in whatever remained of their central missile control, had realized that no one had taken out that supremely, insultingly dangerous bastion of imperialist American interests in the North Atlantic, the United States airbase at Keflavik.

Unfortunately, by then EMP and attrition had compromised the accuracy of their aim. Malibert had been right. No one would have bothered bombing Reykjavik—on purpose—but a forty-mile miss did the job anyway, and Reykjavik ceased to exist.

They had to make a wide detour inland to avoid the fires and the radiation. And as the sun rose on their first day in Iceland, Malibert, drowsing over the boy's bed after the Islandic nurse had shot him full of antibiotics, saw the daybreak in awful, sky-drenching red.

It was worth seeing, for in the days to come there was no daybreak at all.

The worst was the darkness, but at first that did not seem urgent. What was urgent was rain. A trillion trillion dust particles nucleated water vapor. Drops formed. Rain fell—torrents of rain, sheets and cascades of rain. The rivers swelled. The Mississippi overflowed, and the Ganges, and the Yellow. The High Dam at Aswan spilled water over its lip, then crumbled. The rains came where rains came never. The Sahara knew flash floods. The Flaming Mountains at the edge of the Gobi flamed no more; a ten-year supply of rain came down in a week and rinsed the dusty slopes bare.

And the darkness stayed.

The human race lives always eighty days from starvation. That is the sum of stored food, globe wide. It met the nuclear winter with no more and no less.

The missiles went off on the 11th of June. If the world's larders had been equally distributed, on the 30th of August the last mouthful would have been eaten. The starvation deaths would have begun and ended in the next six weeks; exit the human race.

The larders were not equally distributed. The Northern Hemisphere was caught on one foot, fields sown, crops not yet grown. Nothing did grow there. The seedlings poked up through the dark earth for sunlight, found none, died. Sunlight was shaded out by the dense clouds of dust exploded out of the ground by the H-bombs. It was the Cretaceous repeated; extinction was in the air.

There were mountains of stored food in the rich countries of North American and Europe, of course, but they melted swiftly. The rich countries had much stored wealth in the form of their livestock. Every steer was a million calories of protein and fat. When it was slaughtered, it saved thousands of other calories of grain and roughage for every day lopped off its life in feed. The cattle and pigs and sheep—even the goats and horses; even the pet bunnies and the chicks; even the very kittens and hamsters—they all died quickly and were eaten, to eke out the stores of canned foods and root vegetables and grain. There was no rationing of the slaughtered meat. It had to be eaten before it spoiled.

Of course, even in the rich countries the supplies were not equally distributed. The herds and the grain elevators were not located on Times Square or in the Loop. It took troops to convoy corn from Iowa to Boston and Dallas and Philadelphia. Before long, it took killing. Then it could not be done at all.

So the cities starved first. As the convoys of soldiers made the changeover from seizing food for the cities to seizing food for themselves, the riots began, and the next wave of mass death. These casualties didn't usually die of hunger. They died of someone else's.

It didn't take long. By the end of "summer" the frozen remnants of the cities were all the same. A few thousand skinny, freezing desperadoes survived in each, sitting guard over their troves of canned and dried and frozen foodstuffs.

Every river in the world was running sludgy with mud to its mouth, as the last of the trees and grasses died and relaxed their grip on the soil. Every rain washed dirt away. As the winter dark deepened the rains turned to snow. The Flaming Mountains were sheeted in ice now, ghostly, glassy fingers uplifted to the gloom. Men could walk across the Thames at London now, the few men who were left. And across the Hudson, across the Whangpoo, across the Missouri between the two Kansas Cities. Avalanches rumbled down on what was left of Denver. In the stands of dead timber grubs flourished. The starved predators scratched them out and devoured them. Some of the predators were human. The last of the Hawaiians were finally grateful for their termites.

A Western human being—comfortably pudgy on a diet of 2800 calories a day, resolutely jogging to keep the flab away or mournfully conscience-stricken at the thickening thighs and the waistbands that won't quite close—can survive for forty-five days without food. By then the fat is gone. Protein reabsorption of the muscles is well along. The plump housewife or businessman is a starving scrarecrow. Still, even then care and nursing can still restore health.

Then it gets worse.

Dissolution attacks the nervous system. Blindness begins. The flesh of the gums recedes, and the teeth fall out. Apathy becomes pain, then agony, then coma.

Then death. Death for almost every person on Earth. . . .

For forty days and forty nights the rain fell, and so did the temperature. Iceland froze over.

To Harry Malibert's astonishment and dawning relief, Iceland was well equipped to do that. It was one of the few places on Earth that could be submerged in snow and ice and still survive.

There is a ridge of volcanoes that goes almost around the Earth. The part that lies between America and Europe is called the Mid-Atlantic Ridge, and most of it is under water. Here and there, like boils erupting along a forearm, volcanic islands poke up above the surface. Iceland is one of them. It was because Iceland was volcanic that it could survive when most places died of freezing, but it was also because it had been cold in the first place.

The survival authorities put Malibert to work as soon as they found out who he was. There was no job opening for a radio astronomer interested in contacting far-off (and very likely non-existent) alien races. There was, however, plenty of work for persons with scientific training, especially if they had the engineering skills of a man who had run Arecibo for two years. When Malibert was not nursing Timothy Clary through the slow and silent convalescence from his pneumonia, he was calculating heat losses and pumping rates for the piped geothermal water.

Iceland filled itself with enclosed space. It heated the spaces with water from the boiling underground springs.

Of heat it had plenty. Getting the heat from the geyser

fields to the enclosed spaces was harder. The hot water was as hot as ever, since it did not depend at all on sunlight for its calories, but it took a lot more of it to keep out a -30°C chill than a +5°C one. It wasn't just to keep the surviving people warm that they needed energy. It was to grow food.

Iceland had always had a lot of geothermal greenhouses. The flowering ornamentals were ripped out and food plants put in their place. There was no sunlight to make the vegetables and grains grow, so the geothermal power-generating plants were put on max output. Solar-spectrum incandescents flooded the trays with photons. Not just in the old greenhouses. Gymnasia, churches, schools—they all began to grow food under the glaring lights. There was other food, too, metric tons of protein baaing and starving in the hills. The herds of sheep were captured and slaughtered and dressed— and put outside again, to freeze until needed. The animals that froze to death on the slopes were bulldozed into heaps of a hundred, and left where they were. Geodetic maps were carefully marked to show the location of each heap.

It was, after all, a blessing that Reykjavik had been nuked. That meant half a million fewer people for the island's resources to feed.

When Malibert was not calculating load factors, he was out in the desperate cold, urging on the workers. Sweating navvies tried to muscle shrunken fittings together in icy foxholes that their body heat kept filling with icewater. They listened patiently as Malibert tried to give orders—his few words of Icelandic were almost useless, but even the navvies sometimes spoke tourist-English. They checked their radiation monitors, looked up at the storms overhead, returned to their work and prayed. Even Malibert almost prayed when one day, trying to locate the course of the buried coastal road, he looked out on the sea ice and saw a gray-white ice hummock that was not an ice hummock. It was just at the limits of visibility, dim on the fringe of the road crew's work lights, and it moved. "A polar bear!" he whispered to the head of the work crew, and everyone stopped while the beast shambled out of sight.

From then on they carried rifles.

When Malibert was not (incompetent) technical advisor to the task of keeping Iceland warm or (almost incompetent, but

learning) substitute father to Timothy Clary, he was trying
desperately to calculate survival chances. Not just for them;
for the entire human race. With all the desperate flurry of
survival work, the Icelanders spared time to think of the
future. A study team was created, physicists from the University
of Reykjavik, the surviving Supply officer from the
Keflavik airbase, a meteorologist on work-study from the University
of Leyden to learn about North Atlantic air masses.
They met in the gasthuis where Malibert lived with the boy,
and usually Timmy sat silent next to Malibert while they
talked. What they wanted was to know how long the dust
cloud would persist. Some day the particles would finish
dropping from the sky, and then the world could be reborn—if
enough survived to parent a new race, anyway. But when?
They could not tell. They did not know how long, how cold,
how killing the nuclear winter would be. "We don't know
the megatonnage," said Malibert, "we don't know what
atmospheric changes have taken place, we don't know the
rate of insolation. We only know it will be bad."

"It is already bad," grumbled Thorsid Magnesson, Director
of Public Safety. (Once that office had had something to
do with catching criminals, when the major threat to safety
was crime.)

"It will get worse," said Malibert, and it did. The cold
deepened. The reports from the rest of the world dwindled.
They plotted maps to show what they knew to show. One set
of missile maps, to show where the strikes had been—within
a week that no longer mattered, because the deaths from cold
already began to outweigh those from blast. They plotted
isotherm maps, based on the scattered weather reports that
came in—maps that had to be changed every day, as the
freezing line marched toward the Equator. Finally the maps
were irrelevant. The whole world was cold then. They plotted
fatality maps—the percentages of deaths in each area, as they
could infer them from the reports they received, but those
maps soon became too frightening to plot.

The British Isles died first, not because they were nuked
but because they were not. There were too many people alive
there. Britain never owned more than a four-day supply of
food. When the ships stopped coming they starved. So did
Japan. A little later, so did Bermuda and Hawaii and Canada's
off-shore provinces; and then it was the continents' turn.

And Timmy Clary listened to every word.

The boy didn't talk much. He never asked after his parents, not after the first few days. He did not hope for good news, and did not want bad. The boy's infection was cured, but the boy himself was not. He ate half of what a hungry child should devour. He ate that only when Malibert coaxed him.

The only thing that made Timmy look alive was the rare times when Malibert could talk to him about space. There were many in Iceland who knew about Harry Malibert and SETI, and a few who cared about it almost as much as Malibert himself. When time permitted they would get together, Malibert and his groupies. There was Lars the postman (now pick-and-shovel ice excavator, since there was no mail), Ingar the waitress from the Loftleider Hotel (now stitching heavy drapes to help insulate dwelling walls), Elda the English teacher (now practical nurse, frostbite cases a specialty). There were others, but those three were always there when they could get away. They were Harry Malibert fans who had read his books and dreamed with him of radio messages from weird aliens from Aldebaren, or worldships that could carry million-person populations across the galaxy, on voyages of a hundred thousand years. Timmy listened, and drew sketches of the worldships. Malibert supplied him with dimensions. "I talked to Gerry Webb," he said, "and he'd worked it out in detail. It is a matter of rotation rates and strength of materials. To provide the proper simulated gravity for the people in the ships, the shape has to be a cylinder and it has to spin—sixteen kilometers is what the diameter must be. Then the cylinder must be long enough to provide space, but not so long that the dynamics of spin cause it to wobble or bend—perhaps sixty kilometers long. One part to live in. One part to store fuel. And at the end, a reaction chamber where hydrogen fusion thrusts the ship across the Galaxy."

"Hydrogen bombs," said the boy. "Harry? Why don't the bombs wreck the worldship?"

"It's engineering," said Malibert honestly, "and I don't know the details. Gerry was going to give his paper at the Portsmouth meeting; it was one reason I was going." But, of course, there would never be a British Interplanetary Society meeting in Portsmouth now, ever again.

Elda said uneasily, "It is time for lunch soon. Timmy? Will you eat some soup if I make it?" And did make it, whether the boy promised or not. Elda's husband had worked at Keflavik in the PX, an accountant; unfortunately he had been putting in overtime there when the follow-up missile did what the miss had failed to do, and so Elda had no husband left, not enough even to bury.

Even with the earth's hot water pumped full velocity through the straining pipes it was not warm in the gasthuis. She wrapped the boy in blankets and sat near him while he dutifully spooned up the soup. Lars and Ingar sat holding hands and watching the boy eat. "To hear a voice from another star," Lars said suddenly, "that would have been fine."

"There are no voices," said Ingar bitterly. "Not even ours now. We have the answer to the Fermi paradox."

And when the boy paused in his eating to ask what that was, Harry Malibert explained it as carefully as he could:

"It is named after Enrico Fermi, a scientist. He said, 'We know that there are many billions of stars like our sun. Our sun has planets, therefore it is reasonable to assume that some of the other stars do also. One of our planets has living things on it. Us, for instance, as well as trees and germs and horses. Since there are so many stars, it seems almost certain that some of them, at least, have also living things. People. People as smart as we are—or smarter. People who can build spaceships, or send radio messages to other stars, as we can.' Do you understand so far, Timmy?" The boy nodded, frowning, but—Malibert was delighted to see—kept on eating his soup. "Then, the question Fermi asked was, 'Why haven't some of them come to see us?' "

"Like in the movies," the boy nodded. "The flying saucers."

"All those movies are made-up stories, Timmy. Like Jack and the Beanstalk, or Oz. Perhaps some creatures from space have come to see us sometime, but there is no good evidence that this is so. I feel sure there would be evidence if it had happened. There would have to be. If there were many such visits, ever, then at least one would have dropped the Martian equivalent of a McDonald's Big Mac box, or a used Sirian flash cube, and it would have been found and shown to be from somewhere other than the Earth. None ever has. So there are only three possible answers to Dr. Fermi's question. One, there is no other life. Two, there is, but they want to

leave us alone. They don't want to contact us, perhaps because we frighten them with our violence, or for some reason
we can't even guess at. And the third reason—'' Elda made a
quick gesture, but Malibert shook his head—''is that perhaps
as soon as any people get smart enough to do all those things
that get them into space—when they have all the technology
we do—they also have such terrible bombs and weapons that
they can't control them any more. So a war breaks out. And
they kill themselves off before they are fully grown up.''

''Like now,'' Timothy said, nodding seriously to show he
understood. He had finished his soup, but instead of taking
the plate away Elda hugged him in her arms and tried not to
weep.

The world was totally dark now. There was no day or
night, and would not be again for no one could say how long.
The rains and snows had stopped. Without sunlight to suck
water up out of the oceans there was no moisture left in the
atmosphere to fall. Floods had been replaced by freezing
droughts. Two meters down the soil of Iceland was steel
hard, and the navvies could no longer dig. There was no hope
of laying additional pipes. When more heat was needed all
that could be done was to close off buildings and turn off
their heating pipes. Elda's patients now were less likely to be
frostbite and more to be the listlessness of radiation sickness
as volunteers raced in and out of the Reykjavik ruins to find
medicine and food. No one was spared that job. When Elda
came back on a snowmobile from a foraging trip to the
Loftleider Hotel she brought back a present for the boy.
Candy bars and postcards from the gift shop; the candy bars
had to be shared, but the postcards were all for him. ''Do you
know what these are?'' she asked. The cards showed huge,
squat, ugly men and women in costumes of a thousand years
ago. ''They're trolls. We have myths in Iceland that the trolls
lived here. They're still here, Timmy, or so they say; the
mountains are trolls that just got too old and tired to move
any more.''

''They're made-up stories, right?'' the boy asked seriously,
and did not grin until she assured him they were. Then he
made a joke. ''I guess the trolls won,'' he said.

''Ach, Timmy!'' Elda was shocked. But at least the boy
was capable of joking, she told herself, and even graveyard

humor was better than none. Life had become a little easier for her with the new patients—easier because for the radiation-sick there was very little that could be done—and she bestirred herself to think of ways to entertain the boy.

And found a wonderful one.

Since fuel was precious there were no excursions to see the sights of Iceland-under-the-ice. There was no way to see them anyway in the eternal dark. But when a hospital chopper was called up to travel empty to Stokksnes on the eastern shore to bring back a child with a broken back, she begged space for Malibert and Timmy. Elda's own ride was automatic, as duty nurse for the wounded child. "An avalanche crushed his house," she explained. "It is right under the mountains, Stokksnes, and landing there will be a little tricky, I think. But we can come in from the sea and make it safe. At least in the landing lights of the helicopter something can be seen."

They were luckier than that. There was more light. Nothing came through the clouds, where the billions of particles that had once been Elda's husband added to the trillions of trillions that had been Detroit and Marseilles and Shanghai to shut out the sky. But in the clouds and under them were snakes and sheets of dim color, sprays of dull red, fans of pale green. The aurora borealis did not give much light. But there was no other light at all except for the faint glow from the pilot's instrument panel. As their eyes widened they could see the dark shapes of the Vatnajökull slipping by below them. "*Big* trolls," cried the boy happily, and Elda smiled too as she hugged him.

The pilot did as Elda had predicted, down the slopes of the eastern range, out over the sea, and cautiously back in to the little fishing village. As they landed, red-tipped flashlights guiding them, the copter's landing lights picked out a white lump, vaguely saucer-shaped. "Radar dish," said Malibert to the boy, pointing.

Timmy pressed his nose to the freezing window. "Is it one of them, Daddy Harry? The things that could talk to the stars?"

The pilot answered: "Ach, no, Timmy—military, it is."
And Malibert said:

"They wouldn't put one of those here, Timothy. It's too far north. You wanted a place for a big radio telescope that could search the whole sky, not just the little piece of it you can see from Iceland.''

And while they helped slide the stretcher with the broken child into the helicopter, gently, kindly as they could be, Malibert was thinking about those places, Arecibo and Woomara and Socorro and all the others. Every one of them was now dead and certainly broken with a weight of ice and shredded by the mean winds. Crushed, rusted, washed away, all those eyes on space were blinded now; and the thought saddened Harry Malibert, but not for long. More gladdening than anything sad was the fact that, for the first time, Timothy had called him "Daddy."

In one ending to the story, when at last the sun came back it was too late. Iceland had been the last place where human beings survived, and Iceland had finally starved. There was nothing alive anywhere on Earth that spoke, or invented machines, or read books. Fermi's terrible third answer was the right one after all.

But there exists another ending. In this one the sun came back in time. Perhaps it was just barely in time, but the food had not yet run out when daylight brought the first touches of green in some parts of the world, and plants began to grow again from frozen or hoarded seed. In this ending Timothy lived to grow up. When he was old enough, and after Malibert and Elda had got around to marrying, he married one of their daughters. And of their descendants—two generations or a dozen generations later—one was alive on that day when Fermi's paradox became a quaintly amusing old worry, as irrelevant and comical as a fifteenth-century mariner's fear of falling off the edge of the flat Earth. On that day the skies spoke, and those who lived in them came to call.

Perhaps that is the true ending of the story, and in it the human race chose not to squabble and struggle within itself, and so extinguish itself finally into the dark. In this ending human beings survived, and saved all the science and beauty of life, and greeted their star-born visitors with joy. . . .

But that is in fact what did happen!

At least, one would like to think so.

POTS
by C.J. Cherryh

> *Even though the worst may come to pass for
> Earth and our descendants, there is never an
> end to hope if you realize that the scale of time
> in the universe is far vaster than the fleeting
> moments of any civilization. In this way, this
> story is an epilogue to Pohl's tale before it.*

It was a most bitter trip, the shuttle-descent to the windy
surface. Suited, encumbered by lifesupport, Desan stepped off
the platform and waddled onward into the world, waving off
the attentions of small spidery service robots: "Citizen, this
way, this way, citizen, have a care—do watch your step; a
suit tear is hazardous."

Low-level servitors. Desan detested them. The chief of
operations had plainly sent these creatures accompanied only
by an AI eight-wheel transport, which inconveniently chose to
park itself a good five hundred paces beyond the shuttle blast
zone, an uncomfortably long walk across the dusty pan in
the crinkling, pack-encumbered oxy-suit. Desan turned, casting a forlorn glance at the shuttle waiting there on its landing
gear, silver, dip-nosed wedge under a gunmetal sky, at rest
on an ochre and rust landscape. He shivered in the sky-view,
surrendered himself and his meager luggage to the irritating
ministries of the service robots, and waddled on his slow way
down to the waiting AI transport.

"Good day," the vehicle said inanely, opening a door.
"My passenger compartment is not safe atmosphere; do you
understand, Lord Desan?"

"Yes, yes." Desan climbed in and settled himself in the front seat, a slight give of the transport's suspensors. The robots fussed about in insectile hesitance, delicately setting his luggage case just so, adjusting, adjusting until it conformed with their robotic, template-compared notion of their job. Maddening. Typical robotic efficiency. Desan slapped the pressure-sensitive seating. "Come, let's get this moving, shall we?"

The AI talked to its duller cousins, a single squeal that sent them scuttling; "Attention to the door, citizen." It lowered and locked. The AI started its noisy drive motor. "Will you want the windows dimmed, citizen?"

"No. I want to see this place."

"A pleasure, Lord Desan."

Doubtless for the AI, it was.

The station was situated a long drive across the pan, across increasingly softer dust that rolled up to obscure the rearview—softer, looser dust, occasionally a wind-scooped hollow that made the transport flex—("Do forgive me, citizen. Are you comfortable?")

"Quite, quite, you're very good."

"Thank you, citizen."

And finally—*finally!*—something other than flat appeared, the merest humps of hills, and one anomalous mountain, a massive, long bar that began as a haze and became solid; became a smooth regularity before the gentle brown folding of hills hardly worthy of the name.

Mountain. The eye indeed took it for a volcanic or sedimentary formation at distance, some anomalous and stubborn outcrop in this barren reach, where all else had declined to entropy; absolute, featureless, flat. But when the AI passed along its side this mountain had joints and seams, had the marks of *making* on it; and even knowing in advance what it was, driving along within view of the jointing, this work of Ancient hands—chilled Desan's well-traveled soul. The station itself came into view against the weathered hills, a collection of shocking green domes on a brown lifeless world. But such domes Desan had seen. With only the AI for witness, Desan turned in his seat, pressed the flexible bubble of the helmet to the double-seal window, and stared and stared at the stonework until it passed to the rear and the dust obscured it.

"Here, Lord," said the AI, eternally cheerful. "We are almost at the station—a little climb. I do it very smoothly."

Flex and lean; sway and turn. The domes lurched closer in the forward window and the motor whined. "I've very much enjoyed serving you."

"Thank you," Desan murmured, seeing another walk before him, ascent of a plastic grid to an airlock and no sight of a welcoming committee.

More service robots, scuttling toward them as the transport stopped and adjusted itself with a pneumatic wheeze.

"Thank you, Lord Desan, do watch your helmet, watch your lifesupport connections, watch your footing please. The dust is slick. . . ."

"Thank you." With an AI one had no recourse.

"Thank *you*, my lord." The door came up; Desan extricated himself from the seat and stepped to the dusty ground, carefully shielding the oxy-pack from the doorframe and panting with the unaccustomed weight of it in such gravity. The service robots moved to take his luggage while Desan waddled doggedly on, up the plastic gridwork path to the glaringly lime-green domes. Plastics. Plastics that could not even originate in this desolation, but which came from their ships' spare biomass. Here all was dead, frighteningly void: Even the signal that guided him to the lakebed was robotic, like the advertisement that a transport would meet him.

The airlock door shot open ahead; and living, suited personnel appeared, three of them, at last, at long last, flesh-and-blood personnel came walking toward him to offer proper courtesy. But before that mountain of stone; before these glaring green structures and the robotic paraphernalia of research that made all the reports real—Desan still felt the deathliness of the place. He trudged ahead, touched the offered, gloved hands, acknowledged the expected salutations, and proceeded up the jointed-plastic walk to the open airlock. His marrow refused to be warmed. The place refused to come into clear focus, like some bad dream with familiar elements hideously distorted.

A hundred years of voyage since he had last seen this world and then only from orbit, receiving reports thirdhand. A hundred years of work on this planet preceded this small trip from port to research center, under that threatening sky, in this place by a mountain that had once been a dam on a lake that no longer existed.

There had been the findings of the moon, of course. A few artifacts. A cloth of symbols. Primitive, unthinkably primitive. First omen of the findings of this sere, rust-brown world.

He accompanied the welcoming committee into the airlock of the main dome, waited through the cycle, and breathed a sigh of relief as the indicator lights went from white to orange and the inner door admitted them to the interior. He walked forward, removed the helmet and drew a deep breath of air unexpectedly and unpleasantly tainted. The foyer of this centermost dome was businesslike—plastic walls, visible ducting. A few plants struggled for life in a planter in the center of the floor. Before it, a black pillar and a common enough emblem: a plaque with two naked alien figures, the diagrams of a starsystem—reproduced even to its scars and pitting. In some places it might be mundane, unnoticed.

It belonged here, *belonged* here, and it could never be mundane, this message of the Ancients.

"Lord Desan," a female voice said, and he turned, awkward in the suit.

It was Dr. Gothon herself, unmistakable aged woman in science blues. The rare honor dazed him, and wiped away all failure of hospitality thus far. She held out her hand. Startled, he reacted in kind, remembered the glove, and hastily drew back his hand to strip the glove. Her gesture was gracious and he felt the very fool and very much off his stride, his hand touching—no, firmly grasped by the callused, aged hand of the legendary intellect. Age-soft and hard-surfaced at once. Age and vigor. His tongue quite failed him, and he felt, recalling his purpose, utterly daunted.

"Come in, let them rid you of that suit, Lord Desan. Will you rest after your trip, a nap, a cup of tea, perhaps. The robots are taking your luggage to your room. Accommodations here aren't luxurious, but I think you'll find them comfortable."

Deeper and deeper into courtesies. One could lose all sense of direction in such surroundings, letting oneself be disarmed by gentleness, by pleasantness—by embarrassed reluctance to resist.

"I want to see what I came to see, doctor." Desan unfast-ened more seams and shed the suit into waiting hands, smoothed his coveralls. Was that too brusque, too unforgiveably hasty? "I don't think I *could* rest, Dr. Gothon. I attended my comfort aboard the shuttle. I'd like to get my bearings here at least, if one of your staff would be so kind to take me in hand—"

"Of course, of course. I rather expected as much—do come, please, let me show you about. I'll explain as much as I can. Perhaps I can convince you as I go."

He was overwhelmed from the start; he had expected *some* high official, the director of operations most likely, not Gothon. He walked slightly after the doctor, the stoop-shouldered presence that passed like a benison among the students and lesser staff—*I saw the Doctor,* the young ones had been wont to say in hushed tones, aboard the ship, when Gothon strayed absently down a corridor in her rare intervals of waking. *I saw the Doctor.*

In that voice one might claim a theophany.

They had rarely waked her, lesser researchers being suffi-cient for most worlds; while he was the fifth lord-navigator, the fourth born on the journey, a time-dilated trifle, fifty-two waking years of age and a mere two thousand years of voyage against—aeons of Gothon's slumberous life.

And Desan's marrow ached now at such gentle grace in this bowed, mottle-skinned old scholar, this sleuth patiently deciphering the greatest mystery of the universe. Pity oc-curred to him. He suffered personally in this place; but not as Gothon would have suffered here, in that inward quiet where Gothon carried on thoughts the ship crews were sternly ad-monished never to disturb.

Students rushed now to open doors for them, pressed them-selves to the walls and allowed their passage into deeper and deeper halls within the maze of the domes. Passing hands brushed Desan's sleeves, welcome offered the current lord-navigator; he reciprocated with as much attention as he could devote to courtesy in his distress. His heart labored in the unaccustomed gravity, his nostrils accepted not only the ef-fluvium of dome plastics and the recyclers and so many bodies dwelling together; but a flinty, bitter air, like electric-ity or dry dust. He imagined some hazardous leakage of the atmosphere into the dome: unsettling thought. The hazards of the place came home to him, and he wished already to be away.

Gothon had endured here, during his further voyages—seven years more of her diminishing life; waked four times, and this was the fourth, continually active now for five years, her longest stint yet in any waking. She had found data finally worth the consumption of her life, and she burned it without stint. *She* believed. She believed enough to die pursuing it.

He shuddered up and down and followed Gothon through a seal-door toward yet another dome, and his gut tightened in dismay; for there were shelves on either hand, and those shelves were lined with yellow skulls, endless rows of staring dark sockets and grinning jaws. Some were long-nosed; some were short. Some small, virtually noseless skulls had fangs which gave them a wise and intelligent look—*Like miniature people, like babies with grown up features,* must be the initial reaction to anyone seeing them in the holos or viewing the specimens brought up to the orbiting labs. But cranial capacity in these was much too small. The real sapient occupied further shelves, row upon row of eyeless, generously domed skulls, grinning in their flat-toothed way, in permanent horror—provoking profoundest horror in those who discovered them here, in this desolation.

Here Gothon paused, selected one of the small sapient skulls, much reconstructed: Desan had at least the skill to recognize the true bone from the plassbone bonded to it. This skull was far more delicate than the others, the jaw smaller. The front two teeth were restructs. So was one of the side.

"It was a child," Gothon said. "We call her Missy. The first we found at this site, up in the hills, in a streambank. Most of Missy's feet were gone, but she's otherwise intact. Missy was all alone except for a little animal all tucked up in her arms. We keep them together—never mind the cataloging." She lifted an anomalous and much-reconstructed skull from the shelf among the sapients; fanged and delicate. "Even archaeologists have sentiment."

"I—see—" Helpless, caught in courtesy, Desan extended an unwilling finger and touched the skull.

"Back to sleep." Gothon set both skulls tenderly back on the shelf; and dusted her hands and walked further, Desan following, beyond a simple door and into a busy room of workbenches piled high with a clutter of artifacts.

Staff began to rise from their dusty work in a sudden startlement. "No, no, go on," Gothon said quietly. "We're only passing through; ignore us. —Here, do you see, Lord Desan?" Gothon reached carefully past a researcher's shoulder and lifted from the counter an elongate ribbed bottle with the opalescent patina of long burial. "We find a great many of these. Mass production. Industry. Not only on this continent. This same bottle exists in sites all over the world, in the uppermost strata. Same design. Near the time of the calamity. We trace global alliances and trade by such small things." She set it down and gathered up a virtually complete vase, much patched. "It always comes to pots, Lord Desan. By pots and bottles we track them through the ages. Many layers. They had a long and complex past."

Desan reached out and touched the corroded brown surface of the vase, discovering a single bright remnant of the blue glaze along with the gray encrustations of long burial. "How long—how long does it take to reduce a thing to this?"

"It depends on the soil—on moisture, on acidity. This came from hereabouts." Gothon tenderly set it back on a shelf, walked on, frail, hunch-shouldred figure among the aisles of the past. "But very long, very long to obliterate so much—almost all the artifacts are gone. Metals oxidize; plastics rot; cloth goes very quickly; paper and wood last quite long in a desert climate, but they go, finally. Moisture dissolves the details of sculpture. Only the noble metals survive intact. Soil creep warps even stone; crushes metal. We find even the best pots in a matrix of pieces, a puzzle-toss. Fragile as they are, they outlast monuments, they last as long as the earth that holds them, drylands, wetlands, even beneath the sea—where no marine life exists to trouble them. That bottle and that pot are as venerable as that great dam. The makers wouldn't have thought that, would they?"

"But—" Desan's mind reeled at the remembrance of the great plain, the silt and the deep buried secrets.

"But?"

"You surely might miss important detail. A world to search. You might walk right over something and misinterpret everything."

"Oh, yes, it can happen. But *finding* things where we expect them is an important clue, Lord Desan, a confirmation— One only has to suspect where to look. We locate our best hope first—a sunken, a raised place in those photographs we trouble the orbiters to take; but one gets a *feeling* about the lay of the land—more than the mechanical probes, Lord Desan.'' Gothon's dark eyes crinkled in the passage of thoughts unguessed, and Desan stood lost in Gothon's unthinkable mentality. What did a mind *do* in such age? Wander? Could the great doctor lapse into mysticism? To report such a thing—would solve one difficulty. But to have that regrettable duty—

"It's a feeling for living creatures, Lord Desan. It's reaching out to the land and saying—if this were long ago, if I thought to build, if I thought to trade—where would I go? Where would my neighbors live?''

Desan coughed delicately, wishing to draw things back to hard fact. "And the robot probes, of course, do assist.''

"Probes, Lord Desan, are heartless things. A robot can be very skilled, but a researcher directs it only at distance, blind to opportunities and the true sense of the land. But you were born to space. Perhaps it makes no sense.''

"I take your word for it,'' Desan said earnestly. He felt the weight of the sky on his back. The leaden, awful sky, leprous and unhealthy cover between them and the star and the single moon. Gothon remembered homeworld. *Remembered homeworld.* Had been renowned in her field even there. The old scientist claimed to come to such a landscape and *locate* things by seeing things that robot eyes could not, by thinking thoughts those dusty skulls had held in fleshy matter—

—how long ago?

"We look for mounds,'' Gothon said, continuing in her brittle gait down the aisle, past the bowed heads and shy looks of staff and students at their meticulous tasks. The work of tiny electronic needles proceeded about them, the patient ticking away at encrustations to bring ancient surfaces to light. "They built massive structures. Great skyscrapers. Some of them must have lasted, oh, thousands of years intact; but when they went unstable, they fell, and their fall made rubble; and the wind came and the rivers shifted their courses around the ruin, and of course the weight of sediment piled up, wind-and water-driven. From that point, its own weight moved it and warped it and complicated our work.'' Gothon paused again beside a further table, where holo plates stood inactive. She waved her hand and a landscape showed itself, a serpentined row of masonry across a depression. "See the wall there. They didn't build it that way, all wavering back and forth and up and down. Gravity and soil movement deformed it. It was buried until we unearthed it. Otherwise, wind and rain alone would have destroyed it ages ago. As it will do, now, if time doesn't rebury it.''

"And this great pile of stone—'' Desan waved an arm, indicating the imagined direction of the great dam and realizing himself disoriented. "How old is it?''

"Old as the lake it made.''

"But contemporaneous with the fall?''

"Yes. Do you know, that mass may be standing when the star dies. The few great dams; the pyramids we find here and there around the world—One only guesses at their age. They'll outlast any other surface feature except the mountains themselves.''

"Without life.''

"Oh, but there is.''

"Declining.''

"No, no. Not declining.'' The doctor waved her hand and a puddle appeared over the second holo plate, all green with weed waving feathery tendrils back and forth in the surge. "The moon still keeps this world from entropy. There's water, not as much as this dam saw—It's the weed, this little weed that gives one hope for this world. The little life, the things that fly and crawl—the lichens and the life on the flatlands.''

"But nothing *they* knew.''

"No. Life's evolved new answers here. Life's starting over.''

"It certainly hasn't much to start with, has it?''

"Not very much. It's a question that interests Dr. Bothogi— whether the life making a start here has the time left, and whether the consumption curve doesn't add up to defeat—But life doesn't know that. We're very concerned about contamination. But we fear it's inevitable. And who knows, perhaps it will have added something beneficial.'' Dr. Gothon lit yet another holo with the wave of her hand. A streamlined six-legged creature scuttled energetically across a surface of dead moss, frantically waving antennae and making no apparent progress.

"The inheritors of the world.'' Despair chilled Desan's marrow.

"But each generation of these little creatures is an unqualified success. The last to perish perishes in profound tragedy, of course, but without consciousness of it. The awareness will have, oh, half a billion years to wait—then, maybe it will appear; if the star doesn't fail; it's already far advanced down the sequence." Another holo, the image of desert, of blowing sand, beside the holo of the surge of weed in a pool. "Life makes life. That weed you see is busy making life. It's taking in and converting and building a chain of support that will enable things to feed on it, while more of its kind grows. That's what life does. It's busy, all unintended, of course, but fortuitously building itself a way off the planet."

Desan cast her an uncomfortable look askance.

"Oh, indeed. Biomass. Petrochemicals. The storehouse of aeons of energy all waiting the use of consciousness. And that consciousness, if it arrives, dominates the world because awareness is a way of making life more efficiently. But consciousness is a perilous thing, Lord Desan. Consciousness is a computer loose with its own perceptions and performing calculations on its own course, in the service of that little weed; billions of such computers all running and calculating faster and faster, adjusting themselves and their ecological environment, and what if there were the smallest, the most insignificant software error at the outset?"

"You don't believe such a thing. You don't reduce us to that." Desan's faith was shaken; this good woman had not gone unstable, this great intellect had had her faith shaken, that was what—the great and gentle doctor had, in her unthinkable age, acquired cynicism, and he fought back with his fifty-two meager years. "Surely, but surely this isn't the proof, doctor, this could have been a natural calamity."

"Oh, yes, the meteor strike." The doctor waved past a series of holos on a fourth plate, and a vast crater showed in aerial view, a crater so vast the picture showed planetary curvature. It was one of the planet's main features, shockingly visible from space. "But this solar system shows scar after scar of such events. A many-planeted system like this, a star well-attended by debris in its course through the galaxy—Look at the airless bodies, the moons, consider the number of meteor strikes that crater them. Tell me, spacefarer: am I not right in that?"

Desan drew in a breath, relieved to be questioned in his

own element. "Of course, the system is prone to that kind of accident. But that crater is ample cause—"

"If it came when there was still sapience here. But that hammerblow fell on a dead world."

He gazed on the eroded crater, the sandswept crustal melting, eloquent of age. "You have proof."

"Strata. Pots. Ironic, they must have feared such an event very greatly. One thinks they must have had a sense of doom about them, perhaps on the evidence of their moon; or understanding the mechanics of their solar system; or perhaps primitive times witnessed such falls and they remembered. One catches a glimpse of the mind that reached out from here . . . what impelled it, what it sought."

"How can we know that? We overlay our mind on their expectations—" Desan silenced himself, abashed, terrified. It was next to heresy. In a moment more he would have committed irremediable indiscretion; and the lords-magistrate on the orbiting station would hear it by suppertime, to his eternal detriment.

"We stand in their landscape, handle their bones, we hold their skulls in our fleshly hands and try to think *in* their world. Here we stand beneath a threatening heaven. What will we do?"

"Try to escape. Try to get off this world. They *did* get off. The celestial artifacts—"

"Archaelogy is ever so much easier in space. A million years, two, and a thing still shines. Records still can be read. A color can blaze out undimmed after aeons, when first a light falls on it. One surface chewed away by microdust, and the opposing face pristine as the day it had its maker's hand on it. You keep asking me about the age of these ruins. But we know that, don't we truly suspect it, in the marrow of our bones—at what age they fell silent?"

"It *can't* have happened then!"

"Come with me, Lord Desan." Gothon waved a hand, extinguishing all the holos, and, walking on, opened the door into yet another hallway. "So much to catalog. That's much of the work in that room. They're students, mostly. Restoring what they can; numbering, listing. A librarian's job, just to know where things are filed. In five hundred years more of intensive cataloguing and restoring, we may know them well enough to know something of their minds, though we may

never find more of their written language than that of those
artifacts on the moon. A place of wonders. A place of
ongoing wonders, in Dr. Bothogi's work. A little algae beginning the work all over again. Perhaps not for the first
time—interesting thought.''

"You mean—" Desan overtook the aged doctor in the
narrow, sterile hall, a series of ringing steps. "You mean—
before the sapients evolved—there were other calamities,
other re-beginnings.''

"Oh, well before. It sends chills up one's back, doesn't it,
to think how incredibly stubborn life might be here, how
persistent in the calamity of the skies— The algae and then
the creeping things and the slow, slow climb to dominance—"

"Previous sapients?"

"Interesting question in itself. But a thing need not be
sapient to dominate a world, Lord Desan. Only tough. Only
efficient. Haven't the worlds proven that? High sapience is a
rare jewel. So many successes are dead ends. Flippers and
not hands; lack of vocal apparatus—unless you believe in
telepathy, which I assuredly don't. No. Vocalizing is necessary. Some sort of long-distance communication. Light-flashes;
sound; something. Else your individuals stray apart in solitary
discovery and rediscovery and duplication of effort. Oh, even
with awareness—even granted that rare attribute—how many
species lack something essential, or have some handicap that
will stop them before civilization; before technology—"

"—before they leave the planet. But they *did* that, they
were the one in a thousand— Without them—"

"Without them. Yes." Gothon turned her wonderful soft
eyes on him at close range and for a moment he felt a great
and terrible stillness like the stillness of a grave. "Childhood
ends here. One way or the other, it ends."

He was struck speechless. He stood there, paralyzed a
moment, his mind tumbling freefall; then blinked and followed the doctor like a child, helpless to do otherwise.

Let me rest, he thought then, *let us forget this beginning
and this day, let me go somewhere and sit down and have a
warm drink to get the chill from my marrow and let us begin
again. Perhaps we can begin with facts and not fancies—*

But he would not rest. He feared that there was no rest to
be had in this place, that once the body stopped moving, the
weight of the sky would come down, the deadly sky that had

boded destruction for all the history of this lost species; and the age of the land would seep into their bones and haunt his dreams as the far greater scale of stars did not.

All the years I've voyaged, Dr. Gothon, all the years of my life searching from star to star. Relativity has made orphans of us. The world will have sainted you. Me it never knew. In a quarter of a million years—they'll have forgotten; o doctor, you know more than I how a world ages. A quarter of a million years you've seen—and we're both orphans. Me endlessly cloned. You in your long sleep, your several clones held aeons waiting in theirs—o doctor, we'll recreate you. And not truly you, ever again. No more than I'm a Desan-prime. I'm only the fifth lord-navigator.

In a quarter of a million years, has not our species evolved beyond us, might they not, may they not, find some faster transport and find us, their aeons-lost precursors; and we will not know each other, Dr. Gothon—how could we know each other—if they had, but they have not; we have become the wavefront of a quest that never overtakes, never surpasses us.

In a quarter of a million years, might some calamity have befallen us and our world be like this world, ocher and deadly rust?

While we are clones and children of clones, genetic fossils, anomalies of our kind?

What are they to us and we to them? We seek the Ancients, the makers of the probe.

Desan's mind reeled; adept as he was at time-relativity calculations, accustomed as he was to stellar immensities, his mind tottered and he fought to regain the corridor in which they walked, he and the doctor. He widened his stride yet again, overtaking Gothon at the next door.

"Doctor." He put out his hand, preventing her, and then feared his own question, his own skirting of heresy and tempting of hers. "Are you beyond doubt? You can't be beyond doubt. They could have simply abandoned this world in its calamity."

Again the impact of those gentle eyes, devastating. "Tell me, tell me, Lord Desan. In all your travels, in all the several near stars you've visited in a century of effort, have you found traces?"

"No. But they could have gone—"

"—leaving no traces, except on their moon?"

"There may be others. The team in search on the fourth planet—"

"Finds nothing."

"You yourself say that you have to stand in that landscape, you have to think with their mind— Maybe Dr. Ashodt hasn't come to the right hill, the right plain—"

"If there are artifacts there they only are a few. I'll tell you why I know so. Come, come with me." Gothon waved a hand and the door gaped on yet another laboratory.

Desan walked. He would rather have walked out to the deadly surface than through this simple door, to the answer Gothon promised him . . . but habit impelled him; habit, duty—necessity. He had no other purpose for his life but this. He had been left none, lord-navigator, fifth incarnation of Desan Das. They had launched his original with none, his second incarnation had had less, and time and successive incarnations had stripped everything else away. So he went, into a place at once too mundane and too strange to be quite sane—mundane because it was sterile as any lab, a well-lit place of littered tables and a few researchers; and strange because hundreds and hundreds of skulls and bones were piled on shelves in heaps on one wall, silent witnesses. An articulated skeleton hung in its frame; the skeleton of a small animal scampered in macabre rigidity on a tabletop.

He stopped. He stared about him, lost for the moment in the stare of all those eyeless sockets of weathered bone.

"Let me present my colleagues," Gothon was saying; Desan focused on the words late, and blinked helplessly as Gothon rattled off names. Bothogi the zoologist was one, younger than most, seventeenth incarnation, burning himself out in profligate use of his years: so with all the incarnations of Bothogi Nan. The rest of the names slid past his ears ungathered—true strangers, the truly-born, sons and daughters of the voyage. He was lost in their stares like the stares of the skulls, eyes behind which shadows and dust were truth, gazes full of secrets and heresies.

They knew him and he did not know them, not even Lord Bothogi. He felt his solitude, the helplessness of his convictions—all lost in the dust and the silences.

"Kagodte," said Gothon, to a white-eared, hunched individual, "Kagodte—the Lord Desan has come to see your model."

"Ah." The aged eyes flicked, nervously.

"Show him, pray, Dr. Kagodte."

The hunched man walked over to the table, spread his hands. A holo flared and Desan blinked, having expected some dreadful image, some confrontation with a reconstruction. Instead, columns of words rippled in the air, green and blue. Numbers ticked and multiplied. In his startlement he lost the beginning and failed to follow them. "I don't see—"

"We speak statistics here," Gothon said. "We speak data; we couch our heresies in mathematical formulae."

Desan turned and stared at Gothon in fright. "Heresies I have nothing to do with, doctor. I deal with facts. I come here to find facts."

"Sit down," the gentle doctor said. "Sit down, Lord Desan. There, move the bones over, do; the owner's won't mind, there, that's right."

Desan collapsed onto a stool facing a white worktable. Looked up reflexively, eye drawn by a wall-mounted stone that bore the blurred image of a face, eroded, time-dulled—

The juxtaposition of image and bones overwhelmed him. The two whole bodies portrayed on the plaque. The sculpture. The rows of fleshless skulls.

Dead. World hammered by meteors, life struggling in its most rudimentary forms. Dead.

"Ah," Gothon said. Desan looked around and saw Gothon looking up at the wall in his turn. "Yes. That. We find very few sculptures. A few—a precious few. Occasionally the fall of stone will protect a surface. Confirmation. Indeed. But the skulls tell us as much. With our measurements and our holos we can flesh them. We can make them—even more vivid. Do you want to see?"

Desan's mouth worked. "No." A small word. A coward word. "Later. So this was *one* place— You still don't convince me of your thesis, doctor, I'm sorry."

"The place. The world of origin. A many-layered world. The last layers are rich with artifacts of one period, one global culture. Then silence. Species extinguished. Stratum upon stratum of desolation. Millions of years of geological record—"

Gothon came round the end of the table and sat down in the opposing chair, elbows on the table, a scatter of bone between them. Gothon's green eyes shone watery in the brilliant light, her mouth was wrinkled about the jowls and trembled in minute cracks, like aged clay. "The statistics, Lord Desan, the dry statistics tell us. They tell us centers of production of artifacts, such as we have; they tell us compositions, processes the Ancients knew—and there was no progress into advanced materials. None of the materials we take for granted, metals that would have lasted—"

"And perhaps they went to some new process, materials that degraded completely. Perhaps their information storage was on increasingly perishable materials. Perhaps they developed these materials in space."

"Technology has steps. The dry numbers, the dusty dry numbers, the incidences and concentration of items, the numbers and the pots—always the pots, Lord Desan; and the imperishable stones; and the very fact of the meteors—the undeniable fact of the meteor strikes. Could we not avert such a calamity for our own world? Could we not have done it—oh, a half a century before we left?"

"I'm sure you remember, Dr. Gothon. I'm sure you have the advantage of me. But—"

"You see the evidence. You want to cling to your hopes. But there is only one question—no, two. Is this the species that launched the probe?—Yes. Or evolution and concidence have cooperated mightily. Is this the only world they inhabited? Beyond all doubt. If there are artifacts on the fourth planet they are scoured by its storms, buried, lost."

"But they may *be* there."

"There is no abundance of them. There is no *progression*, Lord Desan. That is the key thing. There is nothing beyond these substances, these materials. This was not a star-faring civilization. They launched their slow, unmanned probes, with their cameras, their robot eyes—not for us. We always knew that. We were the recipients of flotsam. Mere wreckage on the beach."

"It was purposeful!" Desan hissed, trembling, surrounded by them all, a lone credent among the quiet heresy in this room. "Dr. Gothon, your unique position—is a position of trust, of profound trust; I beg you to consider the effect you have—"

"Do you threaten me, Lord Desan? Are you here for that, to silence me?"

Desan looked desperately about him, at the sudden hush in

the room. The minute tickings of probes and picks had stopped.
Eyes stared. "Please." He looked back. "I came here to
gather data; I expected a simple meeting, a few staff
meetings—to consider things at leisure—"

"I have distressed you. You wonder how it would be if the
lords-magistrate fell at odds with me. I am aware of myself as
an institution, Lord Desan. I remember Desan Das. I remember launch, the original five ships. I have waked to all but
one of your incarnations. Not to mention the numerous incarnations of the lords-magistrate."

"You cannot discount them! Even you—Let me plead with
you, Dr. Gothon, be patient with us."

"You do not need to teach me patience, Desan-Five."

He shivered convulsively. Even when Gothon smiled that
gentle, disarming smile. "You have to give me facts, doctor,
not mystical communings with the landscape. The lords-
magistrate accept that this is the world of origin. I assure you
they never would have devoted so much time to creating a
base here if that were not the case."

"Come, lord, those power systems on the probe, so long
dead—What was it truly for, but to probe something very
close at hand? Even orthodoxy admits that. And what is close
at hand but their own solar system? Come, I've *seen* the
original artifact and the original tablet. Touched it with my
hands. This was a *primitive* venture, designed to cross their
own solar system—*which they had not the capability to do*."

Desan blinked. "But the purpose—"

"Ah. The purpose."

"You say that you stand in a landscape and you think in
their mind. Well, doctor, use this skill you claim. What did
the Ancients intend? Why did they send it out with a message?"

The old eyes flickered, deep and calm and pained. "An
oracular message, Lord Desan. A message into the dark of
their own future, unaimed, unfocused. Without answer. Without hope of answer. We know its voyage time. Eight million
years. They spoke to the universe at large. This probe went
out, and they fell silent shortly afterward—the depth of this dry
lake of dust, Lord Desan, is eight and a quarter million years.

"I will not believe that."

"Eight and a quarter million years ago, Lord Desan. Calamity fell on them, calamity global and complete within a
century, perhaps within a decade of the launch of that probe.

Perhaps calamity fell from the skies; but demonstrably it was atomics and their own doing. They were at that precarious stage. And the destruction in the great centers is catastrophic and of one level. Destruction centered in places of heavy population. Trace elements. That is what those statistics say. Atomics, Lord Desan.''

''I cannot accept this!''

''Tell me, space-farer—do you understand the workings of weather? What those meteor strikes could do, the dust raised by atomics could do with equal efficiency. Never mind the radiation that alone would have killed millions—never mind the destruction of centers of government: We speak of global calamity, the dimming of the sun in dust, the living oceans and lakes choking in dying photosynthetes in a sunless winter, killing the food chain from the bottom up—''

''You have no proof!''

''The universality, the ruin of the population-centers. Arguably, they had the capacity to prevent meteor-impact. That may be a matter of debate. But beyond a doubt in my own mind, simultaneous destruction of the population centers indicates atomics. The statistics, the pots and the dry numbers, Lord Desan, doom us to that answer. The question is answered. There were no descendants; there was no escape from the world. They destroyed themselves before that meteor hit them.''

Desan rested his mouth against his joined hands. Stared helplessly at the doctor. ''A lie. Is that what you're saying? We pursued a lie?''

''Is it their fault that we needed them so much?''

Desan pushed himself to his feet and stood there by mortal effort. Gothon sat staring up at him with those terrible dark eyes.

''What will you do, lord-navigator? Silence me? The old woman's grown difficult at last: wake my clone after, tell it—what the lords-magistrate select for it to be told?'' Gothon waved a hand about the room, indicating the staff, the dozen sets of living eyes among the dead. ''Bothogi too, those of us who have clones— But what of the rest of the staff? How much will it take to silence all of us?''

Desan stared about him, trembling. ''Dr. Gothon—'' He leaned his hands on the table to look at Gothon. ''You mistake me. You utterly mistake me— The lords-magistrate

may have the station, but I have the ships, *I*, I and my staff.
I propose no such thing. I've come home—'' The unaccustomed word caught in his throat; he considered it, weighed it,
accepted it, at least in the emotional sense. ''—*home*, Dr.
Gothon, after a hundred years of search, to discover this
argument and this dissension.''

''Charges of heresy—''

''They dare not make them against *you*.'' A bitter laugh
welled up. ''Against *you* they have no argument and you well
know it, Dr. Gothon.''

''Against their violence, lord-navigator, I have no defense.''

''But she has,'' said Dr. Bothogi.

Desan turned, flicked a glance from the hardness in Bothogi's
green eyes to the even harder substance of the stone in
Bothogi's hand. He flung himself about again, hands on the
table, abandoning the defense of his back. ''Dr. Gothon! I
appeal to you! I am your friend!''

''For myself,'' said Dr. Gothon, ''I would make no defense at all. But, as you say—they have no argument against
me. So it must be a general catastrophe—the lords-magistrate
have to silence everyone, don't they? *Nothing* can be left on
this base. Perhaps they've quietly dislodged an asteroid or
two and put them on course. In the guise of mining, perhaps
they will silence this poor old world forever—myself and the
rest of the relics. Lost relics and the distant dead are always
safer to venerate, aren't they?''

''That's absurd!''

''Or perhaps they've become more hasty now that your
ships are here and their judgement is in question. *They* have
atomics within their capability, lord-navigator. They can dis-
able your shuttle with beam-fire. They can simply welcome
you to the list of casualties—a charge of heresy. A thing
taken out of context, who knows? After all—all lords are
immediately duplicatable, the captains accustomed to obey
the lords-magistrate—what few of them are awake—am I not
right? If an institution like myself can be threatened—where is
the fifth lord-navigator in their plans? And of a sudden those
plans will be moving in haste.''

Desan blinked. ''Dr. Gothon—I assure you—''

''If you are my friend, lord-navigator, I hope for your
survival. The robots are theirs, do you understand? Their
powerpacks are sufficient for transmission of information to

the base AIs; and from the communications center it goes to satellites; and from satellites to the station and the lords-magistrate. This room is safe from their monitoring. We have seen to that. They cannot hear you."

"I cannot believe these charges, I cannot accept it—"

"Is murder so new?"

"Then come with me! Come with me to the shuttle, we'll confront them—"

"The transportation to the port is theirs. It would not permit. The transport AI would resist. The planes have AI components. And we might never reach the airfield."

"My luggage. Dr. Gothon, my luggage—my com unit!" And Desan's heart sank, remembering the service-robots. "*They* have it."

Gothon smiled, a small, amused smile. "O space-farer. So many scientists clustered here, and could we not improvise so simple a thing? *We* have a receiver-transmitter. Here. In this room. We broke one. We broke another. They're on the registry as broken. What's another bit of rubbish—on this poor planet? We meant to contact the ships, to call *you*, lord-navigator, when you came back. But you saved us the trouble. You came down to us like a thunderbolt. Like the birds you never saw, my spaceborn lord, swooping down on prey. The conferences, the haste you must have inspired up there on the station—if the lords-magistrate planned what I most suspect! I congratulate you. But knowing we have a transmitter—with your shuttle sitting on this world vulnerable as this building—what will you do, lord-navigator, since *they* control the satellite relay?"

Desan sank down on his chair. Stared at Gothon. "You never meant to kill me. All this—you schemed to enlist me."

"I entertained that hope, yes. I knew your predecessors. I also know your personal reputation—a man who burns his years one after the other as if there were no end of them. Unlike his precedessors. What are you, lord-navigator? Zealot? A man with an obsession? Where do you stand in this?"

"To what—" His voice came hoarse and strange. "To what are you trying to convert me, Dr. Gothon?"

"To our rescue from the lords-magistrate. To the rescue of truth."

"Truth!" Desan waved a desperate gesture. "I don't be-lieve you, I cannot believe you, and you tell me about plots as fantastical as your research and try to involve me in your politics. I'm trying to find the trail the Ancients took—one clue, one artifact to direct us—''

"A new tablet?"

"You make light of me. Anything. Any indication where they went. And they *did* go, doctor. You will not convince me with your statistics. The unforeseen and the unpredicted aren't in your statistics."

"So you'll go on looking—for what you'll never find. You'll serve the lords-magistrate. They'll surely cooperate with you. They'll approve your search and leave this world . . . after the great catastrophe. After the catastrophe that obliterates us and all the records. An asteroid. Who but the robots chart their course? Who knows how close it is at this moment?"

"People would know a murder! They could never hide it!"

"I tell you, Lord Desan, you stand in a place and you look around you and you say—what would be natural to this place? In this cratered, devastated world, in this chaotic, debris-ridden solar system—could not an input error by an asteroid miner be more credible an accident than atomics? I tell you when your shuttle descended, we thought you might be acting for the lords-magistrate. That you might have a weapon in your baggage that their robots would deliberately fail to detect. But I believe you, lord-navigator. You're as trapped as we. With only the transmitter and a satellite relay system they control. What will you do? Persuade the lords-magistrate that you support them? Persuade them to support you on this further voyage—in return for your backing them? Perhaps they'll listen to you and let you leave."

"But they will," Desan said. He drew in a deep breath and looked from Gothon to the others and back again. "My shuttle is my own. *My* robotics, Dr. Gothon. From my ship and linked to it. And what I need is that transmitter. Appeal to *me* for protection if you think it so urgent. Trust me. Or trust nothing and we will all wait here and see what truth is."

Gothon reached into a pocket, held up an odd metal object. Smiled. Her eyes crinkled round the edges. "An old-fashioned thing, lord-navigator. We say *key* nowadays and mean something quite different, but I'm a relic myself, remember. Baffles hell out of the robots. Bothogi. Link up that antenna and unlock the closet and let's see what the lord-navigator and his shuttle can do."

"Did it hear you?" Bothogi asked, a boy's honest worry on his unlined face. He still had the rock, as if he had forgotten it. Or feared robots. Or intended to use it if he detected treachery. "Is it moving?"

"I assure you it's moving," Desan said, and shut the transmitter down. He drew a great breath, shut his eyes and saw the shuttle lift, a silver wedge spreading wings for home. Deadly if attacked. *They will not attack it, they must not attack it, they will query us when they know the shuttle is launched and we will discover yet that this is all a ridiculous error of understanding.* And looking at nowhere: "Relays have gone; *nothing* stops it and its defenses are considerable. The lords-navigator have not been fools, citizens: we probe worlds with our shuttles, and we plan to get them back." He turned and faced Gothon and the other staff. "The message is *out*. And because I am a prudent man—are there suits enough for your staff? I advise we get to them. In the case of an accident."

"The alarm," said Gothon at once. "Neoth, sound the alarm." And as a senior staffer moved: "The dome pressure alert," Gothon said. "*That* will confound the robots. All personnel to pressure suits; all robots to seek damage. I agree about the suits. Get them."

The alarm went, a staccato shriek from overhead. Desan glanced instinctively at an uncommunicative white ceiling—

—darkness, darkness above, where the shuttle reached the thin blue edge of space. The station now knew that things had gone greatly amiss. It should inquire, there should be inquiry immediate to the planet—

Staffers had unlocked a second closet. They pulled out suits, not the expected one or two for emergency exit from this pressure-sealable room; but a tightly jammed lot of them. The lab seemed a mine of defenses, a stealthily equipped stronghold that smelled of conspiracy all over the base, throughout the staff—*everyone* in on it—

He blinked at the offering of a suit, ears assailed by the siren. He looked into the eyes of Bothogi who had handed it to him. There would be no call, no inquiry from the lords-magistrate. He began to know that, in the earnest, clear-eyed way these people behaved—not lunatics, not schemers. Truth. They had told their truth as they believed it, as the whole base believed it. And the lords-magistrate named it heresy.

His heart beat steadily again. Things made sense again. His hands found familiar motions, putting on the suit, making the closures.

"There's that AI in the controller's office," said a senior staffer. "I have a key."

"What will they do?" a younger staffer asked, panic-edged. "Will the station's weapons reach here?"

"It's quite distant for sudden actions," said Desan. "Too far for beams and missiles are slow." His heartbeat steadied further. The suit was about him; familiar feeling; hostile worlds and weapons: more familiar ground. He smiled, not a pleasant kind of smile, a parting of lips on strong, long teeth. "And one more thing, young citizen, the ships they have are transports. Miners. Mine are hunters. I regret to say we've carried weapons for the last two hundred thousand years, and my crews know their business. If the lords-magistrate attack that shuttle it will be their mistake. Help Dr. Gothon."

"I've got it, quite, young lord." Gothon made the collar closure. "I've been handling these things longer than—"

Explosion thumped somewhere away. Gothon looked up. All motion stopped. And the air-rush died in the ducts.

"The oxygen system—" Bothogi exclaimed. "O *damn* them—!"

"We have," said Desan coldly. He made no haste. Each final fitting of the suit he made with care. Suit-drill; example to the young: the lord-navigator, youngsters, demonstrates his skill. Pay attenion. "And we've just had our answer from the lords-magistrate. We need to get to that AI and shut it down. Let's have no panic here. Assume that my shuttle has cleared atmosphere—"

—well above the gray clouds, the horror of the surface. Silver needle aimed at the heart of the lords-magistrate.

Alert, alert, it would shriek, *alert, alert, alert*—With its transmission relying on no satellites, with its message shoved out in one high-powered bow-wave. *Crew on the world is in danger*. And, code that no lord-navigator had ever hoped to transmit, a series of numbers in syntaxical link: *Treachery; the lords-magistrate are traitors; aid and rescue—Alert, alert, alert—*

—anguished scream from a world of dust; a place of skulls; the grave of the search.

Treachery, alert, alert, alert!

Desan was not a violent man; he had never thought of himself as violent. He was a searcher, a man with a quest.

He knew nothing of certainty. He believed a woman a quarter of a million years old, because—because Gothon was Gothon. He cried traitor and let loose havoc all the while knowing that here might be the traitor, this gentle-eyed woman, this collector of skulls.

O Gothon, he would ask if he dared, *which of you is false? To force the lords-magistrate to strike with violence enough to damn them— Is that what you wish? Against a quarter million years of unabated life—what are my five incarnations: mere genetic congruency, without memory. I am helpless to know your perspectives.*

Have you planned this a thousand years, ten thousand?

Do you stand in this place and think in the mind of creatures dead longer even than you have lived? Do you hold their skulls and think their thoughts?

Was it purpose eight million years ago?

Was it, is it—horror upon horror—a mistake on both sides?

"Lord Desan," said Bothogi, laying a hand on his shoulder. "Lord Desan, we have a master key. We have weapons. We're waiting, Lord Desan."

Above them the holocaust.

It was only a service robot. It had never known its termination. Not like the base AI, in the director's office, which had fought them with locked doors and release of atmosphere, to the misfortune of the director—

"Tragedy, tragedy," said Bothogi, standing by the small dented corpse, there on the ocher sand before the buildings. Smoke rolled up from a sabotaged lifesupport plant to the right of the domes; the world's air had rolled outward and inward and mingled with the breaching of the central dome— the AI transport's initial act of sabotage, ramming the plastic walls. "Microorganisms let loose on this world—the fools, the arrogant *fools!*"

It was not the microorganisms Desan feared. It was the AI eight-wheeled transport, maneuvering itself for another attack on the coldsleep facilities. Prudent to have set themselves inside a locked room with the rest of the scientists and hope for rescue from offworld; but the AI would batter itself against the plastic walls, and living targets kept it distracted from the sleeping, helpless clones—Gothon's juniormost; Bothogi's; those of a dozen senior staffers.

And keeping it distracted became more and more difficult.

Hour upon hour they had evaded its rushes, clumsy attacks and retreats in their encumbering suits. They had done it damage where they could while staff struggled to come up with something that might slow it . . . it limped along now with a great lot of metal wire wrapped around its rearmost right wheel.

"Damn!" cried a young biologist as it maneuvered for her position. It was the agile young who played this game; and one aging lord-navigator who was the only fighter in the lot.

Dodge, dodge and dodge. "It's going to catch you against the oxyplant, youngster! *This* way!" Desan's heart thudded as the young woman thumped along in the cumbersome suit in a losing race with the transport. "Oh, *damn*, it's got it figured! Bothogi!"

Desan grasped his probe-spear and jogged on—"Divert it!" he yelled. Diverting it was all they could hope for.

It turned their way, a whine of the motor, a serpentine flex of its metal body and a flurry of sand from its eight-wheeled drive. "Run, lord!" Bothogi gasped beside him; and it was still turning—it aimed for them now, and at another tangent a white-suited figure hurled a rock, to distract it yet again.

It kept coming at them. AI. An eight-wheeled, flex-bodied intelligence that had suddenly decided its behavior was not working, and altered the program, refusing distraction. A pressure-windowed juggernaut tracking every turn they made.

Closer and closer. "Sensors!" Desan cried, turning on the slick dust—his footing failed him and he caught himself, gripped the probe and aimed it straight at the sensor array clustered beneath the front window.

Thum-p! The dusty sky went blue and he was on his back, skidding in the sand with the great balloon tires churning sand on either side of him.

The suit, he thought with a spaceman's horror of the abrading, while it dawned on him at the same time he was being dragged beneath the AI, and that every joint and nerve center was throbbing with the high voltage shock of the probe.

Things became very peaceful then, a cessation of commotion. He lay dazed, staring up at a rusty blue sky, and seeing it laced with a silver thread.

They're coming, he thought, and thought of his eldest clone, sleeping at a well-educated twenty years of age. Handsome lad. He talked to the boy from time to time. *Poor lad, the lordship is yours. Your predecessor was a fool—*

A shadow passed above his face. It was another suited face peering down into his. A weight rested on his chest.

"Get off," he said.

"He's alive!" Bothogi's voice cried. "Dr. Gothon, he's still alive!"

The world showed no more scars than it had at the beginning—red and ocher where clouds failed. The algae continued its struggle in sea and tidal pools and lakes and rivers—with whatever microscopic addenda the breached dome had let loose in the world. The insects and the worms continued their blind ascent to space, dominant life on this poor, cratered globe. The research station was in function again, repairs complete.

Desan gazed on the world from his ship: it hung as a sphere in the holotank by his command station. A wave of his hand might show him the darkness of space; the floodlit shapes of ten hunting ships, lately returned from the deep and about to seek it again in continuation of the Mission, sleek fish rising and sinking again in a figurative black sea. A good many suns had shone on their hulls, but this one sun had seen them more often than any since their launching.

Home.

The space station was returning to function. Corpses were consigned to the sun the Mission had sought for so long. And power over the Mission rested solely at present in the hands of the lord-navigator, in the unprecedented circumstance of the demise of all five lords-magistrate simultaneously. Their clones were not yet activated to begin their years of majority— "Later will be time to wake the new lords-magistrate," Desan decreed, "at some further world of the search. Let them hear this event as history."

When I can manage them personally, he thought. He looked

aside at twenty-year-old Desan Six and the youth looked gravely back with the face Desan had seen in the mirror thirty-two waking years ago.

"Lord-navigator?"

"You'll wake your brother after we're away, Six. Directly after. I'll be staying awake much of this trip."

"*Awake*, sir?"

"Quite. There are things I want you to think about. I'll be talking to you and Seven both."

"About the lords-magistrate, sir?"

Desan lifted brows at this presumption. "You and I are already quite well attuned, Six. You'll succeed young. Are you sorry you missed this time?"

"No, lord-navigator! I assure you not!"

"Good brain. I ought to know. Go to your post, Six. Be grateful you don't have to cope with a new lordship *and* five new lords-magistrate and a recent schism."

Desan leaned back in his chair as the youth crossed the bridge and settled at a crew-post, beside the captain. The lord-navigator was more than a figurehead to rule the seventy ships of the Mission, with their captains and their crews. Let the boy try his skill on this plotting. Desan intended to check it. He leaned aside with a wince—the electric shock that had blown him flat between the AI's tires had saved him from worse than a broken arm and leg; and the medical staff had seen to that: the arm and the leg were all but healed, with only a light wrap to protect them. The ribs were tightly wrapped too; and they cost him more pain than all the rest.

A scan had indeed located three errant asteroids, three courses the station's computers had not accurately recorded as inbound for the planet—until personnel from the ships began to run their own observation. Those were redirected.

Casualties. Destruction. Fighting within the Mission. The guilt of the lords-magistrate was profound and beyond dispute.

"Lord-navigator," the communications officer said. "Dr. Gothon returning your call."

Goodbye, he had told Gothon. *I don't accept your judgment, but I shall devote my energy to pursuit of mine, and let any who want to join you—reside on the station. There are some volunteers; I don't profess to understand them. But you may trust them. You may trust the lords-magistrate to have learned a lesson. I will teach it. No member of this mission*

*will be restrained in any opinion while my influence lasts.
And I shall see to that. Sleep again and we may see each
other once more in our lives.*

"I'll receive it," Desan said, pleased and anxious at once
that Gothon deigned reply; he activated the com-control.
Ship-electronics touched his ear, implanted for comfort. He
heard the usual blip and chatter of com's mechanical proto-
cols, then Gothon's quiet voice. "Lord-navigator."

"I'm hearing you, doctor."

"Thank you for your sentiment. I wish you well, too. I
wish you very well."

The tablet was mounted before him, above the console.
Millions of years ago a tiny probe had set out from this
world, bearing the original. Two aliens standing naked, one
with hand uplifted. A series of diagrams which, partially obliterated, had still served to guide the Mission across the centuries. A probe bearing a greeting. Ages-dead cameras and
simple instruments.

*Greetings, stranger. We come from this place, this star
system.*

*See, the hand, the appendage of a builder—This we will
have in common.*

*The diagrams: we speak knowledge; we have no fear of
you, strangers who read this, whoever you be.*

Wise fools.

There had been a time, long ago, when fools had set out to
seek them . . . In a vast desert of stars. Fools who had
desperately needed proof, once upon a quarter million years
ago, that they were not alone. One dust-covered alien artifact
they found, so long ago, on a lonely drifting course.

Hello, it said.

The makers, the peaceful Ancients, became a legend. They
became purpose, inspiration.

The overriding, obsessive *Why* that saved a species, pulled
it back from war, gave it the stars.

"I'm very serious—I do hope you rest, doctor—save a few
years for the unborn."

"My eldest's awake. I've lost my illusions of immortality,
lord-navigator. She hopes to meet you."

"You might still abandon this world and come with us,
doctor."

"To search for a myth?"

"Not a myth. We're bound to disagree. Doctor, doctor, what *good* can your presence there do? What if you're right? It's a dead end. What if I'm wrong? I'll never stop looking. *I'll* never know."

"But we know their descendants, lord-navigator. We. We are. We've spread their legend from star to star—they've become a fable. The Ancients. The Pathfinders. A hundred civilizations have taken up that myth. A hundred civilizations have lived out their years in that belief and begotten others to tell their story. What if you should find them? Would you know them—or where evolution had taken them? Perhaps we've already met them, somewhere along the worlds we've visited, and we failed to know them."

It was irony. Gentle humor. "Perhaps, then," Desan said in turn, "we'll find the track leads home again. Perhaps we *are* their children—eight and a quarter million years removed."

"O ye makers of myths. Do your work, space-farer. Tangle the skein with legends. Teach fables to the races you meet. Brighten the universe with them. I put *my* faith in you. Don't you know—this world is all I came to find, but you—child of the voyage, you have to have more. For you the voyage is the Mission. Goodbye to you. Fare well. Nothing is complete calamity. The equation here is different, by a multitude of microorganisms let free—Bothogi has stopped grieving and begun to have quite different thoughts on the matter. His algae-pools may turn out a different breed this time—the shift of a protein here and there in the genetic chain—who knows what it will breed? Different software this time, perhaps. Good voyage to you, lord-navigator. Look for your Ancients under other suns. We're waiting for their offspring here, under this one."

AN OPEN LETTER
TO THE AMERICAN PEOPLE

Astronauts Francis (Dick) Scobee, Michael Smith, Judy Resnik, Ellison Onizuka, Ronald McNair, Gregory Jarvis, and Christa McAuliffe understood the risk, undertook the challenge, and in so doing embodied the dreams of us all.

Unlike so many of us, they did not take for granted the safety of riding a torch of fire to the stars.

For them the risk was real from the beginning. But some are already seizing upon their deaths as proof that America is unready for the challenge of manned space flight. *This is the last thing the seven would have wanted.*

Originally five orbiters were proposed; only four were built. This tragic reduction of the fleet places an added burden on the remaining three.

But the production facilities still exist. The assembly line can be reactivated. The experiments designed for the orbiter bay are waiting. We can recover a program which is one of our nation's greatest resources and mankind's proudest achievements.

Soon Congress will determine the immediate direction the space program must take. We must place at highest priority the restoration and enhancement of the shuttle fleet and resumption of a full launch schedule.

For the seven.

In keeping with their spirit of dedication to the future of space exploration and with the deepest respect for their memory, we are asking you to join us in urging the President and the Congress to build a new shuttle orbiter to carry on the work of these seven courageous men and women.

As long as their dream lives on, the seven live on in the dream.

SUPPORT SPACE EXPLORATION!

Write to the President at
1600 Pennsylvania Avenue,
Washington, D.C. 20500.